THE MYSTERIES OF PEMBERLEY

AMY DORAZIO

Quills & Quartos
PUBLISHING

Edited by Gail Warner and Jennifer Altman

Proofread by Jan Ashton

Cover Design by Crowglass Design

ISBN: 978-1-951033-39-2 (ebook) and 978-1-951033-46-0 (paperback) the promise from her sister's fingers. "Promise me," Jane urged again. "I must know you will take care of him."

"I shall," Elizabeth gasped. "You have my word. He will be my son, always."

Jane smiled then, the gentle, sweet smile Elizabeth was so accustomed to; her eyes drifted closed and her grip relaxed. For a moment, the death mask slipped away and there again was dear Jane, lovely and angelic in repose. Elizabeth bent, kissing her sister, her lips seared by the heat of Jane's cheek.

A few minutes later, her voice barely audible, Jane said, "Will you tell him about me? Tell him his Mama loved him very much and did not wish to leave him?"

"Of course," said Elizabeth through the sob that choked her. "He will know you, Jane, and he will love you as much as I do. I love you so much, so much and I do not know—" How I can live without you? She could not speak the words; her emotion had closed her throat.

"I love you, too," said Jane. She opened her mouth as if she wished to say more but did not. Her mouth remained open in a frighteningly skeletal gape. After a moment, Elizabeth reached over and pushed her sister's chin up so her mouth would close.

She remained in the room for some time, not even realising that she wept until the nursemaid looked in on her. "Miss Bennet? May I speak to you?"

Elizabeth rose hastily, straightening her skirts and wiping the tears from her eyes. "Of course."

Before she quit the room, she bent, kissing Jane's brow and saying, "Stay, Jane, we need you." Then she hurried out into the hall.

The nurse, a florid-faced lady called Danforth who appeared to be cut in half by her corset, was wringing her hands anxiously as Elizabeth approached her. "Forgive me—I don't mean to speak out of turn but I must say something for the welfare of that little lad in there."

"Of course," said Elizabeth. "What is it?"

"I speak out of turn, do not think I do not know that, but I fear for him, really I do, and I just want him to be well."

"Yes, of course," said Elizabeth. "But what is it?"

"You need to take him from the house," said the nurse. "This disease—I seen it before—it will go through and kill them all. Get him from the house, take him out."

"Take him...out?" Elizabeth stared at the lady. "Where shall I take him?"

The nurse did not answer directly, instead turning and gesturing for Elizabeth to follow her. She led Elizabeth into the nursery where young Charles, only a few months old, was lying in his cradle, contemplating the exquisite creations that were his feet and determining whether he could put them in his mouth. He stopped his endeavour when he saw Elizabeth and beamed with delight, reaching his hands for her and crowing madly with his joy.

His things were packed and ready by the door, and a footman stood there anxiously awaiting his orders.

"There is a lady coming to be wet nurse," explained Mrs Danforth. "He will be needing her in an hour or so."

"Ah..."

"He takes a gruel now twice a day. I shall return to my duties to him soon enough, I think."

"Of course," said Elizabeth, struggling to comprehend the haste with which the lady acted. "But do you not think I—"

"Get him over to Longbourn," the lady whispered. "I know not what might become of him otherwise." Then with a manner most unbecoming in a servant but reflective of her love for the boy, she nearly pushed Elizabeth and the footman out the door.

As it was, she was quite right to do so.

Jane did not last the night. Elizabeth's visit with her sister was the last time she ever beheld her, and as Jane had thought, by that Friday she rested in a grave next to her husband. Mrs Danforth was sadly the next to be stricken, as were several other members of the household at Netherfield.

The frightening plague swept through Meryton, affecting in some manner each of its four and twenty principal families; those at Longbourn were no exception. Both Mr and Mrs Bennet were afflicted, but he recovered while she did not. Lydia was likewise taken from them, and Elizabeth hoped that wherever they were, Mrs Bennet was comforted to have both her liveliest and her loveliest daughters with her.

In spite of the time she had spent at her sister's bedside, Elizabeth was not affected. She had a sore throat, which lasted a week; each day, she expected the fever and chills or the headache that she knew must accompany it. However, these did not come. The dark hand that snatched her sister from the earth passed her by with only a glancing touch.

Little Charles was also spared. Elizabeth supposed she owed Mrs Danforth a debt of gratitude for what she had done in seeing him removed from the house. He never so much as took a fever, instead thriving, laughing, and cooing even on the days when Elizabeth could not stop crying in his presence.

Despite his name, he was in every way her sister. His looks, his gestures, his manner—everything was Jane. He had the same sweetness about him, the same obedience, and the same kindness. At times, he was the only thing that could pull her from the fog of sorrow which threatened to overwhelm her.

ONE

Michaelmas 1816, Hertfordshire

THERE WAS IN THAT YEAR A COLD, A PERVASIVE GREYNESS, WHICH covered the land and made warmth impossible. Spring began late, with snow and flooding interrupting the attempts of the trees and flowers to bud, and killing the rabbits and other small game just as they began their capers and frisks about the land. Summer was little more than a succession of rain, never-ending rain that brought an unseasonable chill to their bones and flooded their roads.

The crops in the field could not withstand such rain and cold and soon died, their bloated, grey-green corpses turning brown and floating into the swollen river. The game were soon to follow—did they leave or did they die? Elizabeth had no idea.

She soon learned that not only Hertfordshire suffered under this strange curse; the effects were felt all over the kingdom, with reports of beggars from Wales who were driven from their home and Irishmen, desperate and poor and facing their starving families, who turned their guns on themselves.

Elizabeth suspected their trials had, in truth, merely just begun. An unprecedented number of their tenants would not make their rents this quarter day. The harvest, such as it would be, was not sufficient to enable many to endure the winter, and already many families had left, seeking employment in factories or other situations.

Longbourn was as prepared for difficult times as any seat of its size, but she knew nevertheless that straitened circumstances were upon them. She worried about it, though it did her little good; her father had never been one to economise or save, and even now, when widespread disaster seemed nigh, her father was as he ever was, more inclined towards making some jest about their misery than seeking to relieve it. So they ate potatoes as often as they could and were thankful they had at least that much.

"Lizzy! Lizzy, come see! Come see!" Little Charles did not intend to await her response; even as he bid her come, he came to her, grabbing her hand and tugging her towards the tree where he had been playing.

She laughed as she rose. "What is it?"

"See! See!" He pointed and gestured towards the house that was visible to them, though Elizabeth had had her back to it. She turned to look.

In front of Longbourn sat an exceedingly grand carriage. It was a regal dark blue trimmed in soft gold and cream. There was a crest on the side of it, but Elizabeth had not before seen it. "Someone has quite made the wrong turn on their way to London," she said to herself.

"London!" Charles replied agreeably.

"Well!" She smiled down at him. "We know how much Grandpapa despises exerting himself for visitors, so let us go rescue him, shall we?"

She watched the little boy bobbing happily along the path before her. He was her light, her small bit of colour in the grey, sodden world she lived in, and she could not begin to think what she would have done had he not survived. She understood now her mother's nerves; truly, nothing was quite so terrible as fully comprehending the dreadful terrors that the everyday world posed to a small child. At times, it seemed that to grow to adulthood was a miracle, and the anxieties provoked in a mother's heart were never ending. How her mother had managed to hold her sanity through five daughters was quite beyond Elizabeth's understanding.

She hastened—as much as a four-year-old boy with the curiosity of six boys would permit her to hasten—back to the house and entered to learn that her father was entertaining one guest, a gentleman who was a stranger to them. Mr Bennet had left instructions with Hill to direct Elizabeth to them in his study as soon as she returned.

The gentleman who sat with her father was a small, well-groomed man. He wore a dark coloured suit and greeted her with the air of a capable man who anticipated the easy disposal of his business.

Her father looked considerably less easy, a worried crease marking his brow. He introduced the man who, it turned out, was the man of business for a gentleman called Darcy from somewhere in the north of England.

"Elizabeth, this is Mr Pritchard," said Mr Bennet. "Pritchard, my daughter Miss Bennet."

"How do you do?" The gentleman offered a correct bow.

Hill had already served watery coffee to the men, and Pritchard, Elizabeth noticed, sipped at it in a fastidious, displeased sort of way. He made her uneasy. His air of competence, his sedate humour, soon seemed arrogant, as if he considered himself far above that which he saw but was enduring it as best he could.

Her arrival into the room required some amount of polite conversation. Observations about the weather were made as well as enquiries into the history of Longbourn. The tedium of it could only increase Elizabeth's anxiety, and soon, she felt she might scream from wondering what all this was about.

"Well then," said Mr Bennet at last. "You were saying before that you are an agent of a man called Darcy. I cannot say I know the gentleman nor can I imagine what business he might have with me, but pray, do speak your piece. Has he died and left some extraordinary sum of money to me?"

Mr Bennet chuckled heartily after the last sentence, and Mr Pritchard acknowledged the jest with a tight smile and a clearing of his throat. "I am afraid not. No, this matter has to do with the boy."

The smile that had lingered on Mr Bennet's lips faded immediately. "The boy?"

"The heir of the late Mr Charles Bingley."

Elizabeth felt her mouth drop as a stab of fear went through her. "What about him?" she asked in a voice that seemed strangely high and rudely loud.

"Mr Darcy is his rightful guardian. Young Master Bingley was left to his care."

"That cannot be true," Elizabeth exclaimed even while her father replied, "And what if he was? Mr Darcy has shown no concern for the boy's whereabouts these four years. Pray, do not suggest he wishes to be an active guardian now."

Stunned, Elizabeth stared at her father. He had not once, ever, suggested that he was not little Charles's legal guardian. Of course she had never asked, but why should she have wondered? It seemed the most sensible course to leave the child among his relations.

"Mr Darcy has been away," said Mr Pritchard. "And much engaged with other business."

"Engaged in business for four years?" Mr Bennet's expression conveyed his doubt with great eloquence. "So much engaged that he was unable to respond to letters?"

"Just so," said Mr Pritchard crisply. "He has only now been made aware that Mr Bingley had issue left behind."

"Not issue," Elizabeth protested. "A son. A living, breathing child."

Mr Pritchard gave her a small nod. "My apologies. Yes, a child. As soon as Mr Darcy knew of it, he dispatched me to retrieve his ward."

"Retrieve him?" Elizabeth exclaimed.

"Mr Darcy lives in Derbyshire," said Mr Pritchard primly. "The boy will reside with him there."

"Derbyshire!" Elizabeth was on her feet before she knew what she was about. "You cannot think we shall allow you to take him to Derbyshire!"

"I am afraid I do."

"I am the only mother he has ever known! This is the only home he has ever known!"

"Unfortunately, in the eyes of the law, that does not signify."

"In the eyes of a child, it is the only thing that signifies!"

Mr Pritchard sighed and raised his hand to rub his forehead. "I do understand that there has been an attachment as well as some expense, and allow me to assure you, Mr Darcy intends to see you compensated for that."

"Compensation? I do not want compensation! I want little Charles to remain where he belongs!"

It went on in the same vein for some time, Elizabeth insisting, in an increasingly heated manner, that the bonds of family and love be considered over the substance of wills and wards and legalities. Mr Pritchard sat calmly throughout, deflecting her assertions with the irrefutable claims of the law. It was a frustrating business, and Mr Bennet, at last, reached the end of what he could tolerate.

"Sir," said Mr Bennet. "While neither Elizabeth nor I can dispute the hold that Mr Darcy has on the child, surely you did not come here today thinking I would immediately remand the boy into your care."

It was the first time in the course of the whole wretched interview that Mr Pritchard was caught unprepared. He blinked owlishly for a moment before saying, "It is naturally my object to take care of Mr Darcy's business."

"Naturally," Mr Bennet agreed. "And yet, why should we trust that you are who you say you are?"

Mr Pritchard was momentarily flustered before drawing up and replying haughtily, "I have a copy of Mr Bingley's last will and testament in my valise."

"What I am saying is that you personally have no more claim on the child than any stranger passing on the street."

With a frown, Mr Pritchard said, "I have a letter of introduction—"

"As I have said, I do not know Mr Darcy, and therefore his letter has no meaning to me," replied Mr Bennet smoothly. "Any one could have penned the letter in your possession and claimed it came from Darcy—I do not know his family or their mark and have no notion of whether it was indeed written by the man himself or by some charlatan in a tavern.

"My grandson is a wealthy little boy. He holds the fortune of several generations in his hands and is an attractive object for an unscrupulous person. I cannot simply turn him over to the first person who presents himself as a man of business for some unknown gentleman in the north."

The panic that had produced nausea in Elizabeth's gut turned unexpectedly to delight. Her dear Papa had found the solution. Call it all a humbug, run the man off, and forget this had ever happened!

Mr Pritchard rose, fastidiously inserting and arranging papers that were lying on her father's desk into his valise. "Alas, I cannot dispute you. I might say it does you some credit although it does make my task more difficult."

"If Mr Darcy wants the boy so badly, he should come himself to retrieve him. It would be a kindness to Mr Bingley's memory to act in the best interests of his son."

"I do not know that Mr Darcy will agree, though he will comply if he thinks it necessary." Mr Pritchard finished with his papers and offered Elizabeth a brief bow. She rose, joining her father in seeing the man to his carriage, which still waited by the front of the house.

She gave her father a glance as the man was handed into the conveyance; it was surely the finest either of them had ever seen, and the four animals that pricked and pranced before it were equally impressive. Her father's gaze was unreadable. His stare into the carriage was unwavering and remained fixed until the wheels began to roll away.

Elizabeth turned to go back into the house, and her father followed her quietly. Once they were safely enclosed within the vestibule, she smiled at him, expecting to rejoice in their victory together. She was disheartened to see his pensive air.

"Papa? Why do you look so?"

"I fear," said Mr Bennet, "that we have not heard the last of this Mr Darcy."

AND SO THEY HAD NOT.

The first thing they did was consult with Mr Willard, husband of Elizabeth's younger sister Mary and a man of the law. Once a clerk for Elizabeth's uncle Philips, he was now his partner, helping Mr Philips extend his business into the nearby villages of St Albans and

Harpenden and even, on occasion, into London. He was a shrewd man and did not believe in hiding the truth.

On Elizabeth's enquiry as to whether or not they could challenge Mr Darcy's claim of guardianship, Mr Willard replied, "Mr Bingley's will is unmistakable in the matter. The best you can hope is that Mr Darcy will willingly surrender the child to your care. Otherwise, it must be put before the courts."

Elizabeth had scant hope of a willing surrender, but as weeks passed, her natural optimism grew. Perhaps Mr Darcy forgot? Or realised that his life would be infinitely more complicated with a small child in tow?

"I wonder whether Mr Darcy is married." she remarked to her father one evening in the drawing room whilst Charles played in front of the fire.

"I heard no mention of a Mrs Darcy."

"A bachelor would surely not wish for the strictures of a child about his neck all the time."

"True," said Mr Bennet, "though any man who could afford that carriage is certainly able to afford an army of servants for the child if he so wished it."

Elizabeth sighed. "But why go to so much trouble only to turn a child over to servants? Are not we, his family, better for his care than even the most loyal servants?"

Mr Bennet nodded. "Perhaps that is why we have seen neither hide nor hair of the man."

It was a dank, grey October; the disappointment of summer faded into a misery-stricken autumn as the failed harvest was passed over, and everyone contemplated the meagre rations that must sustain them through winter. Elizabeth thought herself fortunate to have so many things to fret over that she need not spend all her time fearfully contemplating some stranger tearing baby Charles from her—she could worry about all of them starving to death too.

Each day that passed brought with it a tiny measure more of hope, chasing away the fears that circled endlessly about Elizabeth's head. Each day, she considered the date, thinking that surely this Mr Darcy, if he cared about his obligation to her late brother Bingley, would have already come.

THE HAMLET of Meryton was but half a day's ride from London, yet Darcy felt he had travelled to another world. People gawped at him as if he bore two heads on his shoulders, and the proprietor of the only inn stared at his purse in a manner almost feral. It was a dismal little place, and the people were uncouth, uneducated, and illiberal; he wondered how on earth his late friend had permitted himself to become entrenched in such a place.

He sighed. His disappointment in his friend's choices aside, he did miss the man although it had been above five years since he last laid eyes on him. Five years... How much had happened that he would never wish to live through again, yet how he did wish to return to that simpler, easier time. Do things the right way this time perhaps.

He was a man mindful of his duty, yet time and again, he had failed. Time and again, those whom he loved met a fate they did not deserve because of his negligence.

It would not happen again—in that he was certain.

"Sir, I have arranged our finest chambers for you," the innkeeper was telling him. Lord only knew what 'finest chambers' were like in such a dank hovel as this—likely worse than what most of his servants were accustomed to. "Do you know how long you will be with us?"

"One night," he replied crisply, extracting some coins from his purse. "No more. Can you direct me to Longbourn, perchance?"

WITH GRAIN BEING in such short supply, the bakers had little to offer, so Elizabeth went into the booksellers, an equally disappointing venture. A scant bit of sunshine had tempted her from the house, eager to go somewhere, anywhere, but it seemed Meryton would provide nothing to engage her spirit.

And then she saw him.

That he was a gentleman was immediately apparent, but he was surely unlike any gentleman she had known before. The gentry in Hertfordshire did not have such well-cut, obviously fashionable clothing, nor did they comport themselves in such a way—tall and noble and assured. His was a figure that demanded admiration, though the man seemed unconscious of it.

He spoke with another man who appeared to be a servant, his tone low but with clear authority. The man nodded and asked his master a question; Elizabeth drew near just in time to overhear the gentleman's reply.

"From what Pritchard said, the woman is a bit of an ape leader, clinging to the child as if she had a claim to him. He believed the estate looked desperate for money. I am certain once it is offered, they will forget there ever was a boy."

Elizabeth could not help herself. She gasped and, in so doing, drew their attention. The tall gentleman—who by now she suspected was Mr Darcy—caught her eye then withdrew his gaze, a deeper shade of hauteur spreading over his already-haughty countenance. The shorter man was kinder.

"Miss, pray can you tell us the way to Longbourn?"

The tongue lashing she wished to deliver was overcome by good sense—and a spirit of mischief. She forced herself to drop her eyes and bob a curtsey. "Indeed, sir. You will want to follow that lane about…oh, two miles or so. You will reach an estate called Nether-field; Longbourn adjoins it. There is a smaller road, more of a lane, you can follow southerly."

The man looked about him for a moment; she had to admit, he was a quick study. "Will that not merely turn me about?"

"The bridge is out," she said with a guileless smile—for indeed, the bridge was out over the road that led direct, but it did not follow that another, temporary bridge had not been installed.

"I see." The gentleman sighed, and his manservant said something to him in a low tone. Something about a horse's shoe and arranging a conveyance, but the gentleman shook his head.

"No, no, the walk will do me some good."

"Best be at it then." She curtseyed, and he bowed and, with a few more words to his man, set off as she had directed him.

With studied nonchalance, she examined the cloth in the window of the milliner nearby just long enough to see the gentleman and his man disappear to their various tasks. When they were gone and, God willing, had forgotten all about her, she turned in the direction of the lane that led directly to Longbourn. Picking up her skirts, she ran as fast as her legs could take her.

It was only a mile, but she was gasping and breathless when she arrived, bursting in the door with her bonnet swinging from her hand. "Miss Elizabeth," Hill exclaimed. "Such a fright you—"

"Sorry, Hill!" she tossed over her shoulder as she flung her bonnet on the hall table and raced towards the nursery.

Charles was seated at a small table therein, his rosy cheeks and wildly corkscrewed hair attesting to the fact that he had just awoken from his nap. He stared, dazed and still lethargic, at a dish of tea in front of him.

"Charles! Sweetling!"

Charles startled a bit to find his aunt so near him and so clearly in a panic.

"Come with me! Come let us…let us go see Auntie Charlotte. Would you like to see Aunt Charlotte…and her pug?"

Dazed incomprehension gave way to delight as Charles recalled the squirmy, furry mass he had met at Lucas Lodge recently. "Barney!" he cried out.

"Yes! Barney the pug! Come now, we must not delay."

She reached for him, sweeping him into her arms and knocking the dish of tea with his foot. It splashed and flew, spraying around the nursery but she paid no heed, resolving to clean it later. His coat was hung on a hook in the nursery, and she snatched it up just before she ran out the door.

She carried him down the back stair on silent feet, and they gained the yard with no one else in the house any the wiser. Elizabeth looked around somewhat maniacally before she trotted through the yard but saw no one. The gentleman could not, of course, have travelled almost five miles in the short time that she had run one, but she feared that he had somehow suspected her deception, perhaps had followed her.

Charlotte was only too glad to watch after little Charles for a time. Her very brief marriage had not been blessed with children, and Elizabeth could always tell that Charlotte hungered for a little one. At the age of two and thirty, it was to be supposed Charlotte had likely surrendered any hopes in that quarter; it was not a subject that Elizabeth could speak of to her.

Thus, the visits of little Charles were always welcomed both by Charlotte and her father. They had a small trunk wherein toys were contained, and this trunk had moved gradually from an attic to a guest bedroom and, at last, to the drawing room. It did not escape Elizabeth's notice that the toys contained therein were no longer the old, discarded pieces from Charlotte's brothers; they were newer items, some of them quite expensive in Elizabeth's estimation.

"Perhaps we shall go to the orchard," said Charlotte with a smile. "Maybe we shall find an apple or two."

"No!"

Charlotte drew up. "No? Is he ill?"

"No, but…oh Charlotte, I cannot explain it to you now, but pray, keep him inside, and if any stranger should come to the door, deny his very existence, I beseech you!"

Charlotte's eyebrows flew up, and she surely would have enquired as to her friend's meaning, but it could not be done for Elizabeth had already turned her back, ready to return to Longbourn and await the odious Mr Darcy. "You may depend upon it!" she cried out to Elizabeth's departing form.

DARCY IMAGINED he was played a fool within the first mile of his long walk; by the time he reached Netherfield, he was certain of it. He cursed the impudent little hoyden who had sent him off in such a way. Likely one of those villagers who was instinctively wary of anyone who was a stranger.

The miles gave him a chance to have a good look at the country, and he found little to please him. The environs of Meryton contained the class of people he considered barely gentrified. He saw a few unimpressive estates, some shabby manor houses, and acre after acre of what might, under better management, be called farmland.

It seemed the harvest had come and gone in Hertfordshire with as little creditable result as was seen in Derbyshire. He counted himself fortunate that his storehouses and those of his people had enough laid by to last out this damnable weather; he had often heard of how many were already starving and the winter not yet upon them.

Thinking of that, he did feel something of a pang for the people whose homes and land he viewed. From the look of things, they would not make it through the festive season. He was glad to extricate Bingley's lad from such as this, glad for the chance to give him better than he had seen in the first tender years of his life.

With such thoughts in mind, he arrived at Longbourn. As he approached, he gave it the same appraisal he had given the rest of what he had seen. Nothing of note, he decided. It was likely one of the principal estates in the region, but given the desolation of the area, that was no source of great pride.

The housekeeper took his greatcoat and hat while an elderly manservant took his card to the master of the house. "The name is Bennet, is it not?" he asked her while he waited.

"Yes, sir, Mr Bennet is the master of the house, and his daughter Miss Bennet is the mistress."

"Very good." He nodded, imagining an old man and his spinster daughter.

He was led into a drawing room that was clean if a bit worn, and he was left there for enough time to exhaust his already-limited stores of patience. After all, he was not here because he wished it; he was here to discharge a duty, and no matter what, he would not allow it said that he did not do his duty.

Eventually, the master deigned to join him. He was a scholarly looking gentleman, wearing the comfortable attire of a country squire, right down to spectacles. He held a book in his hand as though Darcy had interrupted his reading but he expected to return to his pastime soon.

"Mr Darcy, I am Thomas Bennet."

"Sir." The gentlemen greeted one another, and Mr Bennet invited him to take a seat. He took the chair indicated, finding it lumpish and lopsided. He twisted in a surreptitious manner, hoping to look as comfortable as Mr Bennet himself did.

As soon as they were situated, Mr Bennet spoke, his eyes twinkling as if he found a great deal of amusement in his guest. "I understand you have come to tear my grandson from his home."

"I do not think I should put it in exactly those terms."

"But so it will be nevertheless."

"I am regretful that you see it as such."

"And your wife? What are her thoughts on the matter?"

Darcy shifted uncomfortably. "I do not have a wife."

Mr Bennet's brows rose to an almost comical height. "You are unwed?"

Darcy replied crisply, "Is that very shocking?"

"What shocks me is imagining that a young buck would wish to undertake the care of a young child."

"I am not a person who shirks my duties, Mr Bennet. My father passed when I was only two and twenty, and I assumed the guardianship of my sister and my family estate at that time. I am no stranger to responsibility."

Mr Bennet did not answer him, instead tilted his head as if listening for something. Somewhere in the house, a door closed and light footsteps approached. Moments later, the door to the drawing room opened.

It was the hoyden! Darcy rose instinctively, taking in her flushed cheeks and untidy hair. He smirked. "Quite a walk from town, is it not?"

Coolly she said, "But a mile. I suppose if one was accustomed to being more in town, a mile might seem daunting."

Mr Bennet, who had not risen, spoke in the same amused tone he had been using for Darcy. "Lizzy, this is the Mr Darcy of whom we have heard much. Mr Darcy, my daughter."

"Miss Bennet," Darcy acknowledged with a slight bow.

"Would you like some tea, Mr Darcy?"

"I thank you, no."

"Mr Darcy was telling me all about his responsibilities," said Mr Bennet.

Shockingly, Miss Bennet took a seat; evidently it was the custom in this house for ladies to take their place among gentlemen, to be party to the business of men and sit as their equal. Darcy frowned at the notion.

He spoke slowly such that she might understand him; he had no wish to be burdened by an excess of questions or feminine sentimentality. "The child was left to my care in Mr Bingley's will. He is, by rights, my child, and I shall remove him from this house forthwith. I thank you for all you have done for him, and if there is any recompense I may offer for expenses incurred, I urge you to submit to my man of business."

So much alike! Mr and Miss Bennet regarded him in like form with amused twinkles in their eyes and heads tilted, one left, one right. As if by unspoken communication, they gave one another a sidelong glance before returning their eyes to Darcy.

"No," said the lady in a pleasant, lilting tone. "I am afraid you will not be taking him anywhere."

TWO

THE TALL GENTLEMAN WITH HIS FINE CLOTHES AND NOBLE COUNTENANCE was nothing short of menacing, but Elizabeth would not show fear, not with the life of little Charles at stake.

"How do you propose to stop me?" Mr Darcy asked.

"Charles belongs with us here at Longbourn," she said adopting the tone of a governess instructing a particularly wilful pupil. "With his family who have cared for him all his life."

"And you have done well," said Mr Darcy in a tone that matched hers, "but legally, he is my duty. I shall not be deterred in discharging my duty to my friend and his heir."

"Your scruple towards your late friend is admirable, belated as it may be. Your friend has lain cold in his grave for many years now."

"Cold in his grave, it is true. But for Bingley, there will be always warmth in my heart."

"But what is a friend to a most beloved sister? Jane was there when I was born, and I was there when she breathed her last. Can you say the same for Mr Bingley, sir?"

"What I can say about Mr Bingley is that regardless of who was present at his birth and his death, in his will, he left his child to my care."

"And my sister, on her deathbed, extracted from me a promise that her child would remain in my care," Elizabeth insisted firmly. "Can the dying gasps of a sister be discounted on the basis of some hastily scrawled notes in a will? I know my brother Bingley, sir, and his will was likely no more considered than anything else he did. He could not have anticipated leaving this earth so soon, therefore what name he pronounced in reply to the question of his solicitor had little forethought ascribed to it."

Throughout this confrontation, Mr Bennet had remained silent. His gaze danced merrily from Elizabeth to Mr Darcy and back again as if this was some marvellous play he beheld. Elizabeth found herself vexed, as often she did, by his tendency to sit back and cast his satiric eye on everything rather than do something.

Mr Darcy raised his hand to pinch the bridge of his nose for a moment. "The length of time that Bingley considered naming the child's guardian is immaterial," he said, speaking with excessive deliberateness. "The will must stand. If you would like to take it before the courts, pray do so. For now, however, the boy is mine, and I intend to see him into my care directly."

The gentleman was completely lacking in feeling. All Elizabeth had lost, the attachment she and young Charles had to each other, meant nothing to him. Likely Mr Darcy had never loved nor been loved by anyone before.

But she had one card left to play, and it seemed now was the time to play it. "Very well, sir, but..."

He stared at her with deadened eyes.

"You will have to find him first."

ELIZABETH'S TURN to be indolent and amused in her chair had arrived; meanwhile, Mr Darcy did his best to find men who would help him search for the boy. Meryton had always been possessed of a friendly character, but a stranger with no claim to anyone, who behaved in such a haughty, authoritative manner, could only give uniform disgust to all he met. Nevertheless, he eventually assembled a group of young ragamuffins from among the stables who made a show of going about to the houses seeking little Charles.

As Elizabeth would have expected of her good neighbours, the answer was no, they had not seen him that day and had not the least notion of where he might be.

"Shall I invite Mr Darcy to dine, Lizzy?" Mr Bennet's eyes twinkled as the last of the boys was returned to the house bearing a negative report.

"I daresay he has not had many meals that were less than two courses," Elizabeth replied. "Longbourn's tables, such as they are now, would disgust him."

"You worry too much." Mr Bennet gave Elizabeth a fond smile and a pat on her back.

And you, not enough. Elizabeth sighed. Those were fears for another day. For today, she would concentrate every effort on keeping little Charles in the bosom of his family.

Mr Darcy's face was nearly purple with rage and a vein in his head jumped and twitched in an amusing manner. These involuntary facial tics were the only things that betrayed his true feelings.

"These sorts of games are likely nothing more to you than a way to pass the evening. You must know you cannot succeed. I shall remove the boy from this place tonight or tomorrow or the next day; it does not signify to me."

"This place," said Elizabeth, "is his home."

Mr Darcy did not give consequence to her protestation. He addressed her father directly.

"See the child ready for travel tomorrow at an early enough hour to make London. I shall return and will not suffer further delay."

He was gone then with a measured step when Elizabeth expected a stomp. Not long thereafter, Charlotte and her father, Sir William Lucas, escorted Charles back into the house.

Charles had borne the travails of the day with excitement and interest. Charlotte had clearly indulged him, playing games and teaching him to write the letters of his name. He was filled with little breathless stories to tell Grandpapa and Lizzy: Barney had managed to catch a small mouse, Charlotte gave him a biscuit, and Sir William said it was going to snow.

Elizabeth heard it all with only one ear for in her mind was a fretful litany that obscured any hopeful chattering: I cannot lose him to Mr Darcy.

MR ROBINSON ARRIVED AFTER DINNER. Mr Robinson was an exceedingly tall, thin gentleman with a shining bald head and a kindly face. As seemed to be the wont for men of his type, he had married a short, round little lady and together they were generally happy and cheerful.

Elizabeth and her father were sitting in the drawing room, reading by the modestly warm fire, when he was shown in. Elizabeth knew immediately it was not a friendly call. Mr Robinson was the magistrate of the area, and his countenance appeared concerned. Nausea immediately twisted in Elizabeth's gut at the supposed meaning of his call.

"You have left the comforts of your own hearth at a strange time, sir," said Mr Bennet.

Mr Robinson nodded. "Business of a particular nature has called me forth."

"Well, out with it then," said Mr Bennet, leaning back in his chair. "Lizzy can hear whatever it is as I should imagine it concerns her too."

Mr Robinson shifted in his seat. "I should think you have already some idea of the nature of my task."

"The matter of the boy," said Mr Bennet. "I am surprised that this Darcy fellow sought you out."

Mr Robinson replied gently, with a steady gaze, "He has the right of it, as I think you know."

There was a short silence while the fire crackled and cast shadows about. Elizabeth thought of how it might have been if her mother were still alive; Mrs Bennet would have shrieked and cried and called for her salts. She would have bemoaned the incontrovertible legal realities of the matter, and she would have refused to see any argument of sense or reason. Elizabeth was determined not to behave as her mother would have.

"Is there…" Her voice emerged thin and high, embarrassing her.

She paused and cleared her throat. "Mr Robinson, what can be done? It is impossible to think this man who we never heard anything about until very recently should be able to tear our Charles from his home and his family!"

"It would be a matter for the courts, I fear."

"The courts?" Elizabeth felt her spirits sink in her chest.

With this. Mr Robinson engaged in a brief but depressing overview of the limited means by which Mr Bennet might reclaim possession of his grandson. There would be two things required that Mr Bennet had in limited supply: money and zeal.

Elizabeth surreptitiously watched her father while Mr Robinson spoke. Mr Bennet listened in a half-hearted manner, casting several longing glances at the book on his lap and going so far as to yawn once. No, Mr Bennet could not be counted upon to fight this particular fight. She swallowed against the painful disappointment lodged in her throat.

"It seems a costly venture," said Mr Bennet when Mr Robinson's summary was done.

"Costly, yes," agreed Mr Robinson. "Costly, prolonged, and unfortunately unlikely to succeed. Mr Darcy is exceedingly wealthy, and he has the means and the inclination to fight you at every step. Furthermore, he is the nephew of the Earl of Matlock."

He did not need to say more. Any one who ever read a newspaper knew of the Earl of Matlock and his influence over…well, nearly everything, it seemed sometimes.

"For reasons only he can know," Mr Robinson continued, "Mr Darcy is as determined to have Charles as you are. Unlike you, however, he has the late Mr Bingley's will on his side."

A tear fell from Elizabeth's eye; she hardly knew it was coming and turned her head too late to conceal its appearance. Both gentlemen looked at her with some alarm, with Mr Bennet offering a mild, "Now, Lizzy."

"Forgive me," she murmured. "I would just…I would do anything to see Charles left in our care."

Mr Robinson took an excessively delicate sip of his coffee, then offered, "Mr Darcy is unmarried."

Elizabeth's mouth dropped and her father's head immediately

jerked towards Mr Robinson. Mr Robinson was sheepish, holding his hands in the air. "Just a thought."

Mr Bennet said, "You cannot mean that Elizabeth should—"

"From the looks of him, I should imagine that he has a very grand, heiress-type bride in his mind," said Elizabeth tartly. "I doubt the likes of me could entice him."

Mr Robinson gave her a kindly grin. "I cannot speak to Mr Darcy's matrimonial ambitions, but I think any man should count himself lucky to have you, Lizzy."

"Robinson, you are trying to remove my grandson and now my daughter from me?" Mr Bennet offered a weak chuckle.

"I only beg that both of you would act with prudence." Mr Robinson set his coffee on the table and crossed his hands in front of him. "The law is not on your side here, and the avenues of redress are few and unlikely. It is a difficult circumstance, tragic really, but I fear that such shenanigans as happened today can do no good. I urge you both to consider carefully whatever further actions are undertaken."

With that, the conversation ended. Elizabeth thought she understood very well what Mr Robinson said: it was hopeless. She would lose little Charles to a man who neither knew him nor loved him—and there was nothing Elizabeth could do about it.

She sat up very late that night in a window seat of the bedchamber she once shared with her sister. The moonless sky watched her as tears came and went, followed by intense rage and then more tears; eventually a headache beset her alongside dispirited ennui. She looked at the bed that was once Jane's. Dear Jane, dear, dear Jane. I have failed in the one thing you have ever asked of me.

THE FIRST FINGERLINGS of another grey dawn were hailed with relief. Elizabeth's fears and sorrows had by then grown tiresome, and she longed to escape the scene of such ponderous regret. She dressed herself quickly, pinned her hair as best she could, and was soon out into the morning.

She could not determine with any satisfaction whether it was raining or merely cold; in any case, she was immediately chilled to her bones, but she began a brisk pace that soon warmed her to a tolerable degree. A good ramble always cheered her or at least helped clear her thoughts.

For an all-too-brief time, she was able to put aside her worries in favour of thinking of the cold air in her lungs and the sights and sounds of nature around her. It was true, the countryside she beheld inspired its own sort of worry—lifeless mud, swollen streams, and no sign of the sun—but it diverted her from her own troubles.

But reality would intrude, and soon enough, Charles was again in her thoughts. Some part of her had begun to accept that he would be taken from her even as the rest of her railed against it and frantically searched for some way, any way, that she could keep a hold of him. Running off with him to the continent was one notion that gained favour with her by the minute—though Upper Canada might do better. With such ideas tormenting her, it was no wonder she did not recognise the odious, looming creature before her in time to avoid speaking to him.

Mr Darcy stood frowning in the morning mist. He greeted her with a grave bow, speaking her name as if pronouncing something of great import. She bobbed an indifferent curtsey. "I am surprised to find you here."

"This is your father's land?"

"No," she said. "This is part of Netherfield."

"Ah." His gaze was assessing and critical as it swept over the land. "Bingley's land then."

"No," she said very deliberately. "My brother leased the manor. He intended to purchase but took ill before he could."

"I see." Mr Darcy nodded, his eyes still traveling over the countryside, swift and dismissive. "Yes, I should have realised that from my study of his books."

"Is that what this is about? My brother's fortune?"

Mr Darcy drew back. "I beg your pardon?"

"You are keen to gain control. Is not fortune generally the inducement in such cases as these?"

Mr Darcy gave a scornful bark of laughter. "In matters of fortune, I am, and always have been, superior to Bingley."

Fortune perhaps, but gentleman-like behaviour? Never. Elizabeth bit her lip to keep the thought from escaping her.

"If anything, I should think that his relations—who are clearly in straitened circumstances—might bear that suspicion more readily than I."

"Straitened circumstances?" She glared at him. "We do face the same problems as the rest of the country, Mr Darcy, but Longbourn is unencumbered by debt, which is more than many can say."

"Unencumbered but entailed away," said Mr Darcy. "Do not think me ignorant of your situation, Miss Bennet."

"If you know so much about us, you will know my father's heir passed without issue," she retorted. "Not that it is any concern of yours."

"No, it is not, but it improves my understanding of why you should cling so desperately to a little boy with one hundred thousand pounds sitting in a bank. What has come of the interest these years, I must wonder."

Elizabeth gasped and felt herself blush scarlet. Hot denial rose to her lips, but she stopped herself before she could speak them. She knew her father would never resort to thievery; however, in a certain circumstance, if it so suited him, she knew he would be able to acquit himself for whatever actions might best serve his purpose, no matter how others might perceive it. But to take money from his grandson? Surely not. But she had enough doubt to prevent her tongue from offering the angry rebuke she wished for.

Her voice shook as she said, "I shall not stand here while you insult me. I am better bred than to reply to your accusations, and in any case, I do not concern myself with such things. I shall bid you good day."

She turned and began to walk away, tears stinging her eyes even as anger rose in her throat. How dare he! Money! As if she had ever cared one bit about Bingley's money or little Charles's fortune!

It would not do. She could not walk away with the cloud of Mr Darcy's suspicion attached to her. She whirled around, facing him once again, her hands on her hips like a scold.

"You are wrong if you think fortune has anything to do with why we wish to keep him here."

"If you love him so much, you should desire the advantages I can offer him. I can give him the life his father and his father's father wanted him to have."

"And you think we cannot?"

Mr Darcy forbore to answer. He stood and stared at her, the mist and his hat rendering his face unreadable and even a bit frightening. She drew her pelisse about her more closely.

"As my sister lay dying, I promised her that I would care for him as a mother would. I solemnly swore it to her. Jane was…she was an angel, too good for this earth, and she never asked anything of anyone. Never wanted to cause any trouble! But in this, she needed my help, and I cannot fail her. Have you never made a promise that was so important you would rather die than fail?"

Something in his face changed then; it grew more stiff, harder somehow. He stared at her until at last her disgust overcame her and she turned from him.

He was lost to every comprehension of kindness, this hateful man. Shocking that she could so heartily despise someone she barely knew, but she did.

"I have disappointed people enough in my life," he said at long last. She turned to face him again while he continued to speak. "While my mistakes have perhaps not been many, they have had dreadful consequences, and it is those consequences that have made me determined not to fail again. Your sister might have asked this of you but, similarly, Bingley has asked it of me. I cannot, nay will not, allow you or any of your family to stand in my way."

"Why now?" she cried. "Why must you remove him from every-thing and everyone he knows?"

"He will learn to know different places and different people, and I daresay it will do him no harm."

"Four years," Elizabeth replied immediately. "For four years, you have been indifferent to his very existence and now you want him?"

"I was not indifferent to his existence," Mr Darcy replied. "I knew nothing of it."

"Is Derbyshire beyond the reach of the post?" Elizabeth retorted. "I should have thought four years sufficient to receive a letter, maybe even two."

"I cannot account for the inadequacies of the post nor explain what came of the letters that must have been sent to me. What I can say is that once I knew I had a duty to my friend, I came immediately."

Elizabeth rolled her eyes. "You mean Mr Pritchard came immediately."

She spun on her heel, intending to storm off towards Longbourn and leave this hateful, odious man behind her. Perhaps she would have some good fortune and he would fall down a ravine or be eaten by some vicious woodland creature.

But such fortune was not to be hers. Instead it was she who fell, slipping on the wet, muddy path. With a small cry, her knee struck a rock and her gloves immediately became soaked and dirty. Mr Darcy was upon her in a trice, his hands beneath her elbows hauling her back to her feet. It was a minor mishap, but humiliation, pique, and the feel of wet mud soaking into her skirts combined to produce mortifying loud sobs nevertheless.

It was the sort of cry that is impossible to suppress; indeed all attempts to stop only made it worse. She pressed her handkerchief to her eyes willing herself to stop, stop, stop—but she could not, not for far too many long minutes.

"Madam, have you injured yourself?" Mr Darcy's attempts to soothe her were as stiff as he was. "Shall I summon assistance?"

"No," she gulped, attempting to restore herself to equanimity. "No, I am not injured."

She swallowed and hiccupped a few sobs while at the same time removing her gloves and shaking them in some vain hope of making them dry—or at least more dry. Her knee, she dared not consider, but it felt bruised, not bleeding. She dabbed and scrubbed at her face, unwilling to suppose how she might look, and at length, her humiliating display ended. Several deep, bracing breaths more and she was prepared to make her last intercession.

Mr Darcy was plainly lost to every sense of decency and civility. He had no feeling, no tenderness, and no better nature to be prevailed upon. So she would degrade herself, desperation providing the impulse.

"What if I came with him?"

Mr Darcy simply stared at her.

"As…as a governess for him. After all, you will need a governess for him soon enough; why should it not be me?"

Mr Darcy's stare had changed from mere indifference to alarm. His mouth hung slightly open, though when he saw her notice, he quickly closed it.

"I loved my sister with all my heart. She was all that was good and kind and sweet, and when I lost her, I knew not what I would do. Seeing Charles leave will be like losing her all over again. I shall do anything I must to avoid that."

To think of that brought fresh dampness to her eyes, but she would not give way again. He made no answer to her plea, staring at the wet ground where she had fallen, no doubt congratulating the mud for having its way with her.

She soon understood he would not reply, and at length, she walked on. He followed her. At least he is silent enough that I may pretend I am alone.

It was not until the gate of Longbourn was within view that she spoke again. "May I ask you something?"

"Of course."

She turned and studied him, this strange, enigmatic man. He bore her examination unperturbed and silent.

"It would be quite easy to leave him where he is. You could be his guardian; we would raise him but still heed your authority. He could be your ward yet our family."

"No."

"Why not?"

Mr Darcy shook his head.

"It answers both your claim of duty and our claims of attachment and affection."

He dropped his gaze. His hand was clenched on his walking stick, and he began to make a slight digging motion in the path with it. She waited with decreasing patience, finally prompting him. "Sir?"

His reply was given in a low voice. "Because I do know what it is to make a promise to someone that is so important that you would rather die than fail, and I do not intend to make a poor show of this."

She did not dare ask more.

She waited several moments and then reduced herself to pleading. "His governess, Mr Darcy. You need not pay me. I only want to stay with him."

He raised his head from the enchanting view of his walking stick. "Pay you?"

She staved off her frustration with a heavy sigh. "To be his governess. I want only to remain close to him, and I shall superintend his education while I am at it."

To her utter amazement a smile seemed to play about his lips. "Miss Bennet, do you truly think yourself capable of superintending the education of a young gentleman?"

"Yes, I think myself perfectly able to manage his education and had already planned to do so."

"And where," Mr Darcy asked carefully, "were you educated?"

They stared at one another for several long moments before she tilted her chin and straightened her shoulders. "Home."

He raised one brow with an imperious look that was painfully insupportable. "You must have been often in London for the benefit of masters?"

"We went but rarely." Against all inclination, Elizabeth felt herself shrinking under the weight of his scorn. "My father is not fond of London."

"I see."

He was back to his careful regard of the path, digging and probing with his stick. With each passing moment, Elizabeth lost what small measure of hope remained in her.

Abruptly, he raised his head, touching the brim of his hat as he turned away from her. "I must return to the inn. I intended to depart today but must forestall until tomorrow."

A short and inadequate delay of the inevitable misery of parting with her boy. Tomorrow! The thought chilled her much more than the weather ever could.

"Sir, please!" she cried out, unable to stop herself, watching him depart. "I beg you. Please permit me to attend him."

And he, without deigning to look back, said, "As you like."

THREE

"THERE YOU ARE." MR BENNET SMILED AT HIS ELDEST DAUGHTER FROM his seat at the head of the breakfast table.

"Did you wait long?" Elizabeth took her seat at the table, smiling at little Charles who sat at his grandfather's right side, happily spooning porridge into his mouth.

"Not at all," her father replied. "How fares our countryside this morning? Any news?"

"Well." Elizabeth made an expressive look towards little Charles. "Perhaps."

Mr Bennet replied to this with a tweak of his eyebrow but said nothing. They finished their meal, allowing Charles to have charge of the conversation. He had a dream to relate to them in painful detail— something about a ship that could sail and fly and drive over the land like a carriage and his nocturnal adventures on this wondrous conveyance—and he would not be swayed from a thorough recounting of it.

When breakfast was over, Elizabeth joined her father in his study.

"I had a most unexpected encounter this morning while I was walking."

"With whom, if I might ask?"

"Mr Darcy. I found him on the path near Netherfield."

"Out having a scornful glare at the fields, was he?"

Elizabeth laughed lightly. "Not seeing anything to please him, to be sure."

She paused a moment. She was resolved, her plan was the only way. The sacrifice must be hers. She had no wish to lie to her dear Papa but neither did she wish for any further opposition to her plans.

Mr Bennet asked, "What did he say?"

"You know, Papa, that I am…I feel it is of utmost importance that we should retain our claim on Jane's son no matter what, and it seems we are doomed in that prospect."

Mr Bennet nodded. "Indeed."

"Mr Darcy has agreed to permit me to accompany Charles to his home in Derbyshire…as Charles's governess."

Mr Bennet stood so rapidly Elizabeth feared for his coffee. "What? A governess! Lizzy, are you mad?"

Elizabeth held up one hand to forestall her father's exclamations of dismay. "I am only determined to fulfil the office with which Jane has charged me."

"Lizzy, I can hardly send my daughter off to live in Derbyshire in the home of an unmarried man."

"But you can send your grandson?"

Mr Bennet studied her for several long moments, then picked up his coffee and went to the window, staring out for some time.

Elizabeth drew a deep, fortifying breath. "I would never wish to go off with such a man as Mr Darcy for my own sake. I want to remain with Charles until…until Mr Darcy realises that the care of the child is more than simply collecting him and tossing him in a nursery somewhere."

Mr Bennet did not turn from his intent scrutiny of the world outside his window. "Firstly, that you should descend to being a governess is—"

"Is my likely fate." He turned back to face her, but she did not back down. "Is it not? Let us speak frankly. When Charles is grown and you are gone, that is likely my fate. I am doing no more than skipping ahead."

With slow heavy steps, Mr Bennet returned to his chair, sinking down into it. "What about marriage?"

"Marriage?" Elizabeth sighed. Her father's wilful blindness was tiring. "Such fancies as those have long ago passed me by. I am five and twenty and certainly no more handsome than I was in my bloom. I have made my peace with the likelihood that I shall remain a spinster."

"I cannot send you off into the care of a man I do not know from Adam. We know nothing of his character, nothing of his morals, nothing of—"

"Yet he will take our Charles."

Mr Bennet stared sightlessly at his desk for a moment.

"Jane would want me to stay with Charles," Elizabeth insisted. "In due time, perhaps Mr Darcy will tire of the needs of a small child in his house. Even better, perhaps you will have time to take it before the courts."

Elizabeth paused for a moment, wishing for her father's avowal to do just that. When such reassurance did not come, she went on, pretending not to notice Mr Bennet's lack of interest in pursuing a legal course against Mr Darcy. "Alas, I see now that everything we have done in this matter thus far has only made Mr Darcy more determined to carry his point."

Mr Bennet nodded thoughtfully.

"However, once the true task is understood to him—when little Charles is in his care—he will apprehend that it is not merely some game, that there is no such thing as winning or losing in cases such as these. Then he may wish to give up the scheme."

"We can dare to hope."

"And perhaps if we are very lucky," she added with a mischievous smile, "he might soon find someone to marry, a lady who dislikes small children, particularly when they are not her own."

"Just take care that he does not fall in love with you," Mr Bennet warned.

"I think I may safely promise you," said Elizabeth as she rose and went to place a kiss on her father's cheek, "nothing of that sort is even remotely possible."

WITH WHAT WAS LIKELY the deference due to him, Mr and Miss Bennet extended to Darcy an invitation to dine that evening. He would have been just as happy having some stew in the public house but felt it would be ungenerous to refuse them.

His horse's shoe was mended—with more skill than he expected should exist in this insignificant hamlet—but Darcy decided to walk. The distance was an easy one, and he reasoned that the fading light would give him an excuse for an early escape from the social requirements.

The air was cold and damp but the walk was brief, and soon he arrived at Longbourn. He paused a moment in the lane to regard it as he had not before, when he was nearly apoplectic with rage.

Longbourn had fine old bones and elegance in its form, but if the tattle he learnt from his man was true, it suffered from the indifference of its owner. It had once brought in two thousand a year, but recent estimates were less, particularly in this most difficult of years. Darcy had no doubt but that he was doing the Bennets an enormous favour in removing the burden of care of the lad from them—and now Miss Bennet too. Unlike Longbourn, he had the means to support them.

He was shown in with more alacrity than he encountered on his first visit and was given directly into the care of the master himself. Mr Bennet received him in his study, again holding what Darcy guessed was an ever-present book.

"You have made my daughter an extraordinarily kind offer, sir."

Less an offer than reluctant acquiescence. Darcy shifted in the uncomfortable chair he had been directed towards. "It seems the path of least misery for us all."

There was a silence during which the two gentlemen regarded one another warily. Darcy, feeling the weight of respect that one must give an elder, deigned to speak first.

"It is clear to me that this family is very attached to the boy. Presumably, the boy is attached to you as well. If I am to assume guardianship of the child, I must begin now doing what is in his best interest. Having his aunt there will be to his comfort, and if he is happy, it will ease my conscience."

"Very good of you. Of course as her father, I must voice my fears of the sorts of behaviour that can sometimes arise."

Darcy felt his cheeks flush but did not know whether it was embarrassment or vexation that yielded the colour. He interrupted Mr Bennet immediately, brusqueness of tone intended to convey his irritation at such an implication. "I assure you, I do not countenance nor indulge any such proclivities."

"I do not intend to insult you," said Mr Bennet. "I speak as a father concerned for the welfare of his daughter."

"Then you should do best to warn her against the scheme."

"And so I have," said Mr Bennet, looking vexingly calm. "But she will not be moved."

A retort came to Darcy's mind—as a father, ought not Bennet have the final say? But he knew how a young lady could prevail against all strictures, and so his tongue was stayed.

"The Darcy family has always held considerable patronage in the Church," he replied stiffly. "And my father exhorted me from a very early age that such patronage should include not only our fortune but our character and our reputations as well. Miss Bennet will be as safe in my home as she is in yours. Moreover, my aunt, Lady Catherine de Bourgh, is also in permanent residence in my house."

"Your aunt?"

Darcy nodded, stiff and small. "My mother's sister."

"I see."

Mr Bennet considered that a moment while regarding Darcy solemnly over his spectacles. "That is some consolation. Nevertheless, I must say to you as my father once said to me: never forget that every lady is someone's daughter, someone's wife, someone's mother, and pray treat her with the respect afforded those stations."

"You have my word, Mr Bennet," said Darcy. Mr Bennet would do well to recall I am obliging them, not the other way around.

The evening passed pleasantly enough. Longbourn retained an excellent cook, particularly noteworthy in such difficult times; the fish, though small, was tasty, and the venison was likewise. The breads were light and crusty as Darcy liked them, and the pudding was among the best he had ever had.

The conversation at dinner was also surprising in its erudition and wit. Mr Bennet and Miss Bennet were both avid readers, and the discussion soon became spirited as they conversed easily about the books they had read. Before long, he realised Miss Bennet played a game of sorts with him.

"Miss Bennet, I begin to think you are fond of professing opinions not your own," he accused.

"Perhaps I do," said she, her eyes sparkling. "Otherwise we might simply agree with each other, and what fun would that be?"

It was then that the most displeasing part of the evening occurred. As he sat there with this lady—the most unattractive sort of country hoyden he had ever known, a lady who would insist on intruding where she was plainly unwanted—he felt an odd tug within him. Along with it, an unwelcome thought entered his mind: she is pretty.

And she was pretty. She was dressed for an occasion—he supposed dinner with a gentleman of good fortune was certainly an occasion—and came to the table in what was undoubtedly her best gown. It did not compare to what he saw in town—or rather what he used to see— but it was well cut and suited her figure admirably.

Rather a light and pleasing figure too.

Accursed thoughts! Yet they were thoughts that proved difficult to dispel. Mr Bennet soon suggested some music in the drawing room, and Miss Bennet, after some pretty little protest, agreed to oblige them. From her demurrals, he expected little of her, but her performance, while by no means capital, was perfectly adequate.

When she sang, it was another matter entirely.

Her voice reached into him, into all the dark recesses of his soul, and offered him light. It was enchanting and enthralling to hear her and watch her, and he was, against all inclination, uplifted. For a brief time—the length of her song—he had a strange sense come over him that he could not immediately identify. Oh yes—it was hope.

He sighed and then recollected his wits, realising he must seem like an imbecile staring at her so. He straightened himself, placing on his countenance his usual demeanour and only then dared look at Mr Bennet.

As Darcy suspected, the gentleman was watching him. When Darcy made eye contact, Mr Bennet half-frowned and murmured coolly, "Someone's daughter, Mr Darcy."

SINCE HER RETURN to the bosom of her family in Hertfordshire, Charlotte Collins—widow of Reverend William Collins—had also resumed her place in Elizabeth's heart. Once childhood playfellows, a strain was introduced when Charlotte married a man whom Elizabeth considered one of the most ridiculous persons she had ever known.

Mr Collins was to have inherited Longbourn on the passing of her father, but a fever took him soon after his marriage, likely the same fever that afflicted her dear sister and Bingley. Since his passing, Longbourn remained entailed, now to some other distant cousin, but alas, it was a cousin too young for Charlotte to marry. She would never be, as Lady Lucas had so hoped, mistress of Longbourn.

She arrived shortly after breakfast with the intention of remaining with Elizabeth for some time. Elizabeth met her at the door and watched as she removed her thick woollen pelisse, noticing that she looked very thin and her skin extremely pale. Though Charlotte was never a handsome girl, her once-lovely, creamy complexion was now faded and grey.

"Charlotte, are you feeling well?" Elizabeth took her friend's arm to lead her into the parlour.

"Do I look ill?"

"No, no, just a bit…well, tired perhaps."

"I am tired," Charlotte admitted, sinking gratefully into the plushy chair Elizabeth offered. "We are down to just one girl to help with the laundry and the cooking. The rest is left to Maria and me."

"We feel very fortunate that Hill has remained with us," Elizabeth said. "So many have gone off to work in factories and the like."

Charlotte shrugged. "The servants must do as they can to survive in these difficult times. But enough about that. What is this I hear about you going to Derbyshire?"

Elizabeth smiled faintly in reply. Charlotte's father, Sir William

Lucas, was a notorious gossip. Elizabeth had no doubt that Charlotte probably knew more about Elizabeth's trip than she herself did.

She began with Mr Pritchard. Charlotte was satisfyingly dismayed and distressed about the prospect of a strange gentleman tearing little Charles from his home, but as Elizabeth's recitation continued, she saw the futility of her protest.

"I began to see that there was little hope of thwarting it," Elizabeth concluded. "I am sure you can imagine my feelings on the inevitability of such a notion."

Charlotte had tears in her eyes. "Oh Lizzy! I do not know how you can sit there so calmly. I am myself about to run mad with the grief of parting from him!"

"I would," Elizabeth agreed calmly, "had I not insisted that I should go along as his governess."

The effect this statement had on Charlotte was not insubstantial. Charlotte was not customarily prone to displays of excessive feeling, but this amazed her and she was silent for nearly a full minute.

"A governess? Lizzy, you surely do not wish to—"

Elizabeth waved aside her concern. "Is it not my eventual fate? Why not hasten to it so that I may remain with my dear little Charles."

"But your marriage prospects—"

"Will not be materially different than they are now, which is to say, improbable if not impossible."

"Oh, Eliza." Charlotte's eyes warmed with compassion. "I do admire your sacrifice."

"Is it not what a mother does? I promised dear Jane I would do as she would have done for him. That is all there is to it."

"You do your sister credit even though I fear it will not redound to your benefit." Charlotte shook her head. "But enough of that. I can see you are resolved, and when Eliza Bennet has made up her mind, there is no sense in trying to persuade her otherwise."

"Quite true." Elizabeth grinned with more confidence than she felt. "So I shall be off to Derbyshire to live in a very grand house with the very grand Mr Darcy and his noble aunt—"

"Noble aunt?"

Elizabeth nodded. "Lady Catherine de Bourgh."

"Lady Catherine de Bourgh?" If Elizabeth thought she exhausted the possibility of shocking Charlotte, she was mistaken. "You do recall my former connexion to that lady, do you not?"

Elizabeth thought for a moment. "The name had some familiarity to me when he said it, though at the time, I thought little of it. A connexion to you?"

"She was Mr Collins's patroness," Charlotte replied. "The lady of Rosings Park?"

"Oh yes! How stupid of me! I cannot believe I forgot!"

"It has been above five years already," Charlotte said with a soft sigh.

"And now she lives with her nephew?" Elizabeth shook her head. "From what you told me, she seemed exceedingly proud of her home. I wonder why she left it."

"It must have been when Mr Darcy married her daughter," Charlotte said.

"Mr Darcy married her daughter? But he is a bachelor."

"Well I am certain they were engaged," said Charlotte. "I know that much is true. I was not long in Kent, but I heard of it often while I was there. Miss de Bourgh said little of the matter herself, but her mother was definite and she is not a woman to be gainsaid."

"Had you met Mr Darcy often?"

"No, I never met him."

"Perhaps he had no wish to marry his cousin?"

"I should think the possibility of having two such great estates, not to mention Miss de Bourgh's fortune, would be sufficient inducement for him."

"That is true. In any case, among noble families, the matches are made more to suit the families than the lovers themselves," Elizabeth said. "No matter the inducement, I cannot imagine tying myself to such a man for my life long."

"If Lady Catherine was your mother, you might think otherwise," Charlotte replied. "A married lady, as you know, is able to preside over her own house and arrange it as she likes, but an unmarried girl must bend to the wishes of her elders."

"You need not tell me, Charlotte." The two friends chuckled comfortably.

"So Miss de Bourgh gained the respectability and relative freedom of a married woman from the union, and Mr Darcy became wealthy."

"No, he was already wealthy. That marriage likely made him one of the richest men in England."

"A splendid payment for what must have been an excessively short marriage," said Elizabeth. "Particularly if they were only engaged while you were married to Mr Collins."

"Yes," said Charlotte. "He must have married her in '12, I suppose. Perhaps she died in the childbed?"

"Likely so," Elizabeth agreed. "But Lady Catherine remains at his house? I wonder that she does not return to Rosings Park."

"I believe someone else lives there now. Mr Darcy must have wished to let it out, though I cannot say for certain. My time in Hunsford parish was so short, I do not have anyone to whom I write nor anyone who writes to me."

"In any case," Elizabeth pronounced cheerfully, "whatever their reasons, I must be glad of them for they serve my purpose now. I shall remain with Charles, and that is all I care about."

"Perhaps not all you care about, Eliza." Charlotte gave her a sly look. "I know it must excite your anticipation to imagine going to Derbyshire. Maybe you will at last see the Lake District."

"It was once a dream of mine." For a moment, Elizabeth was lost in wistful remembrance of the summer she was meant to travel with her aunt and uncle to the Lake District. Jane's marriage and impending confinement led her to decide to remain at home rather than go with Mr and Mrs Gardiner. She would never say that she regretted the decision or would ever choose differently; however, as the letters arrived that summer bearing descriptions of all that was seen and done, she could not deny intense feelings of envy. "Yes," said she with a smile at Charlotte. "At last I shall see something outside of Meryton."

ELIZABETH BEGAN her calls of farewell with her two sisters, both of whom remained in Meryton or close by. Mary, or Mrs Willard as she liked to be called, was the first order of duty.

Mary was married just above three years and had dutifully

birthed two sons to her husband. Arthur, her eldest, was fair haired and pinch-faced, and from the very beginning of his life, carried with him the same faintly disapproving air that his mother always did. Even now, he sat quietly with a set of blocks, creating ramrod straight, square little structures while casting suspicious glances at Elizabeth and little Charles. He did not choose to play with little Charles; Mary explained that young Arthur found it trying on his nerves to be exposed to the high spirits of other boys. With a sigh, Elizabeth looked at the infant sleeping peacefully in his mother's arms. She could only hope that he might be more inclined to liveliness and good humour.

"Derbyshire? Why should you be going to Derbyshire?"

"With Charles," Elizabeth explained patiently. "Your husband must have explained everything to you."

"I was sure he must have heard wrong." Mary pursed her lips and took a dainty sip of her tea. "He thinks you are to go as a governess to little Charles."

"Mr Willard is entirely correct. That is exactly what I intend to do."

It seemed hardly possible but Mary's lips pressed together in an even thinner line and her eyes narrowed such that Elizabeth wondered that she could see. Elizabeth bit her lip, determined not to permit her sister to aggravate her.

"And who," asked Mary in clipped tones, "will marry you then?"

With exaggerated gaiety, Elizabeth said, "There is no doubt I shall boast just as many suitors in Derbyshire as I do here, which is to say none whatsoever!"

Mary's lips nearly disappeared, and Elizabeth hastened to respond in a more serious way. "You know I have no intention to marry, not now."

"Jane never intended that you should become tied to her son while forgoing all other concerns."

Elizabeth rubbed the back of her neck and heaved a sigh. "What concerns have I neglected?"

"Your own," Mary replied primly. "You have no husband, no child of your own. It is not respectable."

Her words stung, but Elizabeth would not permit Mary to know that. Certainly there were changes to her life introduced by the addition of Charles to her care. She could not roam about as she once had —she had the concerns of the household upon her. She did not go to assemblies; she was not often at the neighbourhood parties. Her life had become one common to many spinster daughters: tending a hearth not her own and raising the children of other people.

For the briefest of moments, Mary dropped her usual pompous humour, looking for a moment like she had a true sister's heart. "I worry for you. Do you not wish for your own house and family?"

"I do, of course I do." Elizabeth swallowed. "But this is to be my lot in life, and I intend to find contentment in it. There are no guarantees in this world, and if the only boast I have at the end of my time on this earth is to say I raised one special boy, then I shall be satisfied."

Mary granted only a tight smile and then went on to more pious conversation. Elizabeth had once believed that to be the wife of a parson would have suited Mary very well, but wife of the town solicitor did nearly as well. Mary enjoyed knowing the matters of finance and business for those around her, and she scrupled not to discuss her opinions on how they managed their concerns.

It was nearly an hour later that Elizabeth was able to bid her farewell with a hug and a promise to write often. She gave Arthur a kiss on the head, which alarmed him, and then collected little Charles and went off to Kitty's house.

Kitty had married better than might have been expected. She married Mr Goulding after the death of his wife, unconcerned for the fact that he was older than their father. They had twin girls aged two years, and Kitty spent her days eating cake with Maria Lucas and dreaming of who her daughters might some day marry.

Her visit with Kitty passed easily. Her younger sister cried at the idea of Elizabeth leaving, then engaged her in a violent argument about ancient and irrelevant grievances from back when Lydia was yet alive, then cried again at the idea that Elizabeth would leave Hertfordshire.

Both visits were exhausting—as much from the exertion as from the effort required to bear the silliness of her sisters—and Elizabeth was nearly dead on her feet by the time she arrived back at Longbourn. However, she had just enough time before dinner to write a few letters, for two more sisters were due some correspondence.

The late Charles Bingley had boasted two sisters. Miss Louisa Bingley had married a man of more fashion than fortune and eventually the former had outpaced the latter. With debts mounting, he had abandoned her, disappearing to places unknown.

Miss Caroline Bingley married one Mr John Milne, a man many years her elder who had a sufficient fortune to maintain both sisters in style. They divided their time between London and Bath and felt strongly that the country life was not for them. It was not long into their marriage before children arrived, though alas, Mrs Milne had followed the example of Mrs Bennet and delivered only daughters to her husband thus far.

She was never much interested in her brother's son, but Elizabeth thought she ought to write to her nevertheless.

Mrs Milne,
How long it has been since we last spoke! I do hope you and Mr Milne and Persephone and Helena are continuing on in good health. This dreadful weather we are having has not been any advantage to Hertfordshire, but I understand it is this way everywhere, so likely there is no use complaining about it.

Your brother's son is doing very well. He quite amazed me the other day by counting to one hundred wholly unprompted, and my father has been teaching him all about astronomy and the sciences. Little Charles seems to find it excessively fascinating. Unlike either your brother or my sister, he also enjoys time with his books; nearly anything will capture him, and he often stares at the words on the page doing his best to make them out. Such simple joy there is in seeing the awakening of his mind and wit! I am sure you will encounter such pleasures in your little daughters as well.

Elizabeth went on, relating other little stories from the neighbourhood although it was many years since Caroline had seen any of them. When at last she had exhausted her store of on-dit of little consequence, she came to the true object of her letter.

We had something of a shock several weeks ago—at least to me it was a shock. To my father, it seems the news was not wholly unknown. Evidently your brother, before his death, named an old friend of his as Charles's guardian. Mr Fitzwilliam Darcy is his guardian, and although having had nothing to do with him or us these many years, he intends to take him off to his estate in Derbyshire.

Elizabeth paused a moment, swallowing against the flood of emotion such simple words raised. With a deep breath, she went on.

You might imagine how I perceived such news and intentions, and as such, I have managed to secure a position with Mr Darcy's household. I shall go with Charles to serve as his governess, though he is full young to need one just now. I would say Mr Darcy invited me, but to say he acquiesced to my demand has more truth in it. We shall leave Longbourn shortly, and I shall write to you as soon as I am settled to provide you the direction.

I must presume Mr Darcy is a man of good character as our brother felt it wise to remand his heir into that gentleman's care. Surely you must have known something of him from your younger days, and I pray you will write to me and tell me good things of the gentleman such that my anxieties over leaving my home and entering his will be quelled. I do understand he was once married? I wonder what became of his wife.

Warmest regards,
Elizabeth

FOUR

ELIZABETH TOLD MR DARCY SHE WOULD COUNTENANCE NO LESS THAN A se'nnight before she could leave her home; he told her they would leave in three days for any more would force him to travel on the Sabbath, and he could not abide gentlemen who willingly travelled on the Sabbath. She made certain he knew that her acquiescence was grudging.

Each day brought with it a new reason to dislike Mr Darcy. Although the rumours of his wealth had initially predisposed most of the town to approve of him, his actions during his stay in Meryton were not distinguished by any marks of goodness or charity.

He insulted the blacksmith by remarking on his surprise that his horse should have been so well shod, and he offended Mr Goulding by suggesting improvements to his fields—needed improvements to be sure, but unasked for and, as such, unwelcome.

He sat next to Mrs Long at church one Sunday without speaking a word to her, and when she dared speak to him, she was greeted by solemn hauteur and a reply of the least number of syllables possible. He refused all invitations extended to him and did not show the least inclination towards flirting with the eligible young ladies of the district.

That such a man should have been an acquaintance of the late, beloved Mr Bingley! This was exclaimed in many a drawing room over the time Mr Darcy spent in Meryton.

The letter that Elizabeth received from Caroline did nothing to allay her concerns. Indeed, it achieved quite the opposite.

I find your request that I tell you of Mr Darcy impertinent. Nevertheless, I shall tell you what I can. Of his family, there are fewer better; he is not titled but his grandfather was the Earl of Matlock, and his grandmother is connected with the Devonshires. His income at the time I knew him was around ten thousand a year, but I am certain it is much beyond that now. I do not know whether any other man without a dukedom to his name is as wealthy as Mr Darcy.

This scheme of yours to be governess to little Charles is among the silliest things I have ever heard. There is nothing to gain and everything to be lost. Mr Darcy, for whatever his shortcomings, has all the advantages of a gentleman of rank. I am certain he could raise my brother's son to no dissatisfactory outcome, and you should do best to leave him to it without interference. You will render yourself unmarriageable for no just cause. Why not come to London with Mr Milne and me? I have a number of young gentlemen of my acquaintance who I am sure would be glad to know you, but once you become a governess, I am afraid I shall be unable to say the same.

IT WAS ALARMING to Elizabeth that the best thing that Caroline could say of Mr Darcy was that which she already knew—he was rich—and in the time since Caroline knew him, his prosperity had increased.

"How fortunate is this Mr Darcy," Elizabeth murmured aloud. "In these difficult times when every man, whether prince or pauper, has experienced some sort of decrease, he has managed to increase his own holdings substantially."

She shrugged. It was said the rich got richer and the poor got poorer, and it seemed to be the truth in this case.

A MIZZLING RAIN shrouded the house on the day of their departure. Elizabeth had woken early, determined to have one last ramble around her beloved home before she left it for who knew how long. She briefly entertained the hope that the rain might offer some delay, a short stay of execution, but no; Mr Darcy had expressed his wish to leave, and nothing so inconsequential as rain would likely stop him.

From a rise about half a mile from the house, she was able to view Longbourn, and she was struck—in the way that those familiar are often surprised—by how dreadful it really looked. Too much had been left to the directive of her father's indolence. There were fences that needed mending, the door should have been painted, and the windows appeared very dirty. The roof had a piece that looked like it might be leaking (or would soon begin), and Elizabeth counted three shutters not properly fastened and hung at odd angles. She wondered how much would be left to neglect and disrepair by the time she returned.

"And who can imagine when that will be?" She spoke to no one, permitting herself a moment of anxiety over her impending departure. She had done all she could to push her fears to the side, but now, staring at her home, she allowed them their lead. She knew not when she would return. She knew not how it would be, serving as a governess in a grand estate. She knew not how Mr Darcy would treat her. She knew not whether any of this would do any good to anyone.

"For you, my beloved sister." She spoke it aloud as the rain coalesced into chilled teardrops on her cheeks. Jane had asked her to be a mother to her boy, and a mother would not leave her child, not for anything. She would stay by Charles's side at any cost. In this, she remained resolved.

With a nod, she squared her shoulders and turned to go back to the house. It was time to go to Pemberley.

DARCY BROKE his fast at the inn on the morning of their departure wondering that he felt no relief at leaving this dismal little place. It had been an interminable series of days here—the grey, foggy tedium of the weather an apt metaphor to the grey, foggy tedium of the people of Meryton. There was nothing of note among them, and he wondered that Bingley could have been content with them.

"Not merely content with," he muttered to his coffee cup, "but married one of them."

By all reports, Miss Jane Bingley had been a noted beauty—not a surprise, knowing his friend—though nothing to remark upon in terms of accomplishment or wit. Beauty and sweetness of temper, yet, knowing Bingley, that was likely enough. Unless the girl trapped him somehow? That was very likely the way of things. Jane Bennet had seen her chance to live well beyond anything she had ever known, and she did what she had to do to secure him.

Ah, but what did it matter? Bingley and his lady were both long cold in the ground. He would just need to be certain that young Charles was taught not to lose his head over a pretty face and complaisant temper.

He rose from the small table set aside for his particular use, recalling that he had some letters to post before he left town. He shuffled through them as he walked, ensuring there was nothing neglected. One went to Pemberley, naturally, bearing last-minute instructions for the incorporation of Miss Bennet and little Charles into the household. Several were for Rosings, which made him sigh. Rosings Park required much more of his attention than he wished to allow it. He would need to make a trip, soon; this business with young Charles had distracted him from other obligations.

Ah, but there was one letter he had neglected to write. He hesitated, wondering whether he could forgo another missive, however brief. But no; if he knew anything, it was that ladies required attentiveness and reassurance, and this lady in particular needed more than most.

Turning, he retraced his steps through the inn, returning to the bedchamber he had used these last nights. His men were still removing his trunks, but he waved at them to continue on their way before settling himself at the small desk. The pen was inferior and the ink watery, but he managed to scratch out a few lines on the rough paper.

Anne,
I have no doubt that this estrangement plagues your heart and mind,
but do be assured I shall do all that is within my power to broker
some resolution. What has been done cannot be undone; I cannot
deceive you and pretend I am happy with the way things stand, but
nevertheless I shall continue on.

I shall write you a longer letter later. I am due to depart Hertford-
shire in the next hour with my ward.

As always,
FD

Anne would not find it a satisfying missive, but then, contentment was an unfamiliar feeling to her in general. It would have to do whether she liked it or not.

"YOU ARE STILL DETERMINED to leave me then." Mr Bennet gave a wan smile as Elizabeth came into his study to bid him farewell.

"It has cost John no inconsiderable effort to secure my trunks to the carriage; I daresay he would not permit me to change my mind now, even if I wished it." Elizabeth grinned at her father with more easy cheer than she felt. "My sisters are nearby if you need anything, and little Charles needs me much more than you do."

"That is a question that might be opened for debate," said Mr Bennet. However churlish his words might have seemed, he did rise from his chair and came around his desk to offer his daughter a kiss on the cheek and his best wishes for her travels.

The servants—those who remained—gathered to see her off. Mrs Hill was teary-eyed but understood the necessity of Elizabeth's departure; indeed, if Elizabeth had hesitated, she had no doubt that Hill would toss her into the carriage after the little boy they all loved so dearly.

Despite her newly lowered status, Mr Darcy held to the necessity of chaperonage for her; he employed an older woman from Meryton to accompany them. Elizabeth smiled at Mrs White, who in return could only offer a terrified nod; she had likely never been in such exalted society before.

Mr Darcy's carriage was without question the finest carriage she had ever ridden in—well sprung with deeply cushioned squabs of Mazarin blue. Elizabeth settled Charles into the seat, drawing a rug over his legs and arranging his books and diversions around him. She then situated herself with a rug and a brick at her feet. Mr Darcy paid no heed to any of this bustle. He had his nose already in a book and scarcely looked up to note that anyone had joined him.

Their beginning was quiet. Mrs White was too afraid to speak, and Mr Darcy was disinclined to do anything but frown out the window or into the pages of his book. Little Charles spent some time eagerly admiring the countryside and asking questions about this or that—Whose farm was this? Why were sheep standing there? Did sheep like to eat grass? What if you were a sheep and did not like to eat grass?—but soon enough they were on the turnpike. From there, it was only one dead field after the next. Charles soon tired of seeing the same thing and asked Elizabeth to read him a book. Elizabeth opened the one they had been reading, The Castle of Otranto. It was perhaps a disinterested choice for a child, but Charles delighted in it and insisted upon reading after reading, most enjoying the bit where a man was killed by a large flying helmet.

"Lizzy, how big was the helmet?"

Elizabeth sighed, having answered the same questions many times before. "Very big, Charles."

"Bigger than me?"

"Oh, much bigger."

"Bigger than this carriage?"

"Very likely."

"Whose helmet was it?"

"I cannot say."

Charles considered this for a moment, his thumb creeping into his mouth while he did so. "Did it belong to a giant?"

"I think 'tis very likely." Elizabeth reached out, gently forestalling the movement of his thumb back into his mouth. "One hundred times larger than helmets usually are. I daresay the man himself must also have been one hundred times larger."

"Oh!" Charles exclaimed. "Maybe somewhere a giant was trying to put his helmet on and—oh no!—he dropped it! And it fell on Conrad!"

"That is a very good notion," said Elizabeth. "Shall we read on?"

As it turned out, Charles did not wish to read on. He wished to have Elizabeth read, again, the passage where poor hapless Conrad was found crushed beneath the large helmet. Again and then once again after that. From thence, Charles entertained himself with increasingly fantastic ideas of what must have happened to have a helmet fall from the sky until he fell asleep with his head resting on Elizabeth's legs.

When his soft, baby-breath snore reached Elizabeth's ears, she closed the book and, moving slowly so as not to disturb Charles, replaced it in her valise. She looked up to find Mr Darcy's eyes upon her.

"An unusual choice for a child's reading matter," he said, his displeasure plain.

Elizabeth refused to be concerned. "My father has always believed anything that encourages a love for books must be for good."

"Such things will give him frightening dreams or stimulate an excess of fancy."

"An excess of fancy?" Elizabeth smiled. "Wonderful notion. I think I should like to be in such a way myself."

"These flights of imagination are well and good for a child, but when a boy becomes a man, he must learn to see the world before him and react with soberness and gravity. Fanciful schemes and illogical contemplations are of no use to anyone."

"How fortunate," said Elizabeth, "that the philosophers and poets, the astronomers, and the explorers do not think as you do."

"If young Charles were able to grow to be any of those things, I should say very well, let him dream and imagine as he will. But he will command a great fortune and, one must hope, an estate of his own one day."

"And when that day comes, I daresay he will be well aware that there are not giants dropping helmets out of the sky. For now, however, he is four, and I say it does him no ill to indulge in fanciful notions and imaginings."

Mr Darcy's frown deepened, and he turned back towards the window.

Belatedly, Elizabeth realised she had done herself no favours. True, she perceived she had won the argument, but a governess would do best to act as the master of the house wished. She stifled a sigh, realising the role she had ascribed herself might be more difficult than ever she imagined.

ALTHOUGH DARCY WOULD NOT HAVE ADMITTED it to anyone who asked, he found himself captivated by the young lady who sat opposite him in his carriage. On their first meeting he had dismissed her as plain, but subsequent meetings taught him to appreciate and even admire her appearance. She had remarkably fine eyes, which showed wit and intelligence, and a pleasing and light figure. Her smile was quick and engaging, and she had a playfulness about her that was endearing. Her manners were not of the fashionable world, but they were charming.

She was not a woman who could have ever drawn his notice, and even if she were, his reason and his character should prohibit him from forming any real attachment to her. Yet she drew him, and he found himself often giving her surreptitious glances over the edge of his book or admiring her reflection in his window. It was satisfying enough for the first day, but by the second, he began to crave some sort of conversation with her.

Recommending himself to strangers had never been his strength and particularly so now when there was far more he wished hidden than known. He supposed he could ask her about Meryton, about growing up at Longbourn, but it was not a subject that much interested him. Books had been canvassed and politics were likely unknown to her. What did one speak of with a woman with whom there was little to nothing in common?

"Tell me about your sister's marriage to my friend," he said.

His tone was brusque and the introduction of the subject sudden; he watched as she startled and then composed herself. "Jane and Bingley? What do you want to know?"

"Where did they meet?"

"In Meryton. Mr Bingley leased Netherfield shortly after Michaelmas in '11 and came with a large party of friends. They attended one of the assemblies only a few days after they arrived."

Her words brought fond recollections to his mind. "Bingley loved to dance."

"He did. And the neighbourhood was much obliged to him for it. I do not think there was any lady he left sitting that night, but Jane…"

A faint smile curved her lips as her eyes gazed outwards at nothing. "He had a clear preference for Jane right from that first night with her. They danced…oh, twice at least, maybe three times."

Darcy winced. Three times? At a country ball? No doubt the entire village thought the marriage was all but sealed then and there.

Miss Bennet continued her stories. "They continued to meet at various dinners, parties, and the like, always managing to find a quiet corner to talk together. Then my sister fell ill at Netherfield."

"Fell ill?"

"Bingley's sisters—I believe you know Mrs Hurst and Mrs Milne —had invited her to dine. Jane went on horseback and was caught in a very sudden rainstorm on her way. She was forced to remain at Netherfield for some days with a fever."

Darcy did his best to refrain from rolling his eyes. A cunning manoeuvre that was.

"Bingley loved her very much," Miss Bennet said with a wistful little sigh. "He proposed to her at a ball he gave at Netherfield at the end of November, and they were married within a few weeks."

The end of November? Darcy swallowed against the groan of disgust that rose within him.

"So he had only known her a few weeks when he proposed?" he asked carefully.

"Nearly two months," she replied.

"Rather a short courtship."

"Is there a specific amount of time required?" she shot back.

He did not answer. The nature of Bingley's entrapment was becoming very clear to him; indeed, he could see the true cause sprawled asleep across Miss Bennet's lap.

"And when were they blessed with this little lad?" he asked with deceptive ease in his tone.

It did not fool her. She gave him a severe look but answered in a carefully neutral tone. "Little Charles was born in early July after Jane suffered a fall."

"In July?"

"After an injury. We were exceedingly afraid for him, I assure you. It was far too soon, clearly."

Darcy did not favour her with a reply. It was all quite clear to him now; Miss Bennet's sister had set her cap for Bingley at an assembly, spent some fateful days in his house in October or November, and not so long thereafter, his friend's fate was sealed. It hardly matters now.

"So, married in December, a father by July…" he began.

"Ill by October and dead by November," said Miss Bennet impatiently. "So perhaps it is fortunate that his son was born early; otherwise, he would scarcely have known him at all."

Her tone was brisk but tears shone in her eyes. She quickly turned her head away from him, and it was several minutes until she spoke again in a low tone so as not to disturb the child.

"I see what you are suggesting, Mr Darcy, and I assure you, Jane was not mercenary nor was she the sort to resort to arts and allurements to entrap a man. They loved one another. You should be rejoicing in the fact that your friend's last months were happy ones. He knew he was loved."

"Well then," said Darcy gravely, "I daresay nothing else matters."

"No, it does not," she replied crisply.

He watched her for several moments, staring determinedly out the window with one hand on her side and the other wrapped protectively around little Charles. The hand that held the boy shook, belying her distress, and he felt sorry for having upset her. It was abhorrent to him, these disguises people adopted in order to entrap a person into marriage, but in this particular case, it truly did not signify. Bingley was gone and, along with him, his enjoyment of dancing and his tendency to fall in love with any pretty face he saw. No amount of righteous indignation on his behalf would change any of that.

Darcy swallowed against the lump in his throat. Oh, how he wished he was with Bingley that fateful autumn. Then he would not have been forced to marry a country beauty, required to spend the last months of his life languishing on a rented estate in the middle of nowhere! Indeed, he might not have contracted the disease that felled him. He might yet live.

But then, this boy would not. He studied the handsome little fellow who already bore the strong marks of his friend. I shall not fail you. Darcy made him a solemn, silent vow. I shall be everything you deserve and more.

ELIZABETH'S MIND raced even as she gave every appearance of equanimity sitting across from the odious creature in the carriage with her. How dare he suggest such things of Jane! Fury enveloped her, and she spent some enjoyable moments imagining striking the smug look right off his countenance.

How could she live with such a man? She looked down at little Charles. How could she not? Her duty was clear, but it would not be an easy road, to be sure.

In her mind there was one object, one dearest wish above all: that somehow Mr Darcy's guardianship might be revoked or challenged either in the courts or outside of them. How exactly it might happen, she knew not. She wanted only to return to Longbourn with Charles and live as they were before.

Mr Darcy was clearly an unfeeling man, lost to every notion of decency and kindness. Surely there was something at Pemberley, some shade in his character that would be revealed if only she was clever enough to find it.

With a small glance in Mr Darcy's direction, she made a resolution. She would be on her guard at Pemberley. She would do what she could, so that if the time came and she found a compelling bit of information she might use to broker their release, she would neither scruple nor hesitate to do so.

Charles tugged at her sleeve. "Lizzy, are we soon there?"

"Ah…" She glanced at Mr Darcy. "Are we almost at the inn, sir?"

Mr Darcy did not so much as glance up from a letter he was reading. "About two hours more."

Two hours! It sounded like an eternity. "Very soon," she said brightly to Charles. "I know! Let us look out the window and count how many blue…"

"No!" Charles shrieked suddenly. "I do not want to count, I want to go home!"

Elizabeth closed her eyes a moment, gathering her patience. When she opened them again, she saw that Mr Darcy was peering at them over his letter. "Travel is very tiring, is it not, my sweetling?" she murmured. "But we must not shriek and howl. We must—"

"No-o-o-o!" Charles moaned, tossing himself into her lap. "I hate this carriage."

"Shhhh." Elizabeth reached for him, but it did no more than provoke him. He gave a violent lurch, rolling right off her lap and onto the floor. Along the way he bumped something—his head, an elbow?—and though it was of little consequence, Charles screamed and began a crying fit worthy of a near-death experience.

Elizabeth reached down, pulling him into her lap while glancing at Mr Darcy, who was staring at his letter with a determined look on his face. "There, there," she murmured into Charles's hair. "No need to howl like a wild animal."

But Charles would succumb to his fit. He began to struggle against her, resisting every attempt she made to soothe him, his cries growing more shrill and irritating with every passing second. Warmth flooded Elizabeth's face and body, though whether it was from humiliation or the struggle of keeping him contained, she knew not.

Across from her, Mr Darcy calmly folded his letter in precise thirds, then observed them. Elizabeth continued to struggle but Charles was inconsolable.

"Charles," said Mr Darcy at last. "If you do not stop this behaviour, I shall have to strap you."

Elizabeth gasped while Charles stopped, interested by this new idea. "Strap me?"

"You will do no such thing," Elizabeth protested while Charles asked her what strapping was and whether he would like it.

"The boy has never been strapped?" Mr Darcy raised one brow. "Spare the rod and spoil the child, Miss Bennet."

"He has never required such stern chastening," she replied, wondering why it was she who defended herself. "He is barely more than a baby."

"I am not a baby," Charles protested. "I am a big boy!"

"This is not the behaviour of a gentleman." Mr Darcy met her eye. "I shall expect a great deal better of him, and if a strapping now and again is required to achieve it—"

"Then you will have to go through my dead body to administer it," Elizabeth finished. In her lap, Charles had begun to slowly kick, kick, kick at the seat, his interest in throwing a fit slowly renewing itself. She hissed at him to stop under her breath.

"I have seen far too many examples of spoilt indulgence to permit it in my ward," he retorted.

"And I have seen too many examples of excessive brutality to permit it for my nephew," Elizabeth said, just as feelingly.

He glared at her, and she glared right back even while her mind urged caution and complaisance upon her. Even Mrs White was stirred from her silent corner, clucking something at young Charles and urging him to come to her lap.

Mr Darcy did not break eye contact with Elizabeth, glowering at her even as he raised his fist and thumped sharply on the top of the carriage. Elizabeth felt them come to a sudden halt and her heart lurched.

The carriage door opened, and Mr Darcy stepped out and then leant back in. "Charles, come with me."

Elizabeth opened her mouth to protest but Charles, unsuspecting and trusting, leapt up into Mr Darcy's arms. She scrambled to throw aside the rug on her lap, but it somehow seemed to pin her into place. "Wait!" she cried out as the coachman, evidently not hearing her, closed the door.

FIVE

THE COACHMAN HAD NOT PUT THE STEP DOWN, AND THUS WHEN Elizabeth did at last extricate herself from her lap rug and launch herself from the carriage, she tumbled clumsily onto the road. She fell to her hands and knees, jumping up as quickly as she had fallen down.

Charles's cries filled her ears, and she frantically searched for him, realising belatedly that he was not crying at all.

He was laughing. Laughing and engaging in a game of chase with Mr Darcy in an adjacent field. When they had gone some distance, they stopped, and Mr Darcy bent, picking up something from the ground and then hurling it as hard as he could at a nearby tree. Charles imitated him, and the two were soon engaged in some little game of throwing and tossing. After that, was more running and then a return walk to the carriage, with Mr Darcy speaking to Charles very seriously as little Charles gazed at him worshipfully, nodding eagerly. Elizabeth rolled her eyes. How easily the hearts of little children were won!

"Lizzy did you see me? I won the race!" Little Charles had an enthusiastic report of the time spent with Mr Darcy, which he delivered while Elizabeth fussed over the dirt and mud that she imagined must have stained his clothing. To Mr Darcy, she would give only a scornful glance.

They climbed back into the carriage and re-settled themselves as Charles told her, "Mr Darcy said that if I behave as a gentleman, then he promises to…to…"

Mr Darcy, who had taken up yet another of his inexhaustible supply of letters, said, "I shall ensure that we stop at regular intervals to play a few games and exhaust ourselves."

Elizabeth hardly knew what to make of him. Why threaten violence and then offer play? Teasing, teasing man. It seemed most likely he wished to distress her. Either that, or perhaps the games Mr Darcy liked to play involved tormenting the sensibilities of caring females.

She said nothing while Charles settled himself in, nibbling at a bun they had brought with them and studying the words in Otranto. Eventually, he handed her the remains of the bun and laid his head on her lap for a nap. Elizabeth indulged herself in staring at Mr Darcy until at last he looked up, cocking one brow at her.

"I thought," she said, pronouncing the words with great hauteur, "that you intended to strap him. I was terrified."

"I never said I intended to strap him."

She gaped. "You most certainly did!"

"No," said Mr Darcy with aggravating reason. "I said if he did not stop, I would have to. But he did stop."

"He stopped because you took him out to play!"

Mr Darcy smiled patiently. "A young boy in high spirits is generally only in want of some activity, a brief spell outdoors."

"I know," Elizabeth retorted, feeling vexation flush her cheeks. "I have been raising him these four years."

"And I have been a boy myself for many, many more than four years. Believe me when I say that I know far too well what it is to feel the bite of a strap for my disobedience."

Elizabeth rolled her eyes, unable to summon enough imagination to see Mr Darcy as anything but an imperturbable, tightly buttoned gentleman. "You certainly seemed in favour of it an hour ago."

"I shall never say that it does not have its place in the proper chastening of a child," said Mr Darcy. "But only when all else has failed. I would much prefer that my ward obey me in respect rather than fear."

"And I would prefer that he obey me out of love."

"Love is of no consequence when it comes to unruly behaviour."

"When someone loves someone else they naturally wish to please them."

"Not always," he replied in sharp tones.

The conversation seemed to have taken a turn, or perhaps Elizabeth imagined it. Were they still speaking of Charles? Or was there something else, some hidden meaning to the words?

No matter what, one thing was certain: it was to Mr Darcy to decide how things would be and her feelings on the matter had little to no consequence.

ELIZABETH WAS thankful the next day, on what was the final leg of their journey. Indeed, three days had never seemed as long. Charles had begun the day well, but it was soon tiring to him, Mr Darcy's arrangements notwithstanding.

"Lizzy, when are we there?" He asked for likely the hundredth time that morning.

"Let us ask Mr Darcy," Elizabeth replied. "No doubt he will have the answer for us."

She had disguised herself well for he gave no indication he had heard the impertinence in her tone. "Not long now," he said. "We shall arrive today."

The thought filled her with as much trepidation as relief. Relief to be released from this wretched carriage but trepidation because she and Charles now wholly surrendered to the care of a man who had not impressed her with either kindness or civility, the man who had spent the better part of three days frowning at whatever was outside his window. Mr Darcy had frankly disdained Meryton, but it appeared the rest of England displeased him likewise.

Mr Darcy was as much inclined to silence as anyone she had ever met, and she was resolved to learn her new place; it was easiest to tend to little Charles and disregard the man opposite her. He had a strange habit of staring at her, perhaps cataloguing her faults and repining his decision to bring her to his home.

Charles now sat up on his knees, peering out the window and excitedly exclaiming about the village they were traversing. He pointed at a small boy walking along the road with a cow, and a carriage that was painted a garish rust colour. She suppressed a smile imagining how Caroline Bingley might have thought it handsome, though it would be more likely due to its size and perceived opulence than its actual colour.

Elizabeth joined him, looking out the windows at the unforgiving landscape of Derbyshire. A pang of loneliness struck her as she thought how very far off the rolling hills of Hertfordshire seemed. The deep ravines, ancient oaks, and gnarled yews she saw before her probably appeared sombre in even the best of times; now, set off as they were by leaden skies and starving waifs, the landscape appeared positively menacing.

"It is not long now," Mr Darcy announced, causing her to startle. "An hour at most."

Some time later they turned down a lane, and Elizabeth anticipated an imminent arrival. That arrival was forestalled as they continued on and on and on until Elizabeth wondered whether they would ever see the house. So far away from everything! A sudden longing for the proximity of Lucas Lodge pierced her.

"Shall we reach the house before night, do you think?" She smiled in an attempt to appear light-hearted, but Mr Darcy could only nod gravely in reply.

"Very soon," he said. A few minutes later, quite unexpectedly, he rapped on the roof and the carriage halted. One of the coachmen came to the door and opened it. Mr Darcy exited and turned, his hand extended; evidently, he expected that she should exit as well.

She alit slowly but soon saw the reason for their abrupt stop. Though they were still at some distance from the house, Pemberley stood before them, and she was able to see it as it was best seen.

Elizabeth had wondered what to expect of the home of such a proud man, imagining grandeur on a scale she had not before seen. Indeed, it seemed his pride was warranted, for before her stood a large, handsome, stone building, standing well on rising ground and backed by a ridge of high woody hills. In front, a stream of some natural importance was swelled into greater but without any artificial appearance. Its banks were neither formal nor falsely adorned.

Even such a place as Pemberley could not escape the ravages of the recent meteorological curse, however. The streams were bloated and filled with grey-brown debris of an indeterminate origin; the trees shivered leafless in a damp wind. The fields she could see were bleak and barren and seemed to have been thus for much longer than would be expected in November—no, these looked like February fields.

Nevertheless, Pemberley had not the feeling of neglect and disre-pair she had seen in so many other places. Indeed, Pemberley itself, like its master, seemed to be staring about the landscape with an air of patient disapproval, a grand lady rising up to haughtily pronounce the cold an abomination from which she would remain apart.

Mr Darcy indicated by a wave of his hand that she should return to the carriage, so she did as bid. They began again to move, a quick pace but not for long. Soon after, a peek out the window revealed they were arrived. An army of footmen came to assist them, but Mr Darcy handed Elizabeth and Charles out of the carriage himself.

"Welcome to Pemberley, Miss Bennet and Master Bingley. This is Mrs Reynolds," said Mr Darcy in regards to the kindly looking woman who had come to greet them. "She will see you settled into your apartments."

"Lady Catherine wishes to greet them before I do," Mrs Reynolds added, looking at them with thinly concealed anxiety. When she saw Elizabeth's observation, she quickly made her face blank.

"Very well." Elizabeth took up her traveling case in one hand and held Charles's hand in the other as Mrs Reynolds led them into the main hall of Pemberley.

Their footsteps echoed on the marble floors as they entered an enormous vestibule. Looking around her, Elizabeth could not imagine that even the splendours of such places as Blenheim or Chatsworth could eclipse Pemberley. They followed Mrs Reynolds down a long hall, passing other halls and closed rooms whose purpose Elizabeth could only guess at.

Despite the echo of their footsteps, the silent weight of Pemberley pressed against them; even little Charles did not embark on his usual stream of chatter. He glanced up at his aunt several times as if seeking reassurance in her countenance, but Elizabeth could only pull him more tightly against her as they passed more rooms filled with shrouded furniture and unlit fires.

At last, they arrived to two large, ornately carved doors. A footman opened the door for them and in a deep and ceremonious tone announced, "Miss Elizabeth Bennet," into the drawing room.

The room had not the benefit of afternoon sun; as such, it was shadowy and cold, so much so that Elizabeth scarcely saw the woman who sat within until she rose to extend her hand to them.

"Miss Bennet, I presume. I am Lady Catherine de Bourgh."

Lady Catherine was a tall woman with strong features that suggested she might once have been handsome. She squinted down her aquiline nose as Elizabeth offered the appropriate greeting in return.

"This is the boy, I suppose."

Reaching down around her legs, Elizabeth extracted little Charles who, though not customarily shy, had managed to disappear into her skirts. "This is Master Charles Bingley."

Lady Catherine regarded him dispassionately while Charles fumbled through a little bow and offered her a heart-achingly large smile.

"He is a stout little fellow."

From her tone, Elizabeth could not know whether Charles's stoutness pleased or displeased her ladyship, so she made no reply.

"Your journey was easy, I trust?"

"It was," Elizabeth agreed.

"The roads outside of Derbyshire must have plagued you dreadfully."

"Our journey was as good as any journey in November can be."

"We have had dreadful weather here."

"Hertfordshire has been likewise afflicted," said Elizabeth, feeling warmth against her legs as Charles pressed his body back into them.

Lady Catherine sniffed at that. "Your bedchamber will be in the family wing to be near him."

Family wing? "I thank you, yes."

"We dine at six at Pemberley, the small dining room down the east hall and adjacent to the gallery. Mrs Reynolds, see them settled for me."

Dinner with the new governess? Elizabeth had scarcely any time to consider this mark of civility before Mrs Reynolds, who had lingered by the door throughout their interview with Lady Catherine, came and immediately led them from the room. Then it was down another long, hushed hall and up a stair—the stair was marble, providing them at least the solace of the sound of their footsteps—to yet another expansive hall. Elizabeth pulled her shawl more tightly around her, glad she wore her thickest one.

Their first stop was the nursery, a large, comfortable room with an adjoining schoolroom. It was painted in palest green and there were toys, many toys, scattered about in a neat but cheerful manner. Many of them looked unused, and Elizabeth assumed they were likely new; it was encouraging to think someone had given thought to what Charles might need.

An older woman awaited them, giving her name as Mrs Browning. "I'll see him settled as his supper is on the way." A pang of uncertainty smote her as Charles happily skipped to the other side of the room, taking up a sack of what proved to be tin soldiers and dumping them all over the floor. Mrs Reynolds gave her little time to linger, moving on rapidly to another bedchamber just two doors removed.

"This is yours, Miss Bennet." Selecting one of the keys that hung from her waist, she unlocked the door and opened it. Elizabeth thought it very strange that the door should lock from the outside, but before she could give voice to her question, she was arrested by the sight of the room itself.

The room was charming, in colours of rose, lavender, and verdigris; it brought to mind a meadow in the spring as much as anything she had seen lately. It was a large room yet filled with warmth—a fire was laid in anticipation of her. She sank gratefully into the plushy pink chair next to it. Three days in a carriage had chilled her to her bones.

"Would you like a bath before we dine?" Mrs Reynolds asked.

"A bath?" Elizabeth startled, having not imagined any such thing as a possibility. "Oh...I would not like to be a trouble."

"Nonsense." Mrs Reynolds replied briskly. "A good hot soak will be just the thing to chase off the cold. I shall send Mary to attend you."

"Thank you." Such consideration was certainly surprising, but then again, it was only her first night. No doubt Mr Darcy wished to impress the notion of her good fortune upon her.

That is ungenerous, Lizzy. She scolded herself as she sat by the fire and watched the servants carry in the water while Mary and three other maids arrived to unpack her trunks. It was a task not worthy of so many of them; she had never been a fashion plate, and difficult times had rendered her wardrobe even more shabby than was usual. Nevertheless, the maids treated her clothing as the attire of a duchess, painstakingly arranging her meagre belongings in the massive armoire.

The bath was without a doubt the best she had ever had. The water was at first almost too hot to tolerate—almost. She sank into it, feeling the ache in her cramped, cold muscles give way. It was so relaxing she nearly dozed, recalling herself when Mary asked to assist her.

This governess thing might just be my best idea yet. Elizabeth closed her eyes, inhaling the fragrant steam and relishing the uncommon feeling of warmth.

ELIZABETH DESCENDED the stairway from her guest apartment towards the dining room several minutes before the appointed hour. A footman told her they awaited her in the same drawing room where she met Lady Catherine previously, and after one small misstep in which she accidentally entered a library, she found herself where she needed to be.

More lamps were lit now, and Elizabeth could better see the tall, excessively ornate chair on which Lady Catherine sat, her feet propped on a little stool. Mr Darcy stood beside her, one hand tucked into his coat pocket; it seemed they had been awaiting her in tense silence.

Lady Catherine did not rise to greet her, but Mr Darcy took several steps forward, offering a very correct and formal bow. "Miss Bennet. I trust your accommodations will suffice?"

"They are much finer that I might have expected." When he gave no more response, she decided, strangely, to tease him. "Tell me, sir, do all of the servants at Pemberley have such fine lodgings?"

"Servants?" Lady Catherine asked. "I assure you, the servants at Pemberley are as well cared for as any you will find in any home in England."

Mr Darcy spoke quickly, perhaps to forestall whatever else his hostess might have said. "Charles is not yet in need of a governess, Miss Bennet, and when he is—"

"You were not yourself sent to school," Lady Catherine informed her. "Naturally, we shall seek a woman of superior education herself, one trained at a seminary perhaps, until he is ready for Eton—"

"Perhaps he will go to school," said Mr Darcy firmly. "I have not yet decided."

"The schools are where a young gentleman learns to emulate those of better society, to walk among those who will—"

"Thank you. Your advisements on the matter will be considered."

This did not mollify Lady Catherine in the slightest. "You went to Eton, as did your father before you."

"Yes," said Mr Darcy. "I do remember it."

Her nostrils flared and her eyes narrowed meanly even as her lips pressed into a thin, angry frown for several moments before she turned back to Elizabeth. "In any case, we have not the least doubt that you will soon see that we are perfectly capable of caring for the child."

They were all saved from further argument by the arrival of the butler announcing dinner. Mr Darcy took both ladies on his arm and escorted them into the dining room.

Elizabeth was unsure what to make of the argument. It seemed Lady Catherine considered her unsuited to be governess, and likely her nephew agreed. It was not welcome news. Although she had no wish to lower herself, neither did she wish to be useless. To be useless was to be perceived as a guest, and if she were a guest, then eventually her visit would be over. Lady Catherine's words did nothing but strengthen her belief in that. It was the unspoken conclusion to her ladyship's last sentence: we have not the least doubt that you will soon see that we are perfectly capable of caring for the child—and then you can leave.

He is young. With good fortune, Mr Darcy will have tired of us both before any of these plans need come to pass and will send us both back to Hertfordshire.

In the dining room, it appeared that formality had prevailed over common sense; Lady Catherine had placed herself opposite Mr Darcy at the far end of the table while Elizabeth was on his left side. This meant that on the rare occasions that Mr Darcy spoke to her, Lady Catherine was forced to shout from the other end, "Of what are you speaking? I must have my share of the conversation!" At last she could resist no more and summoned a footman to bring her plate to sit across from Elizabeth on her nephew's right side.

From thence, the discussion was less a conversation than an interview, with Elizabeth as the subject of Lady Catherine's interrogation. Her ladyship began with a compliment of sorts: she pronounced Elizabeth a very genteel, pretty kind of girl. She then began to ask about Elizabeth's sisters: whether they were older or younger than herself, which had succumbed to the fever that took Jane, and who those living had married. She asked whether Kitty and Mary were handsome, where they were educated, what carriage her father kept, and her mother's maiden name. Elizabeth felt all the impertinence of her questions but answered them composedly.

Lady Catherine was much amazed to find that Elizabeth had not herself been afforded the privileges of a governess or any of the masters in London. Her amazement was scarcely less when she learnt that all five sisters had been out at once.

"All five of you out at once! I have never heard of such a thing."

Elizabeth hid a sigh behind a sip of her wine.

"And you, the eldest sister unmarried while your three younger found husbands! That must have grieved you indeed."

"Jane," said Elizabeth with great patience, "was older than I by two years. She was first to marry and then my two younger sisters. By the time they married, I was too busy with little Charles to seek beaux."

"I, too, understood that you were Mrs Bingley's elder sister." It was Mr Darcy's first advance into the conversation for some time. He made his pronouncement with a grave look as if he expected Elizabeth was playing some sort of trick on them.

"No," said Elizabeth. "Jane was the eldest."

"Pray, Miss Bennet, what is your age?" Lady Catherine demanded.

This was too much impertinence to be borne; even Mr Darcy felt it and intervened in his aunt's query.

"Miss Bennet," said he, "cannot be much older than thirty."

"Older than thirty!" Whatever gallantry might have been intended was lost in the age he imagined for her. "You think I am thirty?" Colour flooded Elizabeth's face; although she had never much concerned herself with age and other such vanities, to think she looked thirty or maybe more was distressing indeed.

He gave no answer to her charge, studying her for a moment before dropping his eyes to his plate.

Lady Catherine still stared in expectation of a reply to her rude question. Elizabeth had no wish to gratify her impudence but nevertheless wanted it known she was not nearly as old as they imagined.

"I am five and twenty," she said and the room fell into uncomfortable silence.

At last Lady Catherine, who was exceedingly generous with her advice, offered this, "Five and twenty is not too old to marry. You ought to go to London or Bath to see whether there is some man who will have you. I married when I was only twenty, but not everyone can do that."

Elizabeth murmured some expression of thanks—not because she was grateful but because she thought she should—and the matter was dropped.

The entail was the next source of Lady Catherine's questioning; she was amazed to learn that it was Mr Collins, her former parson, who had been her father's heir.

"These entails are a dreadful business," she said. "It was not thought necessary in Sir Lewis's family."

Elizabeth could offer nothing to this observation.

"But Mr Collins died without issue. Pray tell me, who is your father's heir now?"

"Another cousin," said Elizabeth. "In truth, I know little of him save that he is young."

The expression on Lady Catherine's face indicated that she thought this a lazy reply. "Do you play and sing, Miss Bennet?"

"A little," said Elizabeth but further reply was interrupted by an extensive discourse from Lady Catherine about how all ladies ought to play and sing and that her taste in music and enjoyment of music was superior to any other's.

"Then I must not excite your anticipation," Elizabeth said, "for I play very ill. I never applied myself as I should have done."

"Did not apply yourself?" Lady Catherine recoiled a moment before deducing, "Ah, but you were likely helping your mother. Not everyone has the means nor the situation to pursue a superior education."

"We..." Elizabeth began but then stopped herself. What good would it do to tell Lady Catherine that their mother thought the beauty of her daughters would be sufficient to secure them advantageous matches? That she thought education a waste of time that might be better devoted to the discussion of gowns and gossip?

"You will improve yourself at Pemberley," Lady Catherine announced. "There is a small pianoforte in the room by the servant's hall. You may use that as often as you like."

"Miss Bennet," said Mr Darcy, "may use the pianoforte—and the harp if she wishes—in the music room."

"In the music room!" Lady Catherine's exclamation suggested he had recommended something amazing. They locked eyes, nephew and aunt, and stared at one another in wordless communication. Elizabeth watched with interest.

"In the music room," Mr Darcy repeated firmly. "That is where music is meant to be played, is it not? Else it is merely 'the room'."

Lady Catherine set down her fork carefully and drew a breath. "That room is closed. Most of the instruments are covered."

"Then we shall uncover them."

"Extra work for the maids..."

"The maids will not mind," said Mr Darcy. "It is, after all, their duty, and I daresay they would find it pleasing to hear music as they went about their work."

"It is not necessary to change things for me," Elizabeth protested, unheard.

"Maids do not want music while they work," said Lady Catherine.

"Whether they wish for it or not, I do," said Mr Darcy. "And the last I knew, I was still the master of Pemberley."

This was said in a wry tone but with some warning. Lady Catherine took it with a frown, but she turned her head away from him.

"Miss Bennet," said Mr Darcy. "I shall give orders that the room should be opened for you. I would expect it to be ready within the next day or so."

Not comprehending the strange exchange or the odd anxiety that filled the room, Elizabeth only nodded and murmured her thanks, much relieved when the dinner was over.

There was too much to contemplate, too much newness to be considered, for effortless repose that night. Elizabeth lay awake in her bed, reflecting on this new place she would call home. It was by far the most elegant house she had ever seen. The fires were warm and the bed was comfortable. Her belly, and that of Charles, was full, both of them having enjoyed a tasty dinner with the same anticipated on the morrow.

Despite these creature comforts, Elizabeth could not rest easy. The space of Pemberley was too large. The emptiness swallowed her, making her feel her insignificance, and she heartily disliked the hollow feeling that gave her. She wished for the bustle and jumble that had once comprised a night at Longbourn—the whispers of Kitty and Lydia from their room, Jane's delicate snore, floors that creaked when a maid walked by, and animals outside in their restive nocturnal duties.

At Pemberley, there was only cavernous space and weighty, sombre silence.

It was not so very late. By nine, everyone was drooping from the exertion of travel, prompting Lady Catherine to rise and tell Elizabeth she ought to go to bed. Elizabeth, wishing to oblige for the sake of manners, did so. Mr Darcy also announced his intention to retire early and left the room.

Elizabeth could only hope it would not be so many hours until she slept. She had a book in her valise, but she had finished it already, and it was not so compelling that she would wish to read it again.

When she heard the clock strike eleven, she changed her opinion. Lighting a lamp, she found the book and settled in, hoping to be engaged by the familiar story; it was to no avail. Thus by midnight, she found herself thinking of the impressive library she had stumbled upon earlier in the evening. Though unlit, she had still seen an array of books whose sheer number amazed her; surely among them was something to hasten sleep?

The silence of Pemberley became her true enemy as she crept along the halls, praying she avoided any stray squeaking floor boards. It would not do to wake the master or his aunt, she was sure of it.

"Ahh!" she hissed quietly having come upon a stray object in the hall. A little jewelled broach, delicate and lovely, had nearly become lodged in her foot. Quick reflexes meant it only gave her a good poke. She looked at it in the dim light; it seemed girlish, certainly far too girlish for Lady Catherine to wear. Picking it up, she laid it on a near table; the maids would know where it belonged.

She continued down the hall, hoping she would not be lost. The first door she opened proved to belong to a large drawing room, much larger than the one they had used before. Indeed, use was not anticipated soon for everything in the room was covered by sheets, making spectral beings from the furniture.

The next door she opened was the correct one, and she entered, inhaling the always-familiar scent of well-loved books. She paused a moment, glancing around at the books that loomed on high shelves about her. "So many!" Her father would have thought this heaven, to be sure.

For several minutes, she did no more than walk around with her small lamp, which suddenly seemed very dim in the near-window-less room. It afforded her no more than a few feet in any direction, but the titles she was able to read were enticing.

How long she looked she knew not—there were too many she

wished to read, too many she had never heard of—but at last, she was undecided between two by Mrs Jane West: The Gossip's Tale or The Loyalists. The Loyalists had been published in three volumes, and her father, for perversities known only to himself, had purchased only the second. Elizabeth had read only enough to make her mad to read the rest, and after seeing that all three volumes were present, she decided this would be her selection. A Gossip's Tale was left behind; that would be for another night.

She moved towards the door only to be arrested by what sounded like a horse trotting nearby. A horse? After midnight? She rushed to the window, peering outside to see, though it proved to be little use.

Her first notion was that a horse had gotten out of the barn but that would not answer. It did not sound like a horse that had escaped or was frightened, it seemed like a horse that was being ridden. It proceeded at an orderly pace, fading from earshot within a few moments.

An express then? She waited, listening for the sounds of doors opening or servants attending the front door, but there were none. Indeed, the house remained heavily silent; if anything, it seemed to be listening to her.

She managed to put it from her mind and, taking her treasures, retired for the evening.

It was not until the next morning at the breakfast table, after Mr Darcy announced his intention to ride out, that she recalled it. "I heard a strange sound last night," she said. "After midnight. I had some trouble sleeping and so borrowed a book from the library. In any case, I thought I heard a horse go by."

Mr Darcy raised his coffee cup and took a sip before he replied. "After midnight? I think not."

"I thought perhaps one of the horses may have gotten out?"

Mr Darcy shook his head.

"That is strange indeed. What was oddest of all was that it sounded like a horse being ridden, not a horse running free."

"I assure you, the horses remained as they were all the night long. Even if they escaped their stalls, they would not be able to leave the stable."

"Perhaps," said Elizabeth lightly, "there is a ghostly horseman then."

Mr Darcy chuckled in a strained, unamused way. "I assure you, Pemberley has no ghosts, and I pray you would not even suggest them—some of the servants are easily frightened."

"Perhaps if there is someone riding around Pemberley after midnight, they should be frightened."

"Miss Bennet, I have no doubt that what you heard was merely tree branches or some other usual cause. You are in a new place, and the sounds that are so familiar to me are unfamiliar to you, and your mind will play its tricks on you. I assure you there was no horse and no rider. No-one with even a grain of sense would be riding about without so much as a sliver of moon to guide them, particularly not in Derbyshire, when a step to either side could send the man or his horse towards their sure death at the bottom of a ravine."

It was not enough chastening, it seemed. He rose and tossed his linen onto the table. "My opinion is that you and your very active imagination would do best to remain abed at night rather than wandering about seeking mystery."

With that, he rose and, bidding her good day, left the breakfast room.

SIX

ALONE IN HIS STUDY, DARCY SAT AND RUMINATED. ELIZABETH BENNET would prove to be one of his worst decisions ever, of that he was certain. She was a curious woman, and curiosity was not a quality much prized at Pemberley.

But he had found himself unable to say no to her request to come with her nephew. She did, by some strange inclination, beguile him. There was a sweetness and an openness in her manner that he found endearing, and something in her eyes spoke of intelligence and warmth. She secured her place with him with one simple question: have you never made someone a promise that was so important you would rather die than fail?

He allowed his chin to sink into his hand. Yes, indeed I know what it is when you would rather die than fail, and how deeply one can regret that he did not have that choice. Yes, I know what it is to disappoint someone, everyone. I know what it is to tarnish a legacy. I know what it is to fall short at the very instant that it matters the most and to watch as someone you love bears the consequence.

It was her words that made him feel a kinship with her, feel strangely like he might not be alone, that he might be—someday—understood. And he had invited her in and somehow knew very well that once she was in, it would be exceedingly and increasingly difficult to keep her out.

Her eyes. It is one of life's simpler pleasures to enjoy the sight of fine eyes in the face of a pretty woman.

Could any painter do justice to such eyes? Any artist, any portraitist? Their shape, their colour could perhaps be copied but the expression in them? Never. No artist had sufficient skill for that.

It was while that thought was in his head that his eyes alit on a letter, the most recent. He regarded it, knowing the contents and disliking them heartily. Sudden anger flushed him, and he took up his pen, writing a curt reply.

Anne,
By no means should you leave Kent. You should not come to Pemberley. Leave well enough alone.

FD

LEFT ALONE in the breakfast room—for Lady Catherine had made it clear the evening prior that ladies of elevated status could not be expected to be seen prior to noon—Elizabeth considered her plans for the day. Some time with Charles naturally, but what else?

It was a question not readily answered; for as long as Charles was under her care, Elizabeth had rarely been left to shift for herself. The indulgence of time in which something was not required of her was uncommon and of exceedingly short duration. Elizabeth could scarcely recall what it was she enjoyed doing when at her leisure.

A walk! The perfect thing for an afternoon that followed three days trapped in a carriage. The gloom outside the window might have suggested otherwise to some ladies, but Elizabeth was undaunted.

She set forth upon a ramble, ignoring the mist and rain. The first puddle she stepped in confirmed she would return in disarray, but what did that signify? Mr Darcy already disapproved of her; why not give him just cause?

Elizabeth paused a short distance from the house. Finding herself on a rise, she took the opportunity to survey the prospect about her, unsure which direction to take. She decided to follow the river, walking first through barren fields, her thick cloak failing to protect her from a damp wind

She found herself quite in charity with the rugged landscape. Derbyshire, she observed approvingly, lent itself uniquely to England's current malady. The rocky crags, deep ravines, and shrouding, spectral mists all supported the feeling of crisis and the notion that the world as they knew it just might be at its end.

It appealed to her as no verdure ever could have. Verdure was youth and renewal and hope; she had no use for any of those. Verdure reminded her of the life she had lost: chattering, gay sisters, a life with parties and balls, and a mind filled with ideas of flirtation and possible marriage.

She walked for some time, staying by the river's side, not inclined to lose her way. Eventually, she found herself in a dense wood, and therein she came upon a man. He was some distance away when she saw him, and by his dress, she deduced he was not a gentleman. What he was doing so deep in the woods was unclear; he stood stock still on the bank of the river, staring down at the heaving waters. It seemed he had not heard her approach.

He was a handsome man, tall and well-favoured, though there was something in his bearing that seemed wrong. He was slack where he ought to have been upright, and his mouth hung agape as he stared at the river.

Alarm twisted in her gut although she had no idea why. He appeared perfectly harmless standing there, and she watched him, listening to the sound of her pounding heart in her ears.

Suddenly, he began to make a strange rocking motion, shifting his weight from the right to the left leg, back and forth in a manner that seemed energetic though unconsciously done. Along with his rocking came some speech, though what language he spoke and what he spoke of remained unclear to her. Back and forth, to and fro, his gibberish becoming an angry babble—all of it made Elizabeth's alarm blossom into terror.

She edged backwards, retreating slowly and silently, her eyes trained on the man, fearing he would see her. But he never looked up, instead continuing his frantic, unhappy dance by the river. When she had gotten far enough away from him that she was sure he would not hear her, she turned and gathered up her skirts, increasing the pace of her retreat, faster and faster until she was running, glancing behind her now and again to see whether he followed.

When she had gone some distance, she stopped, turning to find herself alone in the woods, no sound but that of her breath, gasping and deep in her chest. She stood for a moment, recovering herself and feeling all the foolishness of her response.

Naturally, a labourer should be in the woods—perhaps he was cutting down a tree, perhaps he was a forester, perhaps he was a stable boy shirking his duties and having time to himself. None of it posed any danger to her, and indeed, none of it had anything to do with her. Silly girl! Sometimes she forgot she was five and twenty and not fifteen.

Her mind did not wish to accept it, whispering to her that he had not really been attired as a labourer. Not a gentleman, but not a labourer either. Loose-fitting trousers, a sagging shirt, boots but no coat, and a hat that might have been once worn by a soldier. A strange costume indeed.

She entered the house through the carriage vestibule, and it was much to her ill luck to encounter not only Mr Darcy but Lady Catherine as well. Belatedly, she considered her appearance. She had removed her bonnet and a good bit of her hair had escaped its pinnings. The damp had likely caused ringlets to spring up in all directions. Her boots and her petticoats were muddy, and she was yet a little breathless from the rapidity of her return up the river.

As she curtseyed to them, she tucked a curl in and smoothed her skirts, vain attempts to improve matters. Lady Catherine's face revealed that it did not signify in the least.

"I walked down by the river," she said with a sheepish smile. "I saw a man while I was there—"

"You walked in the rain?" Mr Darcy asked. He and his aunt both stared, plainly astonished.

"It is not so much a rain as a little mist," she assured them. "Nothing at all really, and I was desperate to stretch my legs after our travels. But the man I saw had the appearance of—"

Her ladyship said, "You are very nearly drenched to the skin. Do you not fear a fever?"

"I am a hardy sort, rarely ill," Elizabeth assured her.

"You should do best to go put on some dry clothing," said Mr Darcy. "A maid will be along to help you."

"And I shall further advise you to wrap a cloth around your neck with one of Mrs Reynolds's liniments upon it," Lady Catherine added. "I shall send her to you directly."

"Oh I do not think—"

"After all, it would be discomfiting to us all if you were to fall ill and required to take to your bed." Lady Catherine gave her a stern look.

At this, Elizabeth understood. It was not true concern for her welfare that prompted these advisements, but rather a distaste for caring for the ill. Furthermore, they were not interested in the man by the river — likely a servant of some sort, she decided. Nothing of concern to anyone.

"Of course." Elizabeth agreed to their concerns, smiled, and left them.

THERE WAS IN DARCY, as he watched her leave, a sensation he dared not name—though it heated his blood and flushed his skin. It was a sensation that had long since ceased to prick at him, and he had believed it gone for good. Miss Bennet was very pretty, the handsomest woman he had ever known even among those of the fashionable world. Then again, comparing her to a lady of the ton was like comparing a cultivated shrub to a meadow of wildflowers. A beautiful meadow of wildflowers.

But his aunt was speaking to him.

"What?" he asked her, allowing the full measure of his vexation to be known.

She gave him an annoyed scowl. "I said that Miss Bennet exhibits an abominable sort of conceited independence that I cannot like. What can she mean, going out on a day like this and walking three, four, or five miles in mud to her ankles?"

"I see no harm in it."

"You would not allow your sister or your wife to behave in such a way, I am sure."

Darcy clenched his jaw and turned his full attention to Lady Catherine. "Miss Bennet is neither my sister nor my wife, and I do not care what she does. She is here because—"

"Yes, why did you bring her here? She cannot be his governess. She is ill-qualified at best. I should never recommend a woman like Miss Bennet to anyone of higher birth."

"We have already," said Darcy in chilling tones, "had this conversation several times over."

"Not to my satisfaction."

"Then I fear you must resign yourself to dissatisfaction. Pemberley is still my home, and I am still called its master. I shall invite people as I so choose, and I chose to invite Miss Bennet to stay here."

"As my guest," said her ladyship in severe tones. "And if the lady is my guest, I think I ought to look after her. I ought to have some say in what she does."

"Miss Bennet appears perfectly able to care for herself."

"Do not think me a fool, Darcy." Lady Catherine narrowed her eyes and stepped closer to him. She was a tall woman, and broad across the shoulders, but Darcy was yet larger. Strangely, as she came near him, it brought to his mind thoughts of how light and pleasing was the figure of Miss Bennet. What would it be like to have her standing so near him?

"I have learnt," said Lady Catherine, recalling him to his present circumstance, "that her mother's people were in trade. Gardiner is her uncle's name."

"What is that to me?"

"They live near Cheapside. Gracechurch Street, she told me."

"I do not care whether she has uncles enough to fill Cheapside.

She is the daughter of a gentleman and will be afforded the dignity of that station."

"She will never marry anyone of consequence in this world. No doubt she realises that and seeks an alliance of…another sort."

"I beg your pardon?"

Lady Catherine sniffed. "You know exactly what I mean."

Disgust made him flush hotly red.

Lady Catherine continued, "I am not a fool, nor am I unaware that gentlemen have weakness. Ladies of Miss Bennet's ilk will use those weaknesses to their advantage, ply an unsuspecting man with their arts and—"

"Do not be ridiculous," Darcy snapped. "Miss Bennet has not the sort of arts and allurements that would induce me to unprincipled behaviour."

"I should hope not. After all we both know—"

"There will be nothing of that sort under Pemberley's roof."

That pleased her. She stepped back, relieved. "I cannot abide this sort of grasping behaviour."

"Miss Elizabeth Bennet," said he in tones that would brook no confusion, "is nothing to me, I assure you. She is a spinster who will likely remain as such; indeed, her age nearly assures it. Whatever arts and allurements she might possess are similarly lost to my notice. She wished to come, and I agreed, and I think there cannot be too little else said of the matter."

With that, he turned and stalked off, wondering at the phantom sweet scent—her scent, for he already knew that—that seemed to linger in the air.

A SPINSTER? Unlikely to marry? Grasping?

It seemed that Lady Catherine would suppose that her nephew would take another wife or sink to taking Elizabeth as his mistress, and Mr Darcy made it clear he found Elizabeth acceptable for neither of these offices. It was strange how offended she was that he thought her too disagreeable to be his mistress. It is not that I am too much a lady or too well bred—only that I lack the suitable allurements.

Elizabeth scarcely had time to absorb that which she had heard before she realised he had left his aunt and would be, in moments, upon her. She turned the knob on the door nearest her and ducked into the room—an office of sorts, it seemed, perhaps for the house-keeper. There she stood in silent, enraged mortification while she heard Mr Darcy walk past. Seconds later, a swish of skirts told her Lady Catherine had done likewise. She released the breath she was holding.

At the risk of being discovered, she took a moment to quell the rage that had risen within her. You are a spinster, and you do not intend to marry, so what is the harm if he says it too? In any case, it is no surprise they do not wish you here. It is no surprise they disdain you.

She wondered at caring about the opinion of these persons so wholly unconnected to her. What should it matter? I care nothing for their good opinion.

With that, she resolved she would think of it no more. She would concentrate her efforts on finding a way to take little Charles and return to Longbourn.

She hastily changed her clothing in her bedchamber, dismissing the maid who came to assist her and waving off all attempts to administer draughts and liniments. Within half an hour, she was on her way to the nursery, intent on some time with Charles.

She found the boy in a restless, fidgety state while Mrs Browning looked on with the mark of exhaustion plain upon her countenance. On Elizabeth's enquiry into the morning's activity thus far, she admitted, "I had quite forgot how high the spirits of a young boy can be. Too much time indoors, I daresay."

"You are likely quite right." A quick glance at the window revealed there was no remedy for it; rain now streamed down the glass like small turbulent streams. "A day for quiet amusements."

"And we have quite run through all of those."

Elizabeth looked at her with no little sympathy, and Mrs Browning seemed concerned. She straightened and forced a brisk look to her countenance. "But do not think I am unequal to him! He is a delight in every way. Preparing for his arrival took the starch out of me, but we are getting along very well."

"Thank you," said Elizabeth. "I can see that. Pray, do not be made uneasy by my questions. I am only trying to learn the routines and plans of the household. Tell me: what day is yours?"

"Mine?"

"Does the household have a day of rest? Some hours when one may attend to personal matters?"

Mrs Browning appeared baffled by the very notion. "No, ma'am. The mistress, she don't like us to take no days. She says we are born to serve and so serve we must, cheerfully and constantly."

Elizabeth laughed incredulously. "Constantly? Dear me! I do not think anything done constantly can be done to the best of our ability. The body needs respite, as does the mind."

Mrs Browning looked uncertain, as if she wished to agree but did not think it proper that she should.

"Why not take a few hours to yourself?" Elizabeth suggested. "I shall be with Charles, and you can return with his dinner later. Will that do?"

"His...his dinner?" Mrs Browning immediately looked up, her eyes wide with surprise although some interest was seeping into her countenance. Clearly, the poor woman had not had a breath of rest in some time.

"A few hours," Elizabeth urged. "'Tis nothing at all. I know how tiring they are at this age. Go put your feet up, perhaps see to some mending if you feel you must have occupation."

At the mention of having her feet up, Mrs Browning was settled into temptation. "Well...there are some things that need doing. Some...some personal matters as well. I suppose if you are so inclined to be with him, there is no use me being idle up here."

"Just so."

"But do ring for me if you need me. It will not be said that I have shirked my duty to him."

"Of course not. I shall not hesitate to ring, but only if I truly do need you. Otherwise, we shall see you at dinner."

"Four," said the good lady. "I shall see to his dinner at four."

"Very good." Elizabeth smiled as the lady disappeared from the room at a quick pace as though she thought Elizabeth might change her mind. She turned to her nephew who was watching her, fairly bristling with eager anticipation.

"Outside!" He exclaimed happily.

She ran a hand through his curls, feeling a rush of affection for him. "I fear we cannot. Do you see the rain? We should be soaked to our skins immediately! But we can make a fun game inside. What shall we play?"

It turned out that most of what Charles wanted to play required being outdoors, and she sighed, knowing how difficult it was for him to be confined indoors as the weather dictated. She suggested many games to no avail; he wished to run and jump and throw, and nothing else would do.

"What about hide and seek?" she asked at last, to his satisfaction.

"Yes!"

"Shall I hide or do you want to?"

"I hide!" Charles announced. "You count, Lizzy, to six thousand forty hundred seven!"

Obligingly, Elizabeth closed her eyes. "I shall count to twenty, but you must count with me."

Charles agreed with a beaming grin. Elizabeth turned her back on him and closed her eyes. Charles joined her as she began. "One… two…three…four…five… Charles?"

Elizabeth's eyes flew open as she heard the door of the nursery slam closed. She turned on her heel, immediately seeing that Charles was no longer in the room. Going to the hall swiftly, she opened the door and called out for him. "Charles!"

Where had the little rascal gone so quickly? She strode down the hall, pausing at the near intersection of the nursery wing with the larger hall. He was, alas, still nowhere in sight. How much she dreaded raising a hue and cry over this! Mr Darcy would not be best pleased to find a child run amok in his home, of this she was sure.

"Charles?" She stood silent, listening for the tell-tale signs of a little boy at play: a furtive giggle, a shuffle, or a sigh. "Charles?"

She moved back towards the nursery, intent on opening the doors to the apartments she had passed. Just as she reached the nursery door, she heard it: the sound of feet running overhead. Small feet, which likely belonged to a small, impish boy.

"Charles!" she hissed, running to the staircase and flying up the stairs. "Charles, dearest, we cannot have our game all over the house as we do at Longbourn. We must stay in the nursery."

Silence replied to her. The rules of Pemberley were surely much different than the rules at Longbourn, and little Charles must be mindful of that. To be fair, he did not likely know as yet, but it would be no just cause if they were found by Lady Catherine or Mr Darcy.

"Charles!" she half-whispered and half-screamed it. "Come out now!"

She moved down the hall, taking great care to avoid detection. The squeak of a floor board from a closed room warned her of the possible presence of her quarry. She opened the door immediately, belatedly recalling that she had no idea whose room she had just entered. "Charles!"

Small feet protruded from beneath a large bed in the undeniably masculine bedchamber. Praying it was not Mr Darcy's, she knelt by Charles's feet, sliding her upper body under the bed to urge him out. "Come here at once. This is not our room to play in. We are being very rude by entering where we were not invited."

Charles slid out from underneath the bed obligingly. He was generally such a kind and obedient little boy, but his spirits had overwhelmed him. She could surely sympathise with that.

Being a full grown adult, it took her a few seconds more to extract herself from under the bed than it had for Charles, and by the time she was again on her feet, he was off, going through a different door and a large sitting room and disappearing into another bedchamber across. Elizabeth chased after him, resolving to pick him up and carry him back downstairs. "Charles, I am becoming cross with you. You must come away right now... oh!"

Elizabeth entered the room into which Charles had escaped. The room was a part of a tower on the rear of Pemberley and boasted an unusual semi-circular shape. There was an air of disuse about it, a sober vacancy, despite the slippers that peeked from beneath the bed and the shawl tossed over one chair. It looked like someone might return shortly, but it felt very much the opposite. Whoever had gone from this room was gone for some time.

It was fitted up in minutely varying shades of palest blue from the wall coverings to the wool rug on the floor. Whosoever owned the room must have felt like she lived in a cloud, particularly on a day such as this when the windows showed nothing but swirling fog and mizzling rain. Like living in a dream.

Thoughts of leaving were forgot as Elizabeth made a slow perambulation about the spacious room. A woman's room, she had decided, as evidenced by the delicate accessories and bottles of scent on the table. The furniture was eminently suited to a young woman being both light and modern looking—indeed, Elizabeth would have liked it very well for herself. No dust in evidence, apparently the absence of the owner did not lead to dereliction of duties at Pemberley.

There was a small portrait on the bedside table, and Elizabeth picked it up and studied it. A woman, wearing the fashions of some decades past, smiled down at an infant in her arms. Elizabeth contemplated it for several minutes before realising it was a portrait of a younger and happier lady Catherine; the infant was presumably her daughter.

This then must be the bedchamber of the former Mrs Darcy.

For not the first time, she considered the lady who had been Mrs Darcy. Clearly, she was not here and no mention was made of her, so it was safe to presume she had passed away. What happened to her? Had she died in childbed? A fever? Elizabeth yearned to ask about the lady but neither Lady Catherine nor Mr Darcy seemed apt to confide in her.

The sound of something falling over recalled her to her circumstances, and she hastily replaced the miniature to turn her attention back to Charles. The boy was engaged in climbing a bookshelf, knocking over several books in the process. "Charles! Very well, we are done here."

"Read me, Lizzy!" Little Charles thrust a book towards her. Elizabeth took it from him, replacing it and the others that had fallen from the top.

"This does not belong to us and we must—"

"Read, Lizzy, read!"

"Charles, this room and the things in it do not belong to us. How would you like it if someone came into your room and began to play with your toys without your permission?"

This struck him and he fell silent.

"Come now. We must go back to the nursery, but first we shall take a little walk around the house. No more running and no more touching things that do not belong to you. Behave as the young gentleman that you are."

On his agreement, Elizabeth took his hand, and they exited the room.

They had gone down the main stair and made their way into the gallery before she realised Charles still held a book in his hands. "Oh Charles! Never mind that, I shall put it in the library and no one will be the wiser."

She removed it from his hands. Looking at it more closely, she realised it was a journal, likely the journal kept by the young Mrs Darcy. Opening the front page, she saw an elegant feminine hand and immediately closed it again. She would return it to the blue room later.

Pemberley was of such size that even walking its halls was sufficient to tire Charles. The great hall quickly proved an error—there were too many valuable works of art and busts therein to afford her much ease with a four-year-old child by her side. They soon found an empty banquet hall, and Elizabeth surmised it must have once been used for balls of the very grandest sort.

"Ah! I know what we can play!"

"What?" Charles asked eagerly.

"Shall we play country dance?"

"Yes! I love country dance!"

She had begun, when he was very small, teaching him little forms and patterns of dance, reasoning that like his father, he might be quite fond of dancing when he was older. It was true, he scarcely could remember the steps and never would recall any sort of gallantry towards his partner, but the skipping and movement were enough.

They soon became quite silly about it. After some time of dancing, Charles often liked to pretend he was "Mr C" and attempt to step on Elizabeth's toes. "I should never have showed you this!" Elizabeth half-scolded. "A gentleman does not step on his partner's toes!"

"Like Mr C stepped on your toes?"

"Well, yes," said Elizabeth with a smile.

"And that is why you did not marry him?"

One of many reasons. Elizabeth reached down, picking Charles up and resting him on her hip. He was getting somewhat old to be carried around but she would enjoy it as long as she could. "You will have greater chance of success in romance if a lady may be reasonably sure she will not end the dance with bruised feet! Now come along; I think it must soon be time for a nap."

LISTENING FROM THE HALL, Darcy startled and moved away from the door where he had watched them for longer than he would ever dare admit. He hurried back into his study, closing the door silently. He went to the window and stared out at the incessant, infernal grey.

For a moment, he had forgotten it all.

Liveliness, laughter, the sound of merriment—these things were uncommon at Pemberley. How could she smile so? She had lost nearly as much as he but still could pass an afternoon playing and giggling with her nephew.

Rather like building a well. With that thought, his mind slid into an old memory, days long past, when he was just an eager, gangly young lad and his father would teach him all there was to know of an estate. They had ridden out to observe as the men dug a new well. He was amazed when water, clear and fresh, had bubbled up into the new hole, and his father had smiled at his astonishment.

"You dig and dig through the dark earth until, if you have chosen the right spot, you find water. The water springs forth and fills the well."

"And then you can drink it?"

"Aye," his father agreed. "Then you may slake your thirst."

He dug into the mud of Meryton, resenting every bit of effort he was forced to expend, yet it seemed he had struck water, bubbling and clear and delightful. "I did not realise," he murmured, recalling himself to the present, "how very thirsty I really was."

SEVEN

ELIZABETH RELINQUISHED CHARLES TO HIS NURSE WITH SCARCELY enough time to dress for dinner. Lady Catherine's maid, a timorous young thing called Dawson, fluttered about her nervously not wishing to be held accountable for Elizabeth's tardiness to the table.

As it turned out, she need not have worried for Mr Darcy was himself delayed.

"Pritchard arrived," Lady Catherine announced. "Some item of business or another. Mr Darcy saw fit to hear him immediately."

Perhaps he has located more orphans for Mr Darcy to steal. Elizabeth smothered a dark chuckle at the notion.

"Will Mr Pritchard join us to dine?" Elizabeth asked, hoping he would not.

"Pritchard is never one to turn down a meal," Lady Catherine announced in accents that suggested she found him as detestable as Elizabeth did.

As it turned out, Pritchard did not join them. Mr Darcy arrived in the drawing room alone, looking even more pensive than usual.

Dinner that evening was quite the longest Elizabeth had ever endured. Lady Catherine proved herself equal to Mrs Bennet for ignorance, opining on the silliness of the impoverished of the district. Lady Catherine seemed to think that if people starved, it was their own fault for having failed to be born into wealth.

On more than one occasion did Elizabeth find him staring at her. When she first caught him at it, he reddened slightly and turned away, but his eyes were back soon enough. His scrutiny caused her to raise her napkin and dab gently at her lips and chin, imagining she had some crumbs there; but no. Eventually, she decided her only course was to disregard him as best she could, though it persisted not only through dinner but the requisite time in the drawing room. Fortunately, Lady Catherine was agreeably engaged in hearing the sounds of her own opinions and paid no mind to Mr Darcy's strange behaviour or Elizabeth's discomfited silence.

At last, Elizabeth left them. She returned to her own apartment with the intention of collecting the journal of the former Mrs Darcy and returning it to its place before Mr Darcy retired.

As she picked it up from the night table where she had left it earlier, she regarded it for a moment. She had wondered often, in the short time of knowing Mr Darcy, what Mrs Darcy must have been like. Herein were the secrets of that lady.

"It would be terribly officious and rude, Lizzy," she said severely even as the journal beckoned temptingly. "Dreadful trespass, quite rude."

But her curiosity, ever her failing, would undo even her most honourable resolve.

"I have no right," she murmured, opening the first page. Elegant-looking handwriting covered the pages, written evenly and neatly. Surely the lady who had become Mrs Darcy was not so very interesting. She was likely just the same as any other young woman of superior birth.

Elizabeth settled it with herself—just a page or so, enough to satisfy herself that these were ordinary ramblings of a young woman and wife, the once-mistress of Pemberley. Nothing special, nothing worth inducing undue curiosity, and then be done with it. No doubt it was a testament to her loneliness—her general ennui with life and the living of it—that inspired such wonder.

She sank into a chair by the fireplace and opened the book.

My Dearest Beatrice,
Here we are at R, and it is every bit as wonderful as I had imagined. One simply cannot imagine how fresh the sea air is—so very different from D!—and I am positively invigorated by the very feel of it.

We have a charming little house in the most fashionable section of town. Someone with a great deal of taste has fitted it up, for I declare, I am in raptures over every last chair. The tables most particularly are delightful and have inspired me to design my own. Perhaps I shall! Fortunately, I have all my sketch books with me.

Nearly all of us from Mrs B's school are here, and just this morning, we all met to walk along the shore after which we went to a little coffee house and had cakes and talked and laughed until our cheeks ached and the matrons scowled at us. Miss J thinks we shall all find beaux here this summer, and her companion spoke to her sharply for saying so—but I must confess I should think it very diverting indeed if one of us were to have a bit of romance to enjoy along with our sea bathing! I am sure it should not be me, but I should like it very much indeed were I to see one of my dear friends falling in love. Miss L tells us she has already several gentlemen who have spoken with her father of their wishes to pay her court, and she has offered to instruct us on the ways of flirtation—I am exceedingly diverted by the ridiculous things she does with her gloves and fan.

THERE WERE pages and pages of similar musings and exclamations. From what she read, Elizabeth deduced that Mrs Darcy must have written this part while she was yet a young lady, young enough to be still at school but old enough for a schoolgirl's romantic fancies— perhaps fifteen or sixteen? There was something charming and sweet about the way she wrote. She was in every way hopeful and eager, and she saw the world in front of her open with possibility.

The girl wrote of everything and anything: her daily diversions, her opinions of the various coffee shops and tea houses, a gown she saw, a bonnet she wished to purchase. She kept a list of the books she was reading along with a one-or-two-line summary of each. Elizabeth felt strangely pleased to see they shared an interest in books and had to remind herself that it did not matter. This young girl—the girl who had become the woman who became Mrs Darcy—was long gone.

Dearest Beatrice,
I must begin at the very beginning today for I feel it is a day of great importance. A day I shall never forget even when I am exceedingly old.

It began in the common way. I woke and had my toast and chocolate in bed. I told my maid I would wear my new yellow muslin. The other ladies and I had an arrangement to walk along the shore and then take tea in one of the little shops.

Miss L was the first to see him standing along the shore. She has a most dreadful tendency to speak too loudly, so when she began to nudge and whisper, her companion told her to quiet down. However, by then, we all saw him and none of us could restrain our whispers!

I knew him at once—no one could mistake him, so tall as he is and so very well favoured. He was very handsome when we were children and has become even more so now! Such a fine, noble countenance! It was not only I who noticed him—the other ladies remarked on him too—but fortunate girl that I am, I was the only one noticed by him! Miss L was positively agog!

It has been so many years since our last meeting, I wondered how he should meet me. Imagine my delight when he greeted us all with such pleasing manners! He has always been a very gallant, courtly gentleman, and he is no less so now. I was quite surprised with how warmly he greeted me; I should have thought he considered me still a child, but I could not mistake the admiration in his eyes or his voice when he told me I had grown to be a very handsome young lady. Very handsome! I am sure you can imagine my blush! Indeed, I stammered about like a simpleton and likely made him reverse his opinion at once!

The time we spoke was far too short—he is excessively mindful of propriety and could no doubt see that our chaperons had begun to change looks with one another. But when we departed, he asked my permission to call on me. Dare I hope he will call tomorrow?

But it is time to retire now, and so shall my lamp be put out. I do not wonder what my dreams will contain tonight!

With no little regret, Elizabeth closed the journal, forcing herself to rise. She knew she must return the book to its place in the blue room, yet strangely, she found she could not.

Reading the journal was like a return to her former life in the time before plagues and floods and cold overtook her. It reminded her of long days in the drawing room with her sisters and their silly chatter about gowns and dances and bonnets and gentlemen—oh, how it used to wear on her, but she would give anything for it now.

"'Tis as well to be hanged for a sheep as a lamb," she murmured as somewhere in her mind she resolved herself to keep it just a little while longer and perhaps indulge in just a few more of its delightful, sparkling pages.

THE MASTER of Pemberley and his aunt declined attending church services on the Sabbath. Elizabeth was offered the use of the carriage for her own purpose but demurred, wishing instead for the ramble. Lady Catherine found this extraordinary above all things.

"It is above three miles!"

"Not if she walks through the east field," said Mr Darcy. "If you go by the path in the woods, it is not quite two miles."

"Path in the woods! Would you have her set upon by highwaymen?"

"There are no highwaymen lurking at Pemberley, I assure you, and in any case, I would naturally send a man with her."

"No proper lady," said Lady Catherine with disdain, "would consider walking to church."

"Then it is settled," Elizabeth interjected with a smile. "When it comes to a good ramble, I shall always choose to be a hoyden."

The man sent with Elizabeth was called Samuel, a well-muscled young man who appeared to be just a little older than Elizabeth herself. He was red-haired and red-faced, flushed with the distinction of escorting the master's guest; alas, the distinction appeared to render him incapable of speech, and after several failed attempts at getting him to remark on the weather and landscape, Elizabeth decided to question him directly.

"Did you grow up at Pemberley?"

"No ma'am. London."

"How long have you been in this part of the country?"

"Above a year, ma'am."

It was a strange thing indeed to find a servant so far from the home he grew up in, and Elizabeth remarked on it.

"The master offers a good wage ma'am, much better'n most."

"Your family in London must miss you terribly."

"A'nt none of 'em left no more. Me and my sister is all what's remains."

Elizabeth paused to permit Samuel to recover from this extensive sentence.

"Your sister is still in London?"

"No, ma'am, she's here too. An upstairs maid." He was proud of his sister. Elizabeth could hear it in the way he announced her position.

"What is her name?"

"Ruth."

"Oh, Ruth! I suppose I should have guessed from the resemblance you have to one another."

To this, Samuel could offer no greater expression of pleasure than to turn an even deeper shade of red. Claret, Elizabeth decided, and then she wondered whether it was healthy for a man's face to take on such colour.

The small church was full, and many pairs of eyes regarded her with frank curiosity. Some nodded and smiled whilst others only looked; Elizabeth did not mind, she knew how it was in a small town that saw few visitors. The parson nodded her towards the front of the church, to what must have been the Darcy family pew.

The service passed quickly, and when it was done, Elizabeth was afforded a better look at her fellow parishioners. The servants and tradespeople were all towards the back, and the gentry around her were mostly older with very few of an age with herself. It could not signify of course; she was not here for balls and parties, and in any case, most people were in circumstances far too straitened for frivolity.

One lady in particular regarded her with frank curiosity. She was handsome, appearing to be a few years older than Elizabeth, and wore a very fine, beautifully wrought gown. She was helping an older woman, allowing the lady to lean on her heavily while she navigated her out of the pew and situated her with her cane, somehow managing it all while still regarding Elizabeth. Elizabeth offered a small smile, and the lady smiled kindly in return, then turned her full attention to the older woman. Elizabeth found herself wishing she could be introduced to her; it might be nice to have a friend in the neighbourhood.

Being in the front of the church meant she was last to leave, and much of the crowd had dispersed by the time she wended her way forward. The weather did not inspire lingering conversation or walks to church, though Elizabeth did not mind it. She adjusted her pelisse, drawing it closer as she looked around for Samuel to join her again. He was soon by her side, and they began to walk away.

"Miss!" A young female voice called after her. "Beg your pardon, miss!"

Elizabeth stopped and turned around. A small young woman wearing the apparel of a shopkeeper's wife came running after her, holding Elizabeth's reticule aloft. "You left this in your pew," she gasped.

Elizabeth took the reticule gratefully. "How kind of you, and how silly of me. Thank you very much."

The woman smiled and curtseyed. She was younger than Elizabeth had supposed, perhaps twenty, and undeniably plain with hair the colour of a mouse and eyes to match. She had a gentleness about her though, a sort of goodness that shone forth. She seemed like a person who expected very little and was happy with what she had.

Elizabeth shook her head at her own silly thoughts; she imagined a great deal from someone about whom she knew nothing. In any case, the lady had turned to leave, but Elizabeth stopped her. "May I have your name perchance?"

"Oh!" The woman turned back, flushed with the mark of condescension. "I...my name is Giles. Mrs Giles." The Mrs was said with no little pride.

"I thank you again, Mrs Giles. I am Miss Bennet. I shall be staying—"

"At Pemberley." She nodded and looked more relaxed. "I know, ma'am. We all do." She said it with an awkward little giggle.

"It is good to know Derbyshire is not so different from my home county," Elizabeth said with a reassuring smile. "Any stranger is known to us all long before we ever set eyes on him."

"Aye and Yorkshire no different," said Mrs Giles. "That's where my people are from."

"Do you live here in Kympton now?" Elizabeth asked.

"Bakewell, ma'am," she answered. "My husband and his father are the bakers in the square."

"Very good." Elizabeth smiled at the girl. "I am sure I shall be your patron far too often then."

"Be glad to see you, ma'am." The girl curtseyed one final time and was gone.

THE DAYS at Pemberley soon settled into a rhythm—a tedious, lonely rhythm, but a rhythm nevertheless. Elizabeth woke and broke her fast. At times, Mr Darcy joined her at the breakfast table and other times he did not. Lady Catherine never joined them. Then she would walk, then spend time with Charles, after which she would read or write letters. Then dinner, some time in the drawing room—during which she was inevitably asked to do something that excited Lady Catherine's censure—followed by sleep.

Elizabeth had known her society was unwished for, but it startled her to realise how very unwanted she was. Although she was not treated as a servant, neither was she received as a guest. Mr Darcy had condescended to allow her to remain with Charles, but it did not follow that he intended to accept her into his household in any way, shape, or form.

It was therefore no little source of astonishment one morning when her ladyship swept into the vestibule in a mass of heavy skirts and even heavier scent. Two maids attended her. One held charge over her ladyship while the other tended a well-groomed Skye terrier that Lady Catherine enjoyed having with her although Elizabeth had never seen her so much as speak to the creature.

Lady Catherine's eyes swept over Elizabeth's person, and she pursed her lips a moment. After a second of consideration, she must have decided to remain silent for she said only, "Darcy would have you come with me on my calls. Come."

Evidently, whatever plan she might have held for her day did not signify, but Elizabeth, craving some society, acquiesced. She followed Lady Catherine outside, taking only a few minutes to ask one of the maids to get her cloak and bonnet.

A large, gilded carriage stood before them, resplendent and ostentatious in hues of aubergine and garnet to match Lady Catherine's coachmen. Elizabeth's sharp inhalation of amazement was greeted with a pleased nod by Lady Catherine. Her ladyship watched closely as Elizabeth entered the carriage and settled into the overstuffed seats.

"You have likely not been in such a carriage as this before," said Lady Catherine, giving Elizabeth a look as though daring her to dispute it.

Elizabeth shifted in her seat. Indeed, the dark hues of the conveyance, the plushness of the seats, and the overbearing aspect of Lady Catherine produced an uncomfortably close feeling. "Your carriage is exceedingly fine."

"Sir Lewis had it commissioned for my daughter," said Lady Catherine. "A gift for the occasion of her marriage, as a father often does."

Lady Catherine looked at Elizabeth in a piercing way, intent on studying her countenance as if to discern what she knew of the matter. Elizabeth made herself appear complaisant as she searched for words that would receive answers for questions unspoken.

At last, in gentle tones, she said, "It must be very hard to think of that."

"It is hard," her ladyship retorted sharply, "when the very one who has vowed to honour and protect her is instead the instrument of her demise."

"Oh!" Before Elizabeth could say more, the carriage was thrown about, rocking the two ladies side to side. They had hit a rut, it seemed, and it took some time to set things right, sending Lady Catherine into a paroxysm of indignation. Once things were settled, she rapped sharply on the roof with her cane, and when they had stopped, she exited the carriage to ring a peal over the poor coachmen.

When she returned to the carriage, Lady Catherine seemed disinclined to pursue the subject again. Elizabeth could not think of any way to return to it, nor did she know what else she wished to know. As she suspected, Mrs Darcy was deceased, and it seemed Lady Catherine suspected Mr Darcy of bearing some responsibility for it. What could she possibly mean by such a thing?

FROM HIS STUDY, Darcy saw Lady Catherine's carriage as it left the drive bearing, presumably, both Lady Catherine and Miss Bennet, if Mrs Reynolds was correct. He hoped indeed that she was correct for he hoped for time with the boy, and he did not wish for Miss Bennet to find him at it.

After confirming with one of the footmen that Miss Bennet had accompanied Lady Catherine, Darcy went towards the nursery, finding Charles playing quietly at his nurse's feet while she worked at some mending. When she saw Darcy, she rose hastily. "Beg your pardon, sir."

"No, no," he said. "I came to see the lad. How is he doing?"

"He is doing very well," said the nurse while Charles looked at Darcy with plain interest.

Darcy knelt down by him, ignoring the surprise of the nurse. "What is that you have, Charles?"

It appeared the boy was playing with a crude rag doll of sorts, fashioned to look like a horse. It boasted a tail made from yarn and an eye made from a small black button. "Hobgoblin. He was Papa's horse."

"Yes, he was," said Darcy softly, taking the doll from Charles. "I was with your papa when he bought Hobgoblin."

"You know Papa?" The boy exclaimed; evidently, this was a surprise to him. "He died when I was a baby. Lizzy says he could ride his horse very fast and also liked to play country dance."

"Aye, that he did," Darcy agreed. "And he was an excellent shot as well."

"Were you Papa's friend?"

"Indeed, I was. Your papa and I became friends in London," he began, until a different thought occurred to him. "Do you know what London is?"

"Where Uncle Gardiner lives," Charles replied immediately.

Darcy winced. "Ah…yes, I suppose. But there are many different parts to London and your father lived in the part near where I live. His brother—your uncle Hurst—introduced us one night."

Charles looked absolutely blank at the mention of an uncle Hurst, so Darcy asked, "Do you know your Aunt and Uncle Hurst?"

Charles considered it a moment and then asked, "Rupert's mama?"

Was Rupert a Hurst child? Darcy had no idea. "Perhaps?"

Charles wrinkled his nose. "I hate Rupert."

"Oh…well—"

"Lizzy says I must not. But I do. He's bad!"

"Well…yes, we all sometimes—"

"He kicked Rosie!"

Darcy had no idea who Rosie was, but clearly, the child felt this slight keenly. "How dreadful."

"Because," Charles said, "Rosie chewed his boot, and his mama was angry. But he left his boot in the kitchen! Lizzy says Rupert needs to have a care with his things!"

Charles continued, growing more impassioned as he spoke, his curls somehow seeming to bounce and corkscrew more with each word, "Puppies are babies! They do not know! But Rupert is a big boy, and he knows! And Lizzy said Rupert deserves a good kick!"

This made Darcy chuckle, but before he could speak, Charles had added, "But I did not kick him. Lizzy said a gentleman does not kick his cousin."

"Lizzy is right," Darcy agreed. "A gentleman must not kick anyone."

The discussion flagged then as Darcy cast about for something more to say to the lad, finally falling back on their activity during the journey from Hertfordshire.

"Perhaps…would you like to go outside?"

Charles was immediately agreeable to the notion, shouting with delight at the prospect. He ran to retrieve a ball that he might have begun kicking about on the spot had his nurse not urged him outdoors. "Not in here, Master Bingley. Kicking balls is for outside."

"Perhaps the courtyard," Darcy suggested, feeling uncommonly elated by the notion. "It is warmer there and still lots of space to kick the ball."

Nearly two hours had elapsed by the time he returned to his bedchamber, his coat and trousers damp and wrinkled but his heart light. Two hours! He could scarcely credit it.

The past years had gone by at a snail's pace for him. It seemed he was forever looking at time marvelling that only an hour had passed, or he would think it must be time to retire, then recall he had not yet eaten dinner.

And now here it was, the morning half gone, and he had done nothing of use—but he had enjoyed himself. Charles was very similar to his father: he had a great deal of enthusiasm for anything, he liked to talk, and he was eager to partake of any sort of sport or physical exertion. It was a strange sense, this feeling of being with his old friend, yet not.

Charles had a great deal to say about Elizabeth. He spoke of her nearly constantly. It was clear she had donned not only the role of mother but also playfellow and teacher. He had supposed that she was intelligent, and young Charles was the proof of it. He was amazed by the array of things she had taught her young charge. Her education might have been better than he had previously understood it to be.

Miss Elizabeth Bennet was beginning to fascinate him, to engage his thoughts far more than he could ever admit.

ELIZABETH HAD NOT BEEN LONG with Lady Catherine before she understood the great lady's purpose. She believed that most of the misfortune suffered by tenants of the village was the result of their own foolish ways. Her role, her ladyship believed, was to scold them into harmony and plenty. Elizabeth did all she could to soothe, sympathise, and assuage them in the wake of her companion's efforts.

Their last call was not to a villager but to another lady of status. Mrs Lawrence was a widow, and although her estate was by no means the equal of Pemberley, it was large and prosperous. They were shown into a cold room decorated in the fashion of several decades past; it was clean, though Lady Catherine made a great display of using her handkerchief to dust her chair before sitting.

"She scarcely hears," said Lady Catherine as they awaited the lady. "Nor does she see very well."

It seemed the lady had just as much trouble walking for they heard her coming long before she appeared. A slow, shuffling step along with the thud of a cane came painfully towards their room; a young lady's voice was heard murmuring encouragement.

"A new companion," said Lady Catherine with pursed lips. "I should have been well pleased to offer a recommendation, but this housekeeper of Mrs Lawrence's does everything on her own."

Elizabeth could offer no opinion on that and so only nodded.

It was nearly ten minutes before the drawing room door was opened again, and a footman and a young woman accompanied Mrs Lawrence into the room. Elizabeth recognised them immediately; it was the old woman and her young, elegant companion from church. From the smile of recognition on the younger lady's face, it seemed she recognised Elizabeth too.

Introductions were made and Elizabeth learnt the young lady was a widow by the name of Mrs Green. There was an almost-immediate kinship between the two younger women; Elizabeth suspected that

Mrs Green was as lonely as she herself was and eager for friendship. After some minutes of listening to Lady Catherine bellow neighbour-hood gossip at Mrs Lawrence, the pair broke away into their own cosy tête-à-tête by the fire.

"My husband left me with almost nothing," Mrs Green confided. "A few hundred pounds, though no debt. My family is all gone now, so here I am. My days pass very agreeably. She rarely goes out and really just wants someone to sit with her on the few days she feels like sitting."

"And where have you come from?" Elizabeth took a sip of watery tea.

"Derby, though I married quite young. My husband and I lived in London, near Mayfair. We were very happily situated there, and I do miss it sometimes."

"But you must be very happy to return to Derbyshire. Were your husband's people from Derbyshire too?"

Mrs Green nodded. "Alas, they are all gone now. My family, his family. I have no one but Mrs Lawrence."

With that, conversation went flat. Nothing more would be said, it seemed; evidently, Elizabeth's new friend felt some pain at the mention of her relations.

"I am here because my sister's husband left their child to the care of Mr Darcy," said Elizabeth in a rush of confiding spirit. "She and her husband both died. Many people died back then from a fever that swept through our little town."

"Oh." Mrs Green eyes took on a soft expression. "How sad."

Elizabeth nodded. "We were caring for their son for four years. I do not know whether my father was aware of it, but I had no idea of someone else being his guardian until...well, until the day Mr Darcy arrived and announced his intention to remove him from us."

Mrs Green gasped, her eyes round. "No!"

"I am afraid so. It was his right, after all, much as I tried to argue against it. He agreed to allow me to come as Charles's governess, but when I arrived, it seemed my services were unneeded. Now, I suppose I shall just spend my days as best I can, remaining as her ladyship's guest."

"Ah," said Mrs Green. "Well, it could be worse. Pemberley is one of the finest estates in England."

"It is very beautiful."

"Even if its owner renders it somewhat less agreeable."

Elizabeth laughed. How refreshing it was to meet someone so wholly free of artifice. "That," she said, "I cannot deny, no matter how generous he has been to me. Are you acquainted with Mr Darcy?"

"Oh, no, only by reputation. But that is a story for another time. Do tell me about Hertfordshire; I have only ever passed through it."

Time passed too quickly, and before long, Elizabeth was being ordered towards the carriage, but as she went, she hardly knew when she had smiled or enjoyed herself more. Mrs Green seemed to be a true friend of the heart, and Elizabeth found herself quite eager to forward more meetings.

"Pray, call on me," said Elizabeth. "Whenever you would like! Send a note, and I shall be at your disposal."

"Oh!" Mrs Green's face fell. "I cannot...that is, it is exceedingly difficult for me to leave her." She gave a rueful smile and a glance towards the older lady. "Even if she does not need me, it comforts her to know I am in the house. Will you call here? Do you have the carriage at your disposal?"

"I do not know." Elizabeth glanced at Lady Catherine. "Perhaps it would be permitted? I shall send you a note."

"Please do. I am exceedingly fond of good company."

EIGHT

THE DAMP CHILL SETTLED OVER THEM FROM THE MOMENT THEY EXITED Mrs Lawrence's house; Elizabeth pulled her cloak more tightly around her shoulders.

Even Lady Catherine, in all her splendid mature vigour, had the capacity to tire. She fell asleep shortly after entering the carriage and snored, unceasingly and loudly, most of the way back to Pemberley. Elizabeth regarded her with amusement for some time and then turned away, determined to disregard the noise and examine her own thoughts.

How very good it would be to have a friend! Her life was spent too much alone these days.

She could never accustom herself to the loss of Jane. As the years passed and Charles grew, she found herself more often than not sinking into ideas of how it should have been. She should have been married by now with her own house and a child or children. She and Jane would meet in town, or at one another's houses, for extended house parties and endless rounds of diversion. She had pictured them seated side by side on some rolling green lawn whilst their charming husbands did something manly at a distance and their children capered and frisked about them, playing their little games.

Instead, Jane was dead, the lawns were dead, and she was alone.

Scarcely a fortnight at Pemberley and the weight of her solitude was already heavy upon her. She was not wanted, and she had no role within the house to occupy her. How was it that a girl who had once scarcely been able to hear herself think for all the sisters and mother and friends around her was now so very alone? That now, she lived in an enormous house where space and silence were her only friends?

Oh Lizzy! Such maudlin thoughts cannot help you! She gave herself a little shake, determined not to sink into melancholy. She was with Charles, and she might have made a friend. These delights, small though they were, must sustain her. She must hold them close and use them to fill her with joy and not dwell in her sorrows.

"Anne."

Elizabeth was startled from her thoughts on hearing Lady Catherine speak.

"I beg your pardon?" she asked but then realised the lady was still asleep.

Elizabeth watched her, listening closely as she mumbled something about Anne, growing increasingly agitated and unintelligible. It seemed it was apologies and pleadings to Anne, though she could not discern enough of the words to comprehend why.

Eventually, Lady Catherine stopped speaking and sank into deeper sleep, the snores returning to deafen Elizabeth until the very moment they were turning into the lane through Pemberley wood. Then the hapless coachmen struck the same rut as they had before, roughly jolting her ladyship into wakefulness.

She looked at Elizabeth, glaring as though she was quite angry at being disturbed. Elizabeth smiled regretfully. "I fear the bumpy road has interrupted your rest."

"Rest? I was not resting."

"Oh? You seemed quite asleep—"

"Asleep? Oh no, never. I cannot sleep in a carriage, would that I could! But no, I have been spoilt since my infancy by having always the highest degree of comfort in my bed. Alas, it has ruined me for anything else."

Elizabeth, wisely seeing it would not do to attempt to persuade her otherwise, only nodded. In any case, she had another concern to divert her.

Mr Darcy stood at a window observing their arrival. He was tall and still, his face shadowed and unreadable, but there was something in his aspect that seemed disapproving.

IF THE HOURS of play with Charles had passed in a trice, the hours since had elapsed with painful slowness. Darcy had gone to the window more often than he would have ever admitted, wondering when the ladies should return. Thoughts of carriages overturned and marauding highwaymen had just begun to seem like true possibilities when one of the footmen told him the carriage was in the lane.

He stood there a moment, watching the ladies alight while being glad for the shadows that obscured his scrutiny. Miss Bennet exited the carriage with a small, secret smile on her lips. What amused her? Had Lady Catherine said something humorous? That seemed very unlikely, though he knew Miss Bennet well enough to understand that she found sources of amusement wherever she could.

She did not lean on the coachman as she descended, instead making her exit with a little jump that might have seemed undignified to some but to him seemed...well, perfectly in keeping with her character.

She looked around as she moved away from the carriage; her eyes, alight with interest, went here and there, seeing and observing and experiencing. She nodded at the coachman, offering him a kind smile. She spoke to Lady Catherine over her shoulder.

She looked up and locked eyes with him. For a moment, he could see it: himself going to her, helping her remove her coat, inviting her to join him in his study and tell him about her morning.

He jerked back, sudden alarm pounding in his chest. Do not look at what you cannot touch. She is not for you.

He growled, low and angry, in his throat, and spun on his heel, walking away from the wretched window and Miss Bennet's beguiling person.

When had he ever been free? When had his choices ever been his own? Had he erred so grievously as to be denied even the most fundamental of choices?

Frustration propelled him towards his study with quick paces, but before he arrived, he was arrested at the door of the music room. He stood for a moment and then, with a heave and a thrust, flung wide the door and stood gazing at the situation therein.

The harp sat shrouded in one dim corner while the pianoforte huddled under cloths in another. The air had a musty feel, the air of disuse, and he noted the dank cold appeared to have infiltrated the whole place. His shoulders sagged. "Miserable place."

Before he knew what he was about, he had snatched up the sofa cover, jerking it back roughly. It billowed around him, and he tamed it quickly, pummelling it into submission and then tossing it to the side. Several chair covers received similar treatment.

It was a testament to the running of his household that Mrs Reynolds required only minutes to arrive on the scene. "Sir?" She looked around her with alarm.

"Did not Lady Catherine order this room opened?"

"No, sir. She did not."

This news was greeted by the revealing of the harp as he tore the covering from it with sharp vigour. Mrs Reynolds hurried over before Darcy could ball up this cloth, taking the sheet from him and folding it neatly and impossibly quickly.

"She should have," he growled. "I shall not stand for it if she presumes to take the role of mistress in my house."

"Of course, sir," said Mrs Reynolds. "Allow me to summon—"

"Miss Bennet is an excellent musician and requires a place to practice, and even to exhibit for us should she desire it."

"Naturally, sir," she said. "Perhaps, if you would wish to retire to your study, I can send in several of the maids to finish here."

He looked around the room. It was uselessly fine, full of its own importance, and although it was perhaps slightly less desolate than before, it was still a forbidding sort of place. The light cast long shadows over the instruments, and the furniture did not invite harmony. Miss Bennet, he was sure, would not like it one bit.

"Desolate," he muttered. "Who could like this?"

He turned to Mrs Reynolds who regarded him with some alarm. "I apologise, Mrs Reynolds, for my fit of ill humour. Have the maids air and dust this room and then tell Miss Bennet she may have it as she wishes."

Mrs Reynolds nodded, and he left her, exiting the room with the shame of his outburst heavy on his shoulders. Not good; this madness he felt was not good at all.

When he sat at his desk, he considered the temptation before him. There was only one remedy for it: avoid her. Avoid all sight of her, avoid all sound of her. Hope that whatever small strange feeling that persisted in noticing her would die a quick death.

EACH DAY when Elizabeth regarded the little journal, she scolded herself, reminding herself that she intended to put it back. Nevertheless, each day, each time, she picked it up to carry it back, she found herself quite unable to do so.

She would sit, running her fingers over the vellum cover and touching the ribbon used to hold it closed. Then one finger might tug a little, loosening the ribbon, though never quite enough for the book to fall open.

Quite shameful to be so undeniably curious about the affairs of someone so wholly unrelated to her. A dead lady, no less, unable to answer for herself or tend to her own affairs! Quite vulgar, unforgivably rude and impertinent to trespass in such a way. Terrible indeed.

Why then, did her fingers play with the ribbon in just such a way as to unloose the cover?

"Very well, Lizzy. If one cannot resist the temptation of unconscionable intrusion, if one insists on behaving in this most dishonourable fashion, then one might as well get on with it." With that dismissal of justification, she undid the ribbons completely and opened the cover.

She began by reading what she had before—a young lady on holiday at the seaside with her school friends drawing the notice of a young gentleman whom she knew but had not seen since childhood. Strange, now that she thought of it. Would not a lady have seen her own cousin? Of course, it was a considerable distance from Kent to Derbyshire, and her school might have been even farther. So perhaps it had been some time since she had last seen him.

She read on then, to the account of the suitor's first call to his young lady.

I hoped he would call, though I knew not if he would. Indeed, I had nearly persuaded myself he would not. I am not the most handsome of the ladies, and I know that my conversation is lacking. Mrs Y is helping me understand the arts of conversation with gentlemen, but I daresay some of it seems very silly, very cunning. I would much rather have a discussion of serious merit than to rattle on about weather and other inconsequential matters!

But Mrs Y tells me that an education is only good if one has learnt to conceal it. A man, she says, is not interested in arguing or—heaven forfend—feeling stupider than his wife. My friends seem to agree with her, so it surely is so, though I do regret it. I am much better at speaking on serious subjects than the sort of witty repartee necessary to secure a man's affections!

Alas, he did not come today. Such despairing languor I feel! If the day should ever come to pass that I may call myself his beloved, I shall recall this despair as the first and most sure sign of my attachment.

Of course, if nothing ever comes of it, then I suppose all there ever will be is a twinge of anguish.

Elizabeth paused and smiled wistfully at such naive, girlish effusions. Ah, but how it did remind her of her younger sisters! She could almost hear Lydia carrying on about some soldier or another with Kitty as her ardent supporter and second. Mary would of course disapprove of the whole lot of it, and she and Jane would have smiled indulgently and perhaps admonished her to use good sense and modesty with the young man. Such painful, sweet remembrance! Elizabeth heaved a deep sigh before she went on.

Oh my dear Beatrice! He came at last!

Perhaps I should not say it quite like that. He came in due time, two days after I had seen him. Oh, had I dressed in a nicer gown that day! But we had no plans; it was raining and we believed ourselves quite at leisure for the morning. I had a book, and Mrs Y had her letters, and we thought it would pass the day quite pleasurably. The rain made the roads an absolute misery, so naturally we believed anyone of sense would remain indoors.

I could not conceal my shock when he was announced, and I believe I behaved quite stupidly at first. I merely sat, my head bent over some needlework that I hastily snatched up when he arrived. Foolish thing! I did not even have a thread, just the needle that I poked in and out of the cloth!

I am sure I must have imagined it, but he seemed nervous too—we are, both of us, prone to becoming tongue-tied. Mrs Y had to clear her throat several times before I realised it should fall to me to make him at ease.

I did my best. I stammered about the weather and the roads and asked after some long-forgotten relations and friends. Then we talked about Bath and other nonsensical subjects. I despaired that we should be made to spend our time in such a ridiculous fashion, but so it was right up until Mrs Y began to glance over at him from her place by the window. He did not seem to take heed at first, but then he did and even coloured, in a most charming fashion, I must add.

When he rose to leave, I accompanied him, and it was then that he said, in a voice that nearly melted me, "I despise these foolish notions of propriety sometimes."

"As do I," I assured him.

"Perhaps it is best. I would not like to exhaust my welcome."

I did not know how to reply, though I knew very well how much I wanted him to feel welcome to come any time, to stay as long as he liked. I finally said, "That, good sir, would be quite impossible." It seemed to me quite daring, but he did not seem to think ill of me for it! Now I must only hope and pray that he will call again, and soon!

What could be done but to smile at such girlish innocence? There were several pages then of the wholesome amusements of young ladies—lectures and exhibits, teas and afternoons at cards, along with long-winded descriptions of the gardens they visited and ramblings along the shore—until the writer was invited to attend a ball.

We heard talk of an assembly tonight, and I was sure I would not be allowed to go, but Miss J said I should not be such a silly goose. Our older friend sees nothing amiss in the evening. I shall not dance unless the gentleman is family or closely connected; then again, I suppose my desired partner must be considered as such!

Miss L was a sly thing, observing that having had such success obtaining notice in my yellow gown perhaps I ought to wear it again. But no—I am not such a child that I have not something suitable for the evening. My new gown is Pomona green, my favourite colour, and one I think suits me very well although the bodice is quite more daring than I usually wear. I have my mother's combs with their little sparkling gems to put in my hair and my shoe roses are pink.

Everyone is in such agitation waiting for the carriage to take us, there have been giggles alongside tears. But now they are arrived! Off we go, Beatrice, and do not worry, I shall not withhold a single moment from you!

Dearest Beatrice, such a night I have had! It was in every respect a perfect evening, and I daresay if I live to be one hundred, I shall not forget a moment of it.

I saw him immediately when I walked into the hall. He was so tall and handsome, standing near the vestibule; I do not think any man could look finer in evening wear than he does. When he smiled at me, I nearly swooned! I have always thought it very silly to read novels where ladies are swooning and fainting all over the place, but now I understand it very well. My heart pounded so that I felt sure it would leap from my chest!

When he removed from the group of gentlemen he stood with and came towards me, my heart seemed to stop completely. I was sure he would walk right by me, but no. After the most graceful bow I ever saw, he asked me to dance.

I am a poor writer, Beatrice, and have not the words to explain my feelings to you when we danced. It is too much felicity; I know not how I bore it. He is a most elegant dancer, even though he confessed that he obtains little joy from the exercise. And then he said he previously had little joy in dancing until this night when he danced with me. I am sure I blushed scarlet!

The songs we danced to will be forever engraved upon my heart although they passed far too quickly for my wishes. When they were through, he bowed over my hand very low and begged to be permitted another later in the evening. I could not allow it—my companion would have been very cross with me—but I told him as much. He said he would be happy to forgo more dancing merely to spend time with me.

And now I must wonder, dearest Beatrice, how long does it take to fall in love? How many hours must be spent before one can really know? I do not wish to sound like a schoolgirl, but neither can I deny that he is everything a young gentleman ought to be.

"Miss Bennet?" With a guilt-laden startle, Elizabeth closed the journal, leaping to her feet to see Mrs Reynolds standing in the doorway to her apartment.

"Forgive me," said the lady. "I knocked but you must not have heard me. This just came for you."

She extended her arm, and in it, Elizabeth saw a small folded note. Her heart still pounding, she crossed the room and accepted it. She did not recognise the hand that had lettered Miss Elizabeth Bennet, Pemberley across the front of it.

"Thank you. I…my apologies. I did not hear you."

Mrs Reynolds nodded and turned, turning back almost immediately. "Oh, and do tell me whenever you should wish to arrange the music room. I shall have the footmen assist you."

"When I wish to do what?"

"Mr Darcy said you would arrange the music room. Lady Catherine arranged it in its present state—she did not wish her daughter to be exposed to a draught whilst she listened to music."

"And now he wishes me to change it?" Elizabeth stared at the housekeeper, who maintained her stoic, deferential countenance.

"Yes, miss. As you will be the only lady who exhibits, I daresay the ideal arranging of it falls to you."

Elizabeth had not the least notion what to make of such an unanticipated directive. Re-arrange a room at Pemberley? To her own liking and against the express wishes of Lady Catherine?

"It seems impertinent—" she began but Mrs Reynolds interrupted her hurriedly.

"No, no. Pray, do as he suggested. The room is…well, it used to be a lovely place. Miss…Mrs Darcy loved to play and sing all the day long. The sun would shine and she would sing. The parlour maids somehow found themselves dusting there just to hear her. There are no flowers to put in there, but we could find something…colourful to enliven it."

"I am sure I am not nearly as proficient as Mrs Darcy," said Elizabeth. "In fact, I am a poor performer. I would not wish excite anyone's anticipation; no matter how pleasingly the room is arranged, it cannot compensate for the slurring and fudging of the performer."

Mrs Reynolds, who usually appeared to be worried about something, smiled and made a breathy sound that might have been a laugh. "I am certain you are too modest, Miss Bennet. In any case, do let me know when I may assist you."

After the door closed behind Mrs Reynolds, Elizabeth allowed her posture to relax. An extraordinary gesture! And one whose meaning she could not immediately discern. "It did not seem," she mused, "as if refusing was possible."

She rose, intending to go see the room that she might contemplate it further. She gave fleeting consideration to returning the journal to its lovely blue haven, but no, she could not. Not yet.

Elizabeth had seen the music room only briefly before, and it struck her then as a forbidding, unwelcoming sort of place. Minutes later, seeing it again confirmed that belief; it was a formal, discomfiting room that seemed to have been arranged for the express purpose of performing dirges.

She sighed looking at it. "Hardly a room that inspires devotion to the art."

"I agree."

She whirled around to find that Mr Darcy had slipped unheard into the room and stood excessively close to her. She took a step backwards, quelling the desire to gasp or shriek her surprise.

"I beg your pardon, sir. I understood myself alone."

"Think nothing of that. I agree with you."

"So it seems. Mrs Reynolds mentioned you might wish to hear my suggestions for improvement?"

"Not suggestions," he said. "You may change it as you see fit."

"Because you wish for a performer?" She arched one brow at him, giving him a mockingly severe look.

He had the grace to appear somewhat abashed. "I confess my motives are at least partly selfish."

She put her back to him, returning to her regard of the space. "I understand Mrs Darcy was an accomplished performer."

There was a prolonged silence before he offered, "My sister was the true proficient."

Another surprise. She turned back to look at him. "Your sister?"

He nodded.

"I was not aware you have a sister."

"Had a sister." He dropped his eyes to stare at his feet. "She died some time ago while on holiday at Ramsgate. She was but fifteen."

"Oh!" Elizabeth swallowed her fresh bout of surprise and the swell of compassion in her throat. "You have my condolences, sir."

He shrugged, his eyes remaining fixed on his feet. "It was a long time ago."

Silence stretched long between them. Elizabeth watched his face, seeing nothing revealed in his countenance. In gentler accents she said, "How well I know that the pain of losing a most beloved sister is never fully healed."

"Mm," he agreed. He raised his head, and said briskly, "In any case, any changes you make will be improvements, and I shall be indebted to you for them."

With that, he turned and exited the room as quietly and quickly as he had entered it.

NINE

Dinner was yet another strange, strained affair. Elizabeth thought to mention something about the music room to Lady Catherine, but Mr Darcy immediately interceded. From that, she understood it was not to be discussed with her ladyship. The house retired early, and Elizabeth, who was sure she would not sleep for hours, was quick to surrender to the claims of Morpheus.

Then she was on her feet, stumbling towards Charles's bedchamber before she even knew she was awake. A scream. Charles screamed—some part of her mind knew that even while the rest of her struggled to wake and summon what maternal consolation she could. His nursemaid joined her just as she entered his room and saw him sitting bolt upright in his bed, sobbing with terror.

He was still half-asleep, sobbing about the lady who had come in his room, a ghost lady who had threatened to eat his head. "Eat your head!" Elizabeth exclaimed. "No indeed, my sweet, no, no."

"Yes," he sobbed. "She eats your head with her long teeth and scratches your arms with her sharp claws."

A glance at the mantel told her it was just after two. Elizabeth motioned to the nurse that she should return to her bed. She settled in next to Charles and drew him into her arms. They rocked back and forth while he mumbled incoherently about the frightening witch who had come into his room.

"No, no, no," Elizabeth crooned. Ah, how well she remembered the difficulty inherent in being a child with an active imagination! Her mind could never accept that a curtain twitching in the wind was not a restless spirit nor could she comprehend that ghosts rising up from the graveyard and chasing after little girls were not real. To her mind, they had been real. It was not until she was older that she was able to discern the difference between her imaginings and the truth of the world she inhabited.

She did not rebuke him when he shoved his thumb into his mouth; whatever was needed to console at this time of night would be put to use. She continued rocking and crooning while he mumbled about the lady and sucked on his thumb, until at last, his mumbles grew quiet. Eventually, his body went limp and heavy against her side, and some time after that, she chanced laying him back against his pillow and tucking the coverlet up under his chin.

Elizabeth smoothed back the curls around his face, watching him while his breathing changed from the shallow half-sobs to deeper respirations. At last, she rose and stole from the room on silent feet, eager to return to her bed. Carefully she opened the door, having noted its tendency to squeak, and slipped out, turning back to close it without making a tell-tale click that might wake Charles.

And then she nearly screamed when she collided with a sound-less, tall form standing in the hall. A short sound escaped her but then she clapped her hand over her mouth. After a moment, she dropped her hand, releasing her breath in a gasp.

"Is the boy well?" It was Mr Darcy standing there—to what purpose she could not imagine.

"Perfectly so," she hissed. "Pray, lower your voice. I just got him to sleep."

His next utterance was made in an obedient whisper. "A bad dream was it?"

"Yes," she murmured in reply.

"He has them often, I think."

This assertion was correct, though Elizabeth was shocked Mr Darcy realised it. Since coming to Pemberley, little Charles was frequently plagued by the terrors of the night, but who knew from whence those terrors came? Was it all the imaginings of his mind? Or was it the house, Pemberley, which cloaked them all in fear with its cold grandeur? Even her own dreams had taken on a decidedly gothic hue these days.

"Yes, he does," she said finally.

Mr Darcy said nothing after that, merely staring down at her; she was at once conscious of her improper state of dress. Her abrupt awakening meant she had neglected her robe and her slippers, and under his gaze, she felt as naked as the day she was born although, of course, her voluminous gown covered every inch of her. Nevertheless, she crossed her arms over her chest and desperately wished she had her robe.

"Is there anything he needs?" asked Mr Darcy at last.

She shook her head. "He will sleep now. My apologies for the disturbance. I am sure you are as eager to return to your bed as I am to mine."

"Of course."

Was it her imagination or did Mr Darcy cast a lingering glance over her form? The very idea of that made her shiver. He extended his arm, indicating Elizabeth should precede him down the hall. She went with relieved haste, comfortable only when she at last closed the door between herself and Mr Darcy's baffling gaze.

It was only then that she considered why it was that Mr Darcy, in the middle of the night, should be fully dressed.

ALONE IN HIS BEDCHAMBER, Darcy stood, running a shaking hand through his hair, the vision of Miss Bennet's seraphic beauty occupying his mind. She had seemed nearly a vision as she raced into her nephew's bedchamber. He had remained rooted to the spot where he saw her until she emerged again, peaceful with the faint smile that he always noticed after she spent time with Charles.

Of her figure draped in thin white cotton, he dared not think.

Too light for winter, he thought, persuading himself that his only concern was her health. She should have a flannel gown and some woollen stockings. A cap perhaps—but no, no cap should ever be permitted to obscure the loveliness of her wild jumble of curls.

His man arrived in the midst of these musings.

"Morley, what are you doing awake?"

"Waiting for you, sir, naturally." One might have believed it was ten or eleven o'clock from how Morley looked and acted, industriously setting about the business of seeing his master prepared for sleep. He clucked, flicking at some of the horse hairs that clung to Darcy's buckskin breeches but otherwise said very little.

In short time, Darcy was comfortably ensconced in his bed, the lamp burning low and a book in his right hand. It was always thus with him; no matter the hour, he was required to ease his mind's passage into rest with a book. Tonight, however, he did not open the book. Tonight he would reflect on his uncle's letter, the letter that had distressed him so and sent him out into the night in search of resolution.

His uncle was laid low by a series of apoplectic fits; it seemed that his body might never recover from the assault, though his mind was sharp as ever. Confined to his bed or a couch, he contented himself by meddling in the affairs of his two sons and his nephew via letter.

The missive began innocently enough. The doings at Matlock were canvassed along with the health of his various cousins and Lady Matlock. His eldest male cousin, Viscount Saye, was expecting another child with his wife. They had managed only girl children to date, and Lord Matlock was desperate to see an heir, particularly as he felt his own health failing.

He had read the passage so often that he could see it now in his mind's eye.

As you might suspect, with so few balls and amusements in town, the ton has lit upon the breach within the family to exercise their tongues. Nephew, this separation and the remedy for it are in your hands. Anne depends on you, and our very respectability as a family does as well.

The weight of expectation crashed down on him. Anne had created her own problems; why was it to him to serve the remedy? All he wanted was to be free of this black web wrapped around him, ensnaring him most cruelly and squeezing the very life from him. He was yet a young man, only two and thirty. Was it common to see so much grey hair in a man of his age? Did other gentleman feel the sag of their shoulders and an ache in their knees?

He believed he had grown accustomed to it, the feelings of failure and grief and dread that bound him. He reminded himself often that he chose his path and could not return, but some small part of him thought that untrue. Some bit of him clung to a hope that life could one day be agreeable, felicitous even.

Mrs Green sent Elizabeth a note requesting a visit, and Elizabeth was eager to go to her. Feeling she should, she asked Lady Catherine whether she was needed at Pemberley or might she be excused for a morning.

"Need you?" Her ladyship peered down at Elizabeth, and Elizabeth thought it a dear shame that Lady Catherine had not a pince-nez to further emphasise her scrutiny. "Why should I need you, Miss Bennet?"

"I am sure I cannot imagine," said Elizabeth with a smile she hoped appeared winsome. It was not easy, given the sharp reminder that her very existence was superfluous. "It felt improper to go off without asking someone."

"A spinster," Lady Catherine pronounced, "will always do best to amuse herself in any way she can."

Elizabeth pressed her lips together a moment before replying as pleasantly as possible, "Then I shall take my leave of you for the day."

Lady Catherine could only harrumph and mutter her indignation in reply and soon was stalking off down the hall to chastise some poor maid or another. Elizabeth watched her walk off, her pleasant mask falling away. Unneeded, unwanted, unfit. The words buzzed at her endlessly.

Her steps towards the carriage began slowly, but her pace quickened as a determined cheer rose within her. Never mind Lady Catherine. She was going to see a friend and have a nice visit, and to this small pleasure would her spirits be tied.

The journey felt much longer than it was, but soon enough she had arrived at Mrs Lawrence's house. Elizabeth entered and was shown into the same drawing room where she had been on her previous visit. Mrs Green was already there, standing in anticipation of Elizabeth's arrival. She beamed an enormous smile as Elizabeth was announced, and Elizabeth's heart skipped with the pleasure of it.

They offered one another a greeting appropriate to elegant ladies and then, in a somewhat undignified way, giggled. Mrs Green reached out to grasp Elizabeth's hands in her own. "You have no idea how excited I was for your visit!"

"No less so than I," Elizabeth assured her.

Mrs Green led her friend to chairs by the blazing fire and invited her to sit. "I ordered us some refreshments and tea. Mrs Lawrence is unwell this morning, so she will remain in her bedchamber."

"I do hope it is nothing serious."

"Nothing more serious than the consequence of a long life." Mrs Green smiled, but it was touched with sadness. "She is the youngest sister of Lady Catherine's grandmother."

"Lady Catherine's...great-aunt?" Elizabeth felt her mouth gape and quickly schooled her countenance into something less shocked. "Indeed?"

"Aye," said her friend assuredly. "She is above eighty, though she will not tell me how much. Perhaps she does not know herself. In any case, she does have days where leaving her bed proves too much for her. They seem to be coming more often now, I am sorry to say."

"Poor dear," said Elizabeth. "She is fortunate to have such a caring companion for her last days."

"Her family are not kind to her." Mrs Green frowned prettily at her lap. "She has several sons—three, I think—and they all have families of their own, scattered here and there. In the time I have been here, I have only met one of them."

Elizabeth shook her head. "Those of us who have lost the family dear to us know how foolish it is to take such things for granted."

The ladies were interrupted by the housekeeper bearing their repast.

"How long were you married?" asked Elizabeth delicately.

"Seven years." Mrs Green smiled. "You are too kind to ask if I ever had children. No, no I did not, though I assure you it was not for lack of trying."

Elizabeth smiled through the blush that rose quick and hot on her cheeks.

"Forgive me," Mrs Green said, noting Elizabeth's discomfiture. "I forgot for a moment that I spoke to a lady, and an unmarried one at that."

"No, no," said Elizabeth. "Think nothing of that."

"In any case, it suited me very well. Bearing children is quite a dangerous business, and I had no wish to take chances with my life."

"I have heard it said that every man is a potential murderer," Elizabeth offered. "The ones who get their wives with child, that is."

"Aye, 'tis quite true," said Mrs Green.

"I presume that must be what happened to Mrs Darcy."

"Mrs Darcy?" Mrs Green seemed confused for a moment and then recovered herself. "Ah, I should not know. She was long gone when I came here."

"Was she?" Elizabeth gave a little shrug. "She is not spoken of at Pemberley, so I know little of her. I only learnt yesterday that Mr Darcy had a sister."

"Mr Darcy has a sister?"

"She died at a young age," said Elizabeth. "Fifteen, I believe he said."

"I see," said Mrs Green. "So, what is it like living with Mr Darcy? He is much spoken of in these parts as you may imagine. Handsome wealthy and unmarried…a subject of interest indeed, particularly among the ladies!" The two women chuckled.

"The other ladies may have him," Elizabeth declared. "I find him a most disagreeable gentleman although I must acknowledge some gratitude to him for permitting me to stay with Charles. Why he insisted on bringing the boy to Derbyshire, I shall never know. He scarcely says two words to him."

Then she recollected herself. For all Mrs Green's warmth, they were yet strangers; it did not do to bandy about such intimate information.

Mrs Green watched her for a moment, then rose, going to the window and looking out at the gardens below. Elizabeth sat for long moments, her desire to confide in someone beating against her chest. She had been too long without a confidante and too long without anyone to speak to about the truths of her heart. Mrs Green must have sensed her struggle and remained quiet to allow her to deliberate. After a short time, she returned to her seat.

"My greatest fear is that he will ask me to leave," Elizabeth said. "And my fondest wish is that he will allow me to take Charles back to Hertfordshire."

"Of course," Mrs Green murmured soothingly. "Do you think he will?"

Elizabeth shook her head once, quick and decisive, and then stared into her tea, blinking away the tears in her eyes that always appeared when she acknowledged her fate. "He is as determined to have him as I am, though why, I do not know."

"These great men do like to have their way of things," said Mrs Green. "And Mr Darcy has been master of his estate for a long time. He is accustomed to the world arranging itself by his wishes."

Elizabeth admitted, "I did not behave well when he arrived in Hertfordshire. I made a nuisance of myself, and I think it only strengthened his resolve to prevail over me."

"It is likely he intended to carry his point, regardless of how you were. Wealthy men like Mr Darcy are not accustomed to being gainsaid by anyone."

It was then that a strange phenomenon was observed. Pale light, weak and diffuse, had wended its way through the curtains, and feeble though it was, it urged Elizabeth outdoors. Mrs Green was of the same persuasion and offered to show Elizabeth the gardens. "Or at least the place where gardens customarily grow."

They were soon off on a ramble through a garden, which was well-tended though bereft of any true sign of life. Spindly rose bushes stabbed at them defiantly while other dried stems and muddy patches showed them where hedges and flower borders once flourished. But they were outside and it did not rain, and for this Elizabeth was grateful.

For some time they walked and chatted lightly about the state of things, the garden, the weather, and similar matters of no consequence. Then they fell into a companionable silence, walking for some time until Mrs Green said, with some precipitance, "Miss Bennet, I urge you to be cautious."

"Oh?" Elizabeth looked around, thinking there was some danger on the path. "What is it?"

"Not here." Mrs Green shook her lovely curls. "Cautious in your situation. These great men are whimsical in their civilities, and if Mr Darcy wishes you gone, I do not doubt that you will be gone."

"I am well aware of the precarious nature of his hospitality. I only hope..."

She sighed and gave a little laugh while Mrs Green looked at her curiously.

"There are three chances for me to carry my point in this. One was that Mr Darcy should simply tire of the needs of a child in his household."

"Pemberley has so many servants, I cannot think it should trouble him at all."

"True. He scarcely notices that Charles is there." Elizabeth sighed, wondering as always at the vagaries of a man who insisted on tearing a child from his home one day yet ignoring him thereafter. "My next idea was that if he should marry, his wife would not likely want an extra child hanging about. She will wish to fill Pemberley with her own children."

Mrs Green nodded. "This could prove true."

"Though he has no inclination towards marriage that I can see. He has shown little interest in even leaving the house, and there are not many eligible young ladies roaming about Pemberley."

"Save for one?" Mrs Green asked with a sly wink at her friend.

"Do not wish me such ill!" Elizabeth cried out with a little laugh. "Mr Darcy has no leaning in that way, I assure you! Mere disdain would be his warmest feeling towards me."

"So those two possibilities are unlikely at best, then. So how will you broker yours and Charles's release?"

Elizabeth walked several feet more, her eyes roving sightless over the grey-brown garden. Some part of her felt she was confiding too much on too short an acquaintance, but there was something innately trustworthy in Mrs Green's looks. "Secrets lurk in every nook and cranny of Pemberley, it seems. If I should learn…something, no matter how slight, to gain an advantage over him…"

She stopped when she realised how mad it sounded when said aloud. "I sound like some sort of extortionist, do I not?"

The two ladies laughed together for a moment before Mrs Green stopped, turning to her Elizabeth and grasping hold of her arm. "Ladies in the world are powerless enough. If you do know something that gives you some advantage over him, I say use it as you can, nay, how you must."

The ladies were quiet as they took the path leading back to the house. Elizabeth was lost in her own thoughts, and a glance at her friend revealed that she appeared to be the same. It was not until Mrs Green's hand touched the door to Mrs Lawrence's house that she spoke again.

"There have been many deaths at Pemberley. Certainly more than are seen in the great families."

Elizabeth considered that a moment. Mr Darcy was without a person in the world to claim him save for one exceedingly unpleasant aunt. His mother, his father, his sister, and his wife—all dead.

"You do not think—" she began.

"I think nothing," said Mrs Green. "I think it strange, the unlikelihood of so many different sorts of death afflicting one family. That is all."

"It is extraordinary," Elizabeth agreed; but no more could be said than that.

PEMBERLEY WAS silent as a church on Monday when she returned, and her footsteps in the vestibule made a hollow, echoing sound as she moved towards her apartment. She had resolved during her travel back from seeing Mrs Green to indulge herself in a long ramble. It seemed less cold; perhaps the weather was at last due for a change.

She stopped briefly in the nursery. Charles was having a rest, and she promised his nurse that she would return about the time he was expected to wake. Moments later, she was striding towards the outside door, ready to fill her lungs with fresh air and the promise of something like sunshine.

"Miss Bennet."

A curse entered her thoughts but did not escape her lips. She stopped mere steps from the door and turned towards Mr Darcy. "Sir?"

"You have returned from your visit to your friend?"

"I have."

"Ah." He stood, awkwardly shifting his weight. "Was it...did your visit...you found your friend in good health, I presume?"

Elizabeth stifled an impatient sigh. "Excellent health indeed. We had a pleasant time together."

"I am glad to hear it." He paused then added, "I have been reviewing my accounts this morning."

She wondered at his meaning in telling her so. "I trust you found everything in good order."

"Oh yes. Mrs Reynolds is an excellent manager, and my steward is exemplary as well."

"Capital," she replied. She watched him cast about for a moment, seeming to wish to prolong the conversation, for reasons she could not imagine. "I was just about to take a walk. The weather seems more agreeable today than it has been of late."

"Excellent!" He very nearly beamed his approbation, and she had a disconcerting moment when she realised he was actually quite handsome. "I need a few moments to obtain my greatcoat."

Chagrin washed over her as she recognised that her attempt to excuse herself was taken as an invitation. There was nothing for it; he had already summoned a footman to retrieve the needed coat and hat.

"Is there anything particular you wish to see?" He offered his assistance to her as she descended the stairs.

"Nothing particular," she replied. "Is there anything you wish to show me?"

He thought for a moment. "It is a longish sort of walk, perhaps a mile or so to get there."

"A mile? Nothing at all," she replied lightly. "Lead the way, Mr Darcy."

They set out much as she expected they might: silently. For some time there was little but the muffled sound of their footsteps on the mouldering sward beneath them, but Elizabeth could not allow it. He had insisted he come and she would insist that he speak.

"We must have some conversation, Mr Darcy. A very little will do. You could tell me something of the field perhaps, and I shall remark on the trees."

"You talk by rule then when walking?"

"When someone has accompanied me, yes, I do. It would be strange indeed to be in one another's company for so long without some attempt at conversation."

He now seemed pensive but as disinclined to converse with her as ever; with a sigh, she conceded defeat.

"Your parents' marriage must have been a loving union."

An odd and impudent beginning but Elizabeth was glad he said something even if it made her laugh. "Why should you think so?"

"Your father has been widowed some time and does not appear inclined to remarry."

"Perhaps he has not met anyone who suits his fancy," Elizabeth replied. "Longbourn Village and the town nearest it, Meryton, are by no means large nor populous. We dined with no more than four-and-twenty families even before the fever took so many of them."

"He should go to London then," Mr Darcy replied. "An eligible widower with an estate no more than half a day's travel to London would be greatly sought after."

Elizabeth laughed again, and even the spectral mists that crept in around them could not dampen her merriment. "Being sought after is my father's deepest dread. He would much rather be undisturbed in his library."

Mr Darcy offered no reply to her.

"You speak from your own experience," she said, at last, hardly believing her own boldness. "Have none of the ladies in London met with your approval?"

Her eagerness to hear his reply was tempered by her understanding that light-hearted indifference was sure to provoke the truest answer. She did not, therefore, urge him to speak although he seemed to consider her question for an eternity.

"From my experience," he said, "I daresay it is preferable to be alone than to be bound to the wrong person. It seems your father might agree with me even though he requires an heir—as I do."

"My father has chosen his duty to himself over the duty to his estate."

They came to a little rise cut by a narrow path, and Mr Darcy indicated she should precede him. As they began to climb, she heard his reply from behind her.

"As have many men. But it does not mean it will be so forever."

TEN

THE PATH BROUGHT THEM TO THE TOP OF THE RISE, AND FROM THIS RISE, a scene both forlorn and majestic was unveiled. First came a wide stream, the sort that was feral in a pretty way. Beyond the stream, a rolling pasturage led to the remains of what must have once been a grand structure, though whatever grandeur it had once possessed was now far in the past. Nature had her way with it, leaving only a tumble of large rocks and weeds in a shape of what might have been a castle.

It was melancholy to imagine what beauty it once possessed; Elizabeth could almost see the gentleman and ladies who once resided herein sweeping past in farthingales and doublets, while knights jousted on the lawns and fair maidens danced in the wood.

"This, Miss Bennet, is Pemberton." Elizabeth's heart jerked; having been absorbed in her fanciful notions, she was unaware that Mr Darcy had drawn in close behind her. "The Darcy house before there was Pemberley."

"It looks like it was once a princely home, sir," Elizabeth observed with a little glance and a raised brow over her shoulder.

"Aye," agreed Mr Darcy. "Until fire took part of it and flood took the other. But it stood for centuries. I suppose it was time to allow it to rest."

"And the present house? When was it built?"

"It is nearly a hundred years old. Built at the direction of my great-grandfather who was, from what I have heard, an active participant in the building."

Elizabeth laughed. "I should not have imagined your forbearers taking up a shovel."

"The men in my family have long been unafraid to dirty their hands." In an abrupt change of subject, he asked, "Are you fond of ghost stories?"

"Ghost stories?" She considered it a moment while watching the grasses nearest the ruins bend and sway like mourners keening at a graveside. "I cannot say that I am."

"Now that is a surprise, Miss Bennet."

"Why should that surprise you?"

He gave her a wry look. "Because I have seen you reading them to your nephew and presumed you an admirer of the genre."

"Enjoyment of a book can take many forms. Sometimes you enjoy it for the subject, and other times you enjoy it because it gives you a moment of respite from the exertion of chasing a small boy about."

She put her back to the ruins, turning to look at him full on. "I have lost too many who are dear to me to enjoy imagining that the dead should hang about in misery. I should much prefer to imagine them in paradise than in some state of unrest."

"An understandable view," he agreed. "But it is too bad, for Pemberton Castle has a charmingly gothic tale attached to it."

"A young lady crossed in love, no doubt," Elizabeth said. "Is not that the beginning of all such tales?"

"In some manner of speaking. She was a maiden of royal birth who disguised herself as a servant to be with her beloved."

"A good plan indeed!" Elizabeth laughed. "And then when she was discovered…"

"It was she who did the discovering."

It took Elizabeth a moment to understand. "Her beloved was untrue?"

Mr Darcy nodded, his eyes fixed on the stones and rubble in the distance. "So she killed herself. Took some poison right in front of him, then proclaimed his guilt and vowed she would not rest so long as there remained any of his seed on the earth."

"Oh dear," said Elizabeth lightly, turning away from the inexplicably hollow look in Mr Darcy's eyes. "And this wretched scoundrel was your ancestor?"

"Many generations past," he admitted.

"Have you seen the ghostly lady yourself?" Elizabeth asked, hoping to restore Mr Darcy to some semblance of levity. "Does she haunt all the Darcy males or are some generations exempted?"

He gave her a faint, abstracted smile that looked more a reproof than anything. "I hardly put stock in ghosts and fairies and witches. My mind is firmly grounded in the rational world, in things seen and measured and understood."

"Oh." After a moment, Elizabeth nodded. "Very good, then."

At length, she turned and moved back towards the path. Again, Mr Darcy followed her, and when he spoke, she was not sure whether he spoke to her or to himself. "However I cannot deny that those who bear the name of Darcy are unfortunate in affairs of the heart."

On her questioning look, he added, "Wives of Darcy men have a tendency to die too young."

Elizabeth nearly gasped. This was surely more of an admission than she might ever have anticipated, and she hardly knew what to say next. But more conversation was forestalled by the appearance of a man—the mute fellow she had seen along the river on one of her first walks at Pemberley.

The mists had obscured him from their view as they descended from the rise. He stood immediately before them, staring at them both blankly, almost as if he was conjured from the grasses themselves. Elizabeth gave a wordless exclamation of surprise that appeared to equally surprise the man himself who replied with a yelp.

The man recovered from his shock quickly and, after a moment, schooled his countenance into something that looked like a flirtation. "My lady," he said, managing a low, flourishing bow.

Elizabeth hardly knew how to reply but was saved from the necessity of so doing by Mr Darcy, who stepped forward, his face purple with rage. He grabbed her arm and pushed her aside even as the strange man offered a compliment to her. "How very lovely you look today."

"No!" Mr Darcy barked. "Step away at once!"

The man did not appear to notice him, his eyes unmoving from Elizabeth as he stretched his hand towards her. "If you are not engaged for the next..." he began, but Mr Darcy stopped him immediately. "There will be none of that."

Mr Darcy grasped the man's arm firmly and turned him away from Elizabeth. "Wait here," he barked over his shoulder as he began to move the man down the path as rapidly as the man would be moved.

"A very handsome girl indeed," the man remarked conversationally. "Has she any fortune?"

"You will stay away from her," was all Elizabeth heard as the pair disappeared around a bend in the path. Elizabeth exhaled, having not realised she was holding her breath.

Minutes elapsed slowly as she waited for Mr Darcy to reappear. The mists seemed to be thickening, and she shivered a little; she had dressed to walk, not to stand motionless. Eventually, she decided she would begin a slow return to the house. Pemberley had just appeared in her sights when Mr Darcy drew abreast of her.

"I told you to wait." He was breathless, having run to meet her, it seemed.

"I grew weary with the effort," she retorted. "Will you drag me back into the house?"

"That man is a dangerous lunatic. I did as was needed to warn him away from you."

"A dangerous lunatic? Confused perhaps but—"

"You will stay away from him," Mr Darcy told her sternly.

She gave him a sidelong glance. "He seemed simple but hardly dangerous."

"Miss Bennet, look at me." Elizabeth stopped and turned to face Mr Darcy, who spoke to her through gritted teeth and a clenched jaw.

"That man is a threat to any decent lady, and you must stay away from him."

"It is hardly my habit to consort with men unknown to me."

"Has he approached you before?" A vein at Mr Darcy's temple pulsed in an alarming fashion.

Elizabeth chose not to answer. "Who is he?"

Mr Darcy paid no heed to her question. "I must know at once if he speaks to you again. Do I have your word?"

"Mr Darcy," said Elizabeth with a great display of patience, "I have never responded kindly to orders and threats. Perhaps you can explain to me what it is about this man that is so terrible. He had the dress of a gentleman, so I must suppose—"

"You will suppose nothing!" Mr Darcy's rage appeared to be growing. His fists clenched at his sides as his face flushed a deeper red and his posture grew stiff as a board. He seemed to wish to strike something and Elizabeth wondered whether he had taken the man off somewhere and beaten him. She glanced down at his gloves—was that a spot of blood?

"You will stay away from him, and you will tell me immediately if he speaks to you again. Am I clear?"

Elizabeth raised her eyes to Mr Darcy's, feeling a faint flutter of fear as she beheld the fiery anger in his gaze. The angry retort on her lips died unspoken; part of her wished to fight back, to tell Mr Darcy he was not her keeper, but another, wiser part realised she was alone with a furious gentleman who was considerably larger than she was.

She took a careful breath before replying tightly, "I shall tell you directly if he speaks to me again."

They returned to the house in silence, Mr Darcy stalking alongside her with his rage nearly palpable. Elizabeth congratulated herself on being able to show no sign of distress although her mind nearly swam with her feelings on the events of the last minutes.

Mrs Reynolds appeared to assist them in removing their outdoor attire. When he saw her, Mr Darcy turned to Elizabeth. "Have you yet seen to the music room?"

"I confess, I have not."

"Mrs Reynolds, see that the footmen help Miss Bennet rearrange the music room today," he ordered, after which he turned on his heel and disappeared down the hall.

Left alone, Mrs Reynolds and Elizabeth were silent a moment, until Elizabeth, with a light laugh to disguise her pique, said, "It appears I have my orders, Mrs Reynolds. Perhaps someone could help me in an hour or so? I have been away all morning and am in need of a lie-down."

"Of course, Miss Bennet. When you are ready, so will the men be."

With that, the housekeeper left, and Elizabeth was free to return to her bedchamber. She was tired although she had never been one to take such naps or to lie down in the middle of the day. In truth, she needed time apart from everything to ponder the events of the morning, from Mrs Green's observations on the numerous deaths at Pemberley to Pemberton Castle, ghost stories, and then a discomfiting encounter with an idiot who appeared harmless yet drove Mr Darcy to an inexplicable rage. It was too much to make sense of any of it, in truth, and at last she resolved to quiet her mind with some reading.

Alas, her book would not hold her, and soon the siren song of the journal would not be silenced. "I must return this to its rightful place," Elizabeth murmured as she opened the flap and slid into the romantic world of flirtation by the sea.

The gentleman had called and taken the girl walking on several occasions; they had gone on nearly as many drives. He had a friend, a Mr L, who was taken with one of the lady's friends, and it seemed they made a happy foursome.

The young lady was falling in love with her suitor, at least to Elizabeth's view of the matter. Each page contained more about how handsome he was, how witty, how learned. He was praised as much as any man could be, and from the girl's descriptions, it seemed very much like he was falling in love with her too.

Elizabeth paused as she came upon one page containing an account of an evening of music It was nothing extraordinary, merely a discussion of what was played and how it made her feel, but what was interesting was that it was cross-written with a receipt. Elizabeth studied it for a long moment; she never known anyone who cross-wrote something that had no intention of being mailed.

She took a closer look at the receipt.

Havercakes

Put half a pint of buttermilk into a bowl
Add one pint of warm water, hot enough to
bring the mix to blood heat
Crumble in 1/2 oz fresh yeast
Gradually stir in 1/2 pound of fine ground
oatmeal
Stir well then wrap a cloth around the
container and leave in a warm place for an
hour until risen.
Adjust to a thick pouring consistency by
adding a little more meal or water. Grease
the griddle then test for temperature with a
dot of batter. Sift oatmeal onto the riddle-
board.
Pour on a ladleful of batter then spread and
level it by a circular horizontal movement.
When even, slide off onto the linen-covered
spittle board.
With this 'throw' it on to the bakestone
then take up the linen.

How peculiar! I would not suppose that the wife of Mr Darcy should be much interested in baking. Perhaps she ate these somewhere and wished to pass the receipt on to her cook?

Elizabeth turned the page wondering how many other cross-written pages she would find, but the next several pages had lines in only one direction. There seemed to be no reason that she could discern for it, and before too much time had passed, she decided it had no significance whatsoever and turned her attention to what she read.

I am sure I cannot bear my happiness today. Everything has been spoken of; all is now settled. I can scarcely believe it is true that I should have won the affections of such a man as my beloved, but he tells me he knew he loved me even from the very first day he saw me walking along the shore! He told me my beauty vastly outshone the others.

He said such lovely things to me, so charming, so dear, I can hardly bear the sweetness of the memory. He knelt before me and took my hands so gently in his—I thought I might die! But I was so very nervous too, and he told me everything that filled his heart. He said he had scarcely been able to think of anything but me, and he even showed me a poem he had written to me that very first day of our renewed acquaintance. I shall enclose it within these pages and read it at least ten times a day for the rest of my life, I am sure.

Can it be wrong to love someone so? Can it be imprudent to risk whatever you have to pursue your one true love? I used to think Shakespeare such a complicated, uninteresting fellow, but now I understand him in every way.

> "Come what sorrow can, it cannot countervail the
>   exchange of joy that one short minute gives me in
>   her sight:
> Do thou but close our hands with holy words, then
>   love-devouring death do what he dare; it is enough I
>   may but call her mine"

THE POEM MR DARCY had wrote to her must have been lost for Elizabeth did not find it on these or any successive pages. Nevertheless, the meaning was clear: they were in love with one another. Charlotte believed that theirs was an arranged match, but it surely did not seem so. It was difficult to imagine Mr Darcy as the courtly fellow described in these pages, but perhaps his grief had changed him. Despite her vexation with him, she did pity him this.

My beloved has received all that is needed for my wedding, and I am sure I could not be happier than I am on this day. I had thought I should return to London for the clothes, but he is unable to wait. He has promised me that we shall shop for weeks on end when it is done but says he cannot bear to leave R without knowing that I am by his side as his wife. Mrs Y agrees and has urged me to marry here and then enjoy some time at the seaside with my new husband. How lovely it sounds!

Elizabeth smiled wistfully as she turned the page. How well did she recall when she and her sisters discussed such simple dreams as these! She could almost hear them even now: Jane insisting she would have ten children even as Mrs Bennet admonished that, if possible, they should be all sons; Lydia proclaiming loudly that she could never love a man save he was in regimentals and Kitty echoing her; and Mary, who usually only frowned and chided her sisters, would on occasion admit she hoped to find a sober-minded gentleman who enjoyed discussing matters of philosophy and religion with her.

She shook her head and returned to the journal, forgetting silly dreams of the Bennet maidens and instead seeking the reality of Mrs Darcy's wedding.

Instead, she found that page upon page had been removed, some torn neatly, others yanked out, leaving shards behind them. It was difficult to say how many had been removed—perhaps ten, maybe even twenty—but on the next page that remained was a drawing of a cat-like creature. Not a tame cat or even a barn cat; this was more on the order of a wildcat. She noticed the tufts of black hair sprouting from the creature's ears—a lynx?

She studied it for a time but eventually continued reading, finding herself at a point well beyond the wedding and early days of marriage. How far beyond it she was, she could not know. Such details were likely held within the pages that had been removed, and she wondered who had removed them and why.

Life was blissful for the newly wedded Darcys it would seem. There were descriptions of new gowns, new suits, parties, balls, and evenings of music in which Mrs Darcy was often asked to exhibit, though she did not much care to do so. It seemed very gay, though

Elizabeth could not quite shake the sense that the lady was lonely or disappointed in some way.

Then again, perhaps it was only her own feelings colouring this perception.

DARCY SPENT some hours in his study, pacing and fretting and reliving too many old, bad memories to count. He often persuaded himself that he had mastered the monstrous rage within him, but days such as this showed him that he was only deceiving himself and badly at that. He had frightened Miss Bennet, and that notion appalled him.

He did not meet her again until dinner. She entered the drawing room to find him alone with one glass of wine in his hand and another on the table by his side. Her eyes swept the room, no doubt wondering where Lady Catherine was and then she approached him slowly.

"Good evening, Mr Darcy." He noticed she would not look at him.

"Will you have a glass of wine, Miss Bennet?" He picked up the wine on the table beside him and extended it towards her.

"Thank you." She took it from him and then walked past him to stand by the fire. "Lady Catherine is…?"

"Not dining with us this evening. Her ladyship is unwell."

"I am sorry to hear it." She took a sip of her wine. "What ails her?"

"A headache," he replied quickly, though in truth, he had no idea. When Lady Catherine took to her bed, he had learnt not to ask too many questions. Lady Catherine's strange fits and ill tempers generally defied explanation. He thought it likely related to the empty bottles of gin the maids found in her chambers.

"I am sorry to hear it." She looked past him at a point unknown to him. "I could be well satisfied with a tray—"

He thrust his arm towards her. "Let us go in, shall we?"

They entered the dining room in silence. He helped her sit and then seated himself. They were served soup that she ate quietly.

The manservant came to remove their bowls and place before him a cut of venison. He searched it carefully, at last determining where to find the finest piece for her and how best to carve it.

"A man who is master of his estate soon begins to think he is master of everything," she said suddenly, causing him to jerk with surprise.

Warily, he replied, "Only a fool would think himself master of everything. I hope I am not a fool although I have defects in character enough."

"Do you?" She took a morsel of the venison and chewed it slowly, her countenance pensive. "Such as what? Which should you own to?"

He toyed with his venison. "If your idea of conversation is this sort of confessional, perhaps you will indulge my curiosity first."

"You wish to hear of the shades in my character?"

"I do." He offered a smile, which she did not appear to notice.

"Very well." She lifted her napkin and dabbed her mouth. "Mr Bingley's sister Caroline once accused me of possessing a country-town indifference to decorum, and after I had considered it, I had to own she was quite right."

"A country-town indifference to decorum?"

"I believe she meant that I relied more on my sense of what was right and wrong than what society or the ton or even my parents told me to do." She smiled, but her eyes were wistful. "Miss Bingley said so the day after I arrived at Netherfield when my sister took ill. My father could not spare the horses that morning, but I believed Jane needed me, so I went to Netherfield on foot even though it had rained the day before and the mud was deep. Miss Bingley thought it quite scandalous and said I did not need to scamper about the countryside simply because my sister was ill."

Darcy chuckled. "That does sound like her."

She squared her shoulders and looked at him directly. "But so it is with me, and I daresay it is a failing, but one I am not displeased with. My family and how dearly I love them will always prevail over the dictates of society. I bring harm to no one save for myself."

"I suppose I might have guessed this of you already," he replied with a wry smile. "I believe I had some taste of this nature myself in the matter of your nephew."

Elizabeth did not take the intended teasing well. She pursed her lips and took a deliberate sip of her wine before saying pointedly, "There, I have confessed to my defect; what is yours?"

"Mine?" He paused for a fraction of a minute. "My temper I dare not vouch for. It is, I believe, too little yielding—certainly too little for the convenience of the world. I cannot forget the follies and vices of others so soon as I ought, nor their offences against myself. My feelings are not puffed about with every attempt to move them. My temper would perhaps be called resentful. My good opinion once lost is lost for ever."

"A failing indeed," she said, her countenance unreadable. "And one I am not unacquainted with."

"I apologise for the events of this afternoon. They must have distressed you."

"Distressed me? Yes, they did, but even more so, they roused my curiosity. I cannot comprehend what some poor fool might have done to warrant such brutish—"

"That man is dangerous," said Darcy, calmly but firmly. "Any warnings I have served to you with regard to that man are in your best interests, I assure you."

"Blind obedience has ever been a difficulty for me," she shot back. "And now that I am five and twenty, it is even more difficult."

Again came that flash of anger, tightening his chest and causing him to clench his jaw. But it was not anger alone that affected him but also fear. Deep, primal fear on her behalf. He closed his eyes a moment to calm himself.

"Miss Bennet, in bringing you into my home, I have assumed the responsibility for your well-being. It is not a charge I shall take lightly. The man is a danger, and you must, you will avoid him at all costs."

She stared at him with undisguised defiance, though she remained silent.

"I also must insist that a footman attend you whenever you walk," he added. "I cannot imagine what your father permitted, but I shall insist you are accompanied, no matter what."

She protested this at once. "I am not in need of a keeper, Mr Darcy."

"I intend to be quite unyielding on the matter." After a moment's pause, he added, "If I must send you away from Pemberley to carry my point, then I shall." He watched as his words penetrated her consciousness, making her go pale and sink a little in her chair.

There were some long minutes of silence until she at last rose. Very quietly, she bade him excuse her. Without waiting for his reply, she departed, and he did not see her again that night or the day thereafter.

ELEVEN

So there it is. The lines have been drawn in this battle of wills between us, and Mr Darcy shall not scruple to send me off.

Elizabeth paced to and fro in the hall outside her bedchamber. Frustration burned hot within her chest; she could not abide her position—powerless and impotent—subject to the vagaries of this incomprehensible man. Something had to be done and soon, but what?

So far, her stay at Pemberley had yielded little that would prove Mr Darcy an unfit guardian for young Charles. Say what you would of his arrogance or selfishness, Mr Darcy was an able steward to those in his care. His servants and tenants, unlike many, were not going hungry. His people were cared for, and from what she had seen, they all respected him.

The softening of her opinion vexed her, and her vexation propelled her to the drawer where she kept the journal. The answer lay within its pages; she somehow knew that instinctively.

Opening it, she skimmed several pages of sparkling nothings—musings on how delightful was marriage, how lovely their house, how pretty their children were sure to be. Of the latter, she often said how she hoped to be blessed and her dear husband hoped likewise.

Oddly, the parties and amusements of previous pages seemed to have given way to solitude. No mention was made of friends or callers. Similarly, she said nothing of her family. Why had everyone stopped visiting the newly married Darcys?

With a maidenly blush, Elizabeth reminded herself that a newly wedded couple would often seek seclusion in one another, particularly if it were a love match. She shook her head at her silliness and continued to read, hoping to find something more about Mr Darcy's character, something that might be used to broker her release from Pemberley.

Oh, my dearest Beatrice! We have had our first argument, and I am ashamed to say it was entirely my fault!

Well, perhaps not entirely. My husband was not candid on the details of our settlements and pin money, and so I had no notion that what I ordered was too expensive or the bills would come due so soon. He was enraged when he learnt of my expenses, but surely he did realise that I would order wedding clothes.

But no; I must not blame my dear husband, for it is not his fault. I fear I have acted very much a girl in this circumstance. I should have exercised greater economy. It was a largish number of gowns, but Miss Mead had written to me from Madame Comtois' shop with news of some beautiful new silks, and I could not help myself—I added some gowns to what I suppose was already a very substantial order.

His enraged countenance I shall not soon forget. He was red, then purple, though he did not shout. He merely told me we are not as easy as I had supposed we were and any further expenses should be discussed with him for his approval. It seems unfair that...but no. I shall not continue such thoughts for my mind has more serious matters on which to rest.

It seems that his rage was such that he has locked me in my bedchamber.

It was some time until I realised I could not leave, and when I first knew it, I was sure it had been a mistake. But then I rang and rang for my maid, and she did not come. I thought it very curious and had just begun to feel true dread when our housekeeper arrived.

She did not enter. She only spoke through the door to tell me that my husband had decreed I should remain within until he said otherwise. So shall I remain, quiet and more than a little discomfited, dear Beatrice, until he sees fit to release me.

It was on these dreadful words that the journal came to its end. There were no more pages, at least none that were written on. One page had a drawing: a fine house—nothing to Pemberley or even Longbourn, but sizeable and handsome—at the end of a charming, curved lane.

Elizabeth studied it for only a moment before realising what about it was so unusual. It was the perspective that was off. Most houses were drawn from the front to show such features as columns and windows and elegant drives. This drawing focused on the side of the house, with what appeared to be a servants' entrance, though the front could be seen as well. A woman stood on the side of the servants' door in drab raiment, chickens pecking beside her. Was this some statement that the girl felt like a servant in her own home?

"Mr Darcy likes to have women subjected," she mused aloud. "I do hate to disappoint you, sir, but I am not your wife, and I shall not be afraid of you, even if I need to climb out the window to escape you."

A memory teased at her: Mrs Reynolds, on showing her to her room, unlocked the door to this very room from the hall. Doubt pricked at her—was she captive in this place even now?

"Surely not." Would not she have heard footsteps outside the door? A rattle of the doorknob?

But doubt would not be so easily dismissed and eventually she rose, going to the door and opening it just to prove that she had at least her freedom. "For now." Even as she said it, she realised she was not free. She had her own bonds, though not of matrimony; rather, hers was a bond of love for little Charles. As long as he was here, so too would she be, no locked door required.

Just thinking of him brought a smile to her face and she rose, recalling that she had not spent much time with him that day. It would be a welcome relief to her mind to put aside all notions of Mr Darcy and his late wife and the implications of all that lay within the journal. It was likely near Charles's bedtime but perhaps she could read to him.

WITH A GLASS of port in his hand and a closed book on his lap, Darcy sat, his overstuffed chair and thoughts of Elizabeth Bennet surrounding him. Elizabeth Bennet. Did he think of anything else these days? Did his eyes wish to see anything but her? Did his ears want for any sound but that of her dulcet tones?

But this was not the cause of his present alarm. Yes, he was very attracted to her, almost overwhelmingly so. It had begun back in Meryton and grew almost daily. This did not concern him for he knew he could put it aside.

No, what alarmed him now was not his attraction to her but, instead, his attachment to her. He was beginning to realise that his soul hungered for her almost as much as his body did.

My family and how dearly I love them will always prevail over the dictates of society.

How neatly she had articulated everything he felt, all that he believed! How peculiar that this girl from the most backwards place in which he ever found himself, whose upbringing had in no way matched his own, should arrive at the very same beliefs and opinions as he held. She valued what he valued; she believed what he believed.

It added to her many attractions. It made him feel she might one day understand what had happened, how he came to be in the position that he was in.

But could I be happy?

It seemed too much to imagine. Felicity, joy, happiness...even contentment were not things he had dared aspire to of late. An absence of despondence seemed the best he could want.

But he was happy when he was with her. Walking with her, dining with her, reading quietly in the drawing room with her all spoke to him of how it might be, what tender domestic comforts might be his one day.

It was too early to speak to her of a more permanent arrangement of course. The idea of it was so new that his mind could only turn it over and over again, considering it and pondering it.

OVER THE DAYS THAT FOLLOWED, Elizabeth noticed that Mr Darcy seemed to wish to spend a great deal of time with her. Before, she might have passed the entire day seeing him only a few minutes at breakfast and dinner. Now, however, he seemed to find her wherever she was, be it on a walk, reading in the library, or sewing in the drawing room.

Keeping his eye on me? She wondered. Or merely the perverseness of mischance?

The exception to this was, she soon realised, when she was in company with Lady Catherine. Whether it was because Lady Catherine was minding her or because he found her ladyship vexatious, he avoided the two ladies assiduously.

"Have you any plans for the day, Miss Bennet?" he asked one morning as he cut a piece of ham into precise, neatly squared bites.

"Aye," she said, hiding her smile behind her napkin.

He placed one ham square in his mouth and chewed it while giving her an expectant look. Evidently, he wished for her to describe those plans to him, but she would not gratify him until he asked directly. When at last the ham had been thoroughly chewed, he did.

"Will you visit your friend today?"

"No, I intend to go into Bakewell."

"Bakewell?" He seemed astonished.

"It is a town not far from here," she teased. "I daresay it has little of interest to the nobility, but to a simpler person like myself, it offers an agreeable morning spent shopping."

"I know where Bakewell is," he informed her drily. "I am only surprised you should undertake such a venture alone. Fortunately, I am not so engaged this morning that I should not—"

"Lady Catherine will attend me," she informed him, enjoying the fleeting look of confused distaste on his countenance. "And Samuel as well."

"Samuel?"

"A footman."

"Ah, yes, of course. Samuel." He paused a moment, contemplating his neatly squared ham, such as remained.

Elizabeth, considering the subject to have reached its end, laid aside her napkin and began to rise from her seat. "I believe I must prepare—"

"I thank you for your changes to the music room," he said abruptly.

Elizabeth sank back into her chair. She had at last obliged him in his directive to rearrange the music room, strange though it was. Given that she had been ordered to do it, she decided to make the most of it, stopping just short of ordering new paint on the walls.

Indeed, it had not been difficult to improve on it, for whosoever had arranged it previously had made it uninviting. Before Elizabeth's changes, it had managed to be simultaneously cavernous and cramped, with the instruments set apart from the rest of the room at odd angles. Too-large furniture had been shoved together in unusual groupings that seemed to be arranged such that their occupants would not be able to see the performer—only to hear her. Very odd indeed.

So Elizabeth had, with the assistance of two strong footmen, made a more pleasing arrangement. She situated the instruments together and nearer the windows. The furniture, she then placed in less cramped conformations, in ways she believed would allow for both conversation and enjoyment of the music being played.

"I hope the changes met with your approval?"

"Yes, they did," he said. "I think it much more inviting. I wondered if perhaps…"

When the silence had just begun to get uncomfortable, Elizabeth asked, "Perhaps what?"

"It has been some time since Pemberley had parties." He gave a little shrug. "No doubt there were parties in Hertfordshire? Evenings of music, dinner, and the like?"

"No." Elizabeth barely managed to refrain from rolling her eyes. "Never. In the country, we while away our time by stomping through mud and catching fish with our bare hands."

"I only meant to say that no doubt you would prefer to have some similarly lively evenings here."

To say he surprised her was an understatement. She almost wondered if she understood him correctly. "It seems to me that in these difficult times, frivolities and amusements are best suspended."

He shrugged. "Perhaps it is incorrect to allow despair and suffering to overcome us. We might do best to enjoy ourselves as we can, as a distraction from the unhappiness around us."

A party as a distraction from starvation and suffering of one's countrymen? "As you wish, sir."

"WHAT DID DARCY SAY TO YOU?" Lady Catherine asked peevishly as she swept into the vestibule moments later.

Elizabeth, who had been pulling on her gloves, replied, "Mr Darcy? He is gone now." He had left while she finished her breakfast and was no doubt comfortable in his study by now.

"I can see that," Lady Catherine retorted sharply. "Here, come help me with my cloak. I do not have all day to await lazy servants."

Elizabeth took up the garment and helped her ladyship ease into it.

"What did he say to you while you were at breakfast? Of what were you speaking?"

Astonishment rendered Elizabeth mute for a moment. Evidently, Lady Catherine did not mind that Elizabeth should realise she was listening at doors. Her curiosity would overcome any mortification at such a disgraceful practice.

"Mr Darcy intends to have a party," she said at last. "An evening of music—and some supper, I should imagine."

Lady Catherine huffed with no little indignation. "Darcy wishes to play to his neighbours, does he? There is not one of them worthy of his notice."

Elizabeth could offer no opinion on this as she knew very few of the neighbours, isolated as they were. "Perhaps you are right," she conceded at last.

It proved a strategic move. Having secured an agreement of sorts from Elizabeth, Lady Catherine immediately changed tactics.

"Then again, condescension of this sort never goes amiss. He must set an example of better living to them if nothing else."

Elizabeth offered a smile. "In any case, there is nothing quite as pleasurable as planning a party. I am sure it will invigorate us all."

Lady Catherine sniffed. "Then by no means would I suspend your pleasure. Have your way of things, Miss Bennet. I have more profitable claims on my time."

Of course, she had not intended to find herself the hostess of the event! Elizabeth hardly knew how best to reply to this, but decided she must dismiss it. Once the date was set, her ladyship would no doubt take matters in hand.

The ladies exited the house to where the carriage awaited them. "I do hope my lady should not be too busy for such a party? Do you enjoy music?"

"Do I enjoy music?" Lady Catherine asked in tones of great amazement. "There are few people in England, I suppose, who have a more true enjoyment of music than myself, or a better natural taste. If I had ever learnt, I should have been a great proficient."

Elizabeth looked out the window a moment while she suppressed the grin threatening to take over her face. "Then we must have as much of it as we can, I daresay."

"Indeed we must, and if you would practice diligently over the next weeks, I am sure you need not be ashamed to exhibit yourself."

With forced gravity, Elizabeth thanked her for the compliment.

Bakewell was not far away from Pemberley and boasted a bustling market. Elizabeth was pleased by the fabrics and accoutrements she found among the shops. They were the equal of what might have been found in Meryton, though less costly, and she reminded herself of the advantages to be had from the various mills springing up about England. She purchased lengths of fabric for a warm gown for Charles as well as one for herself, and she even found fur-lined gloves that, although not the equal of the ones on Lady Catherine's hands, seemed quite luxurious to her.

"You spend freely for someone in your situation, Miss Bennet." Lady Catherine gave her a disapproving frown after her third purchase.

"Such is not my custom," Elizabeth said, again astonished by the lady's indifference to propriety. "I have not had new gowns for some time, and no doubt my father is concerned about the Derbyshire winters."

"Is he? I never thought a father gave much concern to a daughter's clothes."

"He does not usually," Elizabeth admitted. "Then again, he mentioned that he has dined with our neighbours the Lucases several times since I have been gone. Perhaps Lady Lucas or her daughter, Mrs Collins, encouraged his generosity."

"Mrs Collins?" Lady Catherine enquired.

"Yes," Elizabeth said with a smile. "I believe you must remember her from her time in Kent."

"Oh yes," she said thoughtfully. "The wife of Mr Collins. Very sensible sort of girl. So she returned to her father's house, did she?"

"Mr Collins did not leave her with any settlement she could live on, so she was fortunate her father could take her back."

"I am surprised she did not marry again," Lady Catherine said. "She was pretty enough and did very well with her household and her poultry. I should think some man thereabouts might find it an agreeable prospect."

"Hertfordshire is particularly unlucky in having far more ladies than eligible gentlemen," Elizabeth replied. "And for Charlotte particularly, for she is much the elder of many of them."

"Well if Mr Collins was as dull a lover as he was a preacher, no doubt she is happy to see an end to that business altogether. Do not seem so shocked, Miss Bennet; no doubt you have been around married ladies enough to know some of this sort of thing."

Elizabeth's shock, such as it was, had less to do with Lady Catherine's implication and more to do with the fact that they were on the street with several passers-by within earshot. She had seen more than one lady cast a sidelong glance in their direction.

"Let us see what is in that bakeshop," she said, more to remove them from the area than anything else. Lady Catherine was agreeable to the notion but muttered admonitions of overindulgence and gluttony as she followed Elizabeth into the store.

It was a lovely shop, more like a comfortable parlour than a place of business. Small tables were clustered close to a cheerful fire, and each boasted an arrangement of pinecones or feathers. If the wares were more scanty than was the custom, the baker had done well to disguise it with colourful cloths filling in the gaps and making a festive scene.

"Perhaps some tea?" Elizabeth said to Lady Catherine. The elder woman could not stand for it easily. She made some indignant sputters about condescension and the patronage of the nobility and such, but then her eyes alit on a tart. It was small and had only a pale hint of lemon in evidence, but her ladyship found it inducement enough to sit down and be served.

A sweet-looking young girl came out to wait upon them, her fair hand trembling as she poured for them. It seemed inevitable that she would spill some tea, and Elizabeth could only thank Providence that it was she that bore the splash instead of Lady Catherine.

The hapless girl nevertheless turned the colour of ash, then just as quickly, scarlet burned in her cheeks. "Oh! I am so sorry, Miss Bennet!"

"Never mind that," said Elizabeth with a smile as she used her napkin to wipe her sleeve. She directed her smile at Lady Catherine who looked like she was about to fly into a rage. "It is nothing at all. See, 'tis already gone."

The girl would not have it, fluttering and wiping even as a young man came out from the back, also apologising to Elizabeth. Tears seemed imminent until Elizabeth interrupted her. "I beg your pardon, but how do you know me? Have we met?"

"Yes, miss. I mean, no, miss. I mean, I done seen you in the church and—"

"Mrs Giles, was it?" Elizabeth smiled and laid her hand atop the girl's, gently prohibiting her from further wiping. As it was, she had nearly wiped through Elizabeth's sleeve.

The girl's blush deepened, and she offered a curtsey. The boy bowed and said, "Thank you, miss, for your kindness to my wife. No charge for your tea of course."

"Thank you," Lady Catherine pronounced with great hauteur while Elizabeth demurred.

"Your wife did me a great kindness the day I met her. I was about to walk off without my reticule, and she saved me from the bother."

Mrs Giles ducked her head shyly. "My pleasure to be of service, Miss Bennet. What can I bring for you?"

Lady Catherine asked for the tart, but for Elizabeth, the tea alone would do. As Mrs Giles moved away, however, she suffered a change of heart.

"Mrs Giles. Tell me—do you have havercakes?"

Mrs Giles stopped and looked at Elizabeth. "What would ye be wanting havercakes for?"

"Do you make them here?"

"No." She looked over her shoulder at her husband. "Not here, but I made them often enough when I was home."

"Forgive me, where did you tell me your home was?"

"Loxley." The girl looked down and lowered her voice. "I am from Loxley."

It seemed to bring her some discomfiture to admit it, and Elizabeth permitted her to leave then. She returned soon after with a plate of biscuits for Elizabeth and Lady Catherine's tart and left them. Lady Catherine took a large bite of the tart, pronounced it adequate, and then determined they should depart.

"A moment, if you will," Elizabeth said, taking a sip of her tea. The ladies were quiet as Elizabeth sipped tea and Lady Catherine did likewise. It seemed as though her ladyship was watching her, but Elizabeth would not pay her mind. No doubt her manners offended her ladyship in some way.

Elizabeth could not permit the food to be unpaid for. Though Mrs Giles and her husband seemed well kept enough, few merchants in any of these villages had much to spare, and thanks to her father's unexpected largesse, she did. She left a handful of coins on the table, which scandalised Lady Catherine, and left the shop with a smile at the young couple. Lady Catherine scowled her disapproval all the way from the shop door to the carriage.

It was not long until they were on the road returning to Pemberley, but it felt like an age with Lady Catherine's censorious frown
upon her. Elizabeth pretended not to notice, positioning herself such
that she appeared enthralled by the passing countryside.

"So you like havercakes, do you?" Lady Catherine enquired when
they were about half-way returned.

"I cannot say I have ever eaten one," Elizabeth admitted. "I saw
the receipt and thought they sounded tasty."

"They were a great favourite of my Anne."

Lady Catherine peered at Elizabeth in the darkened carriage as if
waiting to see how she behaved with this small morsel of information
about her daughter. Though Elizabeth was indeed wildly interested
in hearing more about the lady, she instinctively knew that she
should not seem eager. Allowing no more than a polite measure of
curiosity to colour her words, she said, "They must be delightful
then."

"My daughter was not well," said Lady Catherine sharply. "Very
sickly from birth. At times a havercake was all she could manage."

Ill health? Elizabeth had not imagined this. The lady she had
imagined from the journal was lively and amiable. Shy but not sickly.
Then again, perhaps that was why she had been at the seaside during
the writing of her journal.

"I am sorry to hear it."

"But she was a good girl. She never complained, no matter how ill
she was."

Elizabeth had no idea what to say in reply and settled for a
benign, "I wish I might have known her."

"Well, you never will." Lady Catherine shook her head, the folds
beneath her chin quivering. "Her life would have been extraordinary.
She could have been a noted hostess in London, all of the ton just
begging to be invited to her soirees. Every gown she purchased,
every play she attended, every party she graced with her presence
would have been a subject of interest."

"I am sure it—"

"Alas, it will never be as it ought to have been. Those dreams are
nothing now, a whisper of smoke long blown away. A mother's

wisdom is nothing to the base desires of man. A mother may hope and plan, but in the end…"

Elizabeth saw the slight tremor that afflicted Lady Catherine's broad jaw. Her ladyship's expression hardened, and Elizabeth thought she might have clenched her jaw to stop it.

"…n the end, the will of the child must prevail, even when they are wilfully proposing their ruination."

"I am very sorry for it," said Elizabeth with feeling.

"But do not think I blame dear Anne." Lady Catherine shook her head. "No. This tragedy is all to be laid at the door of her husband. The fault is his alone."

TWELVE

WILFULLY PROMOTING HER RUINATION? WAS NOT THE ALLIANCE OF MR Darcy and Miss de Bourgh the design of her relations? And why, if she found Mr Darcy so distasteful, was she in residence at his home?

Elizabeth paused a moment, her mind racing to find the words that would provoke Lady Catherine to further confidences. At last, in a voice scarcely loud enough to be heard and therefore soft enough to maintain Lady Catherine's reverie, she asked, "What did he do?"

"He is an abominably selfish man. Carried her off like a thief in the night, no regard to the wishes of those who loved her. And she, stupid girl that she was, went. Happily. Miss Bennet, should you ever marry, pray give heed to your elders who may see things more clearly than you do, who understand the vagaries of men and their lustful nature."

"They eloped?" Elizabeth asked, but it was too brazen. Lady Catherine was suddenly recalled to herself and realised she spoke to an inferior.

"You are curious today." Lady Catherine gave Elizabeth a look designed to impress upon her what a disagreeable thing curiosity was.

Elizabeth murmured a slight apology and fell into a silent reverie. This was not as Charlotte portrayed matters. Elizabeth pondered, trying to recall Charlotte's exact words, but in the end, could only recall that it was Charlotte's belief that the family wished for the match. Perhaps the family had, but Lady Catherine did not? Nevertheless, Mr Darcy had "carried her off," so to speak. Eloped with her? It did not seem like something he would do, but perhaps he had. From what the journal said, there had been straitened circumstances of a sort—perhaps finding himself in difficulties, he had decided to marry and fill his coffers thusly? From the exchanges she heard at Pemberley, she understood there was little love lost between Mr Darcy and Lady Catherine; perhaps this recent intelligence explained that.

"I did not like that tea place," announced Lady Catherine. "The cake was dry. and the tea was bitter. Those people had airs I could not like. Speaking to us in such an easy way! It was not so when I was a girl. You should not encourage such familiarity."

Roused from her thoughts, Elizabeth knew she should agree, but she did not and she could not. "I found Mr and Mrs Giles perfectly amiable."

Lady Catherine scowled. "I shall thank you kindly to preserve the distinction of rank when in my company, Miss Bennet. I am not used to having such persons as these Gileses speak as if they know me or are entitled to my notice. They would do much better for their little shop if they would pay due respect to the nobility."

With a flush, Elizabeth realised she was likely correct. Ladies like Lady Catherine, ladies who would be valued patrons, were not likely to frequent a place where the proprietors had airs or behaved above their station. The fault lay on Elizabeth's own head; she had forced Mrs Giles to speak to her, only being kind and never comprehending that Mrs Giles might prefer to have her head down and be busy with her work.

"You are correct, ma'am," she said. "But pray, do not think ill of Mrs Giles for it. I spoke to her first."

"See you do not do it again," Lady Catherine said with a sniff.

"Certainly not while you are with me. Should you choose to associate with shopkeepers, pray, make it your own affair."

Elizabeth retired to her apartment immediately on their return from Bakewell. So much of what had been said by Lady Catherine warranted consideration! She was reminded of a game that her father kept in his study, one that had been given to him by his friend Mr Ashby. It was a map on a thin layer of wood that had been cut into many irregular pieces. Mr Bennet had used it to teach his daughters about geography, and Elizabeth could still recall the frustration when she could not fit together pieces that she was certain must belong together.

Such was her stay at Pemberley. Mr Darcy, his wife, and his life before her arrival at Pemberley remained eminently baffling to her. She had developed an unusual attachment to Mrs Darcy, she realised. Something in the lady reminded her of Jane: a girl with a sweet disposition and a happy expectation of life; a girl who was cruelly betrayed by the very hopefulness that defined her.

Perhaps there was another journal? It seemed unlikely.

Mr Darcy, she believed, was away from the house. Charles was napping, and Lady Catherine was doing whatever she did in the time before dinner; therefore, Elizabeth believed she might be able to steal into the blue room in search of another journal.

There was not another journal, but there were papers, a sheaf of them folded crookedly and shoved—or so it appeared—unceremoniously in among the books. Elizabeth wondered at the placement of them, so untidily situated; would she not have noticed that before? But perhaps not. It was Charles, after all, who had removed the journal from the room. Perhaps he had been in here again?

There was no time to consider it. A sound from the hall made her heart drop into her boots, but it proved to be nothing. Rather than tempt fate, she would remove herself. Moments later, she was in her bedchamber, eagerly looking upon the first page of the bundle.

Dearest Beatrice,

It has been quite too long since I have written, and for that, I can only apologise. I should like to pretend I am so full of the delights of marriage to have had time to write, but I fear I cannot lie to you, dear Beatrice.

Let me assure you that I remain delighted with my dear husband. He is everything any lady could wish for: handsome and witty and learned. I never doubt his ability to care for our home or me, and should our union be blessed with children some day, I have not the least doubt that he will be a splendid father to them.

It is I, dear Beatrice, who continues to fail so grievously to please him. I fear I am quite silly at times and possess a knack for erring in the simplest of tasks. The servants mind me very ill and have not yet learnt how he likes things—indeed, I am still learning it myself! He has a very high standard, and I can only admire him all the more for it.

Elizabeth paused. Had a more faithful portrait of Mr Darcy ever been painted? Exacting, precise, demanding; yes, this was the Mr Darcy to whom she had found herself attached. For a moment, she recalled the manner in which he ate meat, any sort of meat: cutting it into small, precise squares that he would then nudge into straight lines before he ate them. And his writing! His writing was telling: tightly circumscribed, upright lines, consisting mostly of words of at least four syllables. Yes, indeed, exacting, precise, and demanding were apt descriptions of the Mr Darcy she had come to know.

She read on, her innate sympathy and affection for the unknown girl causing anxiety to twist in her gut as she did. The young Mrs Darcy made a number of missteps for which her husband responded with increasing ire.

Elizabeth observed on earlier pages that the girl seemed to be disappointed or lonely, and these pages confirmed it. The gaiety of their earlier days had given way to isolation and solitude. She pleaded with her husband to visit this friend or that or attend this concert or that assembly. Such applications only fed his vexation; he seemed to think it some affront to his own character, that his wife sought the society of others.

His answers to such aggravation increased in severity. He began by stern admonishment then proceeded to send her to her bedchamber for the remains of the day, sometimes even two. Elizabeth's brow wrinkled when she saw this; how very peculiar to treat your wife as one might an unruly child!

Such treatment became more common as the pages went on. He treated her thus for the most minor of infractions, from dirtying her attire to failing to pass a message to a footman, censuring her by sending her to bed without supper or making her remain in her bedchamber a day or two—once for three days together! Elizabeth could not imagine or accept that any grown woman should tolerate such indignity.

"Perhaps," said Elizabeth to the journal, "the life of a spinster does boast some advantages."

All of this paled in consideration of what was to come. It was a beautiful day, and Mrs Darcy's young friends were walking in the park. Some had beaux to attend them and others had companions, and it seemed the young lady could not resist the temptation to be among the party. Her husband was absent on business that would require his full day; she saw no harm in some amusement for herself.

It turned out there was a great deal of harm in it, for her husband was not best pleased to find her absent when he came home. When she returned, they had a fierce row over her disobedience and his feeling that she had humiliated him, and the result of it all was that he hit her.

Elizabeth drew in a sharp breath reading the words.

He slapped her across her face. She had not detailed what precisely it was that provoked him to such an action, but he appeared to repent of it immediately, gathering her into his arms, begging her forgiveness and promising it would never happen again.

Until it did, not long after.

Young Mrs Darcy did not always date her entries so Elizabeth could not know if a week or a month or an hour had passed before there was more. Again they were arguing and again he was roused to violence, this time grabbing her by her arms and slamming her into the wall behind her.

Elizabeth's hands began to shake, and her vision clouded with tears of sorrow and rage. Hateful, despicable man! He degraded and disparaged her, thoughtless and cruel to the very one he should have most protected.

She skimmed the subsequent pages, seeing more evidence of barbarism and cruelty. Tears leaked down her cheeks as she read of days spent locked in her bedchamber, humiliation in the marital bed, and increasing episodes of physical violence—increasing both in frequency and in severity.

Pretty words and expensive gifts always followed such episodes. They swayed her at first, induced her forgiveness but it was not many pages before she greeted them with dutiful and insincere pleasure. It made Elizabeth burn, this idea that the young lady should be forced to put on a pretty smile for such gifts! For such a man's ego!

A knock startled her, and she leapt to her feet, shoving the journal under her pillow and wiping the evidence of grief from her eyes. It was the maid, come to dress her for dinner, and she succumbed, unable to imagine how she might sit across the table from such a man and not lose her appetite.

"NAN!"

The young maid startled and dropped the chamber pot, the porcelain landing hard on her shod foot before bouncing up to clip her smartly on the ankle. She repressed a cry. At least the chamber pot was not full as it had been the last time she dropped it.

Mr Mackay was muttering something about how stupid and clumsy she was, but she pretended not to hear him as she bent and picked up the chamber pot. "He wants more water," said Mr Mackay. "If you think you can get it up there without spilling it all over the place."

She went stiff. "More...more water?"

"Are you deaf, girl? Or merely stupid? Wa-a-a-te-errrrrrr. You know, that wet sort of stuff we sit in to clean ourselves? Perhaps you have heard of it?"

Shame brought a hot flush to her cheeks, and she looked down so he would not see the tears stinging her eyes. "Yes, sir."

"Be quick about it, and mind, he wants the water hot not just warm. He likes a very hot bath."

It was not her duty to take hot bath water to the young earl, but that hardly signified. How could she refuse any request that came from him directly, especially when it was his own man who brought the charge? Even if she had wished to protest, even if it was not miles beyond her courage to oppose such indecency, Mr Mackay was gone too quickly to have heard it. She stood in silent humiliation until she realised Mrs Sloane was looking at her, a mixture of contempt and pity on her face.

Nan fixed her hopes on the pity. "Mrs Sloane, I…"

"No one wants to hear your complaining, girl, least of all me. Get going with it." The woman turned her back and went about her business.

Nan sighed. She had been warned by Sarah, the upstairs maid who had suffered the advances herself for many months: avoid dark corridors and empty rooms, and for pity's sake, subdue that bosom of yours. The latter was the most difficult for her; her figure had for many years now been well formed. But Sarah obligingly bound her in strips of Holland cloth, and Nan hoped it would be enough.

Only recently had his lordship deigned to leave Sarah to her duties. "How?" Nan had asked her. "How did you make him stop?"

Sarah had twisted her mouth in an expression of regret and admitted, "Why it was once you were hired. You are younger and prettier that I am, and you turned his eye."

Despite her dread, she made a quick business of obtaining the water, reasoning if she could not avoid it altogether, then she might well get it over with. Very soon, too soon, she was outside his bedchamber, knocking and entering on his call. "Your water, sir," she called out, edging close enough to his dressing room to be heard. "Where shall I leave it for you?"

"I cannot hear you," came the bored reply from the dressing closet. "Come in here."

With a fortifying breath, she pushed the door open. His lordship reclined in his bath, one naked leg tossed over the side of his tub and a condescending grin on his face. Idly, she wondered if things had been different, if he might have been a suitor for her. He had just turned thirty and possessed both a venerated name and a magnificently bloated fortune. That might have been sufficient to overlook the fact that he was a rake and a scoundrel.

She stood in the door, holding buckets that were growing heavier by the instant, and waited for him to tell her where to put the water. "There's a good girl," he drawled, his eyes going hungrily over her body as if she were the one unclothed. "Pray, do not be shy. I shall not bite."

"Where would you like the water, sir?"

"Bring it here."

No escaping it then. She knew how it would be from the moment he asked for her. She trained her gaze on the floor as she edged closer, lifting one bucket to pour it into the tub.

"I think, dear Nan, I shall require your assistance."

One bucket was in, and there was just one more.

"Aye, sir."

"I cannot reach my back."

Her eyes were still trained on the floor but she could hear the mocking smile in his tone. "I shall be glad to summon Mr Mackay for you."

"Oh no, not Mackay." With a great whoosh of water, his lordship stood and grabbed her wrist such that the bucket tipped, splashing hot water onto her legs and feet. She cried out and attempted to pull away from him, leading to more spillage, this time higher on her thighs. She dared not think of how she must look, wet from the waist down, her skirts clinging to her in an indecent way.

She dropped the bucket, hearing it clatter away from them. "Please, sir!"

He was too strong; she could not pull her hand away even when he said, "Do you not know how to wash a man?"

"Pl-please...I...I..."

"Just like this, my dear."

She kept her eyes averted as he took her hand and pressed it to his body, forcing it in a circle on his stomach. She prayed he would not go lower, knowing she could not prevent him if he did. "I... please, sir... I must... my duties..."

"Do not be shy," he drawled. "We can be great friends, you and I."

She felt him moving her hand lower, feeling rough hair that

acquainted her as to her location on his anatomy. Tears sprung into her eyes, and she squeezed them closed, squeaking, "Please, sir, I beg you would stop."

Shockingly, he did, releasing her wrist abruptly and causing her to stumble backwards, nearly tripping over her bucket which lay on the floor, thin rivulets of leftover water streaming from it. "See that you clean that," he said, sitting back down into his bath and leaning his head against the towel on the edge, his eyes closing almost immediately.

She bent, picking up the buckets with trembling hands. A used towel nearby sopped up most of the spilled water around the tub. She worked quickly, but his lordship did not again open his eyes or move towards her. He seemed to have forgotten she was there, saying nothing as she left the room.

Caught between anger and distress, she hurried to the small bedchamber she shared with Sarah. As one might expect at this time, Sarah was off attending to her own duties, so Nan knew she could count on time alone. She would not cry; indeed, she refused to cry.

Nan had one small trunk that held her most valued possessions; she was even able to lock it, making it valuable in itself. She pulled it from under the bed and withdrew the key from her shoe, where she always kept it. Opening the box, she beheld the contents.

It soothed her immediately to see them sparkling and winking at her. Her little treasures, not heirlooms of course, only trinkets and baubles of little distinction that no one would miss but their owner, and heaven only knew, she was long gone. To her, these little jewels were a promise, one she made to herself, a promise for a new life. Someday soon, she hoped, she would run, for this purgatory she had found herself in could scarcely be borne another day.

But they were not enough. I need more.

It had been unhappy news to her to learn from an overheard conversation that selling such items as these did not yield nearly as much as was expended on them. Particularly when—as was her case —the items would not be sold to a jeweller who might recognise them but to a pawnbroker.

It was dangerous, what she did to obtain these items. Dangerous with great risk of discovery. Yet what choice did she have? To endure days and weeks and years as a servant, subject to the whims of a noble reprobate?

America.

The word itself sounded hopeful. She imagined herself in one of the cities she had heard of, New York or Boston, or perhaps even in the southern colonies where there were large plantations, built to look just like the country houses of England. Carolina, she thought they were called. Surely school teachers were needed in all of these places? School teachers or governesses—she had always loved children and would love to teach them most of all.

With a wistful sigh, she went to close the box, opening it once more to look for something particular. A little brooch—she was certain she had it in there.

She rifled through the items, but the brooch was not there. What had happened to it? It was not so valuable, certainly less so than many of the other things, but she liked it and thought it might fetch a bit to help her.

But it was gone, so no use repining that. Perhaps she had dropped it. She shrugged, secured her valuables, and rose. Her skirts appeared dry, though they had a cool damp feel where they touched her legs. For a moment, she thought of changing but someone might notice and ask why, and that would not do at all. Keep your nose clean and your head down. That had been the advice she received, and she thought it sound. As little attention as could be given her, the better.

Miss Bennet was quiet at dinner, her lowered countenance pale as she pushed her dinner about her plate. Several times when he spoke to her, she startled, and her answers to his questions were given slowly and with great deliberation. It mattered not to their always-verbose dining companion, Lady Catherine; she went on about a subject always dear to her heart: the importance of preservation of rank.

Humour had never been his strength, but he considered what his cousin might do in such a circumstance. His cousin, once his dearest friend, was not considered handsome nor did he have the advantage of fortune. Nevertheless, he was always a favourite with ladies and gentlemen alike, always able to enter the conversation with levity and wit. Alas, Darcy did not share his gift and was yet casting about for something to say when Lady Catherine interrupted her monologue to say, "You are very dull this evening, Miss Bennet."

"Forgive me." Miss Bennet raised her head and smiled, in a wan, distracted way. "I do not mean to seem inattentive. I find your ideas quite…illuminating."

Darcy was moved to pity by the expression on her face, such was the contrast with her usual appearance. Likely his aunt's dreadful prattle sounded officious and arrogant to Miss Bennet. He decided he must speak. "I fear these ideas are those of an older generation, ma'am."

Lady Catherine was unprepared for such impertinence. After a moment to understand his meaning, she turned a narrow-eyed gaze on him. "You, more so than anyone, must agree that preservation of noble blood lines—"

"Is useless," Darcy concluded, enjoying the thrill that his uncharacteristic incivility gave him. "England is filled with idle, dissipated nobleman. I do not think preserving that sort of thing is much benefit to anyone."

"So you would have heiresses married to farmers would you?"

"Marriage is a complicated business. I daresay that considerations of fortune and family only make it worse."

Miss Bennet was staring at him now. Did he fool himself that there was admiration in her eyes? Or merely astonishment? Whatever it was exhilarated him.

"When two of noble birth are united—"

"You see the same thing as two people of common birth united. Children, a family, gains or losses of fortune, struggles, triumphs, old age, and eventual death. The only difference is how large the roof over their heads is and whether they eat venison or gruel."

Lady Catherine glared meanly for several moments before suddenly relaxing, straightening in her chair, and allowing a smirk to breach her countenance. "Darcy, you very nearly persuaded me you were in earnest."

"I am entirely in earnest."

"I know what you think." She shook a finger at him in a most vexatious way. "I know you do not agree with such impolitic unions as you describe."

At once his delight in his own daring vanished. How dare she say such things! And at his own dinner table with Miss Bennet looking at them both with undisguised curiosity.

He did not reply for some time, too long. Dinner was being cleared around them, and he waited until the servants had removed themselves before he stood, tossing his napkin on the table. "I daresay what I think might surprise you both."

His study could not contain him. Agitation, jubilation, and disgust all warred within him, and he knew not how to think or feel or simply be with so much rioting emotion within him. He paced, schooling himself into the sort of sobriety for which he was known, and once he had achieved it, he left again, moving towards the drawing room at quick paces, hardly daring to admit to the cause of his eagerness.

Lady Catherine sat alone in the drawing room, frowning at a letter. He gave her a cool nod of acknowledgement.

"Darcy, your dining table is not Cambridge," she said without looking up. "One cannot simply bandy about outrageous notions with a young lady of inferior birth—"

At that most inauspicious moment, the door opened and Miss Bennet returned. There was no doubt she heard Lady Catherine—her cheeks bore a scarlet flush and her chin was held up too high to doubt that—but she did not remark on it. "Charles is still having frightening dreams," she said. "It seems to help if I am the one to settle him into his bed."

"You will spoil him," Lady Catherine warned.

"Frightening dreams?" Darcy smiled at her as she sat down and picked up her needlework.

"He is certain a lady comes in at night who wishes to eat his head." She gave a half-shrug. "He seems to think that as long as he has his copy of Otranto with him, he will be safe. I suppose he thinks he might summon the giant to drop a helmet on her head."

Darcy chuckled and decided he would dare to sit next to her. She had chosen a settee but had settled herself in the middle of it. "May I join you?"

She gave him a brief surprised look but obligingly moved to the side. Indeed, she could not have chosen better; it was the settee farthest from her ladyship, who was already drooping over her letter. Darcy stared into the fire, willing Lady Catherine to drop off to sleep so that he might talk with Miss Bennet.

"I hope the conversation at dinner was no source of distress to you."

"It was not. But perhaps her ladyship had the right of it. Perhaps you were pretending to opinions not your own for the sake of conversation."

"Do you think it unlikely that I should hold the opinions as I stated?"

"I have rarely seen a man in your position who does not have a more practical view of marriage," she replied, watching him carefully. "Everyone wants to marry in some way that will raise them."

"Perhaps that is so, but I have never been one who simply yields to the common opinion."

"I see." She smirked in a teasing way. "You congratulate yourself on a better understanding than most men, is that it? Superiority of mind?"

Her words might have offended him but for the sweetness, the archness in her manner. It made it impossible for her to offend him. He leant closer to her.

"Oh, I have faults enough but not, I hope, in understanding. My temper, I dare not vouch for."

In a trice, all light-hearted gibes were dismissed. Miss Bennet stiffened, drawing away from him, and she dropped her eyes to the neglected sewing on her lap. Mere seconds later, she stood, the noise causing Lady Catherine to snort and sputter in her chair.

"I fear my headache has returned. If you will excuse me, I believe I shall retire early this evening." She strode from the room with energetic steps to Darcy's great dismay. She had already gained the hall when he decided to follow her.

"Miss Bennet," he called as soon as he was in the hall.

She froze, seeming as if she expected a dagger in her back. Slowly, she turned to face him, her countenance a stone mask of indifference, and her eyes carefully fixed to the side.

"It seems my remarks have distressed you."

She shrugged elaborately, then raised her eyes to his, a challenging expression on her countenance. "I have recently known of a situation where a young lady lived with her husband who had violent fits of temper. It is not my idea of gentlemanly behaviour."

"I could not agree more," he agreed quickly. "Pray, do not think I speak of my temper as an indirect boast. Indeed, I think a gentleman ought to know his weaknesses and seek to regulate them."

Her eyes slid away, but she did not run off. "Miss Bennet..." he began, having no idea what he meant to say. You make me want to be a better man? I wish I had not the mistakes of my past to taint me? I can do better this time, I promise?

"Sir?" she asked when the minutes had drawn long.

"You need fear for nothing," he said, even as he wondered where the words came from. "I want you to be...to be happy here."

Her eyes lit with curiosity, and he wondered whether she knew they did that. She was always pretty, but when her eyes were truly alive—with delight, with anger, with wonderment—then her beauty was quite extraordinary, well beyond anything he had ever seen before.

"Do you think me afraid, Mr Darcy?"

"No," he said immediately. "No, of course not, but...but if you are, do not trouble yourself. Ever."

For long, painful moments she considered him, her eyes seeming to carefully assess the truth in his looks. At last she nodded and offered the slightest bob of a curtsey before moving down the hall away from him.

THIRTEEN

My temper I dare not vouch for. You need fear for nothing.

The words haunted her through the night and into the next day as she took her breakfast from a tray in her apartment; then again as she dressed, as she played with Charles, and as she rode in the carriage to see Mrs Green.

My temper I dare not vouch for. I want you to be happy.

The hot brick at her feet and the rug across her lap were nothing to the shivery fear she felt at the thought of it. It was not unlawful for a woman to be chastened by her husband but to do so in such a degrading manner as she had read was despicable. But then he said he wanted her to be happy. He said she need fear for nothing. Why did he speak so?

The wind blew cold and raw against her back as she left the carriage and hurried into the house where her friend awaited her. "You could not have come at a better time," said Mrs Green as she squeezed Elizabeth's hands in greeting. "She is unwell this week, and I have gone mad from the tedium."

Elizabeth looked into Mrs Green's kind eyes and, in a rush, knew she must confide in her. Everything was a jumble in her mind; she needed to speak it out, to make it known to someone who could help her apprehend the meaning of it all.

"I have gone mad as well," she began slowly. "But not from tedium."

"Oh?" Mrs Green led her out of the vestibule, taking her into the drawing room where a merry fire blazed. She invited Elizabeth to sit, but Elizabeth took a moment by the fire, stretching out her hands to ward off the chill that had sunk into her bones.

Elizabeth wrapped her arms around herself and turned from the fire, warmer but not warm. She slowly sank into the chair next to her friend's and said, "I have done something quite dreadful, and I pray you will not despise me for it."

"I am sure I shall not." Mrs Green smiled and patted her hand. "Tell me."

Elizabeth began slowly. "It was clear to me from the first that Pemberley was a house of mourning. Furniture is covered, the servants are sober, and there is simply an air of...of sorrow."

She went on to describe what she knew: Mr Darcy had been engaged and thereafter married to Lady Catherine's daughter, his cousin; plainly Mrs Darcy was no longer in residence; and her bedchamber was kept to its former state.

"You are certain it was hers?"

Elizabeth nodded. "It could not be anyone else's. It is too new, too young, to have been the bedchamber of his mother. In any case, the journal I found has erased all doubt from my mind."

"How did you find it?"

With a grimace, Elizabeth explained it to her. Mrs Green covered a giggle with her hand as Elizabeth told her of Charles's capers. "It was, of course, less amusing when it happened," Elizabeth acknowledged. "To my shame, I did not immediately return the journal and... and still more to my discredit, I have...I read it as well as some papers that attended it."

Mrs Green raised her eyebrows.

"Quite dishonourable indeed, and I cannot excuse myself but to say that I am...well, Pemberley is a lonely place. Lady Catherine and Mr Darcy have made no pretence of their wish to see me gone, and I am afforded only basic civility, not kindness and certainly not friendship."

"But Lady Catherine did bring you here," Mrs Green observed. "She must spend some time with you."

"Her civilities are in accordance with her own will; she is not prone to confide in me." Elizabeth sighed again. "In any case, the journal delighted me. From the first, I felt a sort of kinship with the writer…with the former Mrs Darcy. She was not what I expected based on her mother and her husband. She seemed like someone I could be friends with."

"You grew attached to her by reading her thoughts."

A smile stole across Elizabeth's face. "I did." The smile faded as she recalled her more recent remembrances. "Which makes what I have read of late even more painful."

She told Mrs Green as much of it as she could recall, as much as her mind would permit her to remember. The distress she felt was yet fresh; her hands trembled at bit at the recollections.

Mrs Green was looking at her lap when Elizabeth finished. She cleared her throat delicately before speaking. "A man, as you know, has every right to correct his wife as he sees fit."

"Yes, I do know that, but does it not seem vastly wrong? Every feeling within me revolts at his treatment of her! The humiliations she has suffered!"

"And who is Beatrice?"

Elizabeth shrugged. "I have no idea. To my understanding there has never been any such person either present or past at Pemberley."

"Perhaps she was a school mate or a friend?" Mrs Green suggested. "A beloved servant even."

Elizabeth shrugged. "That is possible. I cannot think the name signified; it might be no more than a name she liked and gave to her journal."

"Perhaps she is not dead," Mrs Green offered. "Maybe she ran away from him to escape his harsh treatment of her."

Elizabeth considered the idea. "But he has her money and her mother. Where would she go?"

"True. A lady has not many choices if a return to her family is out of the question."

"Lady Catherine herself said that he...that her daughter's husband was the instrument of her demise."

Mrs Green nodded. "And then, of course, there is the matter of his sister."

"His sister?" Elizabeth looked at her friend curiously. "She died as a young girl."

"Or so it has been said." Mrs Green gave her a significant look. "I have asked a few questions of the servants. Miss Darcy, you see, was in love with a man who was a second son, and that man was in love with her. It was all settled that they would marry when she turned eighteen."

"And the family naturally despised him because he had no fortune?"

Mrs Green smiled faintly at Elizabeth's wry tone. "No fortune at all, but he intended to make a study of the law. With her fortune and his occupation, they would not have gone hungry, but neither would she have been the society mistress that her family thought she ought to be."

"But then she died?"

"She did; but not before she had made some provision for her lover."

"She left him money?"

"Her fortune was ample," said Mrs Green. "Thirty or forty thousand pounds at least, and she wished for her lover to live as he should. Alas, her brother denied it."

"That is dreadful! It was her money to do with as she chose!"

"A girl of that age naturally has no say over her fortune. No real control or power; but her brother should have done as she wished. Why the girl begged from her very death bed! Pleaded with her brother to care for the gentleman! But it was nothing to Mr Darcy. He denied it, and that was that."

"He is certainly heartless enough to do so; I have seen it myself. Rich men are accustomed to doing as they please, and Mr Darcy is no exception." Elizabeth shook her head. "The world should know what he really is. Handsome as a devil with the same disposition."

"You think he is handsome?" Mrs Green laughed but soon grew

serious again. "I daresay he is. Pray, Miss Bennet, use caution. Do not be seduced by him or his wealth."

"Seduced by him?" Elizabeth laughed far more heartily than she felt. "I assure you, there is absolutely no possibility of that. No, what I want from Mr Darcy is the very same thing I have always wanted: freedom for me and Charles."

"Well, then you must ask him for it, demand it even."

"How can I do that?

Mrs Green smiled again, but it was a mean smile, cold and cruel-looking. "Why, you should tell him you intend to expose him."

ELIZABETH RETURNED from Mrs Lawrence's home with scarcely enough time to dress for dinner. Mrs Green had been a most excellent host, gently steering the conversation to pleasanter subjects. In retrospect, Elizabeth decided she had not understood her correctly when she suggested exposing her suspicions of Mr Darcy. It had been said in jest, naturally.

But she had made two excellent suggestions, and Elizabeth intended to follow through with them forthwith. The first was to finish the journal, and the second was to go to the Darcy family in search of Mrs Darcy's grave. Surely it would not be so difficult to find, and then she would at least have confirmation that there was a Mrs Darcy and she had died. "But that will be for tomorrow," she said, glancing regretfully at the clock. "For now, we must dine."

Dinner passed as it usually did: Lady Catherine talking and Mr Darcy only occasionally contributing to the discussion. There were several times when he seemed to be attempting to draw her out, asking her odd questions about disconnected subjects. Lady Catherine would hastily interject and add her opinions to the matter, so he soon quit the endeavour.

At last, she was returned to her apartment and able to read the journal.

My dearest Beatrice,
My husband is an excessively confusing man, and I never know who he is in truth. Is he the tender lover I once knew? A man who is

merely driven to cruelty by my stupidity and insolence? Or is he inherently bad? I have long believed it to be the former. I hoped every day that even I, stupid, naïve, and childish though I am, would be able to fix this, to do better, to be the wife he deserves me to be.

Alas, I begin to fear it is the latter. I fear he is—and has always been—evil, and no matter what I do or how well I do it, there will always be within him that need to hurt and injure and anguish me.

He came to me in my dressing room this morning as I was at my toilette. He had arrived at the worst, most embarrassing possible moment—I begin to think he does that on purpose, hoping to shame me. In any case, there was little to be done for it save to carry on what I had begun and wish him and that terrible gaze of his away. When I was finished, he said, speaking ever so sweetly, that I was just the same as my chamber pot. Painted up on the outside to look like something of worth but containing nothing but filth and waste inside.

Such things lack power over me now. I do not cry as I once did. I only feel tired, so very tired. I wake in the morning wishing for nothing more than to stay abed all day long, but I cannot do that. He cannot take away my respectability; appearances must be kept although I cannot think we fool the servants as much as we think we do.

After shaming me so and saying such cruel things to me, he told me he wished to take me riding. It was a most unlooked-for treat, and thusly, I was suspicious of it. But I dressed and away we went. He was, as often he is, sorrowful and regretful. He wept as he told me of the cruelty he has encountered in his life, the people who were unaccountably against him, and the shortcomings he sees within himself. As we went on, the beautiful hills and forests bearing witness to us, he made me promise after promise to change, to become a gentleman worthy of me.

It stirs nothing in me now, these pretty speeches he makes. I know they mean nothing.

He is coming to me now. What will it be this night? Will he desire me? Will he be cruel to me? Will he kill me? I cannot say. Perhaps all three.

I can hear him now in his bedchamber preparing in that fastidious way of his for whatever the shadows of the night might bring. I shall bid you adieu, Beatrice, perhaps for now or perhaps for always. Only morning will know the truth of it.

Elizabeth drew a shaking breath, having reached the end of the pages. Her cheeks were damp; she had cried at some point in the narrative. Poor girl. Poor, poor girl! She folded the pages and hugged them to her chest. For a time she did no more but contemplate the life that was held in the writings, both the journal and these spare pages —the hopes that had flared and died, the romance that had turned too quickly to despair.

She needed to return the journal to its rightful place. Now that she knew how Mrs Darcy had been abused, it mortified her to have read her private thoughts. Had not the girl suffered enough? Had she not been punished for her crime of loving a man?

Yet Elizabeth meant no disrespect. Indeed, she had grown to admire the girl. She wished ardently that she could have known her, that she might have been her friend.

"I am her friend," she whispered. "And in my first act of friendship, I shall return her to her bedchamber."

She left her chamber quietly, stealing down the darkened hall with the journal held behind her lest a servant was about. It was too late at night for such consideration, but she did it nevertheless.

The blue bedchamber was full dark, and Elizabeth cursed herself for having failed to bring a lamp. Dare she light the one that rested on the mantel? The sharp bite of her shin against a chair persuaded her she must, if only to ensure the journal returned to the proper spot.

Once she had some dim light, it was an easy matter to find the appropriate place on the bookshelf. She bent, inserting the pages in a position behind the journal. She had just removed her hand from it when the door burst open, hitting the wall behind it with a force that made Elizabeth jump up and shriek. Her heart nearly stopped when she beheld Mr Darcy towering over her, the darkness of the room failing to conceal his rage.

"What are you doing?"

"I…forgive me I…" He loomed over her, and she tried to creep backwards. Failing that, she coiled inward, wishing herself small and hidden.

"This room is not to be entered, not by you, not by anyone!"

"Apologise…I…"

"What have you been doing? How long have you been in here?"

"N-nothing. Not long. I was not—"

"Who let you in here?"

"The door was…it was ajar and I—"

"This door is kept locked at all times!"

His rage was terrifying, and she found herself quite unable to breathe or think or say anything of sense. She had no right to be in the room, and she had intruded where she ought not to have gone.

"I do apologise," she said in a voice so small she scarcely recognised it herself.

He glared at her, and she watched his fevered respirations, in and out and in and out, as if he had run a mile to get here. She quaked observing him; when she realised it, she drew in a shaking breath and ran her hands over her skirts, her hair, in an attempt to compose herself. It did not work.

"Mr Darcy, I pray you will forgive my impertinence and my intrusion into this room. I—." She paused, unsure what reason or excuse could be given. There was none. "I am sorry. You may be assured it will not happen again."

He did not indicate that he heard her, not immediately and not for some minutes after. She began, at length, to edge quietly towards the door. When she reached it, she again apologised, in a whisper of a voice and repeated her avowal that she would never enter the room again.

He said nothing more to her, merely watched her make a quick exit.

SLEEP ELUDED her that night as she sat on her bed, awash with guilt and mortification—and yes, also fear. Of what might such a man be capable? She was in his house; she was under his power. She spent hours staring into the darkness, seeing nothing more than Mr Darcy towering over her in righteous fury.

When the sun finally rose to the greatest, greyest extent that it could these days, she decided to dress, not summoning a maid but helping herself as best she could, twisting her hair into a simple style. She had just finished when there was a knock on her door. Ruth, the upstairs maid, entered, her eyes firmly affixed to the floor.

"Mr Darcy wishes to see you in his study, miss."

Fear knifed through her gut. Summoned to Mr Darcy's study? Her mouth went dry at the idea of it, and she longed to cry out to Ruth—Why? What does he wish to do with me?—but she would not surrender her dignity. She had done wrong, and it seemed it was time to pay for it.

Her legs shook and trembled so that she thought she must look drunk, shambling down the hall as she did. I must apologise to him. Even as the thought ran through her mind, she thought how much in charity she was with the girl in the journal. It was frightening to be powerless, to have made a mistake, and to know one might pay dearly for it.

She paused outside of Mr Darcy's study, hoping to gather her wits and her equanimity. Eventually, as composed as she could be, she knocked and entered on his bidding.

"G-good morning, sir." She managed a shaky curtsey which he did not see because he was intent on whatever it was he was writing.

"Sit there, Miss Bennet." He indicated the seat opposite his desk with his pen, still not looking at her.

She sat then for interminable minutes as he scribbled and scratched carefully, seeming unaware of her. At last, when it seemed the letter was approaching an end, she ventured to say, "I know that it was dreadfully rude of me to—"

He raised his head to look at her, and she was struck by the look in his eyes. His rage had given way to pain and something else—

sorrow? Mortification? Whatever it was, it was not the ire she had expected, and it made her silent.

"What were you looking for?" His voice was deep but calm, his words measured.

"I...I..." She had considered this last night. A full confession was likely best, but surely if he knew she had learned his secrets, then he would send her off? Artifice and cunning were both deplorable to her, but she could not risk immediate departure, departure without Charles. The very notion of it made her blood run cold and easily tossed aside any principles.

Once she remembered that, the words fell with ease from her lips. "I recently finished A Gossip's Tale and wanted to find the second volume of the tale." He seemed to wish for further explanation, so she added, "It is called A Legendary Story."

"And did you find it?"

Elizabeth touched her tongue to her lips before answering. "I did not."

He said nothing else then, only staring at her for long, long minutes until at last, he turned away, looking out the window nearest him.

"Sir?" When it became clear he would not look at her again, she continued. "Sir, I am very grateful to you for your hospitality, and I sincerely regret that I have repaid that goodness by entering into places I was not meant to go. You may be assured I shall not do any such thing ever again."

He turned back to her and gave one small, tight nod, his eyes dark and inscrutable. Unable to account for it, she blushed and immediately dropped her eyes. They remained thusly for some time until at last, very gently, Mr Darcy dismissed her. "You will likely wish to have breakfast."

She nodded and rose, leaving with some haste.

He watched her leave with a heavy heart.

The night had not been kind to him. Rage had propelled him to his bedchamber where he tore his cravat from his neck with the savagery of a jungle beast, throwing it onto the chair before doing the same with his jacket.

The thin sliver of pale light he saw beneath the door had ignited futile hope within him, but it was not the death of that hope which angered him. No— his anger was born of the fear of Elizabeth being in there, knowing things, discovering what secrets lurked in Pemberley's shadows. Rage swelled within him, and before he knew what he was about, he had burst in on her, ringing a peal over her such as she had apparently never before seen.

What will she think of me if…no, when she learns the truth?

The sight of her quaking before him was nearly his undoing. In a trice, he was appalled by his own behaviour, and he knew not, even now, how to undo the damage he had wrought. She was wary now, pale and humble and silent; she had offered her apology with a meekness he could not abide. It did not suit her, such diffidence, and he had forced it on her with his black rage.

He ran a hand through his hair, raking his scalp. It was not his way to apologise, and indeed, she was undoubtedly wrong, being in a place she had no right to be. Nevertheless, he knew he must fix this and quickly.

Less than an hour later, Darcy mounted his horse, intended for Chesterfield where a particular bookseller kept his shop. Darcy had patronised the shop all his life, as had his father before him. The man, of an age with his father, had an engaging array of tomes, and what he did not have on hand, he was quick to procure. Darcy anticipated an agreeable hour or two spent searching for that which Pemberley lacked; but the real object of his journey would be to the benefit of Miss Bennet.

When he entered the store sometime later, he greeted the bookseller by name and asked immediately about her desire. "A Legendary Story by Mrs West. I must have a copy."

ELIZABETH HAD BEEN at the instrument for some time, amusing herself with a Scottish air she had recently learnt when the quiet click of the door being opened made her aware she was no longer alone. She was positive it was Mr Darcy and decided she would pay him no mind even if a minute tremor in her fingers threatened to betray her uneasiness. She persevered through the piece, appearing to be just as she was previously: indifferent, felicitous, and wholly engaged in her little song.

He stood slightly behind her, and she felt a queer flutter in her breast along with vexation that she should be made anxious by him. Her fingers struck a bit harder and her gaiety was forced, but she persisted.

He moved, standing in her peripheral vision now, only partly hidden by the curls that whispered and shook at her temples. As he stepped into full view, she saw, without looking, solemnity bordering on severity on his countenance. He stood quietly watchful, his arms folded behind his back.

At the first convenient moment, Elizabeth turned her face up to him, forcing a smile to her lips. "You mean to frighten me, Mr Darcy, by coming in all this state to hear me? I am sorry I must tell you that I shall not be alarmed. There is a stubbornness about me that never can bear to be frightened at the will of others. My courage always rises with every attempt to intimidate me."

"I shall not say you are mistaken," he replied, "because you could not really believe that I entertain any design of alarming you."

Careful to retain a teasing note in her voice, she said, "Oh! But I do indeed, Mr Darcy. I think you might enjoy a proper apprehensive reverence in my regard."

He walked closer to her, still with his arms behind his back, and came to loom above her. She considered rising, but given the difference in their heights, he would still tower over her, so why should it matter? She would remain comfortable on her bench.

A book was thrust towards her with a simple, "Here."

A Legendary Story. She looked at it with no little surprise. "Where did you find it?"

She was bemused to see colour rise into his cheeks. "I…it was…I had it on the bookshelf in my bedchamber."

Mirth tickled the corners of her mouth. "I should not have thought you a fan of Mrs West."

"I enjoy some novels."

"And did you like this novel?"

"Ah…" His colour deepened. "No."

"No? Why not? 'Tis a very popular book, you know."

He shifted on his feet. "Mass appeal is not equivalent to literary merit."

"Yet if the purpose of a book is to engage the collective psyche, what better measure is there than the ability to enchant the masses?"

"As a man of sense and education, I fear I require more in a book than mere titillation. For me, enjoyment must extend beyond readability into an acknowledgement of the author's skill in telling his or her tale."

"Both literary merit and the skill of the author are rendered meaningless if no one wants to read it." She smiled to remove the barb from her teasing. "And which was it that you found deficient in the case of this particular book?"

He shifted again. "Forgive me I…what I meant to say, when you asked if I enjoyed it, was that I did not read it. It was in my bedchamber, but I do not recall reading it. Perhaps I shall when you have finished it."

His eyes moved over her face, and she wondered what it was he looked for. "I shall begin reading it tonight."

"Excellent." He bowed then, not seeming to wish for any further discourse, and hastily excused himself from the room.

She looked over the book—which she had wished to read by the by—at last opening the cover. A small bit of paper fell out and drifted to the floor. She bent and retrieved it, opening it to find it was a bill of sale, dated for that very day.

FOURTEEN

As they prepared for bed that night, Nan whispered to Sarah, "The next night that is fair, I shall need to absent myself for a time."

"Absent yourself?" Sarah stood as she believed a lady would, with her nose in the air and her hand on her hip. "Ain't we taking some airs!"

Nan lowered her head and blushed. It was not the first time the other maids had accused her of acting above herself, and although they did so lightly, she despised these little missteps. In any case, she could not afford to vex Sarah, not when she needed her so.

"Next you'n be wanting us to call you 'ma'am' just like that old bird Jenkinson up there. Thinks she's so high, just because she's her ladyship's companion. I know the truth of that one. She ain't no lady, nor ever was!"

Nan had her own opinions of Mrs Jenkinson of course. Although she was employed as companion to her ladyship, she always seemed to be lurking about the servants' quarters, watching over things. It was not an opinion she could share with Sarah, however, and so she only remarked, "Mrs Jenkinson has always seemed quite genteel to me."

"Airs," Sarah replied in a matter-of-fact tone. "All airs. She was a nurse and then someways got herself raised up to be our lady's friend. Can't say's I know how she done it, don't even know where she come from—she only hired on about the same time you did."

That would be agreeable to be taken on as someone's companion and live as the better folk did. But she did know how Mrs Jenkinson had done it and did not choose to follow suit.

Sarah uttered a small curse, her attention having been drawn to her skirt. "Ah, but ain't that a miserable shame!"

"What is wrong?"

"Am I not already too tired to see straight and now this!" Sarah glared at the skirt, then showed Nan a small tear.

"Let me mend it for you."

"No, no, I can worry about that tomorrow."

"Nonsense. Unless you have spare skirts to wear, you will need this tomorrow. You know how Mrs Cole hates when we are not neat."

"That she does." Sarah sighed and looked longingly at the bed. "No, I canna ask you, not when you're just as dead on your feet as me."

"I'll be needing your help soon enough," said Nan. "Now give it here."

Sarah gratefully surrendered the article to Nan and then clambered into the bed, sinking in with a little sigh. Nan allowed herself a half-smile, watching her, glad she could do a favour to repay Sarah for some of the things Sarah had done to help her. Sarah had a man— a useful sort of man—who held a trusted position in the stable and did not mind keeping his mouth shut when one of the horses got some exercise at night. Sarah naturally made sure he got his thanks for his assistance even if the thought of that made Nan feel quite wrong.

From the bed, Sarah said, "You can count on me, Nan. I told you from the first, whether or not I know your tale for truth, I still want to help you. But if you get yourself up the pole, there'll be little I can do."

Up the pole. Nan, her head already bent over Sarah's skirt, smothered a smile. Did Sarah think she was sneaking out to meet someone?

Sleepily, Sarah warned, "Mrs Cole's a good 'un, but you go to her with your belly full, she will turn you out straightaways."

"I daresay she would." Nan finished with the stitching and rose, brushing the skirt and laying it on the chair where they put their uniforms. "You need not fear for me; it is nothing like you suppose. I cannot think of anything I would like less than a sweetheart."

DARCY ENTERED THE BLUE ROOM, pausing for a moment to look around. Nothing had changed in these many years. Indeed, he could almost see her: a child with her hair down her back and hollow-eyed grief in her eyes. He had wanted this room to be special to her and urged her to decorate it as she liked.

"Blue," she told him. "Everything blue."

"Blue? I thought ladies liked pink and lavender and yellow."

She shook her head, quite definite on the matter. "I want it to look like the sky, so I can pretend I am a bird."

That made him chuckle, though he regretted it when she gave him that look of bruised offence. "No, of course. Do not we all wish to be birds sometimes?"

"Perhaps not," she replied with as much hauteur as a ten year old could summon. "But I do. How delightful it must be to simply fly away whenever you wish! To look out upon a sunny day and soar high above everything! Every problem, every concern, just fading away while you soar and swoop—it seems quite enchanting if you must know."

"Hmm," he teased gently. "That does sound splendid. Perhaps I shall do the same to my bedchamber?"

That elicited a giggle, which was well worth anything to him in those days. Their father had just passed, leaving an uncertain girl, with him as her equally uncertain guardian. The house had been as much like the family tomb as anything in those days.

Recalling himself to the present, he mused, "Not much better now."

The notion of choices had been much on his mind of late. He had, he realised, spent much of the last years railing against the unfairness of the decisions that had been thrust upon him and the tragedies into which he had stumbled. Yes, most of it his own doing. Nevertheless, he had to admit to some smallness of character, some resentment, that could not comprehend why he was so different than any other man who earned a wife, children, a happy home with relative ease.

Alas, he had permitted himself to languish in that bitterness. People had tragedy in their lives, and they survived it, they recovered. They did not punish themselves endlessly. They did not entomb themselves in their remorse as he had.

Quite without realising it, Miss Bennet had rolled away the stone, so to speak. The question was: Could he emerge? Would he? Dare he believe in felicity? Dare he hope for the future?

These were questions whose answers as yet eluded him but one thing he knew: it was time to release the ghosts of the past. Taking firm hold of his sense of purpose, he went to the bookcase, removing the tomes he knew were her journals. The books, he decided, could remain, but a box that he believed contained letters was removed.

Then the miniature, a few ribbons, and some other odds and ends; anything that might be evidence of what once was. He carried them across the room they had called their private drawing room and into his own bedchamber.

A fire awaited him there, and he tossed the items into it, sitting down to watch it all burn. When it was done, he stood for a moment at loose ends, uncertain what to do with himself. A ride, he decided. I shall ride.

THE NIGHT HAD BEEN EXCEEDINGLY long for Elizabeth as she tossed and turned, trying to make sense of what she knew and to learn a course of action from it. The sad story of Mr Darcy's wife spun in her head; felicity, hope, and trust fading into humiliation and despair and, eventually, death. Mr Darcy's bilious countenance, black with fury, insisted on being at the forefront of such thoughts.

As dawn approached, she rose and, taking up a piece of paper, began to write rapidly all that she knew. She did not make any attempt to make sense of anything or draw any conclusions; it was mere thoughts expelled onto paper.

When she was finished, she sat quietly, her face turned towards the window, seeing nothing. "Nothing is certain," she was forced to admit to the hazy dawn. "There is truth here, but I could not accuse him with any degree of real certainty."

For after all, no matter how much she believed he might have hurt his wife, the fact remained that it was likely she died in childbed or by illness. He had been a brute of a husband, but it was not easy to connect that with the death of his wife.

She sighed heavily. She needed to leave, and for that, she required Mr Darcy to release Charles. For a moment, she wondered whether she might make Mr Darcy angry enough to hit her, then the resulting gift might be to go home.

But what about Charles? Would Mr Darcy hurt Charles? Somehow Elizabeth did not think so. After all, he had wanted the boy here, but now that Charles was in residence, he barely saw him. Of course, Charles had had some little fancy about Mr Darcy playing with him in the courtyard, but then, such was the age. Dreams were often confused with reality in four-year-olds. Charles also thought there were dragons in the river and tribes of errant knights roaming the woods, eager to be vanquished by a four-year-old.

With a sigh, she put down the pen. It was too early to eat breakfast, and she decided she would walk. She had not as yet, she recalled, visited the grave of this lady to whom she had formed such an attachment. She would do so this morning—if she could find it.

Minutes later, she was striding towards the church at a brisk pace. The woods were silent and still, not yet fully returned to life after the long night. As she walked, snow began to drift down, stinging her cheeks and wetting the path in front of her, and delight in it caused her pace to quicken into a sort of run. She arrived at the church yard breathless, her bonnet dangling down her back in a manner most often seen on young girls.

As might have been anticipated from such a family, the Darcys were buried in a tomb, the names engraved neatly on an outer stone with birth and death years recorded. The Darcys were indeed an ancient family, and had recorded their dead faithfully it seemed.

There was one Anne Darcy which gave her a start until she realised from the dates it must be the present Mr Darcy's mother. She searched and searched, seeking a younger female Darcy but there was not one. When she had concluded that it was not there, she stood a moment, pondering the meaning of it. "Perhaps she did not die?" Elizabeth said aloud. "Perhaps she was buried in Kent? Or London maybe?"

"If she takes her own life she ain't to be buried Christian-like."

The male voice, spoken so close behind her, made her shriek. She spun on her heel. It was the simple man she had seen before. He rocked back and forth on his heels, looking sideways at nothing.

"I beg your pardon," she said.

He seemed not to know how to reply and so repeated himself. "If she takes her own life, she ain't to be buried Christian-like."

Elizabeth smiled kindly at him, even as her eyes roamed his face. He had a curious wound, she observed, a sort of sunken-in part of his face. The skin around it looked tight and shiny, contributing to the overall misshapen effect. He had once been a handsome man, but now that male beauty was distorted.

But whatever had disfigured him was old and healed; other wounds, fresher and angry-looking, informed her that he had been recently beaten—severely beaten. One eye was blackened, and there was an extended cut along the side of his face that was turned partly away from her. It looked like one of his teeth was missing, though how long it had been gone was hard to tell without peering at him too closely.

"Sir, you are hurt," she said gently.

"He was very angry," he said, increasing the speed of his rocking. "Very, very angry."

"Who was angry?" she asked; then nausea made her turn cold as she realised she knew who had likely beat the poor idiot. The day she had walked with Mr Darcy and they came upon this poor soul in the woods. Mr Darcy left her then, she remembered, and returned breathless and agitated. "Sir, was it Mr Darcy?"

This made the man look at her with alarm, his rocking growing even more agitated. "Oh no," he moaned. "Oh nooooo."

She stepped forward, holding out a hand. "He is not here, I promise. Let me help you."

The man jerked away from her. "Not Mr Darcy! No!"

"No, I do not mean—"

"Noooottt Darcy. Noooo!" He wailed.

"Forgive me." She tried to smile, tried so soothe him, but she had distressed him too much. He began to scuttle away from her, his speed surprising.

Elizabeth stopped her efforts to console him and merely watched him go. Tears stung her eyes and fury burned hot within her breast to watch the pitiable creature—and know whose hand had rendered him thus.

Her anger propelled her down the path that would return her to Pemberley. She stalked along as a woman possessed, her mind swirling with scenes in which she told the dastardly Mr Darcy precisely what she thought of him and his abuse of those too helpless to defend themselves. Was this how he had done it to his young wife? Perhaps the idiot was correct; perhaps he had merely beset her with helpless anger until, unable to do anything else, the madness drove her to take her own life.

She was nearly returned to Pemberley when she saw him, mounted on his horse and trotting slowly through the woods. He looked as though he had not a care in the world, and she despised him for that. Too late she considered whether she ought to conceal herself; he had already nodded his head to acknowledge her and was preparing to dismount.

"You are out early today, Miss Bennet," he said with disgusting easiness while tying his horse to a nearby tree.

"I was just in the churchyard," she replied, wishing she might induce some discomfort. "Paying my respects to those of the parish whom I shall never know."

"You should not walk alone. Samuel or one of the other footmen should always be glad to accompany you."

"Yes," she said, drawing the word long. "I thought as much when I saw the poor idiot that we have seen before. He has been beaten severely, I am afraid. Tell me, do you think it was highwaymen who did it?"

She asked it with deceptive sweetness, but Mr Darcy understood her immediately. His expression hardened from geniality to anger in a trice, but he controlled himself, speaking in tight accents. "You take an eager interest in that gentleman's concerns."

"Who could help but feel utmost compassion for the poor creature!" Elizabeth cried. "But then again, sympathy has not been your strength."

Her accusation seemed to catch him off-guard. His eyes narrowed as he studied her. "I have not the pleasure of understanding you."

Had wisdom prevailed, she should have retreated, perhaps even apologised. But she was too angry, and angry people are not often wise.

"Yet I daresay I understand you completely," she retorted. "You scruple at nothing to have things in accordance with your will. Never mind the defenceless small creatures who are trampled in your path, whether they be idiots or children or women."

"Is this again about little Charles? He was left to my care! You could not have expected me to delight in such a state as I found him."

"Such a state as you found him?" Elizabeth echoed with a weak, incredulous laugh. "He was well fed, well rested, well clothed, and most of all, well loved."

"He was living on the charity of relations whose situation in life was decidedly beneath his own."

"In case you have forgotten, Bingley gained his fortune from trade," Elizabeth retorted sharply.

"I do not forget that, nor have I forgot that it was the dearest wish of Bingley's father to see his son and grandsons become gentlemen. Bingley never did purchase an estate, but under my direction, his son will fulfil his grandfather's wish."

"I am not sure I like your idea of running an estate. Pemberley is a frightful place, everything covered up in secrets and sorrow. Your servants do not even have an hour they may call their own—though they at least do not appear to suffer abuse."

"Pemberley may have suffered some neglect in recent years," he said with an air of affected tranquillity. "I shall own it even if I am not proud of myself for so doing. But no one suffers abuse."

"You can say so now," she said, even as reason and logic

attempted to prevent her. But the truth was coming up too fast to be restrained. "But there was one who did, indeed, suffer a great deal by your hand."

His eyes narrowed, he took a step nearer her. "Of what do you accuse me?"

"I think you are a murderer," she said, the words shocking even her. She stopped, knowing she should not have said it. But it could not be taken back.

The response of Mr Darcy shocked her even more than her candour had. The cloud of fury that seemed to attend him disappeared; instead, there was sorrow. He seemed somehow smaller as he turned his face away from her. "A murderer," he mused. "Yet what is a murderer? Someone who kills? Or someone who merely wished to kill?"

He turned then to look at her full on. "If I am not a murderer," he said quietly, "it was only because I lacked the courage to carry through with it."

Elizabeth gasped at the plainness of his speech.

"There are some people, Miss Bennet, who do not deserve the breath of life."

"After such an admission as this," she said, tightly controlling her words and her voice, "you can hardly expect me to remain here with Charles. We are not safe."

"If that is how you feel," he replied, "then, by all means, go."

"Consider it done." Shaking with emotion, she turned and began to move away from him at a quick pace, only permitting herself a look behind her when she felt a sufficient distance had been gained. She saw that he was back beside his horse. He had placed one hand on his horse's neck and leant his head against his forearm.

The oddity of such a posture after the heated nature of their argument made her curious, and she continued to look over her shoulder as she walked.

It proved a grave mistake. Moments later, in an unfortunate convergence of the tattered lace of her petticoat, loose rock, some mouldering leaves, and the edge of an old well, she slipped.

There was no time to scream, no time to think; she could only react, and she somehow found herself clutching bits of rotted vegetation while her body dangled over the gaping maw of the well, prone against the earthen walls. She gasped, fearful and shaking, as reason struggled to assert itself through the din of terror.

Her first instinct was, of course, to pull herself up. Doing so resulted in the release of a clump of rotted vines, which fell useless into the chasm beneath and caused another wave of intense fear to go through her. A million frightened thoughts raced through her mind that she would die here alone, painfully, and Charles would be left to the mercies of Mr Darcy.

An attempt to climb up the slick, slimy walls was likewise unsuccessful, the toes of her boots scrabbling for purchase in vain. She found, briefly, a foothold in a rock that jutted from the wall, but merely touching it with her foot caused it to crumble away. She whimpered, already feeling the ache that would fatigue her arms, her fingers slipping on the vines that barely held her from death.

Was Mr Darcy still there? Could he see her, and would he know where she had gone? Did he exult even now in knowing that her foolish pride would cause her death? It was a superb irony that the man she had just accused of being a heartless killer was now the only person who could save her from death.

Would he come if she called? Surely he could ride away, having ostensibly never seen her. Hours from now when they realised she was missing, he could say he had no idea what had become of her. Her body would never be found, and she would be yet another of Pemberley's mysteries.

Another shower of dirt and small stones rained down upon her, and she cried out.

"Miss Bennet?" His voice sounded curious at first and then alarmed. "Miss Bennet? Where are you?"

There was nothing for it. She would have to trust him, it was her only hope. "Please help me!" Her voice broke on the last word as tears began to roll down her face.

She heard footsteps, then running, towards her. "Where are you?"

"I fell down the well," she said, half sobbing and half laughing. "Careful, you would not wish to slip."

"Good God." He had come to the edge of the well. She heard him take a deep breath, and when he spoke, his voice was calm. "I am going to pull you up. Do not be afraid, just hold on. Can you do that? Hold on until I say you may let go. Do not let go until I say so."

"Ye-yes."

She felt him grasp her wrists and pull, but it was no good. His feet, too close to the edge, sent another flurry of loose stones and earth over her, and she screamed, feeling some give in the vines she grasped.

"Let me lie down." He stretched flat on his stomach and again grasped her wrists to pull her up. But such a position could only decrease his strength, and he tugged her to no avail.

Her arms were afire with the effort of remaining where she was, and she knew not how much longer she could hold on. "It is no use," she said with a little sob.

"I shall be damned if I see you fall," he swore. "See here. I am going to get some rope to help secure us while I pull you up. Just stay put until I get it. Can you do that? Just hold on."

She smiled, weak and half-hearted. "I shall certainly do my best."

He left her then, very briefly; from the sound of his steps, it seemed that he took off running. But although he was fast, it seemed an eternity, as sweat beaded on her back and her arms screamed, afire with the desire to simply let go.

When he returned, he spent a moment doing something nearby— tying the rope to a tree she imagined. Then he was leaning over her again, reaching to tie the rope around her waist. "You are tied to the tree and to me. We just need to pull you out. Are you ready?" She felt him grasp her wrists even tighter. "I shall begin counting now. One, two, three!"

Elizabeth began to scrabble up the wall even as Mr Darcy pulled with all his might to yank her back from the edge. A large shelf of dirt, moss, and stone gave way as it happened, and for a moment, Elizabeth thought all was lost, that she was falling and falling…

But then she felt the warmth and solidity of Mr Darcy's body somehow beneath hers. He felt so sturdy, so definite, and she sobbed with the relief of him. His arms tightened around her, holding her, as he asked, "Are you hurt?"

She could not speak. A fever broke over her, causing her to shiver and shake and feel faint all at once. She worried she would vomit or scream, or cry; she worried the well would somehow suck her back in, pulling her down to her demise.

"No," she managed to choke out. "Just scared."

His arms, already tight around her, tightened more, and he murmured something that sounded like "I almost lost you." It seemed natural to feel his lips on top of her head, planting gentle kisses, and even more natural to raise her face and kiss his chin. His kiss moved from her hair down her forehead and then onto her cheeks; from there, it was but a short distance to her lips, and he kissed her with all the ardency of a true lover.

For a moment, she enjoyed the solace and comfort his attentions gave her, but then horrified comprehension pierced her.

"Mr Darcy!" She jerked away from him, jumping up and straightening her skirts. The rope was still around her waist, and she began to tug at it with little effect.

He rose with astonishing equanimity, though he was not able to meet her eye. Reaching towards her, he loosed the knots that tied her to him, allowing the rope to fall away from her. There was too much to be thought and said to do anything, so Elizabeth allowed instinct to prevail. Taking hold of her skirts, she took off at a run, exceedingly grateful when Mr Darcy did not attempt to pursue her.

FIFTEEN

HE WATCHED HER RUN FROM HIM AS IF DEMONS PURSUED HER. WHEN SHE had gone from his sight, he sank down again, next to the same hole that had nearly claimed her life.

What had he been thinking to give way in such a manner? To kiss her as he had wished to kiss her for…well for many weeks now.

Strangely, it was his father's voice he heard in his head, admonishing him for giving way to his impulses, his lusts, his dark desires. There was so much to be felt that it was impossible to name them all. Disbelief, fear, dismay, terror, but most of all, disappointment. Crashing, crushing disappointment. How he wished to purge himself of the past, but his past would not be purged. It would always rise to join him, to stain and plague him. His history was what he was; there was nothing else to him.

He had come to see her as his salvation. She was the light to his dark, the one who could break the curse that bound him. Yet what had he done to deserve it? Taken her from her home, using a child held captive between them. Was it any wonder she thought him capable of murder? Indeed, although he had the will to murder, he had not the capability; if he had, George Wickham would be mouldering in a pauper's grave even now.

He ran a hand over his mouth. How had she seen that blackness within him? Did it exude from his pores? Was it a cloud about him? He had nothing to offer her but a fine house richly furnished but missing its soul. As the grey mist settled in around him and the dampness of the earth crept into his joints, he felt himself becoming one with the mournful wood. This was where he belonged, this place of darkness and death.

WISHING TO SEE NO ONE, Elizabeth entered the house by a side door, passing by the stairs leading to Mrs Reynolds's room and the servants' hall. Her strides long, she nearly missed what lay on the floor in front of her, and she made an inelegant little hop, having almost tripped over a round, grey tabby who was sunning herself. With her nerves nearly torn to shreds, it was just what she needed.

She sank to the floor next to the cat, offering her apologies for almost stepping on her. At first, the cat did not care much for Elizabeth, giving her no more attention than the swish of her tail and a sidelong look, but then Elizabeth began to pet her, running her hand down the cat's back in long, languid strokes. Her efforts were soon rewarded by a low, throaty purr.

At that moment, Lady Catherine swept around the corner, pausing for a moment in appalled astonishment. "Why is that here?"

"The cat?" Elizabeth rose. "She was sitting here enjoying the bit of sun, such as it is. Is she someone's pet?"

"She used to be." Lady Catherine began then to clap and make shooing motions at the cat. "Beatrice! Shoo! Out of here, now! Shoo!"

The cat gave her a disdainful glare and rose slowly. Elizabeth bit her lip at the seeming defiance and watched Beatrice stroll away languorously, her head in the air. At least now I know who Beatrice is.

Lady Catherine shook her head. "I have always said cats belong in the barns, but you young ladies have your own notions. It is hardly fashionable to have them lurking about the house as if they belong. People will think we have mice."

She paused then, looking more closely at Elizabeth. "What have you been doing? You have no bonnet, and I have seen farmers with less dirt on them."

I accused your nephew of murdering your daughter and then almost died. "I fell," Elizabeth answered simply.

"Well, are you hurt?"

Elizabeth realised that her arms and legs ached miserably. "Nothing that a hot soak will not remedy."

Lady Catherine sniffed disapprovingly. "There can be no good to come by all this scampering about the countryside as you do. You should learn to ride better, Miss Bennet. I shall send Dawson to attend you with a bath; get along to your apartment."

Elizabeth gave a disinterested nod and then moved down the hall as quickly as her aching limbs would permit, her mind going along at a much quicker pace, though with less progress. Mr Darcy's words to her, the poor beaten lunatic, her near-death experience and unexpected rescue by the man she accused of being a killer—it all did nothing but jumble and tumble about in her mind. Only one fact was clear: he said she could take Charles and go. That was the only truth that mattered after all, and she decided she would visit the nursery while her bath was prepared to tell Charles the good news that they would go home to Hertfordshire soon.

Expecting to find little Charles at play, she was surprised to hear Mrs Browning had put him to bed. "I did not like the sound of his chest."

"Oh no!" Elizabeth rushed to Charles's bedside. She laid her hand against his forehead. "Is it a fever?"

"Not yet," said the nurse. "But I do not think we can be too cautious."

Charles opened his eyes. "Charles," Elizabeth asked anxiously, "where does it hurt, angel?"

He gave a barking cough in reply, and Elizabeth looked worriedly at Mrs Browning, who said reassuringly, "It might be nothing, but I thought it best to be prudent."

Elizabeth could not speak for a moment. Yes, indeed, prudence was critical. Ever since Jane…but no, she could not think of that. Illnesses meant more to her now, now that she knew a trifling cold one day could mean a trip to the graveyard the next. With a deep breath, she asked, "Is there fever powder? I shall need—"

"Mr Darcy has been in to see him this morning," Mrs Browning told her. "He was eager to summon the doctor in Lambton, but I said I thought we might try some pectoral drops first."

"Mr Darcy was in this morning? Why?"

Mrs Browning looked surprised. "Why they often have some little game together in the morning, kicking a ball or throwing something about in the courtyard beneath us. He has promised to teach him to ride when the weather is favourable. But our poor little boy did not even plead for it today; he wanted only for a book to be read to him."

This news was too extraordinary to be considered in light of her more immediate concerns. "Have you any experience with these drops? My mother always believed in the home remedies."

"These will do him, I assure you. Some rest is all he needs."

Assurances meant very little to Elizabeth, and she decided she would read to him, never mind the bath or her muddy dress. She sat with him the rest of the night, feeding him broth when he would take it and encouraging him into repose as soon as she could. As the nursery windows faded from dim into dark, she returned to her bedchamber for a mere moment to select a warm blanket that she wrapped around herself in Mrs Browning's chair.

It was only then that she permitted herself to consider the implication of Charles's illness for her plans to leave Pemberley. No matter how much she might like to run off immediately, she would wait patiently. No doubt Charles would be soon improved, and they would make their plans then. She could only pray that Mr Darcy would give her a wide berth in the meanwhile.

But Mr Darcy had been to visit Charles? Had played with him? It defied explanation or understanding.

The night was very long. Charles slept fitfully, tossing and turning, and Elizabeth remained by his side, anxiously pressing her lips against his head to judge for fever. His cough was alternately barking and hacking, and she tormented herself that it was worsening.

He fell into a deeper sleep towards morning, his cheeks flushed and his cough at last subsided. Elizabeth rose, her muscles and joints protesting the lack of sleep that night had afforded her and went in search of some coffee or tea.

At some time during the night, a note had been placed in her bedchamber beside what appeared to be a small purse.

Miss Elizabeth Bennet,
I pray that you will forgive me any insults I have offered from the first moment of our acquaintance, as well as my ungentlemanly presumptions this afternoon. I can offer no reason or justification for anything I have done to offend you but will only subject myself to your superior benevolence and mercy.

I intend to leave Pemberley at first light for London where I shall remain for several weeks. I have no wish to detain you from your departure and therefore will only say that I shall regret your absence. I shall not shirk my duty as guardian to Charles Bingley but, as you have suggested in the past, will henceforth discharge that duty by acting in accordance with Mr Bennet.

The purse is for the comfort of your travels. I pray that your journey will be easy and your health will be good. My best wishes for your future endeavours.

I shall only add, God bless you
F. Darcy

Laying aside the note, she opened the purse. The amount contained therein caused her to raise her brows. What was this? Some attempt to buy her silence? But even as she tried to be offended by it, she found she could not. What did any of it mean? Confusion was her only clear reply.

It would be useful to have money for her journey, though she certainly did not require as much as this. She would write to her father immediately, requesting his assistance in returning to Hertfordshire, but experience had taught her that Mr Bennet would likely to be tardy in his reply. While a gentleman might have the luxury of hieing off at a moment's notice, things were more complicated for a lady who intended on making a journey with a small child.

THE NEXT DAYS were such that Elizabeth would not wish on her worst enemy. Charles came down with a fever and a cough that racked his body. Elizabeth would not leave his side, finding herself sleeping on her feet while she attended him. Mrs Browning pleaded with her to rest ere she find herself with two sickbeds to mind, but Elizabeth could not obey.

At last—and Elizabeth knew not the precise number of days required—the fever broke. It was a joyful day when Charles grew querulous from the tedium of lying abed. She and Mrs Browning celebrated by conscripting one of the other maids into watching over him while they both took a much-earned nap.

"And...Mr Darcy remains gone?" Elizabeth asked carefully when she joined Lady Catherine for dinner. "London, or so I was told."

Peevishly, Lady Catherine said, "He did not see fit to say anything of the matter to me. Here one day and gone the next with no thought for those of us who might rather he stay."

Despite having napped, Elizabeth was yet worn from caring for little Charles and, as such, did not exert herself too far to be an agreeable dining companion. Lady Catherine appeared to be of a like mind, and thus did the ladies take their meal in relative quiet, both retiring early.

The next day was similarly sedate. Lady Catherine declined to emerge from her apartment for reasons known only to herself. Elizabeth occupied herself with quiet pursuits, first writing another letter to her father to request his assistance in her return home with Charles and then playing some games with the boy. She was relieved to see him with healthy colour in his cheeks as well as some measure of his usual irrepressible vigour, and she could only hope her father would reply soon that their travel might commence.

She had just settled in the drawing room with a book when Mrs Reynolds entered, her hands twisting before her and a worried expression on her face. "Forgive me, Miss Bennet, but...but there are some guests arriving shortly. They are just now coming up the lane."

"Guests?" Elizabeth exclaimed. "What guests?"

The lady shifted on her feet. "Mr Darcy's relations. It is the carriage of his Matlock cousins, but I know not who is in the carriage exactly."

"I see," said Elizabeth. "But why do you tell me? Surely Lady Catherine is able to receive them?"

Mrs Reynolds shook her head. "Lady Catherine will not receive them, not in these or any other circumstances."

"Really?" Surprise made Elizabeth more frank than was her custom. "But why? Are they not her relations too?"

The housekeeper lowered her face before her reply tumbled from her in a rush of words. "She will not receive them. The last time they were here, I was made to know in very plain terms that she would never extend her hospitality to them and I should not trouble her with such requests ever again at the risk of losing my position."

Nonplussed, Elizabeth responded, "But…I cannot think it would be anything short of abominably rude to receive them myself. Likely, they would not wish for it in any case."

Mrs Reynolds raised her head and gave Elizabeth a silent, pleading look. "I think they will not mind it, and really, it is not too much an impertinence, I am sure."

Elizabeth rose. "I shall go speak to Lady Catherine—"

"Please, Miss Bennet!" Mrs Reynolds sounded almost desperate but recovered herself immediately, drawing upright and lowering her voice to a more respectful tone. "Miss, if you would please oblige me —I do not wish to turn them away but neither do I wish to risk the displeasure of her ladyship."

"But Mr Darcy—"

"Is not here." Mrs Reynolds smiled worriedly before saying again, "Please?"

Elizabeth pursed her lips a moment before asking, "Are they very disagreeable people?"

"Not at all. Indeed I…I quite like them, and I daresay you will, too."

"I do not understand—" But no more could be told to her. Voices were heard from the vestibule, hearty male voices. Evidently, these relations of Mr Darcy did not intend to wait until they were bid to enter. "It seems there is nothing to be done save for me to take it on myself to receive them."

With a relieved nod, the housekeeper curtseyed. "If you need me, do ring."

Elizabeth had scarcely a moment to recover from her astonishment. Seconds later, the door was again thrust open by a handsome gentleman, elaborately dressed and coiffed. Elizabeth took a step forward, ready to speak to him when he turned away, crying out over his shoulder, "I found her."

Elizabeth sank into a curtsey. "How do you—"

"Oh, none of that bother." The man approached with several large paces, stopping just short of her, and examined her for a few moments before returning to the door.

"Lilly, refresh yourself later, you simply must come see this girl Darcy has been hiding. Very pretty, very pretty indeed." The voice of a lady was heard at some distance, though Elizabeth could not make out what she said. "Lady Saye, you will come to me at once! I command you! As your husband!"

With a broad grin, he looked at Elizabeth. "She is an impertinent puss. I guarantee that speech of mine did nothing but vex her. How do you do? I am Saye, Darcy's older and more handsome cousin. He is wealthier than I am, and taller too, but I am vastly more fun at parties."

"I am Miss Eliz—"

"Yes, yes, I know who you are. We all know and have been quite mad to meet you. I simply could not comprehend you would be so pretty, although I admit I have heard the women from Hertfordshire are uniformly quite pretty, beyond all others. Something about the rivers, or so I have been told."

"Here I am." A lovely young woman, heavy with child, puffed into the room. "But not on your order, Saye, and I thank you not to speak so to me. You roused my curiosity, and I found that more urgent than my annoyance with you. Did he introduce himself properly, Miss Bennet? Or has he been spouting nonsense at you?"

"Nonsense of course," Saye answered. "I thought it best to begin how I mean to go on."

The door again pushed open, leaving Elizabeth to wonder what

had become of the manservant and all the footmen. Another gentleman, not handsome as Lord Saye but with an amiable countenance,
entered.

"Richard, at last. We are all getting to know Miss Bennet, and you
are off wandering the place. Where is your wife?"

"She is gone upstairs." The man called Richard gave his brother a
look and then turned to Elizabeth. "You are at a disadvantage, Miss
Bennet, for we all know you, but you know none of us at all."

"It is a disadvantage indeed," she said. He came closer to her,
bowing low over her hand. "General Richard Fitzwilliam, younger
brother of this reprobate. I trust our little visit will not inconvenience
you. We want for very little, I assure you. A crust of bread and a bed
in the scullery will do."

"Ah...well, you see Mr Darcy—"

"Is gone;, yes, we know," said Lady Saye with a beaming smile.
"If he were here, we would never have made it past the gate."

"Oh," said Elizabeth. No more reply was necessary or possible,
for at that moment, the door was again opened—this time by a
footman—and another lady entered. She was a slim, pale creature
with the sort of pinched face that rarely foretold an amiable character.
She also boasted a rounded stomach, though smaller than that of
Lady Saye; however, it was her eyes that stirred sympathy within
Elizabeth. They were red-rimmed and swollen.

"How does your mother get along?" Saye enquired.

Mother? Elizabeth tried not to gasp.

"That horrid beast up there," said the lady, "does not deserve
such a title. I... I..." With this she began to cry, ugly, gasping sobs
coming from her. General Fitzwilliam was quick to go to her and
press her into his chest, murmuring soothing sounds while her
narrow shoulders shook.

"Pray, forgive my wife for this alarming scene, Miss Bennet," said
he with a charming smile, once the worst of her sobs had subsided.
"She and her mother—"

"Do not call her that!" came the strangled protest from his chest.

"...that is, she and Lady Catherine have been estranged for some
time—"

"Since I dared have an opinion on whom I might like to take as my husband!"

"...and it grieves her—"

"I am not grieved! She may happily rot in hell for what I care!"

"Do not speak so," he said softly. "For she is, above all, your family."

"She is a gin-soaked harpy!" The lady pushed back from him, sent him a fierce glare, and turned on her heel. "I shall be in my bedchamber resting."

She turned to Elizabeth, asking, "Where will you have us, Miss Bennet? Darcy has so much of the house all covered up! It looks like the house is closed —has he not opened it properly since he returned from abroad?"

"I..." Elizabeth floundered a moment before saying, "Pray, permit me a moment to speak to Mrs Reynolds."

Her mind was reeling. She felt like an actor thrust into the middle of some play, one who had missed the first act but was expected to play her role nevertheless. The other three looked at her with varying degrees of expectation on their countenances, and strangely, the advisement of her mother came into her mind.

No matter what else might have been said of her, Mrs Bennet had always managed to set a good table and see that her guests, both expected and not, were cared for. Thusly did Elizabeth rise to this occasion—wherein guests not her own and the role of host were thrust upon her—due to the training bestowed on her by her mother.

"Permit me to ring for something to eat, and perhaps then we may sit and get ourselves better acquainted while the maids prepare rooms for you."

A QUICK CONFERENCE with Mrs Reynolds allowed Elizabeth to determine where to put these people who had unaccountably decided they were her guests. The servants were ready with the food and soon all, save for Mrs Fitzwilliam, were settled comfortably in the drawing room with plates and cups and full stomachs. They began to know each other in the way most strangers do; Elizabeth acquainted them with her home and her family, including those who had been lost to her. Charles was brought from his nursery and gave them no little delight with a short song he sang, even if he did dissolve into coughs and giggles throughout.

Elizabeth learnt the brothers were from Matlock, less than 10 miles away from Pemberley, and that Lord Saye was a viscount who would succeed to the earldom of Matlock when his father died. Lord and Lady Saye had two daughters in addition to the child who would arrive in the next months. Lady Saye was the former Miss Lillian Goddard of Oxfordshire and had married the viscount six years ago.

But it was the history of General and Mrs Fitzwilliam that served to astonish and dismay her most. Mr Fitzwilliam was a former major general in the army who had resigned his commission on the conclusion of the war. "My wife insisted," said he with a grin. "Said it was time to come home and conquer domestic life."

"And your wife is the daughter of Lady Catherine?" Elizabeth asked carefully.

"She is."

"Has Lady Catherine many daughters?"

General Fitzwilliam shook his head. "Anne is her only child."

He continued offering his thoughts on family estrangement and the bonds of maternal affection, but Elizabeth could not hear him, her thoughts filled with one sentence alone: Anne is her only child.

In abstracted tones, she said softly, "I cannot imagine what could have caused such a breach."

The door opened, and Mrs Fitzwilliam entered the room, still red-eyed but with an air of determination about her. "It started because I refused to marry Darcy," she announced. "Never mind that we never had the least inclination towards each other. She wished it so and told us fantastic tales about how she promised his mother. As if I should live my life by the dictates of a dead woman!"

General Fitzwilliam turned to Elizabeth. "Lady Catherine and Darcy's mother, Lady Anne, were very close you see. Lady Anne was the elder by less than a year, and from what I have heard, they were never apart. Whatever they did was done together, and when their marriages separated them, both were heartbroken."

"So they thought they would simply arrange their children's lives to suit themselves," said Mrs Fitzwilliam bitterly. Her husband offered her a brief smile and a pat on her hand.

"Pray forgive my astonishment," said Elizabeth. "I understood that…"

"That I was dead?" Mrs Fitzwilliam asked bluntly. "I am not dead. She tells people I am dead. It seems she would prefer to think me dead than disobedient."

Elizabeth laughed with some discomfort. "I confess…I did think you had…well, I believed you had married Darcy and then…then died."

"Darcy has never been married," Saye informed her.

"And I am very much alive," said Mrs Fitzwilliam. "We did it over the anvil in Scotland, just to send her into vapours."

"Not true," General Fitzwilliam interjected. "You wanted to see Scotland, and the family was…well, it was a difficult time for a proper wedding."

"Then I am wrong on all accounts." Elizabeth smiled, her mind still whirling with surprise and dismay. Surprise that so much of what she thought she knew was incorrect. Dismay that her prejudice had coloured the scant information she had.

She managed to put aside her considerations for later, her efforts best directed at serving as host to the entertaining group from Matlock. Indeed, they wanted for very little; they were a jolly group who treated Pemberley as their own home.

"So where has Darcy gone?" asked General Fitzwilliam at length. "How long will he be away?"

Elizabeth coloured but replied calmly. "London, and he said he would be there for several weeks."

He looked at her for a moment too long. Then with a little nod, he turned away, seeming to accept the fact that more remained unsaid than said. Fortunately, his brother began a discourse on prawns and how he felt about them, so their discomfort was subsumed into matters of no consequence to anyone save Lord Saye. However, when at last Elizabeth was able to raise her eyes, she found the general's gaze upon her—frank, interested, and too knowing by half.

SIXTEEN

Darcy has never been married.

Had his lordship struck Elizabeth, he could have scarcely shocked her more.

Mrs Fitzwilliam née de Bourgh had married…but not Mr Darcy. No, the cousin she married was General Fitzwilliam, and the house she lived in was Rosings—never Pemberley. She had made a few, rare visits to Pemberley—due to indifferent health—but she had never lived there. And a blue room? No, Mrs Fitzwilliam's favourite colour was grey. A most interesting colour, grey, she told Elizabeth earlier that evening. It could be grey-blue, grey-purple, grey-green, even grey-yellow. Blue was quite a dull colour by comparison to the wonders of grey.

And Darcy had never been married. Never been married and therefore had never abused a young wife. Had never been cruel and unfeeling and humiliating. Had certainly never been the instrument of anyone's demise. Who then wrote the journal? Did it even matter?

Charlotte had not been incorrect, Elizabeth learnt. When Charlotte was in residence at Hunsford, separated from Rosings Park by only a small lane, it was indeed the design of Lady Catherine to see her daughter wed to Mr Darcy. But somehow that plan had gone off and now General Fitzwilliam had her. Was this why Darcy despised his relations? Had the General stolen his bride?

Sleep shunned her that night, and as she lay, tossing, turning, and being in all ways miserable, she suddenly recalled a most important truth: I may leave. I am free to go. All of this—the strange diaries, the enigmatic Mr Darcy, and his life and goings-on (along with the humiliation of her presumptions and accusations)—could all be left behind her.

Such thoughts arrived with both relief and dismay. A most peculiar reluctance plagued her, and she could make no sense of it. This was what she had wished for ever since that wretched day when Mr Darcy appeared in Hertfordshire! She wanted to be free to return to her life at Longbourn with Charles! Why, then, did the idea of it make her feel so very hollow?

No. This is what I have longed for; this is what has been my object throughout this ordeal. To take Charles and leave is my dearest wish. Charles was in good health now, and there was nothing to stop her. She resolved that in the morning, she would speak to Mrs Reynolds directly about her plans to depart in a few days hence.

Unbidden, her mind recollected the feel of Mr Darcy's lips on hers. "I almost lost you." That scene had taken on the hue of fantasy in her mind. She almost wondered whether any of it had happened— the woods, falling, Mr Darcy kissing her—but Mr Darcy's absence persuaded her that it was indeed quite real.

Having had little sleep, Elizabeth rose early. As she dressed, she decided two days would surely be sufficient to make her preparations. Her possessions were few and her acquaintances even fewer; indeed, it was only Mrs Green who might rightly expect a call of farewell.

She found Mrs Reynolds standing with a homely-looking man in clerical garb who bowed to her but did not speak. "Miss Bennet, what may I do for you?"

"I can come back."

"No, no," said the man. "I require only a few minutes of this good lady's time."

So Elizabeth waited idly while they finished their business, making a disinterested perambulation of the housekeeper's office. It was a neatly kept space, bright and comfortable. A window looked over the pond, and the desk situated beneath it suggested that its user might indulge in that view as often as she could. A second chair in a cheerful yellow fabric was by the fire.

When the man left, Mrs Reynolds turned her attention to Elizabeth. "Mr Darcy has given the parish three hundred tons of coal," she began but stopped when Elizabeth exclaimed over it.

"You think it imprudent?"

"Oh! No, of course not. I was only surprised, that is all."

Mrs Reynolds puffed up. "Mr Darcy is the soul of generosity. You will not see people starving nor freezing hereabouts, and the credit will be laid to him." She made a wry little smile. "Not that he would accept it of course. That is why he has me meeting with the curate in the early morning hours."

"He donates food as well as coal?"

"All those in the parish, according to their need, have been receiving an allotment of bread and cheese every week. Now that winter is nearly upon us, he has agreed to fund the provision of soup as well," Mrs Reynolds informed her proudly.

"But he wishes it to remain secret?"

"Aye," said Mrs Reynolds. "And I beg you not to speak of it. It is no false modesty, I assure you. He truly believes that charity should be done in silence."

"I daresay he is correct," Elizabeth answered.

This answer seemed to give Mrs Reynolds undue satisfaction. She smiled and folded her hands in front of her, seeming to receive some second-hand adulation brought by Elizabeth's slight approval of Mr Darcy. Then she asked, "What brings you down here this morning? Did you wish to make a change to the meals?"

"Oh…ah, no." It was difficult to continue in the face of Mrs Reynold's apparent good cheer, but Elizabeth nevertheless did. "I only wished to tell you that with Charles no longer ill, we shall make our arrangements to travel."

"Travel?" Mrs Reynolds stared at her blankly. "Where are you going?"

"Home." Elizabeth felt awkward under the weight of Mrs Reynolds' stare. "Mr Darcy gave us leave to return to Hertfordshire."

The effect on Mrs Reynolds was shocking. The good lady appeared to sink into herself, all signs of prior glad-heartedness gone. Elizabeth felt compelled to turn her gaze to the view over the desk. When it had gone on far too long, she looked back at Mrs Reynolds, shocked to find her dabbing at her eyes with her handkerchief.

When the housekeeper saw Elizabeth had noticed her, she began a profusion of apologies, her skin turning the colour of a ripe strawberry. Elizabeth had no notion how to answer save for meaningless demurrals and assurances.

"Pemberley is a delight," she said as a means to forestall awkward conversations. "But naturally, I wish to be at my home with my father. I am grateful for the hospitality shown me but—"

"Miss Bennet." Mrs Reynolds spoke in low but fervent tones. "Miss Bennet, I implore you to remain."

Elizabeth stopped speaking. Her eyes searched the older lady's countenance, seeing the strain, the fatigue, which she presumed had always been there. To add to that now was some desperation, but though pity stirred within her, she was resolute. "I am afraid I cannot stay."

Mrs Reynolds composed herself, reaching up to tuck a strand of hair beneath her cap and smoothing her apron over her legs. "Excuse me. Of course you wish to leave, and who am I to stop you? What good could it do?"

"Really I must go. Mr Darcy would not be best pleased to return from wherever he is and find me here."

"Did he say that?" The housekeeper had a sudden sharp-eyed look.

"No, not...well, I asked him whether I could leave, and he said yes."

"He does not want you gone," said Mrs Reynolds. "I am certain he would prefer you to stay here."

"I do not think you know his mind in this," Elizabeth insisted gently. Her words gave Mrs Reynolds pause, and she looked at Elizabeth carefully, unlike the manner of a servant. She glanced over her shoulder, seeing that the hall was yet empty and carefully closed the door. She invited Elizabeth to sit in the yellow chair, and Elizabeth accepted, sitting there silently while Mrs Reynolds dragged the desk chair closer.

She began in low tones. "Miss Bennet, Pemberley needs you, and Mr Darcy sees that."

"I...I cannot think what you mean."

"It has not always been this way. It was, before, quite different, very different, and I began to believe it would...that maybe things could be as they once were.

"Pemberley had once the soul of felicity. When I came here, Mr Darcy was a wee tyke of four—just like our little Charles, he was—and a sweeter, more generous boy could scarcely be known. Oh, one could not have asked for a finer situation than to be in service at Pemberley! Lady Anne was beautiful, and old Mr Darcy was gallant, and they had their dear little son. They were good to us, them that work here. We never wanted for anything.

"They were happy times," she continued, her tone growing wistful and her eyes distant, no doubt looking upon years gone by. "I can still see that little boy scampering about the lawns, running off from his nurse to look at the horses. Oh, but he loved those horses! He was just happy all the day long, always in some little game with his friend George.

"Things began to change when Lady Anne died. 'Tis no great surprise, of course, a death of a charming woman in the prime of her life—old Mr Darcy simply could not recover from it. I want to believe his death was an accident. Perhaps it was. Guns sometimes do go off while their owners are cleaning them."

Elizabeth swallowed a gasp.

"Of course, Mr Darcy did not generally clean his guns himself. Plenty of people around here to do that sort of thing. In the end, I believe solitude got to him. No matter how reserved a person is, to be always alone, to feel that there is no one to belong to..." She shook her head, clucking softly.

Elizabeth thought how she felt ever since Jane died—like there was no one who truly knew her. She was not alone, not by any stretch of the imagination, but neither did she have anyone.

"That was ten years ago now, but you can see why I worry.

Twenty-eight years, Miss Bennet; I have known him almost his entire life, and he is the closest to a son I shall ever know."

Elizabeth did quick calculation in her head. "Mr Darcy was only twenty-two when he became master of this estate."

"Aye, and a creditable job he did from the first. He is a fair and generous master. No matter what difficulties he faced, he has always been good to those of us below stairs."

"Has he faced many difficulties?"

Mrs Reynolds glanced over her shoulder again at the closed door. "Yes," she said, her voice near a whisper. "And I shall not say I know them, because in truth, I do not, not completely. But five years ago, Miss Darcy died, and this place has been in mourning ever since."

"Five years? I understood that Mr Darcy was an adolescent when she died."

"No," said Mrs Reynolds. "Miss Darcy was fifteen, but Mr Darcy was her senior by twelve years. He was her guardian, you see, from when his father died."

Elizabeth swallowed. "How did she die? Was she taken ill?"

Mrs Reynolds shook her head. "No one knows. She had gone to Ramsgate with her school friends, you see, and a companion—a good lady called Mrs Younge who came highly recommended. Mr Darcy had decided to seek a wife that year, and once he had finished in London, he was off to some country house parties. There was one in particular that took him out to Lancashire. He was not sure he should go—he was of a mind to join Miss Darcy at Ramsgate—but his cousins persuaded him to go to Lancashire."

She laughed ruefully. "I thought we would hear an announcement when he returned, but there was nothing. He and his sister usually came to Pemberley at the end of the summer, but that year, we had word that he was fixed in London. Then, some months later—I daresay it was February— Lady Catherine arrived with her daughter and General Fitzwilliam and informed us that Miss Darcy had passed away, and Mr Darcy was travelling."

"Where did he go?"

"I cannot say," said Mrs Reynolds. "We were told to close up the house save for apartments for Lady Catherine and Miss de Bourgh, as well as for General Fitzwilliam. It was not too many days later when the two young people made off for Scotland."

It took Elizabeth a moment to comprehend her. "Oh! Miss de Bourgh, who is now Mrs Fitzwilliam."

Mrs Reynolds nodded. "Lady Catherine swore from there that she would never speak to her daughter again, and I guess she intends to keep her word although it has been some years and caused her a good bit of sorrow."

So much had been said, and Elizabeth knew it would be some time before she was able to make sense of any of it—if indeed there was any sense to be made.

Mrs Reynolds continued to speak. "I cannot say whether Lady Catherine knew where Mr Darcy was, or why he stayed away so long—"

"How long was it?"

"I do not truly know, for I have no idea when he left. He only just returned this past May, so it must have been four years or so."

"And did he tell you where he was all that time?"

"He will not speak of it, not to anyone," said Mrs Reynolds. "But you can imagine my alarm now, seeing that something has gone off and he has again left us."

There was silence as Elizabeth felt the crushing weight of her thoughtless words in the woods. Mrs Reynolds could not know what guilt, what repentant spirit, she placed on Elizabeth's shoulders with her recollections and the glimmer of tears in her kindly eyes.

Elizabeth could not meet those eyes when Mrs Reynolds spoke again. "Miss Darcy was a true proficient with her music. She loved to play and sing all the day long, and Mr Darcy liked nothing more than to draw up a chair and listen to her. He would sit in there with her for hours. Then one day after her death, I saw the chairs were all pushed around quite oddly, in a way that made it very awkward for any exhibition of music. I believed he intended that there should be no more music at Pemberley."

She smiled then, a rare brightness that pushed her face into long-forgotten contours. "I thought it quite a good sign when he asked you to fix it, Miss Bennet. When he seemed to like to hear you play—a very good sign indeed."

In a feeble small voice, Elizabeth said, "Mrs Reynolds, I am not...I cannot..."

When she stopped speaking, Mrs Reynolds prompted gently, "Cannot what, dear?"

What she wished to say was that she could not fix Pemberley. She could not be the one who rescued Mr Darcy from his solitude. She had been an abominable guest, trespassing and spying and drawing the most terrible conclusions possible. Shame washed over her; she was deeply embarrassed by her silly imaginings. Had she grown so accustomed to reading novels that she thought herself alive in one?

"I cannot stay," she said at last, in a small voice.

Mrs Reynolds made no attempt to disguise her sorrow and her disappointment, but her words were kind enough. She reached over and patted Elizabeth's hand. "I understand."

Elizabeth wished to explain so much more. Her fight with Darcy, her mistakes, her stupidity— for Mr Darcy to return and find her still at Pemberley would be indeed the most humiliating presumption that ever was. Even now, she wondered what he might think if he knew she was playing host to his relations.

Guilt made Elizabeth walk slowly as she left Mrs Reynolds and moved towards the breakfast room. Though part of her mind struggled to understand what had happened, another part of her was awash with dismay. How different Mr Darcy was from the villain she had painted him! How different she was from the clever miss who thought she could thwart him!

Even Pemberley was misunderstood. She had seen the closed-up rooms as frightening and cold, but it must have been by design. After all, her own room was not cold, was it? Nor was the nursery or the drawing rooms or any of the other places they inhabited. Mr Darcy, it seemed, was practicing economy, for how could one wantonly and unadvisedly heat rooms that were not in use when all around them people were freezing?

How happy Pemberley could be when the curse of the chill was gone and the grass turned green, the trees had leaves, and laughter echoed in the halls. It was an elegant home, once it was done being austere.

"Miss Bennet." She nearly shrieked; General Fitzwilliam had approached on silent feet and startled her from her musings.

"Oh! General Fitzwilliam, forgive me, I—"

"No, I must beg you to forgive me," he said with an easy grin. "I still have a soldier's habit of rising at first light. It will be hours before anyone else shows their face."

Elizabeth shifted awkwardly on her feet. She did not want company. She wanted to be alone to cry or pack or search her mind for some understanding of the truth here at Pemberley. She did not wish to make polite chatter with General Fitzwilliam. "Excuse me, sir, I—"

"I am glad to catch you alone," he said, holding his arm out to her. "I was hoping the two of us might be better acquainted, and it seems now is as good a time as any."

How STRANGE TO BE IN London! Darcy walked streets he had known his entire life, yet they were as foreign to him as the deserts of Arabia. There were even more ruffians on the streets these days, and they had encroached even into Mayfair, but he was able to fend them off easily enough with a handful of coins.

He could only bear the contemplation of his house a short while. Lord Cathcart had it now and had made purchase offers to him on a number of occasions, but Darcy would not part with it. No, it seemed some wretched hope must remain within him for he persisted in maintaining the trappings of a "Gentleman of Consequence."

Odd that he could imagine her in it. He could clearly imagine walking down this very street with her—they had been shopping and a footman had gone ahead with their packages. He had indulged her, and she had teased him with that pursed lip and sparkling-eyed smile of hers and then he would lean over and kiss—

But no. His kiss was an unpardonable liberty. A fever of relief had seized him that she was alive and well. To hold her tightly, to kiss her, was instinctive.

Their last meeting he could never forget, for what had she said to him that was not true? Selfish? Yes. Negligent? Yes. Arrogant and presumptuous? Yes and yes. A murderer?

"No," he muttered. "But only because blasted George Wickham was such a swimmer."

His temper, that foul monster, had risen up within him when she referred to George as a "poor creature," but truly, what could he expect? That she was tender-hearted and kind, he knew, and she had not the benefit of knowing the monster George Wickham once was. She was ignorant to the fact that George Wickham had gambolled about the countryside seducing innocents and mounting debts he could not pay. Miss Bennet had no idea that George Wickham had persuaded Georgiana to marry him, made her believe he loved her, and beat her black and blue when she could not release her fortune into his grasping hands.

He never thought of it if he could help it. Even now when he saw George, he forced his mind away from that terrible, cursed night when he chased him, keening like a madman, out into the night, his arm bloody yet steady enough to fire one deadly shot. He remembered how George had turned back to look at him at the last moment and the way his eyes looked when he stumbled over the edge of the icy bank.

Darcy took a deep breath. This would not do. He must instead consider what, if anything, he should do concerning Miss Bennet. As he had written her his short little note, the temptation to lay it bare before her was nearly irresistible. But he had stopped himself, reasoning it did not signify. Miss Bennet and Charles would go their own way, and he would remain the haunted, solitary figure at Pemberley.

Something in him wanted her to know, wanted her to understand that he was not what she had perceived him to be, at least not at heart. Perhaps he had behaved as a villain but he knew he could be a hero if given the chance.

He moved slowly, passing all the scenes he had once known so well; for one mad moment, he considered entering his club. But no— it was not the time for reunions and fond where-have-you-beens.

He resumed his walk a fraction of a minute too late. His uncle exited the club, his man by his side to help him walk. Though his lordship's body was impaired, his mind was sharp as ever, and he quickly spied his nephew on the street. "Darcy? Darcy, is that you? Come here, boy, I am delighted to see you."

There was nothing for it but to obey. Darcy would not disrespect his uncle right in the midst of London with all of society around them yearning for some morsel of scandal. He forced a genial smile to his face and walked over to his lordship, bowing and permitting the older man to lean heavily on his arm as they walked to his carriage.

When they were settled into their seats, Lord Matlock leant back and favoured Darcy with a broad smile. "What brings you to London?"

"Business," said Darcy. "I am surprised to find you here."

"Had to do my shopping," Lord Matlock declared. "Father Christmas has quite a surprise for your aunt this year."

"Ah yes, Christmas." It had been so long since Darcy paid any heed to the festivities of Christmas and the New Year he had nearly forgotten they existed.

"Christmas," his lordship repeated. "An excellent time of year to let bygones be bygones and heal old wounds."

Darcy chuckled and sighed simultaneously.

"It is not right, you know. Your cousins, your aunt, they love you, care about you. All we wish for is to move past the tragedy that has afflicted us all. You most of all, of course, but we have all suffered."

It was an old admonishment, one he had heard tens or dozens or hundreds of times since returning to England. Somehow, though, he heard it differently this time. He was tired of being bitter and angry, he realised. Worn with the effort of being entombed in sorrow. He could not be happy, but perhaps he could be less miserable.

"Darcy, who knows if this latest illness will take me, but should I not have the comfort of knowing that my family, at least, is well and whole?"

"What does your doctor say?" Darcy asked with some alarm.

Lord Matlock waved his hand impatiently. "Never mind my doctor. What I need to regain my strength is to be relieved of the burden of worry for my family. Could we all sit down and talk?"

"I...yes. I suppose it would be good to do that. I shall return to Pemberley in a few days—"

"Pemberley? Splendid. Everyone is already there!"

SEVENTEEN

"Everyone already at Pemberley?" Darcy felt his brows shoot to the top of his head. "Who?"

"Your family." Lord Matlock smiled. "All those who love you dearly."

"Fitzwilliam and Anne? Because I assure you, Lady Catherine would have disposed of them straightaway."

"Miss Bennet is there," Lord Matlock replied. "She will take care of them, I am sure."

"Miss Bennet will be leaving shortly," Darcy informed him. "Perhaps she is already gone."

"Not according to Saye," Lord Matlock informed him. "He finds her utterly beguiling, as does Lady Saye, and sent me a note saying as much."

"She was leaving," Darcy insisted. "No doubt she is gone now, and perhaps my cousins along with her."

"I suppose we shall find out once we get there. I shall tell them to remain, call a family meeting of sorts. The advantage of being near death," Lord Matlock proclaimed, "is that people are more inclined to oblige you. This could be my last Christmas, you know."

"Your colour is much improved."

"No, it is not," Lord Matlock said. "In fact, I daresay it is a little worse. And such frightful pains I have in my legs! I can scarcely sleep most nights."

"But what exactly is the nature of your illness?" Darcy asked, leaning forward to inspect his uncle's countenance. "Perhaps someone who had studied on the continent—"

"What I need is my family all around me," Lord Matlock insisted. "To heal the breach Darcy! Then I may die in peace."

Darcy by now suspected that his lordship was nowhere near dying. He was, after all, only sixty or thereabouts, and Fitzwilliams were known for long lives. "Very well," said Darcy. "Off to Pemberley, and whoever is there will receive my attentions."

"Excellent." Having settled their plans, Lord Matlock asked Darcy where he should leave him. "Did you walk from your house? Or is your curricle lagging about somewhere?"

"I walked."

"You know, given these afflictions of mine, I have come to believe walking is a very healthful habit for a man," Lord Matlock mused. "A man ought to walk as much as he can, be it in town or while in the country. Ladies too! Darcy, when you marry, pray encourage your wife to walk as much as she is able."

An image of Miss Bennet with pink cheeks and tendrils of hair springing loose all around her face arose in Darcy's mind. Without thinking, he said, "Miss Bennet enjoys rambling about more than any lady I have ever known."

"Does she?"

Darcy cursed himself as he observed the keen interest lighting his uncle's eyes. "Or so I have been told."

"You have said scarcely anything about the lady," Lord Matlock said, affecting an air of nonchalance.

"As I have been with you less than a quarter-hour, I daresay there has been scant opportunity."

"She is a beautiful young lady living in your home. Such a situation as this is bound to raise curiosity."

Darcy immediately snapped to full attention. "She is the guest of my aunt, and who said she is beautiful?"

His lordship chuckled and settled back in the seat. "The colour on your cheeks said all I need to know."

"Has there been talk?" Darcy was not mollified. "I shall not stand for gossip that might be injurious to Miss Bennet's reputation, as well as to my own."

"Stand down, son. The curiosity I speak of is my own." Lord Matlock grinned.

"She is leaving Pemberley, so it does not signify whether she is pretty or not."

"Saye reports she is handsome, and Richard said she is witty and kind-hearted."

His lordship waited a reply to that with rapt attention; it did not appear that the man so much as drew a breath. Reluctantly, Darcy said, "I did not think her pretty at first, likely because she vexed me so greatly; but for some time now I have considered her the hand-somest woman of my acquaintance."

"That is a recommendation indeed!"

"It does not signify."

"Not signify? You are a young man and she is a young woman; therefore, it signifies."

"A young woman of no fortune, connexions to trade—"

"And you are an unhappy young man who has endured a great tragedy." His lordship shrugged. "If there is anything being ill has shown me, it is that life is very brief. Why, it seems just the other day that I was courting your aunt, that we were a young newly-wedded couple, that I was dandling Saye on my knee. All gone now. I am on that long slope of infirmity, with nothing but my grave to anticipate."

Darcy rolled his eyes.

"Happy days are fleeting, Darcy, and you need to grab as many of them as you can."

"I do not even recall what happiness looks like. At any rate, I cannot marry anyone while at any moment the truth could rear up and smite me. It would not be fair to the lady."

"Perhaps you should take her into your confidence."

"No," Darcy replied shortly. "Again, I must remind you: she will leave. Any further business between us will be conducted by her father."

He swallowed heavily. No more walks with her, no more talking over dinner. No music, no laughter, no arguing over books. Just Mr Bennet to perhaps speak of her now and again. Mr Bennet who would inform him— perhaps—of when she married, when she became a mother.

Tearing his mind from such troubling notions, Darcy said, "Sir, I must go to Meryton on our way north to speak to Mr Bennet."

They had arrived at the place where Darcy was keeping rooms, and he moved to alight from the carriage. His uncle stopped him by placing his hand on Darcy's arm and holding him tightly in an awkward bent-over position.

"We have all lost those who we loved Darcy. You do not need to spend the remainder of your life in penance and mourning." Lord Matlock gave him an encouraging smile. "The door to the prison is open, but you will need to walk out on your own strength."

Darcy did not offer the reply that sprung immediately to his mind: the door was indeed open, but the chains that bound him within were as present as ever.

General Fitzwilliam was in person and address very much the gentleman. Elizabeth suspected, based on knowing him only the evening prior, that she might have become friends with him under other circumstances. This day, however, she had no stomach for the sort of civilities he required. She wished for nothing more than to disappear into her apartment and contemplate all she had learnt.

Courtesy dictated she do otherwise, and so she did, sitting with General Fitzwilliam in the breakfast parlour. They chatted easily for a time, and she found herself telling him about her first impressions of Mr Darcy. General Fitzwilliam winced and then laughed when she told him about Mr Darcy's unflattering comments. "Ape leader! How prodigiously uncivil! But Darcy is not often seen in the best light on first meeting; I daresay he must have improved in your estimation?"

At this remark, Elizabeth's face flamed, and she dropped her eyes, willing herself to calm down. Do not blush, she urged herself, which had the effect of making her blush several degrees deeper. When she dared look up, Fitzwilliam (for he had asked her to assume some familiarity with him) was regarding her with an air of amused surprise.

She hardly knew how to explain herself. No matter how kindly Fitzwilliam was, she would not confess to all that she had done, to the prejudices she had fed. "Mr Darcy and I saw each other little in the course of our days."

"I am sorry to hear that," Fitzwilliam replied with real feeling. "For I have rarely known any man as in need of a friend as Darcy."

"You care for him deeply," she observed even as some part of her mind wondered at the devotion that seemed to surround Darcy.

"He is as dear to me as any other person could be, and so it has been our whole life long."

"But you have been at odds of late?" Elizabeth asked in polite accents. "I only surmise as much, for when you arrived, you all said that had Mr Darcy been at home, he should not have received you."

General Fitzwilliam laughed with genuine good humour; another man might have taken offence at her frank speech, but he did not. "We have a difference of opinion between us that we have been unable to overcome."

"I am sorry to hear that," Elizabeth replied when it seemed no more would be said. She considered a moment and then said, "What then was your purpose in coming here?"

The general shrugged. "My wife is expecting our first child and—"

"Old Dickie here finally figured out how these things worked!" Saye proclaimed, entering the breakfast room. "And now we shall have an heir to Rosings Park."

Fitzwilliam rolled his eyes. "I was busy leading men into war, Saye. 'Tis a tricky business to begin a family from another country. In any case, Miss Bennet, my wife, being with child, has felt a greater urgency to reconcile with her mother."

"Alas, yet again, Lady Cattle-prod will have nothing to do with her."

"Do not call her that, Saye."

"If she behaves like a cow, then I shall refer to her as such."

"In any case," said Elizabeth gently, "I hope she has some success in her endeavour. I have reason to believe that it might weigh on Lady Catherine far more than one might suppose."

"My aunt believes in propriety and maintaining the family name above all things," Saye told her. "She cannot forgive them for running off and risking scandal as they did."

"Miss Bennet." Mrs Reynolds entered, bringing their conversation to a temporary halt. "I beg your pardon. I wondered whether you need Samuel to escort you to church this morning."

Uncertain, Elizabeth looked to her companions. "Sirs, are your family in the habit of attending services?"

"We are, but it is an irregular habit at best." Colonel Fitzwilliam grinned broadly. "But let us not disturb Samuel. I shall escort you to church myself if you do not mind it."

"I do not mind it at all." She smiled at Mrs Reynolds. "Tell Samuel he is freed from his obligation today."

When the housekeeper had gone from the room, Elizabeth looked at Fitzwilliam expectantly. "It will make a grand tale for our walk," he said with a joviality that seemed more than a trifle forced.

It was not long after that when they found themselves on the path, walking towards the church with only a fat hound to accompany them. December had surprised them all by being uncommonly warm and dry; it was genuinely shocking after so many long months of unusually cold and wet. Alas, it did no more than to intensify the reek of decay pervading the forest.

"America is just the same you know," Fitzwilliam told her. "Snow in May, all the crops ruined. Had it first hand from a friend of mine."

Elizabeth stopped in her tracks. In later reflection, she could not have said why it was that his words delivered in such a disinterested way struck her so keenly. Suddenly she just knew. Darcy had been in America. It was nearly audible, the sound of pieces neatly fitted together, clicking into place, the picture emerging clear in her mind. "He went to America."

"Who did?"

"Darcy." She looked up at Fitzwilliam. "Of course! But why he could not be reached is the bit I cannot make out—then again, perhaps he did not wish to be found?"

The general was staring at her, dismay breaching his countenance. "Um...I do not mean to imply that—"

"Is this dreadful weather what brought him back?" she asked. "I have heard it said that he had just returned in the spring. Perhaps he saw the sufferings abroad and could not remain apart from Pemberley?"

The general flushed. "Miss Bennet, do not—"

"For whatever had taken him away," she mused, only barely aware of the general's growing distress, "the notion that people might suffer or starve should bring him back. He had to know his tenants, his people, were well. His sense of true charity would demand it."

Though dismayed, Fitzwilliam chuckled. "Miss Bennet, you are an uncommonly clever sort."

"So I am right," she concluded. "He was in America following his sister's death?"

Fitzwilliam stared at her for some time, but he no longer appeared shocked. He was an uncommonly clever sort himself, it seemed, and she concluded that he had already adapted to the knowledge that she knew more than he had believed she did and his mind was already shifting to the necessity of discerning precisely what it was that she knew.

"If you were sworn to secrecy," she said, "you need not break your vow for my sake. Your silence is confirmation enough."

Fitzwilliam would say nothing, but offered a slight chuckle as he looked away from her. "Let us proceed," he said at last. "Else we should be late for church."

As it stood, they were indeed late for church, and Elizabeth blushed with shame as they made their way to the seats reserved for Pemberley. They settled in as a hymn was sung by their fellow church-goers and gave the service such devout attention as was rarely seen.

It was not until the service had concluded that Elizabeth looked around, hoping to see her friend in attendance. "There is my friend, Mrs Green," she told the general. "She is a companion to your relation, Mrs Lawrence."

"Whose relation?"

"Yours," Elizabeth replied. "Mrs Lawrence? I believe she said that Mrs Lawrence was Lady Catherine's aunt?"

Fitzwilliam was looking at her as if she had gone mad. "I beg your pardon, Miss Bennet, but I do not know any Lawrences."

"Oh." Elizabeth felt herself blush. "I must be mistaken. In any case, do excuse me while I greet her." She looked around the crowded room, but it seemed Mrs Green had evaporated into thin air.

Fitzwilliam saw her confusion and raised himself up, using the advantage of his height. "Is she the lady in the yellow gown? The one who has just smiled in this— Oh, no, it seems she was smiling at that gentleman over there."

"Mrs Green was wearing a dark blue dress," said Elizabeth, while craning her neck to look around. "I do not see her anywhere. She must have been in haste to leave."

More to herself than to Fitzwilliam, she said, "I could have sworn she said Mrs Lawrence was Lady Catherine's aunt. I thought it quite extraordinary."

"My father and Lady Catherine have one aunt alive," said Fitzwilliam. "Lady Tilbury. She lives in Bath, though if you asked her, she would likely tell you she lives at her ancestral home, a place called Baldock Abbey. Poor dear is quite gone daft—Baldock Abbey was levelled by fire nearly twenty years ago."

"Strange indeed," said Elizabeth. She cared not a bit about Lady Tilbury. She was certain beyond anything that Mrs Green told her Mrs Lawrence was a relation of the Fitzwilliams. "But why would she lie?"

"I believe I have heard something of this Mrs Lawrence," said Fitzwilliam. "That is an old scandal if I am thinking of the right people. She was the governess at Blenheim some generations ago, and Admiral Lawrence saw her and made her an offer on the spot. He was a good bit older than she was, too, just to give the wagging tongues more cause to move."

Elizabeth thought of the old lady she knew and could not help the laugh that escaped her. "Positively disgraceful! Ah, but in the end, it does not signify, does it?"

"Anyone who cared about it or gossiped about it is long gone," Fitzwilliam agreed. "Such is life! But at least she has her memories."

On Monday morning, Darcy arrived with his uncle in Hertfordshire. After installing his lordship at the inn, Darcy rode to Longbourn.

Meryton looked very different to him now. There was a little ribbon shop where Elizabeth might have found her accoutrements, and there was a bookstore, likely the very one where she bought little Charles his dreadful but beloved Otranto.

He was shown into Longbourn directly on his arrival whereupon he found a young woman awaiting him in the sitting room. He knew her—he had met her the last time that he was here—but he could not immediately recall who she was.

"How do you do, Mr Darcy?" she said, rising.

"Uh…how do you do…?" He smiled, feeling all the awkwardness that comes from forgetting an acquaintance's name. "It is a pleasure to be here."

She invited him to sit, and he did, sensing that the room was different than the time he had been here before. He could not quite place his finger on it, but it seemed newer somehow than on his prior visit. Fresher? More yellow?

To his great relief, Mr Bennet arrived only moments later. "Mr Darcy. This is an unexpected pleasure."

"Is it?" He felt himself redden. "I beg your pardon, sir. I wrote to you last week with the matters I had hoped to—"

"Last week?" Mr Bennet chuckled then gave the woman an expressive look.

"Last week?" she echoed. "Oh dear. I think it is likely in one of your piles."

"I daresay it is. Shall we send Hill to find it?"

"Let us not trouble Hill. I shall find it." She rose and quit the room moments later.

Mr Bennet smiled genially at Darcy. "I find that if I wait a fortnight or so to open my letters, all the little trials and tribulations within them tend to have worked themselves out."

"I am sorry to hear that," said Darcy, "for had you read mine, it might have better prepared you for the conversation I wish to have about Miss Bennet and Charles."

"Indeed? Well, I must say—"

They were interrupted by the return of the lady. Mrs Collins! Yes, Darcy remembered it now. But why on earth was she here with Mr Bennet? How did she take such liberty as to enter the gentleman's study and rifle through his letters?

She had Darcy's letter in her hand, and as she entered, she extended her arm towards Mr Bennet. He took it with an excessively courtly bow and then sat down again.

"Thank you, um, Mrs Collins," said Darcy. His pronunciation of her name caused the lady and Mr Bennet to startle. Mrs Collins pressed a hand to her lips, and Mr Bennet looked like a boy caught with his finger in the jam bowl. Darcy glanced back and forth between them, silently bidding one of them to speak while wondering where he had erred.

"My dear," said Mr Bennet, "have you not written to Elizabeth?"

"I have not, my beloved," answered the lady, "for you told me that you wished to do it."

Mr Bennet chuckled. "In the future, my dearest, pray recall that my intentions rarely do succeed into action. I am afraid my natural inclination to procrastinate won out in this circumstance."

Mrs Collins laughed, an affectedly girlish giggle. "Oh, my dear, whatever shall I do with you?"

"I have a few suggestions but they are not fit for polite society." He gave a little leer and Darcy nearly gagged, permitting himself only a wince instead. Did this silly banter mean what he suspected?

Mr Bennet turned towards him. "Mr Darcy, you will find I am quite unrepentant in my indolence! Just a glance at a book and all my plans are for nothing. In any case it is much pleasanter to share such news in person."

"Yes, my dear, but we did not know we should have such an opportunity as this," she scolded. "Really, Eliza should know."

"She should," said Mr Bennet. "And she will quite soon I daresay."

"Pray, forgive me for being rude," said Darcy at last. "I have not the pleasure of understanding what news there is. Should you deem me fit to hear it, I would be much obliged."

There was a final smiling look between the other two, an

unspoken communication that seemed to establish Mr Bennet as the teller. From his chair, Mr Bennet made a grand waving gesture at the lady. "Mr Darcy, it gives me no little amount of honour to introduce to you my wife, Mrs Charlotte Bennet."

The half an hour that followed was simultaneously tedious and enlightening. Mr and Mrs Bennet appeared determined to "my dear" and "my darling" one another to death but insensible of any dismay that might result from a childhood friend becoming a stepmother. It was a subject he broached gently when Mrs Bennet took her leave of them so that the men might discuss Darcy's business.

"Oh, Elizabeth will be delighted," Mr Bennet replied. "Charlotte has always been a great favourite, and in any case, Lizzy is five and twenty now and hardly in need of any mothering."

Darcy cleared his throat. "That is true."

"And," he said with a little twinkle of his eyes over his spectacles, "I have seen no indication that she wishes to leave Derbyshire!"

Likely because you have not read her letters.

"Lizzy must realise her old papa still wishes for some companion-ship." Mr Bennet smiled broadly. "Mrs Bennet is a useful sort of girl, well accustomed to economy and industry. She will have Longbourn humming along before long and, supposing we are very fortunate, even provide it with an heir. You have your estate, Mr Darcy; I trust the importance of an heir is not lost to you."

"Pemberley is not entailed," Darcy replied. "Whoever I choose may inherit Pemberley."

"Ah! Well done indeed. Alas, it is not so for Longbourn." He chuckled. "Mrs Bennet has been singularly fortunate in that regard. Her first husband, Collins, was my cousin and eventual heir."

"He was?"

"Oh yes. I did not know him until he came back in the autumn of '11—the same time as Bingley was here. That proved an eventful time for he proposed to Elizabeth on the same evening Bingley proposed to Jane, though with a far different outcome."

"Proposed to Elizabeth? But how then did he come to be married to…" Darcy trailed off, realising the truth was likely best left unsaid.

"Oh, Mrs Bennet—rather Miss Lucas as she was then—invited

him to dinner the very same evening that Lizzy refused him, and it all fell into place from there."

"So soon after he offered for Elizabeth?" Darcy asked with some horror. "Had he no feelings for your daughter?"

"Oh no, and Lizzy had positively no regard for him. Bit of an odd fellow, that Collins, but he's dead now, so no use thinking of that. Yes, so Charlotte got him, but then he died around the same time as Elizabeth's mother did. And, now here we are."

Here we are indeed. Bit of an opportunist are you not, Mrs Bennet? "Seems that your Mrs Bennet was nearly destined to become the mistress of your house."

"Indeed it does." Mr Bennet nodded in an agreeable sort of way that gave Darcy a hot flash of anger all over his body. Was Mr Bennet's own comfort his only consideration in any of this? He knew then that the unpleasant duty would fall to him to tell Elizabeth of the state of affairs at Longbourn, and he also somehow knew that it would not be received gladly.

And perhaps even change her mind about leaving? He quieted that selfish thought at once. In any case, Miss Bennet was an independent sort. Likely she had already left Pemberley and was well on her way to Longbourn.

"I have trespassed far too long on your time already, so do let me come to the purpose of my visit. In short, Miss Bennet and Charles intend to return to Longbourn—"

"Come to Longbourn? Well that is good of her to pay every civility to her new mother. How long would she wish to remain?"

Darcy repressed the desire to roll his eyes or box Mr Bennet's ears —perhaps both. "No," he said patiently, "I mean to say that she wishes to return here to live."

"Oh." Mr Bennet waved his hand. "Well you do not wish that. Just tell her no."

"I have agreed to the scheme."

"You have?" Mr Bennet looked concerned.

There were folded papers within Darcy's jacket pocket, and he withdrew them. He had spent considerable hours outlining a scheme for guardianship that seemed prudent to him, and his solicitor had drawn up information about a shared guardianship. He handed the papers to Mr Bennet and proceeded into a short explanation of what was written therein.

Mr Bennet did not deign to look at the papers Darcy handed him, holding onto them loosely as though he feared the taint of obligation might bleed through. He merely cocked his head and watched Darcy give his exposition but made no outward appearance of acceptance or refusal.

When Darcy concluded, the two gentlemen sat in silence for a moment until Mr Bennet sighed heavily. "Well, this is...I mean, Elizabeth should not have presumed that I would wish for this."

Darcy said nothing.

"I see now that I should have perhaps informed my daughter of my own situation before all of these plans were made and situated. A man who is newly married does not always wish for grown children to be about the place."

"Do you mean to say she is unwelcome?"

Mr Bennet removed his spectacles and scrubbed at his eyes. "What I mean is that when a man remarries, sometimes the things of the past are less...well, Lizzy is grown, she is a grown woman, all of my daughters are. It is a new day at Longbourn."

"A new day?"

"I suppose she could come live here, but to be guardian of Jane's boy is quite another matter. And what if Lizzy would marry? What then?"

Darcy silently reached over and took the papers, replacing them in his pocket.

"Lizzy should marry," said her father. "I am sure Jane did not intend for her to give all that up for the boy."

"Your grandson," said Darcy. "And I daresay Elizabeth loves him as a mother would."

"Of course," said Mr Bennet. "But she would have no legal obligation to the child whereas I would...I am no young buck, Mr Darcy. What if I should take ill?"

"You seem healthy—"

"Mrs Bennet and I have plans to travel! She has not been to France and with the war ended—"

"Miss Bennet could, even now, be travelling here."

"Oh...well, if she arrives, she will shift for herself. Lizzy has always been good at that. There are plenty of people about, she will not want for company." Mr Bennet offered a regretful smile. "I am afraid I am just not prepared to agree to this scheme. Lizzy can live where she likes, but I cannot be a party to this guardianship business."

"This is unfortunate indeed, for I do not think it prudent for me to allow my ward to live over one hundred miles away from me with no one to oversee him as a guardian."

Mr Bennet smiled, obviously relieved. "Sir, we are in agreement. Lizzy must remain at Pemberley."

She has no wish to stay there! Darcy wondered that the contrary nature of this man had not been plain to him earlier. And selfish! If Elizabeth thought him selfish, what must she think of her own father?

When he thought of that, his heart melted a little. Poor, poor girl, with no place to really call her own. Her father did not want her to return, and Darcy had made Pemberley such a dreadful place that she wanted only to escape it.

He had not considered before how it must have been to arrive there knowing she was exceedingly unwanted. To have walked through the dark, shrouded halls, to have heard all the whispers of secrets around her. Had he done anything to see that her life was pleasing? No, he been well occupied in stewing in his misery.

He rose from his chair. "Mr Bennet, I shall relay this information to Miss Bennet and see that she is well cared for at Pemberley."

EIGHTEEN

I NEED TO SORT THINGS OUT.

Elizabeth sat with Charles one morning, absently playing alphabet blocks with him while thoughts and theories and conjecture swarmed about in her mind.

A mere fortnight ago, she laboured under the belief that Mr Darcy's wife had been the resident of the blue room and Mr Darcy was a brutal monster who beat her and either murdered her or caused her to commit suicide. And what evidence had she of these beliefs? The word of Charlotte, who had supposed him engaged, coupled with the fact that he insulted Jane (in fact, little Charles had arrived rather quickly, had he not? And likely at her own mother's urging to Jane), called Elizabeth thirty, and had the audacity to take charge of the ward he should have had all along.

As it stood, there was no wife, only a younger sister in the blue room. And Mr Darcy a monster? Hardly. He was a man who gave food and heat to the poor, who had lately suffered the death of his young sister, his only surviving family member, and who appeared to love Charles as a father might.

For the more that Elizabeth enquired, the more examples there were of Mr Darcy's superlative care of Charles. He played ball with him. He read to him. He called for a physician when Charles was ill, and despite every inclination protesting against it, allowed his favourite aunt to come along and live with him.

Even his interactions with her had begun to take on different hues. Had he not urged her to make free with his library? Had he not walked with her many times? And how many times did they talk of books and news and politics? Another man might have felt it impudent or not ladylike, the manner in which she argued, but he had seemed to enjoy it, to encourage it even.

But he hates you now. Surely he hates you now.

Her mind would not put it aside, instead returning, as it had so often, to the well. Even through her terror she could recall the feel of his strong arms wrapped around her and his lips on hers; even now she could hear him say "I almost lost you."

Oh Lizzy why do you think of such things? She shook her head, vexed at herself for thinking so frequently of her fall into the well. Determinedly, she changed her mind to other subjects.

Who wrote the journal? Surely not the deceased Miss Darcy? She was too young to have married, and the journal had indicated that her family approved. Who was the lunatic, and why was he so often wandering about Pemberley? She oft reminded herself that it was of no consequence to her. She ought to stop playing at being a Bow Street Runner and arrange her travel back to Hertfordshire. The notion of Mr Darcy returning to Pemberley and finding her still there induced panic, to say the least. It would be mortifying to have remained where one was so deeply unwelcome.

Elizabeth could not recall when she last had a restful night's sleep. Thoughts, worries, fears all consumed her as she lay in the dark hours puzzling over all that had been said and done, all that had been misunderstood and misinterpreted. She had, she saw now, been quite abominable in her actions towards Mr Darcy. No, he had not been everything a gentleman ought to be, but it had not given her license to behave as she had, to think the thoughts that she did. She was heartily ashamed of herself and simultaneously hoped and feared meeting with him again that she might tell him so.

Her father had not replied to her letter begging his assistance to return home, and she began to despair that he ever would. She had sent another and then another, but no reply was as yet given. It was maddening, but perhaps it was for the best. Perhaps she should be made to stay and face Mr Darcy.

She began to imagine how it would be when he returned. Scenes played in her mind; most were humiliating sorts of scenes in which she begged Mr Darcy's forgiveness, and he replied with disdain and hauteur. The more such scenes were imagined, the more she realised that she must pray to be gone before he returned. Perhaps, she decided, she must act without her father; perhaps she must arrange her travel on her own.

"Lizzy, not there. George sits there."

"Who is George, darling?" Elizabeth replaced a fallen alphabet letter on Charles's little table.

"My friend."

"Your friend?" Elizabeth looked to Mrs Browning for clarification; Mrs Browning gave her a surreptitious little grin.

"George is our new playfellow here in the nursery, ma'am. Comes and goes as he pleases, does George."

"George," announced Charles, "is not a he. George is a girl."

"A girl named George?" Elizabeth asked.

Charles did not look at her, busily arranging the blocks on the table. "George is a girl, but she still has good stories."

"Well, I am a girl too, and I flatter myself that I have good stories." Elizabeth smiled and pushed a lock of hair from Charles's eyes.

"Not as good as George's stories," Charles informed her. "George can fly."

"He...she can? How marvellous."

"On her horse, she flies," Charles added. "The whole way over the river!"

"Oh my! George must have quite a horse," Elizabeth teased while making a show of looking around her. "Is George here now?"

Charles looked—in only the way a four-year-old can—like she was mad. "Of course not. George only visits at night-time."

"Only at night-time? Does not George sleep?"

"She takes care of a little boy like me, except he is not a little boy. He is a grown-up boy, but he is as naughty as a little boy, so she can only come while the little boy sleeps."

"I see," said Elizabeth. "Come now, we should have some porridge for breakfast."

The door clicked open, and Mrs Fitzwilliam peered in. "Good morning," she said to Elizabeth. "May I join you?"

"Of course." Elizabeth motioned to the chair beside hers. "I hope you rested well?"

"Oh, no, I never sleep. Did not sleep before this," she gestured to her stomach, "and sleep even more poorly now." With that, she was off on a litany of complaints, from dyspepsia to insatiable hunger, then swellings of this or that, a pain in her hips and her ribs, and etc. Elizabeth made sympathetic murmurings throughout, which seemed enough to satisfy her.

"But we need an heir to Rosings Park," she concluded. "So here we are."

"How good that you were able to travel."

"I should have thought that my mother would want to put all this nonsense aside to see me," said Mrs Fitzwilliam. "After all, it was she who was always telling me about ladies dying in the childbed! Why I could be gone tomorrow for all she cares."

"She does care," said Elizabeth soothingly. "I know this separation troubles her exceedingly. Perhaps once the baby is born—"

"If anything, the actual presence of a child could only dismay her. She has never been very fond of children." Mrs Fitzwilliam gave an elaborate shrug. "She would not even permit Georgiana at Rosings until she was at least twelve. She thinks it unseemly for children to travel."

Elizabeth hardly knew what to say to that.

"But I had an excellent nurse, very loving. She stayed with me all my life, for I have always been of a delicate constitution. I miss my darling Jenkinson exceedingly."

"What became of her?"

"My mother released her," said Mrs Fitzwilliam. "She said if I was strong enough to elope then I should not be in need of a nurse."

"I am sure your mother found her a good position," said Elizabeth, more from politeness than true feeling.

"She is companion to an older lady in Loxley, a dowager countess of somewhere I cannot recall. I hope so. Such a position would be agreeable to her, I am sure."

THE JOURNEY back to Pemberley drew long. Muddy roads, his uncle's poor health, and his own impatience stretched the three-day journey into five and made it feel like ten. But as impatient as Darcy was to be back at home, he was equally dreading the scenes that must arise.

His uncle clutched his arm as they made their way slowly into the front hall where Mrs Reynolds met them. Darcy was surprised to see her; he could not say what it was exactly, but there was a cheer to the older woman that he had not seen for some time. She almost seemed younger in some ways, though he would not have said anything of the like to her. No, he had learnt his lesson by guessing Miss Bennet's age.

The greetings were given and their coats and hats taken. "Lord Matlock," said Mrs Reynolds, "your wife has arrived only this morning. Would you like to join her in her apartment?" Lord Matlock, whose face bore the strains of travel fatigue and carriage sickness, was quick to agree and followed her as rapidly as his gouty legs and cane would permit.

And just like that, Darcy was alone in the hall, feeling the strangeness that comes from an absence. The house even smelt different and had an air of unfamiliarity he could not place.

He decided he would make his way to his bedchamber but met his cousin before his foot touched the bottom step.

"Darcy." Fitzwilliam halted immediately, colour suffusing his face although his bearing remained upright and unabashed.

Darcy knew not what to do for a moment and settled for a stiff, formal bow. "General Fitzwilliam."

Fitzwilliam's eyes narrowed; he was ever the tactician, always calculating how things were and what was best done. "Should you like me to call you Mr Darcy?"

"Darcy will do."

"So will Fitzwilliam, then, or Richard." He cocked one brow. "As in our earlier times."

Darcy nodded.

They stood, regarding one another warily for several moments until Fitzwilliam added. "You are no doubt surprised to find us here."

"Your father knew you were here."

"My father?"

"He is gone to see Lady Matlock. He withstood the journey well, but he was tired."

"Excellent," said Fitzwilliam. After a shorter pause, he added, "My wife wished to see her mother in hopes that some reconciliation might come forth. It has not. If you wish us to leave—"

"You may remain."

"Very good."

In the following silence, Darcy glanced around the hall while Fitzwilliam rocked back and forth on his heels. There were things that needed said but he knew not how to begin. Perhaps now was not the time. "If you will excuse me I shall—"

"How long will this go on?" Fitzwilliam burst out. "How long must my wife and I pay for the iniquitous sin of eloping?"

"I do not care one bit how you married your wife," Darcy replied sharply.

"I have months of silence and curt replies that say you do."

"The unfortunate effect of selfishness is that one finds oneself quite alone to bear the consequences." How well do I know that!

"Selfish?" Fitzwilliam growled. He made a disgusted sound, looking to the side at an unseen sympathiser. "See here, I—"

"I was in the midst of tragedy," Darcy replied, barely remembering to lower his voice.

"As was I! I was her guardian too! This was as much a failure in my oversight as yours!"

"If we must have this conversation now, let us at least closet ourselves," said Darcy through gritted teeth.

After a deep breath, Fitzwilliam nodded his agreement and followed Darcy to his study. Though his mind was on the conversation to follow, Darcy could not fail to notice that curtains had been changed out, allowing light to penetrate the formerly shrouded halls. Furniture covers had been removed, and in the distance, he could hear Saye, with his dreadful attempts at being a tenor, singing Christmas carols. Despite himself, he smiled.

Even his study was improved, he noticed. Lighter and brighter, with a festive arrangement of pinecones and red berries on his desk. On closer examination, he realised the berries were pebbles painted red. One did as they must in difficult times, he realised, even if it meant paint on a pebble to mimic good cheer.

He gestured to his cousin to sit and then joined him. A servant had already been in to light a fire for them, and he drew near it, eager to chase away the chill of travel.

When the silence had drawn long, Fitzwilliam said, "I did look for you, you know."

"I was not where you left me."

"I gathered as much."

Darcy shrugged. "It seemed best to hide myself, try to create a new life."

"We never intended that you should stay there."

"But I thought that I should," said Darcy. "I believed Fitzwilliam Darcy was no more and in his place, George Walter."

"George Walter?" Fitzwilliam gave a snort of a chuckle.

"Your middle name and mine," Darcy replied. "Common enough that no one should connect them to us, or so I hoped."

Fitzwilliam nodded slowly. "In any case, it does not signify does it? Nothing to hide from now."

"Do you think so?"

"George Wickham is not dead."

"Perhaps I did not remove him from this mortal coil, but I took his life from him, to be sure. He is a senseless lunatic in a cabin in the woods."

"And better behaved than he ever was," Fitzwilliam retorted. "We should have knocked the wits out of him a long time ago, before ever he set his sights on Georgiana."

Despite himself, Darcy smiled a slight, faint smile. "Not so well behaved. He has regular beatings administered by the brothers of young ladies in Lambton and Kympton. Takes more than a wooden post to the head to remove some instincts I daresay."

Fitzwilliam chuckled. Both men studied their hands, their feet, the fire for a moment until Fitzwilliam offered, "Do you want to know why we eloped?"

"You wanted Rosings, and she liked the way you looked in regimentals?"

"Hardly," Fitzwilliam said. "But yes, I did need something to live on. I am not asking if you know why we married, I am asking if you know why we eloped."

"What I know," said Darcy, careful to keep his voice steady, "was that mere weeks after…after…you and she were off on a honeymoon while I—"

"Not at all," Fitzwilliam interrupted. "Darcy, it is not the truth. I could not be so unconcerned, not when Georgiana was gone, and you were hiding with your family name held in the balance."

"But I thought—"

Fitzwilliam leant forward. "I eloped so that in the future, if anything were to come out, any hint of any of it, it would be me who bore the scandal. If there was someone in the family believed to have eloped, then the stories would mix and mingle; the gossips would be assuring one another, 'oh no, you are mistaken it was Miss de Bourgh and her cousin who eloped, not Miss Darcy.' We played the active decoys if you will."

The realisation hit him hard. He had not ever considered that Fitzwilliam's actions were anything less than wholly self-centred. He only knew he was sitting in the outer reaches of the Scottish highlands, hiding from anyone and everyone, imagining the horror of being hanged—and through it, he believed Fitzwilliam was prancing about with Anne, having completely forgotten about Georgiana.

"I was surprised that you married her," Darcy admitted.

"We were hardly in love," Fitzwilliam admitted. "It was Anne who thought of it. I had just met with one of my investigators who had again failed to find any sign of Georgiana, and he asked if there was any evidence that Georgiana had married. Naturally, I said no but when I sat with Anne that night, we feared it had begun to come out. So Anne said, 'let us change the story to our own.' and we did."

Darcy felt a strange sensation when Fitzwilliam said that, like a chain that had bound him falling away. An odd need to laugh burbled up within his chest, so he looked down at his feet; it would not do to begin behaving like a lunatic himself.

"I misunderstood you completely," he said softly.

Fitzwilliam, who likely knew it was as much an apology as he would ever get, grinned broadly in reply. Darcy reached towards his arm, punching it lightly with his fist.

"Well, if it is not Darcy!" Saye cried, entering the study. "Good to see you old man. Any chance you have a lyre anywhere?"

Such an incongruous enquiry after so many years made Darcy laugh aloud. "I am afraid not, Saye."

Saye cursed. "Would the stores in Lambton have one?"

"Have you been by the music room?" Fitzwilliam asked. "I feared someone was killing a cat in there earlier."

Saye rolled his eyes. "The sounds of battle have obviously affected your hearing."

"I prefer the sounds of battle to whatever it was you were doing in the music room."

"I like my voice," Saye replied blithely. "And Miss Bennet had the most lovely idea. Annabelle and Claire came from the nursery with Charles, and we taught them all some little songs. They will entertain us later, our own little musicale, but if only we could find a lyre, it would be done to perfection."

To hear her name spoken so easily from Saye's lips dropped Darcy's spirits. She hated him, and if she knew the truth she would... well he had no idea.

"Miss Bennet," he began, but his demurrals died on his lips. What did she know? He had no idea, but she had somehow arrived at the notion that he had murdered someone. "I do not know what Miss Bennet might think or know about any of this business. She thinks Georgiana died, and that is the beginning and end of it."

"Are you certain of that?"

"Why do you ask?" Darcy asked Fitzwilliam.

"Has she asked many questions about Georgiana?"

Darcy shook his head. "No, not really."

Fitzwilliam nodded. "I noticed that too. In my experience, a person like Miss Bennet—someone who is given to a natural curiosity —will ask either too many or too few questions. The latter is most alarming for generally it means she intends to find the answers for herself."

"So you believe I should speak to her, tell her everything?" Darcy shook his head, imagining such a scene. "I cannot. I shall not."

"She lives here, Darcy," Fitzwilliam told him. "If you do not tell her, she will likely come to her own conclusions. I daresay you should rather have her learn yours."

ALTHOUGH SHE KNEW that he was coming, the news that Darcy was actually at home electrified Elizabeth. She knew not how to behave. Should she apologise? Attempt a quick escape? Act like nothing had happened? No possibility seemed to have any merit whatsoever.

It was while dressing for dinner that the notion of sending a note occurred to her, in concert with the idea of not going down for dinner. Yes, she absolutely must permit Darcy time with his relations without her presence to dismay him. He had surely no wish to see her and certainly not at his dinner table.

She was already dressed to dine, but it did not signify. She sat staring into space for several minutes before deciding what to write.

Mr Darcy,

No doubt you are surprised to find me still at Pemberley after our exchange before you departed for London. As you know, Charles became ill, and I thought it best to remain until he was well. Following that, your relations arrived and prevailed upon me to remain; I could not deny them their pleasure. Please do be assured, sir, I could not have trespassed on your hospitality were it for any less urgent situation than this.

With regard to my unjust accusation—the presence of Mrs Fitzwilliam here at Pemberley has made me feel the fullness of my error with keen certainty. I am most ashamed of what I have thought, particularly in light of your generosity and goodness towards Charles and myself.

I expect to hear from my father within the next day or so regarding my journey home. Until then, I shall remain in my apartment, beginning with this evening's dinner.

My deepest apologies for everything,
Elizabeth Bennet

There. No doubt Mr Darcy was already dressing, so it would likely be best to summon Ruth to send the letter through Mr Darcy's valet. She hurried to ring the bell, hoping she was not too late, that Mr Darcy would not have already descended to the dining room.

While she awaited Ruth, she went to the window, her eyes seeing little as her mind insisted on rehearsing the facts of all she had learnt. The blue room? Miss Darcy's. Beatrice? Miss Darcy's cat. The elopement? That belonged to Darcy's cousins. The lunatic? No one knew. For a moment, Elizabeth's thoughts lingered on what Mrs Green had once told her, the tale of the second son that Miss Darcy had loved. But no, that likely meant nothing at all to any of this, and in any case, Elizabeth began to wonder about some of the things Mrs Green had said, wondering whether any of it should bear out.

A knock at the door interrupted her musings. "Come in," she called while going back to the desk to retrieve the note. The door did not open, so Elizabeth walked over and opened it herself.

Mr Darcy stood on the opposite side of the door, his face averted and awkward and his hands tucked behind his back.

"Oh!" Elizabeth's hand flew to her mouth even as the other almost dropped her note. "Oh! Mr Darcy. You are returned. I mean of course I had heard you were returned. Welcome home. Forgive my impertinence in saying so—who am I to welcome you to your own home? But I am glad to know your journey was safe."

"It was." Mr Darcy sounded coldly polite, and it served to help Elizabeth regain her equanimity. It would not do to be a silly, prattling miss when she had already importuned him so much.

"May I escort you to dinner?"

"I was not...I had not intended..." A blush burnt over Elizabeth's face. "I did not intend to go down."

"I hope my family has not been too trying."

"Of course not, no, I enjoyed them exceedingly."

He dropped his eyes and seemed to clench his jaw, and in a moment, she realised he believed it was his presence that rendered it disagreeable to her. In a rush, she said, "I had thought you might wish to be with them alone, or rather, in my absence."

He still seemed doubtful so she thrust the letter towards him. "Would you do me honour of reading this letter?"

He took it, sliding it into the pocket of his jacket. "If you have no cause to object to dinner," he said, "I would prefer you dine with us."

Should she? It did not seem she should or could decline. "Very well," she agreed.

He offered his arm, and after a moment, she laid her hand upon it. He did not begin to walk immediately. "Following dinner," he said, "I need to speak with you in my study."

Her nerves, quelled into some semblance of calm in the last moments, cried out their alarm. "Of course," she said, keeping her tone sedate. "After dinner then."

NINETEEN

THE FITZWILLIAMS NEVER PERMITTED ANYTHING LESS THAN A BOISTEROUS, lively meal. Saye was on some new regimen guaranteed to give him a dewy complexion and thicker hair, and he regaled them all endlessly with the dire consequences sure to result from the things on their plates. Lady Matlock fretted over her husband's plate, doing all she could to tempt his appetite with morsels of this or that but only managing to vex him. Anne was peevish, speaking at length on the predicament of being a woman with child who also had to manage the concerns of her general state of indifferent health. Fitzwilliam tried to join every conversation at once.

Throughout, Miss Bennet remained silent. She seemed to have little appetite, pushing her food around her plate; at some point, Darcy believed he saw her slipping a bit of fish to something under the table. When he looked, he saw Beatrice, Georgiana's old tabby. One could not know that half the country is starving by looking at that creature.

When the ladies rose to leave, he rose with them. "Darcy," Saye called. "I know it has been some time since you have been in society, but do keep with the men, sir."

"I have some business to attend in my study."

Miss Bennet startled and flushed on hearing his words. She met his gaze, and he nodded to let her know she should join him.

The other ladies walked ahead while Elizabeth dropped back, glancing behind her to see that Darcy followed. He gestured in the general direction of his study, and she moved in the way he indicated.

They entered the room and he gestured towards the chairs across from his desk. She sat, looking surprised when he chose to sit next to her rather than on the opposite side of the large walnut desk but said nothing. Silence then ensued as he thought of a way to begin the subject he supposed would distress her most. Somewhat idly, he noticed a ray of sunlight had pierced the room; it touched her hair, awakening marvellous hues of chestnut, amber, and molasses.

The extended silence prompted her speech. "Mr Darcy, sir, if you will please allow me to tell you how extremely sorry I am for the base-less accusations that I made." Tears sprung to her eyes, but she laughed a rueful laugh. "Your cousins arrived right on time. I was only begin-ning to feel my stupidity, but when I met the very person I thought... when I met Mrs Fitzwilliam, I felt my absurdity quite keenly."

What could he say to this? That he would never hurt another soul? But he had. He knew now that he was capable of killing some-one, that anything was possible in someone who had been pushed beyond their reason, beyond the strictures with which they had been raised, even beyond their own will. There was a dark place within him—a place tightly held and vigorously guarded that had, neverthe-less, escaped. It had held sway for at least one dreadful night. Who was to say it would not happen again?

His eyes devoured her, haloed by that one determined shaft of sunlight that continued to enter the room. She was lovely, from the long lashes that brushed her fair cheek to the small white hands that twisted anxiously in her lap. How he longed to reach over and cover her hands with his, to feel their cool delicacy within his grasp, perhaps even to draw her to his chest.

But he could not. He would not love her no matter how his heart yearned for it. He did not deserve such a being as her.

"It was an understandable error."

"Understandable?" she cried. "No! I took gossip and a pilfered journal that I had no right to read—"

"Journal?" Darcy asked quickly. "What do you mean? What journal?"

Her hands shook so that it was visible even to him; he could not take his eyes from them, though he was in a panic wondering whose journal she had read. Her voice shook as much as her hands when she at last found courage sufficient to reply. "The day you found me in the blue bedchamber—"

"My sister's bedchamber."

She swallowed hard. "Yes, Miss Darcy's bedchamber. I was not honest with you when I told you I had come looking for a book. In truth, I was returning a journal I had no right to read, and I should have admitted as much to you when you found me out."

After another, shorter silence, she added, "I am terribly, dreadfully sorry."

Georgiana's journals left in her girlhood bedchamber could have nothing of concern in them. Tedious stuff of school and friends and gowns most likely. "What exactly did you read?"

This surprised her. She raised her head, and although her eyes glimmered with tears, there was curiosity there too. "You have not read them?"

"I am not in the habit of reading the private journals of other people."

It came out sharper than he had intended and made her flush scarlet. She lowered her eyes again, but not quickly enough that he missed one fat tear rolling down her cheek. "I have certainly learnt my lesson in that regard, sir."

He looked away as she dashed her hand against her cheek. "It was likely the journal of her girlhood. I should not have imagined it held anything of great interest for anyone but Georgiana herself."

Again, Elizabeth gave him that quick, curious glance. "It did begin that way," she admitted. "The usual things of concern to a teenaged girl. I daresay that is what induced me to read further."

She smiled faintly. "It made me think of my own youth, of the days when my sisters and I were all at home. Happier times. Alas, the journal did not contain only that sort of thing."

"What else was written?"

"A story," she began, but her voice squeaked and she paused, clearing her throat. "A story of a lady who fell in love and was married to a man who…who unfortunately was not what he seemed. A man who abused his position as her husband and abused…abused her."

A chill pierced his heart as he considered that. Georgiana suffering disillusionment, pain, the solitude of a dreadful mistake… He swallowed against the pain such thoughts produced. Yet she loved him still, he thought, remembering her cries, her pleadings on Wickham's behalf.

But surely she had not written of this in her journal? She had not returned to Pemberley after her marriage; any journals or papers she had at Ramsgate were long since destroyed.

"My sister," he said, "was also a lady with an active imagination. In any case, she was only fifteen and had never been married."

"Of course." Elizabeth raised a handkerchief to her eyes, touching first the right then the left before lowering it again to her lap where she twisted it. Suddenly she stood.

"Likely you have been long desiring my absence. I shall go now and begin the preparations for my depart—"

"Sit down, Miss Bennet."

"I should have been long gone by now," she said, ignoring his directive. "Charles took ill, he had a cough and a fever, and I am sure you can imagine how that frightened me, but once he was well, your relations arrived, and I had hoped my father would write back to me, but he did not, but in any case, you may be assured that I shall go immediately."

He paused a moment to be sure her burst of speech had concluded. "Miss Bennet, pray, sit down."

This time she did, albeit with some reluctance.

"I called you in here because I have something particular to speak to you about. It does not concern any of the business…" He trailed off but saw that she understood him. "It is a matter of particular concern to you."

She raised her eyes to his, awaiting what it was he had to say. There was nothing for it but to begin.

"I went to Longbourn, on my way north from the city. I intended a meeting with your father to discuss the guardianship of Charles."

Elizabeth nodded, and Darcy had to look away from her, running his hand over his mouth.

"I sent him a letter to inform him of the need for my visit, but he did not...that is to say, I surprised him."

She nodded, her curious eyes never leaving his face. "That sounds like my father."

"A lady received me. I knew her from my previous visit, and I recollected her as an intimate friend of yours, but I could not recall her name. When I did remember her name—Mrs Collins—she corrected me." His eyes now fixed on her face, he added, "She is called Mrs Bennet now."

For a moment, Elizabeth only stared at him, then she burst into laughter, her hand quickly rising to cover her mouth. "Forgive me, Mr Darcy, but did you say...Mrs Bennet? Charlotte said she was Mrs Bennet?" This sent her off into another burst of giggles.

"She did indeed, and your father confirmed that they were lately married. I believe they said the happy event took place on the 26th of November."

"My father and Charlotte married?" Another gale of laughter, bordering on the hysterical. "Oh, Mr Darcy, I do apologise," said Elizabeth, her mirth plain on her face. "I see what happened. My father did read your letter, and they obviously decided to have some fun at your expense. It was badly done, to be sure."

Darcy reached across his desk, retrieving the letters Mr and Mrs Bennet had written to Elizabeth that he had lain there previously. He silently handed them to her, watching as her mirth slipped away and, in its place, wariness. She unfolded her father's letter first, reading through it with an impassive expression, though her complexion went very pale. When she was done, she re-folded it carefully and laid it aside. Mrs Bennet's letter was next; during this reading, tears formed in her eyes and angry blotches appeared on her cheeks. She tossed the letter carelessly onto his desk when she was through.

"Ridiculous!" she fumed. "What is the meaning of this?"

She rose with haste, her chair squawking in protest, and stalked across the room. "Charlotte Lucas? Well, she was always determined to be mistress of my mother's house. But this? Oh if my mother was still alive... She always said, 'those Lucases are very artful people, they are all for what they can get,' but this is really...this is simply beyond the pale!"

Darcy did not know what to say and so cleared his throat in what he hoped was a sympathetic way. Although he felt in some ways that he knew Elizabeth very little, somehow in this, he had known her mind. He had anticipated no little distress over this news, though what he had anticipated was still much less than what she appeared to feel about it.

"My mother is rolling in her grave, I shall assure you of that. She always dreaded giving way to Charlotte, though she believed it would be when the Collinses claimed their rightful inheritance. But this! To steal my mother's husband? It cannot be borne!"

"It does seem—"

"What does she think she will do? Bear my father an heir?" Elizabeth laughed again, but it was a bitter angry sort of laugh.

"Your father did mention that."

This seemed to shock Elizabeth more than anything and she gasped, "Oh! Oh!" several times before falling silent. Her breath came quick and hard, and he saw her struggle with her equanimity.

"A glass of wine?" he offered. "Shall I get you one?"

At her mute nod, he rose and went to the small cabinet wherein he kept some libations. He poured her a generous drink and took it back to her, urging her take her seat again and sip the wine. Elizabeth sat and took several tiny sips, barely wetting her lips, but it seemed to fortify her.

"My father has always been a self-indulgent man. He indulged himself in the pleasures of misery for many years, and now he will indulge himself in marital felicity."

Darcy nodded.

"And this is why he did not answer me? Have Charles and I been so quickly supplanted in my father's care?"

Darcy offered awkwardly, "Your father obviously cares for you deeply."

She scoffed and said nothing to that. "He does not want us home, does he?"

Her eyes fixed on his in a penetrating manner; he could not have disguised the truth even if he wished it, but he did do his best to soften it. "Your father and Mrs Bennet," he said gently, "have some plans of their own, some travel and the like. So the long and short of it is that your father has not...that is to say, at the present time, it is not within his capabilities to share the guardianship of Charles with me."

Elizabeth stared at him a moment, the look on her face one he had never seen. Shock, despair, anger, and disappointment made her eyes nearly black. Her naked agony was nearly too much to be borne. Then she covered her face with both hands and began to sob, and that was much, much worse. He watched with compassionate silence for some moments and then, recalled to his manners, withdrew a handkerchief from his pocket and pressed it into her hand.

When she had calmed herself, she sat with his handkerchief pressed to her chest while her eyes stared at nothing. "So what you really mean to tell me, is that I have nowhere to go."

A fat tear rolled down her cheek, but she continued to stare off. "Such is the lot of a spinster." She swallowed audibly. "Shuffled to and fro to whosoever will take her."

"Pemberley is your home." On her look, he repeated it. "It is. Pemberley will be your home as long as you wish to remain here."

"How can you say so?" She shook her head. "After what has passed between us? I could not, even if I wished it, tread upon your generous nature."

"I want you to stay," he repeated. "I urge you to stay."

"Charles will stay," she replied woodenly, as more tears gathered in her eyes. "I cannot drag a child about the country. Lady Catherine will help me find a position, I hope."

"You and Charles will both stay here, at Pemberley."

"I suppose I should not be so surprised," she mused. "He was always an indifferent parent. Why alter his custom now?"

Darcy had no idea what to say to that.

"I cannot stay," she said with a sudden air of resolve. "How could I when I have insulted you so unforgivably?"

"It is not unforgivable because I have already forgiven it," he replied. "Dare I ask the same?"

"What do you have to be sorry for?"

"For my conduct in the woods that day. Another lady might have demanded a proposal of marriage."

"Yes, the woods were alit with the scandal." She gave a tired wave of her hand. "Sensibilities were high for us both. It was of no consequence."

"Thank you." Except it had been of great consequence to him—but he could not say so, not now.

"This is all frightfully ironic," she said thoughtfully. "First I thought you a…a…" She gave him a helpless look, and he understood she was referring to her prior belief that he had killed his wife. "And then you had to save my life, to pull me out of the well. Then I thought I wanted nothing more than to leave Pemberley only to find I have nowhere to go. Once again, you are forced to rescue me."

She gave him a wan smile; it was half-hearted, but it was enough to enrapture him. "It is my privilege," he said, in a voice gone slightly hoarse.

They sat in silence for a time then. She was staring at some point of nothing on the floor, and he was watching her, waiting to be of use to her. A strange thought occurred to him as they sat there: he wanted to tell her everything. All that had happened, why it happened and how; the words fairly thrummed in his throat, begging for release.

Almost as if she had heard his thoughts, she said, "You may be assured that I shall not pry into your affairs; rather, I should not pry further into your affairs." She smiled at him again, and if it was a trifle forced, it was nevertheless lovely. "We are all entitled to our secrets."

An unexpected impulse arose within him. Perhaps it was the nature of their discussion or the recent events that had plagued them, but no matter why, he felt the need to tease her, to laugh with her.

Therefore did he say, "I believe I heard something in Hertfordshire about one of your secrets."

"Mine?"

"Quite the scandal, it seemed." He waggled his eyebrows mockingly.

It seemed that she too was eager to leave the heavy-laden moments behind them for a time. With delighted alarm, she cried out, "Oh no! What did you hear?"

"Something about the heir to Longbourn," said Darcy with feigned guilelessness, "a proposal gone awry which was then followed almost immediately by a second proposal to the lady's friend."

Elizabeth laughed, a true, merry laugh, her eyes sparkling. "Oh my... Well, yes, that is a bit of a story, but not one that reflects well on any of us."

LADY CATHERINE REMAINED steadfast in her resolution to cast off her daughter and went so far as to remove herself from Pemberley to Matlock. This troubled the rest of the family not at all. They threw themselves into the festive season, playing games, singing songs, and, on occasion, dancing. The music room was again rearranged, this time to remove much of the furniture so that dance sets could be formed. Elizabeth was delighted to play at such gatherings while Saye, Fitzwilliam and Darcy partnered variously with Lady Matlock, Lady Saye and Mrs Fitzwilliam.

"Oh these dances are going to shake this child right out of me," Lady Saye cried out one such evening. She nearly fell into Elizabeth's arms. "Saye," she called over one shoulder, "partner with Miss Bennet. I simply must rest. Do you mind, dearest?" The last was directed at Elizabeth who froze on her little bench at the very idea of dancing.

"I had not thought of dancing, and in any case, who would play for us?"

"Me," Lady Saye smiled brightly. "Do dance with him and wear him out for me? It is like having a puppy, one must wear them out else they keep you up all night."

"I have not had a dance these five years together." Elizabeth demurred. "I daresay I scarcely remember how."

"Then we must waltz," Saye declared. "For there is nothing required for a lady during the waltz; she need only hang on."

Mrs Fitzwilliam—perhaps sensing Elizabeth's discomfort but maybe merely seeing the suggestion of a slight to herself—immediately spoke in a disagreeable, whinging tone. "Saye, you have not yet asked me to dance. This always happens during these sorts of parties, one lady gets exhausted by the effort while the rest of us are—"

"Saye, ask your cousin to dance," Lord Matlock barked from his chair while a murmur of disagreement and soothing went up from everyone else.

Saye rolled his eyes, looking every bit a boy and not at all like a lord. "Very well!" he snapped. "Come, Anne."

"Come?" Mrs Fitzwilliam stared around the room in exaggerated astonishment. "This is how he asks me to dance? Come?"

An argument ensued briefly. Mrs Fitzwilliam began to cite old insults and injuries to her by her elder cousins while Saye proclaimed that any lady of the ton, no matter who she was, would have danced with him on the basis of a mere crook of his finger. This prompted General Fitzwilliam to observe that the ladies of the ton were notoriously indiscriminate.

Elizabeth watched them all with a mix of alarm and amusement and did not realise Darcy had moved close to her until he spoke, in a tone meant for her ear alone. "Perhaps you would dance with me."

"Oh!" She turned, seeing him standing very near the instrument. "Beg your pardon, I did not know you were standing there."

"Would you like to dance?"

"I do not know how. The waltz was still seen as far too scandalous in my days of parties and balls."

"I assure you it remains just as scandalous," said Darcy. "But evidently, society has decided we shall accept it anyway. I have been told it has been danced at Almack's for several Seasons now, and even at court just this year."

He cleared his throat, looking uncomfortable but also pleading. "As Saye so aptly put it, the lady really need only hang on."

Hold on to Mr Darcy as Mr Darcy holds on to you. The thought made her flush a little. In a low tone, she agreed to the dance, unable to look at him.

He led her towards the middle of the room where they had been dancing, and his relations paused in their bickering. "Anne," said Saye tiredly, "the set is forming. Are we or are we not going to waltz?"

"Very well," Mrs Fitzwilliam replied primly, "but I must tell you it gives me no pleasure."

"Mother," Fitzwilliam called out. "Pray do not make me remain on the side. I love a waltz."

Lady Saye had taken up her perch at the instrument and played a few chords to hasten the dancers to their places. Elizabeth glanced at Fitzwilliam and Saye, observing how they put one arm around their partners' waists and held the other up and it seemed inconceivable that she should find herself thus with Mr Darcy. But he reached for her, sliding his hand around her back, and she put her arms where they belonged, and suddenly they were moving.

It was peculiarly exhilarating to be swept along, and she immediately understood the appeal of the dance. Mr Darcy had strong arms and kept her tight as they swirled and dipped along, and it was some time before she truly appreciated the intimacy of the dance. They were very close, and he did not remove his eyes from her once.

She cleared her throat. "This dance would be a trial if one were not particularly acquainted with your partner."

"An absolute punishment if you disliked your partner," said Darcy. "Such as if you were dancing with Mr C."

"Mr C?" It took her a moment to connect what he said to her game with Charles. She blushed again and looked down. "That would be problematic indeed."

"I may only hope it is not too great a trial to waltz with me."

His eyes had remained on hers throughout the exchange and his countenance had not altered—though somehow it had. His eyes became warmer or deeper; she felt as if he was seeing her very soul. Oh this is complicated, to be so close to a man. One cannot hide a thing, so I suppose it is best not to even attempt it.

"A trial? Not at all." She smiled up at him as warmly as she could. "I am enjoying it very well indeed."

His lips curled in the barest hint of a smile, and he kept his eyes upon her, though she blushed and had to remove her gaze—only to find Saye standing very close to them. She gave a started yelp and halted immediately, making Mr Darcy halt as well.

"Saye? What in the devil—"

Saye quirked a brow at them, the look on his face unmistakably gleeful. "In case you had not noticed—and I daresay you did not—the music has ended, and therefore, the dance along with it. Unless you are setting a new fashion? Darcy, do not make this more scandalous than it already is."

TWENTY

THE LADIES RETIRED LONG BEFORE THE GENTLEMEN WERE INCLINED TO DO so, and therefore, as was once their custom, the gentleman moved to the billiards table to finish the evening. Even Lord Matlock looked alert and lively and proclaimed that although he might not play, he would certainly watch from a comfortable chair in the corner. Darcy could not deny that it was good, very good, to be within the bosom of his relations once again.

Such thoughts, however, could only be succeeded by a rush of guilt. Georgiana should be here too, except for his misdeeds. She never would be here again, and the guilt of that rested on his head. Determinedly, he pushed that notion away, choosing instead to recollect his dance with Elizabeth: the feel of her light figure within his arms, the gracefulness of her movements...the pink of her cheeks and the sparkle of her eyes. An alarming flush spread over his body, suggesting that perhaps these thoughts, too, must be set aside while in the presence of his relations.

As if he could read Darcy's mind, Saye spoke up. "Fond of the waltz, Darcy?"

Darcy did not look at him, choosing instead to study the table. "It was pleasant, though I do not think I should make a habit of it."

"I would hope not," said Saye. "Not if you intend to do it like that every time."

"What do you mean?" Darcy asked sharply.

Saye gave his father and brother an expressive look. Lord Matlock only chuckled delightedly while Fitzwilliam proclaimed, "Darcy and I have only just reconciled; I must allow at least a week before I vex him again."

"Always to me to do the heavy lifting," Saye huffed. "Darcy, you seemed terribly comfortable with Miss Bennet in your arms."

"Miss Bennet is at Pemberley to care for her nephew," Darcy replied sharply. "Nothing else."

"Come now, Darcy. We are not stupid you know. It is scarcely a day, and I can see how taken you are with her."

"I cannot recall the last time I have seen you so," Fitzwilliam added.

"Perhaps that is because I have been on another continent, hiding from the arm of justice," Darcy retorted sharply.

An immediate pall fell over the room. At length, Fitzwilliam offered, "I only mean to say that it is good to have you back, good to be welcome in your home and good to see you..."

Happy, Darcy finished in his mind. Darcy understood what he meant to say and why he could not say it. Darcy was not truly happy, not really. Certainly not in the sense that most people wished to be. "I am as happy as I ever have any reasonable expectation of being."

"Why so?" Fitzwilliam asked gently.

Darcy replied with only a look that he hoped communicated how ridiculous he found the question.

"Surely you do not intend to live as a monk for the rest of your life?" Saye asked.

"I do not consider it living like a monk so much as receiving my due," Darcy replied in a tone he hoped would forestall further enquiry. Alas, even if his cousins might have been put off by it, his uncle was not.

"Foolishness!" He declared. "You are a young man, and a wife would be just the thing to help you forget."

"I shall never forget," Darcy replied softly. "But I have more to alarm me than this."

"Mrs Younge," said Fitzwilliam.

Darcy nodded. "We have never learnt what became of her after that dreadful night, did we?"

"I believe she must be in hiding," said Fitzwilliam. "Took whatever she had and made a new life for herself."

"She believed my sister would make her rich. I cannot think she gave it up so easily."

"If there is one thing marriage has taught me," Saye interjected, "it is that when a woman is dissatisfied with her end of things, she will be dissatisfied forever if need be."

Fitzwilliam agreed with a strong nod. "And if she appears to be silent on the matter, it is only because she is waiting for the proper time to string you up by the ballocks about it."

Darcy chuckled quietly while Lord Matlock clucked worriedly and wondered aloud whether he should fear for his sons' marriages.

"Mrs Younge has a great deal to be unhappy about, I fear," said Fitzwilliam. "I did manage to confirm she and Wickham were lovers. Based on letters read and individuals spoken to, Mrs Younge believed that she and George would gain control of Georgiana's fortune and use it to begin a life together."

Saye snorted. "Did they think Darcy would be so stupid as to give it up? Fifteen is a long way off from one and twenty."

Fitzwilliam grimaced and glanced at his brother. Saye did not see it, but alas, Darcy did.

"Whatever it is, I beg you would tell me," Darcy insisted.

"I saw the marriage articles."

"What?" Lord Matlock asked. "What articles?"

"The ones where Darcy ostensibly signed to allow his fifteen-year-old sister to marry."

Darcy clenched his jaw against the expletives he wished to utter.

"But Darcy!" Lord Matlock turned towards him. "Surely you never—"

"Of course not."

"Evidently, Wickham forged them," Fitzwilliam explained. "Very well, in fact. Had Darcy's seal and made his mark better than Darcy himself could have."

"Easily enough done when two men are raised as brothers," Darcy muttered.

Fitzwilliam continued, "He was uniquely situated to perpetrate this hoax, and he took full advantage of that, writing to include the proviso that if Georgiana died before she turned one and twenty, he should receive her fortune."

"That is not uncommon," Lord Matlock said soberly. When the three gentlemen looked at him, he added, "A lady is as likely to die in childbirth as anything else. A woman who marries before the age of her majority could have one or more little ones before the childbed takes her, and then where should her money go?"

Darcy said, "I daresay they had no intention of waiting for childbirth to take her."

Fitzwilliam shook his head gravely.

"In any case, she is dead, and no claim has been made against her fortune," Saye said.

"Wickham, the person who could make such a claim, is an idiot," said Fitzwilliam. "I would be shocked if he had any comprehension of a wife or money or anything like that. But my belief is that Mrs Younge does know and remembers very clearly what she might have had."

There was a brief silence. The gentlemen all considered what this most recent intelligence meant to the situation at hand, if anything, and Saye took it upon himself to pour generous servings of Darcy's brandy for them all.

"In the years since," said Fitzwilliam. "Mrs Younge has never turned up any place that I looked. It is possible that she resolved herself to accepting the money given to her and began anew somewhere else."

"Perhaps suckling at the teat of some other poor young heiress," Saye offered.

"But the other possibility," said Darcy, "is that she is, as yet, continuing to pursue a way to get the money."

"Blackmailing you further will not work," Fitzwilliam said. "I made sure of that much."

No one asked how he had done it. As is common among good and honourable men in Fitzwilliam's position, he was acquainted with many bad and dishonourable men. He was often heard saying that when one was dealing with pigs, it was sometimes necessary to dip into the mud.

"So if she wants more money, she needs something more," Darcy surmised. "It is possible she has been seeking Georgiana herself, or perhaps she is trying to find some way to have at me."

"It is possible," Saye offered, "that she has given up the fight. It has been many years now."

"Possible," said Darcy. "But alas, not probable."

"Do you recall," Saye asked at breakfast the next morning, "when we were children and our parents would permit us to buy presents for one another for the Christmas feast?"

As he spoke, he was industriously heaping a generous amount of jam on his bread.

"What happened to your diet?" Fitzwilliam asked, agog at the amount of jam Saye intended to consume.

"My diet is succeeding splendidly. I thank you for noticing."

"I am disgusted by the amount of jam you are eating," said Fitzwilliam.

"I need it," Saye explained, taking a large, vulgar bite that caused his cheeks to bulge. "For reasons too complicated for a soldier to comprehend. Now, the presents—do you remember that?"

"I remember it," Darcy replied. "In fact, I still have a fishing knife that I daresay one of you gave me."

"So why not resurrect the old custom? Would it not be sublime? I love getting presents."

"Christmas is in two days," Lady Saye interjected. "Is there time enough?"

"Oh yes! We do it all in one day," Fitzwilliam said. "We should all go into Bakewell today, see what we can find."

"But the rule is that no more than a few shillings are spent," Saye told his wife. "We all change names, and husband and wife cannot buy for each other."

Mrs Fitzwilliam clapped her hands, her first display of real enthusiasm since her arrival. "Yes! This sounds like great fun."

Elizabeth's immediate instinct was to demur. It had occurred to her some late night in the recent past that her finances should be regarded as uncertain at best. Her father was neither prone to keeping to a budget nor concerned for his daughter's welfare. He sent irregular sums of money over the past weeks, but she had no idea if she could expect the same to continue. He had never before left her desperate, but then again, it seemed that anything was possible where Mr Bennet was concerned.

"I shall take Miss Bennet," Lady Saye announced with a big smile. "I know just the thing I should like most to give you."

"No, no," Saye scolded his wife mockingly. "We cannot say who is giving what to whom! We draw names from a hat, very secretive, and we reveal it during the feast."

"Or," said Fitzwilliam, "we might keep it a secret for an extra bit of fun?"

"Yes, let us do that!" The cries went up around the table.

"What is our limit?" Saye looked around the table while Elizabeth gathered her courage to speak. She wished to participate—it sounded quite fun, and she loved buying presents for people—but surely whatever sum they proposed would be quite beyond her touch.

"What about a crown?" asked Mr Darcy, his attention on the bread he was buttering.

A crown. Elizabeth silently sighed with relief. A crown was within her means if the others agreed to it. She waited silently while others voiced their support of a limit of one crown. Indeed, no one objected save for Mrs Fitzwilliam who rapidly whined about luxury and her entitlement to it and was just as rapidly hushed.

"One crown it is," Saye crowed, seemingly delighted with the novelty of economy. "Now we must draw names. But shall we do the children too?" It was determined that the children should also receive gifts, nothing of great value, but then again all of them were of an age to be delighted with anything.

It was surprising, how enlivening an excursion to shop could be. Everyone left the breakfast room chatting and laughing, walking back to their various apartments to change clothes or refresh themselves.

Elizabeth followed behind them all, hearing the happy voices echo in Pemberley's halls. As she walked, she looked around her. They still kept many of the rooms closed, not wishing to burn coal needlessly, but covers had been removed and curtains were opened. With the sounds of a festive season in the air, Pemberley was a charming place. The house, like the people within it, only wanted for some liveliness to revive it.

"Pleasure is an enslaving thing, is it not?" Elizabeth jumped, not realising that Mr Darcy was close behind her.

"Sorry?" She asked, glancing at him over her shoulder.

He cleared his throat. "I only mean to say that people have an inherent and undeniable need to be amused and delighted. It is almost as compelling a need as food to eat and air to breathe."

Elizabeth laughed. "I do think people have an impulse towards happiness, but why should we not? I daresay we are all given our fair share of trials and tribulations, but nothing is gained from languishing in them."

"Perhaps you are right," he said thoughtfully. "Though seen in another light…"

The others had disappeared into their bedchambers by then; Elizabeth stood alone with Mr Darcy in the hall. By his looks, it seemed he had something on his mind and, surprisingly, wished to speak of it with her.

"Yes?" She prompted gently.

He did not look at her, fastening his gaze on the carpet beneath them. "You asked me once whether I had ever made someone a promise that was so important I should rather die than fail. I believe I told you I had."

Elizabeth nodded. "As have I."

"I wonder at times whether it is an offence to those I have injured to be happy." He paused and then said hurriedly, "It does tempt me —although I am perhaps a more sober-tempered person than some, I have never been a soul to delight in misery—but it seems cruel to indulge myself."

Although it should have been obvious to her before, comprehension at last dawned on her. Mr Darcy suffered a weight of guilt for sins that were yet unknown to Elizabeth. Having lost so much of her own family, it was not a surprise. She understood very well what it was to lie awake wondering why it was not she who had died, how it was that she had been spared and for what purpose.

"I have thought so myself, wondering how I can possibly laugh or tease or worry about inconsequential matters when my dear Jane lies in the churchyard and her son does not know his mama."

Darcy smiled faintly at that.

"My father is a great fan of the Greek philosophers and there is a quote from one of his books that always stays with me. Pericles it was, or so I believe, who said, 'What you leave behind is not what is engraved in stone monuments, but what is woven into the lives of others.' I like to think that Jane has left her sweetness and goodness woven into my own tapestry, and thus, I have determined to live joyfully, that I might show the same to others. It is no offence to them, but rather a tribute."

She could see him contemplating her words for several moments.

"Georgiana," he said but then paused, seeming to gather some courage. "She was very sweet as well, a sweet child. I was looking forward to knowing the lady she would become."

He bowed then, jerky and hurried. "You will likely wish to gather your things," was all he said before he turned and left her.

THEY DREW names from a hat in the vestibule while awaiting the arrival of the carriages. Lord and Lady Matlock would join them but wished for their own conveyance, sure that his lordship would not be able to remain as long as the younger people did. Elizabeth was not sure whether it was more a source of dismay or relief to pull Darcy's name from the hat.

She would never have been able to answer for it, particularly given her initial dislike of him, but she felt a desire to find something that would bring him the happiness he sorely lacked. She had seen him smile on rare occasions, and to be the inducement for such a smile would be a wonderful thing.

They were a merry party on their way to Bakewell, with much laughter and conversation. The market was bustling; fair weather and the proximity of Christmas had brought many people from their homes to shop.

Saye had abandoned them straightaway for some concern of his own, and Darcy begged them to excuse him for a few minutes. The three ladies walked through the town, Fitzwilliam loosely attending them as they paused over ribbons and other wares in the shops. Fitzwilliam soon looked like he wished he had absconded with the other gentlemen.

"See this fabric?" Mrs Fitzwilliam caressed a bolt of heavy maroon silk. "I daresay it should make up very nicely for me."

"It would suit you admirably, my dear," said Fitzwilliam but Elizabeth noticed that his tone was one of a man who has given the expected reply many times over.

"You do not think it would make me look tan?"

"How would it make you look tan?" Saye had returned just in time to torment his sister-in-law. "I have eaten blancmange with better colour than yours."

Mrs Fitzwilliam paid no attention to him. "I think an overdress picked out in gold thread—"

"Would look hideous," Saye opined, tapping the material with one gloved finger. "There is one thing this fabric is suited for, and that is ugly curtains."

"A curtain?" Mrs Fitzwilliam gave him an aggrieved look while his wife issued a playful swat to his arm.

"Not just any curtains." He smirked. "Ugly curtains. The kind of curtains one hangs in the guest apartment to be sure the guest does not stay too long."

Fitzwilliam roared with laughter, earning a disgusted look from his wife. With a pinched, vexed little face, she said, "Saye, you know nothing of ladies' fashions."

"I know more than you," Saye informed her blithely. "When was the last time you were in Paris?"

"You know that my health has always been far too indifferent to entertain the possibility of frivolous travel."

Saye smiled in a vexingly superior way. "Then I daresay you should do best to defer to my judgment. This, madam, is a curtain."

As the two continued to bicker, with Fitzwilliam quickly offering his own appeasing commentary, the door to the shop opened, and a lady walked through; behind that lady was Mrs Green. Elizabeth was delighted to see her friend, having been unable to call on her since the arrival of Mr Darcy's relations at Pemberley.

"Mrs Green!" She exclaimed. "How good—"

To her deepest shock and consternation, at the sound of her voice, her friend startled. In the work of a moment, she turned on her heel, exiting the shop as quickly as she had entered it.

Elizabeth could not account for such a response, and before she thought of it overmuch, she was pursuing the lady onto the street. "I beg your pardon," she called after her, watching as her slender friend went weaving through the crowd. "Mrs Green?"

Passers-by stared as Elizabeth pushed by them, moving quicker and quicker in pursuit of her friend. Once she believed she saw her look behind her, straight at Elizabeth, and Elizabeth called out to her. Then, in the blink of an eye, she lost her. Mrs Green had somehow managed to disappear into the populace, leaving nothing but a baffled and slightly sad friend behind her.

Have I angered her in some way? Elizabeth waited some moments, scanning the crowd in hopes of seeing her again, but it was not to be. She turned and walked slowly back to the shop, her concerns for her friend heavy on her mind.

When she entered the shop again, it was to find that there was an agreed-upon scheme of dividing themselves. "'Tis difficult to purchase secret presents when we are all together," Saye informed her. "I am already done, so I shall escort you unless you have some objection?"

"Of course not, my lord." Elizabeth smiled through her consternation, resolving to put it behind her for now.

They set off wandering about the streets. Elizabeth looked at this and that—a toothpick case, a snuff-box, some fine linen she idly considered making into handkerchiefs for him—but nothing met her approval. She appreciated the diversion from her troublesome thoughts that kept intruding upon her, persistent in reminding her that Mrs Green had snubbed her.

"Something for Darcy?" Saye asked finally.

"What? Um, ah, no." But nevertheless, she blushed scarlet

Saye rolled his eyes. "I knew it must be either him or me, and as you did not object to travelling about with me, I surmised it was him. But the things you are looking at are all wrong."

"I have never bought a present for a man before."

"Never?"

Elizabeth shook her head. "And then to find something for Mr Darcy, a man who already has so much! I fear the task will prove impossible."

Saye stood for a moment, peering at her closely. He seemed to hold some secret to himself, repressing a grin until at last, he asked, "How adventurous are you?"

"Why?"

"I know just the thing, but you will have to trust me."

"Can you tell me—" Her words ended abruptly as Saye took hold of her elbow and began to move her forcefully and quickly through the market.

Elizabeth found herself in an almost-trot, torn between laughing and gasping for breath. "Where are we going?"

"No more questions!" Saye pulled them between two buildings that looked like a person could scarcely fit between them, all the while urging her to hurry. The little alleyway stank of rotted fish and decay. Elizabeth wrinkled her nose against it, but it was no good; she still choked and coughed as they pressed forward into ever-deepening shadows.

They stopped in front of a door made of rotted planks that Saye pushed open with his foot. He nudged Elizabeth ahead of him into a small room, dark and dank, wherein sat a group of men—labourers it seemed—who were engaged in drinking very heavily. Gin. She knew well the smell of it by now, courtesy of Lady Catherine.

The air was close and hot, and the scent of gin mixed with the reek of many unwashed men. Saye walked in front of her, and she shrank behind him murmuring into his ear, "Saye, I cannot be in here. Surely there is nothing here Mr Darcy would wish to purchase."

He did not listen, putting his hands on his hips as the men regarded them warily. At last Saye found who he sought, crying out, "Gertie, you fat rascal! Come meet me!"

A man, thin to the point of emaciation, rose slowly from where he had been sitting on half a barrel in the deepest recesses of the room. He strolled towards Saye while the other men watched them from hooded eyes. Elizabeth noticed that one man had laid his hand on a dagger at his side and she shivered.

"Well if it ain't the prince," said the thin man—Gertie presumably. "You han't been by of late, thought the comfort piece must have tied you down."

"Oh, she does," Saye replied amiably. "But she sets me free once she's done with me."

This made all the men roar, though Elizabeth did not understand the joke. The man with the dagger relaxed, and the others went back to their own conversations. She released her breath gratefully.

"Have you The Widow?" Saye asked. "I need the best bottle you have."

"I do," said Gertie and named a sum that was well above a crown. Elizabeth had no idea what "the widow" was or why she commanded such a price, but she was well pleased to say thank you but no and quit the horrid place. Saye, however, would not hear of it.

A violent row ensued. Saye accused Gertie of being a thief and a whore, and Gertie told Saye to take a golden pickaxe and shove it right up his golden— But he stopped then in some deference to Elizabeth's presence, or so she supposed. In any case, she believed she could guess at the remainder of his insult.

At last, after several rounds of vicious argument, Gertie took Elizabeth's crown and disappeared into an adjoining room, one that appeared even darker and smaller than the first. He returned with a dark bottle bearing a jonquil-coloured label and handed it to Elizabeth for inspection.

Confused, she took it, reading the label aloud. "Veuve-Clicquot. Champagne." From the corner of her eye, Elizabeth saw Saye shoving a fistful of coins at Gertie. She turned quickly, "My lord! I cannot allow you to give more than is the prescribed amount, particularly when I cannot pay—"

Entirely unabashed, he pressed his gloved finger to her lips. "Shhhhh."

He turned and bowed to Gertie. Gertie replied by curtseying, causing all the men to roar again with laughter. "Gertie, you are a fine gentleman, and we thank you kindly." He took Elizabeth's arm then and almost forcibly propelled her from the horrible room.

The alley was positively fresh by comparison, and when they at last emerged into the marketplace, Elizabeth breathed deeply, relishing in the crisp air before turning to Saye for some explanation. Saye scolded her in a somewhat indifferent manner. "Gertie is a great friend of mine. Not only is his wife increasing but his mistress as well. He needs the money, so consider it well done."

"But I cannot repay you, sir. I am, as you know, in limited circumstances."

"Get Darcy drunk on it; that will be repayment enough."

TWENTY-ONE

Everyone had an air of mischievous delight when they convened at the bake shop, having assigned their mysterious parcels to the footmen who had accompanied them for just that purpose.

"It is a truth universally acknowledged," announced Fitzwilliam, "that shopping is best followed by eating. Shall we?" He gestured to the bakers behind him and cries of assent went up.

"I believe almost all of Derbyshire must be in here," said Mr Darcy in low tones. "They must be good bakers."

"They are." Elizabeth smiled over her shoulder at him. "Even Lady Catherine could not dislike them although she thought I was too friendly with the shop girl."

"I am sure you were," said Mr Darcy with a slight smile. "I have noticed that about you; that you are as kind to a pauper as you are to a king."

Elizabeth blushed, thankful for the crowds that somewhat disguised her awkwardness. "I have always believed that how you treat people is more a reflection of your own character than that of another."

They reached some little tables where they would enjoy their repast, and Mr Darcy helped her sit as Fitzwilliam and Saye were both assisting their wives. Nearly as soon as they sat, Mrs Giles appeared, full of deference and awe and eager to please them all.

The shop was exceedingly busy—it seemed that even the straitened circumstances of the area would not dampen enthusiasm for the festive season. The air was close and warm, and the small space was filled with a multitude of conversations; thus it was that Elizabeth nearly missed it when Mrs Giles leant into her and murmured, "There be havercakes right in the back."

Elizabeth nodded. "Havercakes? Oh, no, I think I shall have—"

"Oh, but you must try a true Loxley havercake. I think you should like 'em very well, miss."

Elizabeth turned to look at Mrs Giles, whose broad, shiny face pleaded for her to acquiesce. Elizabeth smiled warmly. "Pray, do bring me a true Loxley havercake."

"Come in the back with me," Mrs Giles urged. "They taste best when they are right off the rack."

Mr Darcy was examining a newspaper while Fitzwilliam argued with Mrs Fitzwilliam about something in hushed, hissing tones and Saye looked on with interest. "Excuse me," Elizabeth said to the table at large. Mr Darcy was quick to rise, assisting her from the chair he had given her only moments earlier.

"I shall not be a moment," she told him, then turned to follow Mrs Giles back a long hall into the kitchen.

Somehow, the kitchens were even hotter and busier than the shop itself. There were several bakers at work kneading and mixing, while a bevy of young girls buzzed about scooping flour and scrubbing pans. "We are making the bread for distributing with the soup," Mrs Giles announced proudly. "Lady Catherine de Bourgh, and none other, feeding those less fortunate."

Mrs Giles seemed to watch Elizabeth very carefully as she spoke. "I have much to thank her for."

"Do you?"

In rushed and hushed tones, Mrs Giles said, "Aye. I should not have found myself able to marry for many years were it not for her.

She gave me a sum so Mr Giles could take me, else I should still be in the scullery at Halliday Abbey."

Elizabeth wrinkled her brow. It seemed an unlikely tale as Lady Catherine had been so disgusted by her own friendliness to Mrs Giles on their prior visit. "Why would she do that? Was she acquainted with you in some way?"

There was a shout then and several people bustled through with arms heavily laden with pans and bread loaves. "Mrs Giles," a man called out. Elizabeth recognised him as her husband.

"I need to return to the front of the shop," Mrs Giles whispered. She fumbled in her apron for a moment, then thrust a small bundle in Elizabeth's direction. "Here."

"What is this?"

"Something you might want," Mrs Giles said, her words coming still quicker as she took Elizabeth's arm, almost pushing her out of the kitchen. "I thought you should know what to do with it."

Know what to do with it? "What is it?"

"Don't open it until ye leave; pray, do me this much." Mrs Giles was nearly pushing Elizabeth out the door. No more could be said. Mrs Giles curtseyed and left Elizabeth by the door with the small bundle in her hand and confusion in her mind.

She walked back to the table slowly, bemused by the strangeness of the whole thing but soon decided to put it away from her mind until she was back in her own bedchamber at Pemberley. Likely a little gift to me. Perhaps she did not wish the others to see? But why would she give me a gift?

It was not until the shopping party had returned to Pemberley and Elizabeth was alone in her bedchamber that she unwrapped Mrs Giles's little parcel. Inside was a pin—an ordinary little pin, something like a schoolgirl might wear on her cloak—fashioned in the shape of a lily.

"Pretty little thing," Elizabeth mused aloud while turning it over and examining it. It held no clues as to its meaning or purpose, and Elizabeth soon decided there was nothing to be made of it but mere friendship.

CHRISTMAS DAY dawned in a way none of them had seen for quite some time: warm and fair. Darcy stood at the window of his breakfast room, a lightness in his being that did not know he even deserved, and he wondered whether it was a harbinger of happier days to come. Certainly, the land was still dirty and blighted, the rivers swollen and brown, and the fields barren, but where there was sunlight, there was hope. One could almost imagine on such a day the return of verdure, singing birds, and frolicking game.

The rest of the family were quick to join him—Fitzwilliam first, followed by Miss Bennet and Lord and Lady Matlock. Saye and Lady Saye were last to arrive, save for Anne. Christmas or not, Anne would remain abed most of the day.

"The children have heard that there are to be gifts," said Miss Bennet. "They are scarcely able to contain themselves for the excitement."

Miss Bennet almost looked like a child herself, her eyes sparkling and her cheeks nicely rosy. My Christmas present to myself is that I shall admire her unabashedly today. And in his heart was a feeling much like being outdoors, warmth basking on the muddy ruination and trying to return it to what it once was.

When everyone had their plates full, Darcy cleared his throat. They all paused and looked at him expectantly.

"I have decided something that I think will be for the good for us all," he said. Unexpectedly, his voice trembled, but he pretended not to notice. The gazes around the table were fixed on him, and he found himself seeking Miss Bennet's eyes. She was watching him with a compassionate gaze although she could have no idea what he intended to say, and he drew strength from that.

"I intend to put a marker in the churchyard for Georgiana."

Silence fell immediately as he had expected it would. His eyes slid from face to face, seeing their reactions. Fitzwilliam grew immediately sober, and Saye looked thoughtful. Lord Matlock nodded once, very firmly, and Lady Matlock smiled encouragingly, though she raised her handkerchief to press into the corners of her eyes.

Fitzwilliam was first to speak. "I daresay it is time."

A chorus of assent went up around the table, but Darcy could only watch Miss Bennet. What did she think of it? Did she wonder at it all? Having made the announcement in her presence, Darcy knew an explanation must be proffered, and he intended to give her one. As terrifying and exhilarating as it might be, he needed to tell her, to unburden himself. Living with the dread of discovery had proven painfully exhausting.

There was some little discussion thereafter—what sort of marker, would he hold a ceremony, what would be written on the stone—but it died down soon enough. Miss Bennet was silent throughout.

"And when shall we do presents?" Saye asked as the conversation came to its natural conclusion. "Immediately if not sooner is my hope."

"Miss Bennet? What did your family do? Did you give gifts to your sisters?" Lady Saye asked kindly and at once all eyes were on Elizabeth, who blushed.

"No, we never exchanged gifts, only dinner followed by games and songs. The neighbours generally visited one another. My father used to have a sleigh, and he would take us out in it if we had snow."

"Sounds charming," said Fitzwilliam. "Too bad we do not have snow. Darcy, do you still have that ancient sleigh of yours? That thing was enormous."

"Quite large," Darcy agreed. "Snow is definitely required, else I should kill my horses."

Saye clapped his hands together just once. "Very well. No sleigh. What I am hearing is that we shall open our presents immediately—"

"Immediately after dinner," Fitzwilliam interjected. Saye protested vigorously but was forced to concede by the others. An afternoon of music and games and other amusements was decided on. Everyone rose, intent on quitting the breakfast room and going on with the day. Darcy watched them all leave, hoping Elizabeth would lag behind. She obliged his silent entreaty, lingering over one last swallow of tea before rising and carefully placing her napkin on the table.

As the door swung closed behind Lord Matlock, Darcy spoke, "Miss Bennet? I wonder whether I might prevail upon you to take a walk."

"That sounds lovely."

He held out his hand to stop her. "I...if you would oblige me, I have something I wish to discuss with you."

Her eyes went wide, and her hand rose to touch the curls at the nape of her neck. Her habit, he had noticed, when she was anxious.

"No cause for alarm," he reassured her.

She forced a small smile. "I immediately wondered what other of my relations might have married my friends and required you to give the news."

"No, not that. I wanted to tell you about my sister. That is, if you wish to hear it."

Her eyes searched his face, and he forced himself to be calm. "I need a minute to gather my things," she said at last.

True to her word, she was in the vestibule before he had even enough time to tell Mrs Reynolds their plan. He was still walking down the hall when he saw her standing in a serviceable woollen overcoat, her hands in gloves that had seen better days, and a bonnet that was likely as old as the gloves. The pure beauty and goodness of her was almost too much to be borne. He stopped in his tracks.

I cannot tell her. What will she think of me?

She saw him and smiled, taking one small step towards the door, and he knew his fate was sealed. *I must tell her. I can bear the weight of my secrets no more.*

He offered his arm silently, and she took it. They exited the house speaking of the most commonplace of things: how shocking to see the sun, how excited were the children, and how quickly the month of December had passed. She snuck small glances in his direction when she believed he was not looking, and at last, he said, "You likely wonder why, after so long an effort at secrecy, I have decided to confide in you."

"Yes, I do."

"Secrets are dreadful things. The uncertainty, the worry, and the fear that someone might find out are exceedingly weighty. I used to think that the worst possibility was for someone to know, for the Darcy name to be shaded. But now I simply cannot live this lie any longer, not when it comes to you, who are living in my very household. You must know even if...even if I suspect you will think me the most pitiable excuse of a gentleman there ever was once you know of it."

To his relief, she did not reassure him with pretty words and falsehoods.

"Mr Darcy, permit me to say just one thing to you. I must thank you for your unexampled kindness—"

"No, I am not kind, not really."

"But you are." She stopped and turned to him, earnestness shining from her dark eyes. "I have seen the goodness in you, especially for your kindness to me and to Charles, and I have always believed that goodness will always be the victor over evil. So whatever has been done or left undone in your past, know that I shall forgive it."

"Do not speak so," he said at once. "You know not the manner of evil I shall tell you."

"If you are ready to tell it, then I am ready to hear it."

They walked again, her arm still upon his, her step matching his, even their breath coming at the same pace. Telling her began like falling from a precipice; he plunged heedlessly into it, terrified and uncertain, in the middle before he knew he had begun.

"In '11," he began, "my sister was fifteen years of age. She was in school but she was finished with it. I might have wished for another year for her, but many of her friends were leaving and she begged to be allowed to leave too."

"For a girl of fifteen," said Elizabeth, "the fact that her friends are doing it is reason enough for nearly anything."

"Just so," he agreed. "However, not only did she want to leave school, but she also wished to make a visit to the seaside—Ramsgate specifically. Some of the young ladies were taking houses with their various companions, and Georgiana wanted to do likewise. Haply, I had just learnt of a woman in need of a situation, a Mrs Younge. Very well regarded, excellent references, and known among the better families of Derbyshire because she had grown up in Derby.

"It is not my custom to be so free with her care, but Mrs Younge was very well recommended and seemed far older than her years."

"How old is she?" Elizabeth asked.

"The same age as I, but there was a sobriety in her appearance that inspired trust. She was a larger woman, nearly as tall as Lady Catherine, and somewhat plump. I had not the least doubt that she could manage Georgiana and shield her from harm."

They paused a moment, Darcy uncertain which path might interest Elizabeth the most. How he longed to show her Pemberley in all its glory! The rare sunlight notwithstanding, the land was still bleak, muddy, and raw. But Elizabeth wished to remain in the sun, it seemed, so off they went into the barren remnants of his mother's rose gardens.

"Alas, it was not long before I suspected I had made an error. I cannot really say what it was exactly—her letters to me showed Georgiana was having as much wholesome enjoyment as any lady should expect to—but I grew uneasy. I tried to reason it away, requesting assurances from her in my letters, but it would not do. I continued to feel that sense of something amiss, I and soon decided nothing else would do but to visit her at Ramsgate and see how things were for myself.

"Unfortunately, I found myself detained along the way." Darcy paused, the memory of his failures stinging at him. Elizabeth looked up at him, so trusting, so pure. It astonished him that he could walk side by side with her and his iniquity could co-exist with her innocence.

"There was a lady," he said abruptly, turning his gaze downward to avoid hers. "She was at some house party in Lancashire, and Fitzwilliam urged me to go there with him rather than to Ramsgate. He ascribed my feelings to unreasonable suspicion, and I soon believed him—mostly because I wished to. I forgot my duty, and so it was, that when I had had my share of the diversion in Lancashire and went on to Ramsgate, my sister was"—his voice cracked—"gone."

Elizabeth murmured something; he knew not what. Some syllables of dismay no doubt.

"In fact, by the time I arrived, she had been gone for several weeks. No note, no forwarding address, no sign of anything to do with her. So began the worst months of my life."

He inhaled deeply, using his walking stick to push some debris out of their way on the path. "I shall not relate all the money and time spent, the visits to this town or that. Such details do not signify.

All that truly did signify was that I soon learnt she had eloped, and not long after that, I discovered who her suitor was."

"Did you know him?"

"I did," said Darcy quietly. "I still do. He is a man known to me my entire life long, raised up next to me like a brother, given a gentleman's education although he was but the son of my father's steward. Yes, I knew him very well indeed. His name is George Wickham. You have seen him as the man who roams about the countryside hereabouts."

"The lunatic?" Elizabeth's mouth dropped into a perfect, round expression of surprise. "But he is...your sister eloped with him?"

"He is an idiot now," Darcy said glumly. "But then he was charming and handsome, and my poor sister likely thought he was in love with her. Ladies were always in love with Wickham, high-born and low. He had the gift of being uniformly pleasing to all he met, though it was nothing more than an illusion. Inside, he was black as night.

"We searched for them everywhere, and I soon realised he was keeping himself a few steps ahead of us, moving from situation to situation, so I decided that I would do as I must to make him come to me, to flush him out, if you will."

"How did you do that?"

"Her fortune was no doubt his object from the start, and I cut them off. It was a risk; I did fear for her abandonment. But I was out of ideas by then. As I suspected, it soon brought him to me directly."

Coming to this part of the narrative made him shake. The rage was still there, coupled with sorrow and anguish for what had followed. It required some effort, but he did manage to speak calmly.

"He surprised me in London one evening when I was unwisely alone after nightfall. It was raining and the streets were mostly deserted, as I daresay was his wish. I knew he was desperate, and he had clearly taken some effort to seclude me, so I was glad I carried my pistol in my jacket as sometimes I do.

"He was in a hack chaise and bid me join him. We went to a filthy small house on Wapping Lane down near the docks, and therein was my sister." Darcy closed his eyes a moment against the wash of pain that the memory of her, bruised, bedraggled, and fearful, brought him.

"The sight of her made me wish to kill him right then and there, I was enraged from the start. Then he spoke to her, speaking like a lover, but I could hear the mocking in his tone. He said, 'Speak sense to your brother, Mrs Wickham,' and it was all I could do not to pull my pistol on him right then."

"So your sister was married?"

"So it seemed at the time, but we learned later, she was not. The entire marriage ceremony was a hoax performed by some man who had no authority whatsoever. She believed she was married, but she never really was.

"Wickham and I began to argue. He uttered every manner of oath and foul invective against her and me, and she sobbed in a corner while I vented my spleen against him. He said unspeakable things, things he had done to her, things he would do if he did not get her fortune, but he did not persuade me. I was firm in my righteous anger and would not bend. As generally happens in such cases, things became violent.

"The recollection is a jumble to me now—Georgiana screaming, Wickham and I fighting. In the course of things, he managed to stab me with a small blade he had on him; in reply, I withdrew my pistol. He ran out of the door, into the street, and I went after him.

"Likely he believed I could not shoot him out in the open like that, and I daresay I would not. But we continued our battle down by the water, and somewhere in the course of our struggle, I struck his head against a wooden post.

"He lost consciousness immediately and fell, then suddenly, he slipped from my hands. I was shocked to see that the blow, such as it was, had rendered him helpless, and in my shock, I allowed him to fall over the edge of the dock into the water below." Darcy sighed again very deeply and looked over at Elizabeth. "I did not attempt to save him. God help me, I turned and walked back to the house."

What she thought of that, he knew not for she made no comment, only continued to walk beside him. At length, Darcy continued the vile story.

"When I returned to the house, Georgiana was gone. There was, in her place, a letter ordering me to pay thirty thousand pounds for her safe return."

Elizabeth halted in her steps, turning to look at him. "Who wrote the letter? Did you know?"

"I did. The letter came from Mrs Younge. I had suspected for some time that she and Wickham had worked together to defraud my sister, though I could never have imagined anything like this. I believe she and Wickham were lovers; the entirety of this scheme was no doubt concocted to obtain Georgiana's fortune, after which, she would have been abandoned so they could go off together, begin a life together."

"Such evil!"

Darcy could hear the shock in her voice yet knew he had not told her the worst of it. He considered for a moment whether he should spare her, but something in him urged a full confession.

"There is more," he said, his voice shaking. Tears sprung into his eyes, but he did no more than blink them away. "With the letter was…was something quite horrible. Something I…I can scarcely bear to think of, though there have been weeks, months, where I dreamt of little else."

Elizabeth dropped her hand from his arm, and he felt the achingly sweet consolation of her reaching for his hand, weaving her fingers into his and pulling close to his side. It made the ache within him that much more poignant.

His voice was hoarse, and he could scarcely utter the words, but he forced himself to tell her. "It was her finger. She was a talented musician and Mrs Younge…"

Elizabeth whispered something beside him, and although it was low, he heard the horror in her voice. Darcy found he could not go on. Already the tears were stinging his eyes threatening to spill over, and nausea churned within him just remembering it. He heard a small sniff beside him and presumed to imagine that Elizabeth was also affected.

They walked for several minutes until he could speak again. "I was given three days and the arrangements for the money were detailed to me, but I was proud and arrogant even in this, my deepest fear and sorrow. I believed I could outwit her, and so, with

Fitzwilliam's assistance, I set up a trap. We involved several able men that he knew, and we believed we had the matter well in hand.

"The day arrived, and the meeting was set. Then…somehow it all went off. Mrs Younge never came, it all just went sour. My sister disappeared, and Mrs Younge with her." Darcy shook his head. "Foolish, foolish pride. What is money when one might have had a beloved sister safe at home?

"But I was stupid, eaten up with pride, and now, here I am, my sister having suffered every manner of torture and torment, with nothing but my pride to console me."

His breath was fast and his heart pounded so loudly that he nearly missed her next words, softly spoken as they were.

"You were right to be angry."

Incredulous, he turned to her. "How can you say so? Do you not see what my bile has wrought?"

She reached out to him, laying her hand on his arm and squeezing him gently. "They betrayed you, did they not? A man who called himself your friend, a woman who assumed the role of confidante, and even a sister who had been raised to protect herself from such as this. It was a deep betrayal on all fronts, and I do not blame you a bit for your anger."

He could not reply to her. He stood staring at her, his breath coming fast, his eyes locked onto the sympathy in her eyes, and somewhere within him, the tight iron band that had encased his chest for all of these years was loosened. She understood it better than he did himself. She had neatly captured that dark kernel within his soul, the bit that was angry with poor Georgiana for having brought this upon them, and she accepted and forgave it. He might have wept were it not for the joy in it.

Somehow he found her in his arms, pressed tightly against his chest with every bit of strength he possessed. "Yes," he said. "Yes."

And then she tilted her face up towards his, rose up on her toes, and kissed him gently on the lips.

TWENTY-TWO

FOR A BRIEF MOMENT, SHE WAS HORRIFIED BY HER BRAZENNESS. EVEN AS she felt her lips pressed against his, she doubted herself. Had she really just kissed him?

But soon her shame was forgotten as he pulled her to him so fiercely she could not have breathed if she wished it. His hands—his large, hot hands—were splayed out over her back, pressing her close, and she had nothing to do but to make their clasp even tighter by winding her arms around his neck. Her bonnet went crazily askew as he moved one hand up to thrust into her hair.

He kissed her with such hunger it was nearly frightening; he seemed to wish to mould himself to her, to brand and own her with his lips. She found she liked it almost as much as it scared her. Soon, too soon, his kisses slowed, became less fevered yet, somehow, still more sweet. He seemed unable to remove his lips from her, gently touching them to her cheeks, her forehead, even her nose, over and over again.

"You must know how I feel about you," he murmured.

She laughed, breathless and surprised. "No, I confess I...I do not."

"Elizabeth." He sighed it more than said it, his forehead resting against hers. "I love you. I do truly love you, and that is why I—"

Although her soul thrilled at his words, she was alarmed by his tone, a tone that contradicted the joy that should come with such words.

"What?" she asked, reaching with one hand to touch his cheek. "Do you think I do not—"

He pulled back. "How can I ever be worthy of you? How could I possibly make you happy? Would I merely destroy you? Would it not be the most unselfish, loving thing to do to order you away from me?"

"No," she cried out. "Because I have no wish to be away from you."

"You must understand," he said with great earnestness. "I do not know if I can be a husband, a father. I wish to, I want to desperately, but it is probable I shall fail as miserably as I failed my sister. I cannot bear it. I cannot bear to bring you misery."

He stepped back and her arms fell away, hanging empty by her sides.

"I know you feel like this now," she said softly. "But you will change. Your heart will heal, you will go on. As painful as it seems, you will, and I shall help you do it."

"You have already helped me more than you will ever know," he said, taking her again into his arms. "You made me realise that despite the fact Georgiana was dead, I am not, and I can make a new life."

Conversation was forgotten then as they engaged in a far more agreeable occupation. At length, Elizabeth pulled back, murmuring, "I wonder whether the others will worry about what has become of us, having been gone so long."

"They will not worry, but Saye will perhaps indulge himself in some plot to embarrass us, and thus, it is best to return. I am accustomed to him, but I do not like him to tease you."

They set off then, Elizabeth's hand tucked happily in Darcy's arm. Her mind was nearly completely filled with the happiness she found in him. A small part of her, however, could not forget the things she had found—the inconsistencies, so to speak, in the story.

"May I ask just one thing?"

"You may ask anything," he replied. "You know the worst of it; I have nothing to hide from you."

That earned a smile from her. "Are you satisfied beyond doubt that your sister is not alive? I wondered because of the—"

"Elizabeth." He shook his head. "Do you know what the worst part of hope is?"

She regarded him expectantly.

"Hope lives hand-in-hand with despair," he said. "I have come to realise that it is my worst enemy in all of this. As long as I cling to the false hope that she is alive and will somehow emerge from all of this, I cannot rid myself of the despair and the guilt that accompany me. It is time."

He inhaled deeply. "Five years. Five long years filled with fruitless searches. It is time to let it all pass and acknowledge what has been true all along: she is dead. I shall place a marker in her honour, and I shall grieve her as she deserves to be grieved, and in so doing, I pray I shall heal. This chapter will be closed."

Elizabeth glanced up at him, seeing the resolution on his countenance. He needed to accept that his sister had died—now, before useless hope and regret drove him mad.

"You are right," was all she said.

ELIZABETH LAY awake in her bed long into the dark night, the festivities of the day having exhausted her body but not her mind.

The exchanging of gifts had been a rousing success, among the children most particularly. Charles was delighted to receive little tin soldiers and a new book from his Grandfather Bennet, as well as a cricket bat and ball from Darcy along with the promise to teach him to play. Elizabeth had been surprised that Darcy remembered him in such a way—surprised and pleased. She had knitted all the children new, thick woollen stockings and enclosed within each pair an orange, candy, and a few coins.

For the adults, there was equal delight, no matter what the gift. Elizabeth had received from Lady Saye a beautiful new fan and was still admiring it when Darcy opened his gift from her.

"Veuve-Clicquot," he said in a flat voice that seemed to conceal some amusement. "Thank you, Miss Bennet. I must admit, it is a favourite of mine."

She smiled. "I was well advised, then."

"Well advised, perhaps, but not well chaperoned." He turned to Saye. "You did not take her there, did you? Not among those dreadful—"

"Who Gertie? He is as good a gentleman as anyone," Saye protested. "It was the middle of the day. Miss Bennet withstood no harm to either her person or her reputation."

"If you ever take her there again," said Darcy calmly, "I shall harm your person, I assure you."

Saye shrugged. "So? Are we going to have some?"

Very deliberately, Darcy had placed the bottle behind him. "I shall save it."

"Save it? For what? 'Tis Christmas, as good an occasion as any. Come Darcy, let us drink up."

"No."

Elizabeth nearly laughed aloud seeing Saye with an expression on his face like a child denied a treat and Darcy, looking smug and aloof, being the one to deny it. Even now, lying in her bed, it made her smile to think of it.

It was not until much later in the evening, after they had all gathered around the pianoforte to sing carols and played games of the season, that Darcy whispered to her, "You and I shall have this on some occasion special to us both."

And she smiled then and now, thinking what that occasion might be. An engagement? It was what she hoped for, and she hoped he did too.

Of course, we might also drink it in celebration of finding Miss Darcy. The idea popped right into her head unbidden.

Elizabeth could not quite believe that Miss Darcy had died. There were too many oddities, too much folly, surrounding the circumstances of her disappearance to accept it. It does not make sense, she continued to tell herself. We are adding two and two and getting three. Somewhere there are extra bits that have not been considered fully.

She chuckled softly at herself. Would her daring never cease? Her first attempt at solving the mysteries of Pemberley led her to accuse Mr Darcy of killing his wife, thereby making an utter fool of herself. And now?

Asking a few questions could not hurt, she reasoned. She would just need to avoid asking Darcy; she did not wish to destroy his attempt at acceptance and his path to healing his wounded heart.

Knowing that General Fitzwilliam was awake with the dawn, Elizabeth went into the breakfast parlour at a very early hour the next day. She had the good fortune to find Fitzwilliam seated with a nearly empty plate and the newspapers spread out around him. He rose quickly to help her sit in the chair next to his. "You are an early riser."

"As are you."

"Military life," he said ruefully. "You can leave the military, but it never leaves you, or so I have been told."

"I am glad to find you alone. I was wondering whether you would answer some questions for me."

"I daresay I could," he said cautiously. "Questions about what?"

Elizabeth shifted in her chair. "Mr Darcy, as you might know, has confided in me regarding the events surrounding the death of his sister."

Fitzwilliam nodded, his eyes never leaving her. "Do you have some questions about the veracity of the account?"

"I do not doubt what I was told, but I do have some questions." Elizabeth took a deep breath. "Mostly I wondered…is it possible that Miss Darcy did not die after all?"

Fitzwilliam did not shrink from the question nor did he appear surprised to receive it. He took a sip of his drink and asked, "Why do you think so?"

She recognised it for what it was—an attempt to make her talk more, perhaps revealing something of herself to him. Therefore, she turned it about on him, replying with, "Likely the same reasons you have thought it yourself."

He threw back his head and laughed. "Well done, Miss Bennet. No old interrogation tricks for you then."

He leant back in his chair, rubbing his face for a moment. "Darcy no doubt told you of Mrs Younge and what she did to Georgiana, how she asked for a ransom."

"He did," said Elizabeth. "And then how, inexplicably, it all went off."

"Yes," Fitzwilliam confirmed. "So our first conclusion— and the most likely one—is that the object ransomed—Georgiana—got away from her either through death or escape."

"Could Mrs Younge have killed her?" Elizabeth asked.

"It might have been accidental," Fitzwilliam replied. "Georgiana might have been more grievously injured than we knew, or Mrs Younge, on learning of Wickham's fate, might have wished to hurt her more."

It was a plausible sequence of events. Elizabeth had considered it as well. Perhaps Mrs Younge in her furious zeal had injured poor Miss Darcy mortally. "But could she have escaped?"

"It was naturally our hope, and to that end, we searched diligently for her these past years. No sign of either her or Mrs Younge has ever been found."

"None?"

He shook his head. "I looked, I hired people to look, I used men under my command to look. There was no sign of her, not then and not now."

"It seems very strange."

"You must understand, Miss Bennet, a lady such as Georgiana was unlikely to have made it far without the assistance of family or friends. She was witty in the way gently bred ladies were supposed to be; that is to say, she spoke good French and could arrange a dinner party to perfection. But the skills to survive against people like that? No, not at all. She had no access to money or her possessions, and she was very, very young." He sighed. "Fifteen. Have you ever noticed, Miss Bennet, that if danger will befall a lady, it usually happens when she is fifteen or sixteen? A dangerous age for a young lady in my opinion—it seems they believe they are grown when the truth is they are not."

Elizabeth smiled faintly, the distant memory of Lydia at fifteen calling to her. Yes, goodness only knew what Lydia might have got up to had she lived. "Not a girl but not yet a woman."

"Exactly. And my cousin was even more so than most."

Elizabeth considered that. "Did you ever know anything about her journal? Not one she kept as a girl, but a journal from her courtship and marriage."

She had surprised him; his brow wrinkled and he leant towards her almost unconsciously. "Where was it found?"?

Through a deep, mortified blush, Elizabeth told him of the journal she had come upon in the pale blue bedroom.

"And you read it?" He seemed more amused than appalled by the idea.

"Curiosity has always been my failing." She offered an abashed half-smile. "In any case, I found it strange that such a journal was here at Pemberley in her girlhood bedchamber."

"It is very odd," he said absently, pondering the implications of it. "And you say you read it? It was about courting him? Wickham?"

"When they met, when they married, and…"

"And?"

Elizabeth swallowed. "Abuse," she said quietly. "Her husband went from being all that was gallant and kind to hitting her, humiliating her. It was dreadful."

Fitzwilliam's face lost its mask of genial detachment, and for a moment, she saw the real pain that he must have worked so hard to conceal. He silently mouthed a word that made Elizabeth blush.

"And it was right there in her bedchamber?"

Elizabeth nodded and Fitzwilliam sat silently for several minutes. He stared at nothing, evidently contemplating the meaning of a journal written after his young cousin's marriage appearing in her childhood bedchamber.

"But she never visited Pemberley after her marriage?" Elizabeth asked though she knew Miss Darcy had not.

Fitzwilliam slowly shook his head. "She must have given it to Darcy? But he never mentioned it, and surely it should have been examined for possibilities? It could not have been in her bedchamber all this time. I searched it myself, many, many, times, seeking something, anything to help our efforts. I would not have overlooked a journal."

He considered it more before coming to some conclusion that

made him sigh. "Nevertheless, whatever value the journal might have had to us has long since expired. Perhaps I shall ask Darcy for it though...but no, there is nothing to be gleaned from it."

"But perhaps there is," said Elizabeth quickly. "There were some entries which were odd: a picture of a lynx, a receipt for havercakes, a drawing of a servant girl outside of a house."

"It likely means nothing," said Fitzwilliam. "Georgiana loved to draw. She drew everything she saw."

"But she would not have seen a lynx," Elizabeth observed.

"In a book, yes, she might have," said Fitzwilliam. "As for the receipt? Havercakes you say? Well, perhaps she had some and liked them. Maybe she cooked for Wickham, I have no idea.

"No matter how we twist and turn it about, we arrive at the same conclusion. She must have died. No matter where she was in '11 or '12, drawing lynx and writing journals, the fact remains that we have seen no sign of her. She would have come to us by now; of this I am certain."

"Unless she feared bringing shame on her family," Elizabeth said. "If she was anything like Mr Darcy, then family duty and a wish to uphold the name—"

"Was important above all." Fitzwilliam nodded in agreement. "So yes, perhaps she would remain away from us, but think of what that means. What choice is there for a desperate young woman with no fortune, no family, out on the streets on her own?"

Elizabeth fell silent as the grim reality of that fell upon her.

"Trust me when I say I should sooner believe her dead," he said quietly.

There was but one last consideration: the lily pin that Mrs Giles had given her. Elizabeth removed the pin from the pocket in her gown and extended towards Fitzwilliam. "What about this?"

He glanced at it. "What about it?"

"I was given it by someone who suggested it might be important. Does this pin hold any significance to you? Did it belong to Miss Darcy?"

Fitzwilliam took it from her, examining it closely before shaking his head. "No. Forgive me, Miss Bennet, but this is just...well, allow me to say that Georgiana's jewellery was all heirloom pieces given to her by her family. Nothing as…"

It was clear what he was trying so desperately to say, so Elizabeth saved him from his agony by teasing gently, "I think you mean to say she should not have worn anything as inexpensive as this? That it lacks the dignity to be present on the chest of any Darcy?"

"I see you cut right to the home truth!" He chuckled. "Yes, for lack of more delicate meaning, Georgiana would not have owned a pin of paste and tin such as this."

"Very well." It was time to concede defeat. Fitzwilliam, an able soldier of senior rank, had already devoted himself to this cause. If five years, experience, and a limitless supply of assistance had yielded nothing to him, why should Elizabeth think she might find something? It seemed presumptuous now that she thought of it.

Fitzwilliam finished his food and rose, saying something about horses and morning air, and Elizabeth waved him off. She sat, more indolent than was her wont, just enjoying her tea and the morning sun coming through the windows of the breakfast room.

Sometime later, Lady Saye entered the room. She chatted about this and that, remarking mostly on the children, the appearance of sunshine, and how difficult it was to have a day without the aid of the servants.

"Mr Darcy is good to give them the day," said Elizabeth. "He was quite shocked when I told him the nursemaid had not any time to herself in a week."

"Oh, Lady Catherine abused them all abominably," Lady Saye agreed. "I wonder whether she will ever return. She is likely terrorising the help at Matlock. Oh, but look at that!"

Lady Saye had spied the pin next to Elizabeth's tea saucer. She took it up, twisting and turning it, seeming strangely delighted by it. "Wherever did you find this?"

"Someone gave it to me in Bakewell the day we were all there. Do you like it?"

"This pin," said Lady Saye in an amused voice, "was given as a prize at the school I went to. It was for the girl with the best comportment, but really, it was much more than that. You had to have a certain grace and to have reached a certain proficiency in your subjects. It was much coveted to earn one. I can assure you I never did." She giggled at the end.

"No?"

"Oh!" She flapped her hand a little. "No, I was forever vexing my masters. My only real talent is figuring out how little I can do without angering people. I never excelled at anything but spending money and thinking up new ways to have my maid arrange my hair."

She laughed again but Elizabeth scarcely heard her. "Did Miss Darcy go to the same school you did?"

"Yes, she did," said Lady Saye. "Mrs Botwright's School for Ladies. Perhaps this belonged to her?"

"Yes," said Elizabeth thoughtfully. "Perhaps it did."

"Beg your pardon, Miss Bennet." Mrs Reynolds had entered the room bearing a small folded paper. "This came in the post."

"You need not have troubled yourself," said Elizabeth warmly. "You are meant to be lolling about on a settee somewhere."

"Oh! Goodness, I do not think I should even know how!" The lady laughed and then turned to leave while Elizabeth regarded the note. The hand was familiar to her, and it gladdened her heart to see it, though she opened it with some trepidation.

My Dear Miss Bennet,
You cannot imagine with what shame I realised it was you who called after me in the market in Bakewell that other day! I quite mistook you for another, less beloved, acquaintance, and therefore wished to avoid the meeting. But I could not feel so for you, I assure you!

Pray, forgive me and pay me the honour of a visit as soon as is convenient for you, and if you cannot, do write to me and tell me you have accepted this poor explanation along with my sincerest apologies.

Always your friend,
Mrs Green

Is not that a relief? Elizabeth sighed and resolved to visit her at once, perhaps even tomorrow.

SARAH FELL BACK onto the bed with a sigh. "Ah, but don't Boxing Day go by in a wink! I just as soon wonder what I shall do with myself and it's gone."

"Quite true," Nan agreed, looking into the small parcel she had been given by her ladyship. All the servants had received one, and she had to admit, it was very generous. *If I am ever in a position to treat my servants, I shall be sure to…but no, that is foolish.*

It almost seemed as if Sarah had read her thoughts. "They do us well here."

"Aye."

"Must have been the same for your'n people?"

Nan turned to cast a shrewd eye upon her. "My people?"

Sarah said, soft but insistent, "Aye. At the place you come from."

"I have no people," she said quickly, turning her back on her. It was not the first time Sarah had cast her line for information, but she could not give her any. Not when she was so very close to her leave-taking. Not when the end was in sight.

"But you did once?"

Reaching a quick decision, Nan took her parcel, crossed the room, and took a seat on the bed next to Sarah, laying it beside her. Sarah eyed her curiously.

"I want you to have it."

"Quiet me up, will you?"

"You deserve it," Nan told her.

Sarah nudged the parcel back in Nan's direction. "I can't take yours."

"I insist." Gently, Nan pushed it into her hand. "You have been a friend, and I know not where I should be without all your help."

"Ah, you'd do good enough."

"Really. I have not much to offer you, but I can give you this much."

Sarah eyed her sceptically. "There's a crown in there, new stockings, and new gloves."

With gentle persistence, Nan said, "If you have no need of them, sell them, or save them for when you do need them."

"Don't they wear stockings where you be going?"

Did they? Nan had no idea. Her plan was to depart on Twelfth

Night. Halliday Abbey would hold a ball that night, attended by nearly a hundred guests. When those guests left, one would be the unwitting conveyor of Nan, who intended to conceal herself in a trunk. From there, it was on to Birmingham and a ticket to the farthest place she could go with the least amount of money. It was not an ideal plan, but neither was it the worst she had suffered.

But this little gift to Sarah was her way of expressing thanks. All the night-time rides and the fortune she had amassed in so doing had been because Sarah helped her. All the times she had avoided the wrath of Mrs Jenkinson or the advances of Lord Halliday were because Sarah had come to her rescue. She owed her far more than a crown and some stockings.

"Take them," was all she said. "In any case, the gloves would look dreadfully silly, would they not?" With a rueful smile, she fluttered her mutilated left hand at her friend. It did not bother her any more to see it, not the way it once had. The only time she had ever even cried over it was when she realised she could never wear a wedding ring. In retrospect, she understood that was likely done on purpose. In any case, no one would ever marry her, so what was the purpose in thinking of it?

"How did it happen?" Sarah lightly brushed Nan's hand, her touch fleeting but compassionate.

"Oh!" Nan shook her head. "Just an accident. Just one of those things."

She could see that Sarah did not believe her, but she let the moment pass. But it was some minutes later as they lay side by side in the dark that Sarah said,

"I know you's not one of us, not really. I suspect you are running, hiding from something, I know not what, but it must be fearful bad for you to descend to this. Just know I shall never give you up, you can be sure of that much. All's I say is that if them's who love you are still around, you should make sure they know you are well. Not knowing is the dreadful thing, that's all."

I wish I could, she thought. But alas I cannot. I am honour bound. It was part of the agreement.

She could not admit anything so merely replied, "Your silence is much appreciated. You are a good friend to me, Sarah, and I shall not forget you."

She felt the bed shift as Sarah moved a little. "I had a sister once," she said quietly. "Older sister. Found herself in a difficult way and ran off, likely 'coz she knew Pa would have her hide. But there's worse than facing that sort of thing. Next Pa knew of her, she was on the streets, doing the unspeakable just to stay alive. Came down with the French disease, she did, died not long after. But at least we knew."

Nan had no idea what to say to that and so offered only, "I am sorry to hear it."

TWENTY-THREE

"AND WHAT," ASKED DARCY WITH A SMILE UPON HIS LIPS, "HAVE YOU planned for your day, Miss Bennet?"

It was two days after Christmas, another fair afternoon. Elizabeth had begun to think the worst of it was far behind them and had even dared imagine Pemberley in the springtime.

"May I tempt you into walking with me again?"

"I should very much enjoy a walk with you." She met his smile with one of her own. "But first I must go to call on my friend, Mrs Green."

"Mrs Green?" Darcy frowned in a mockingly severe way. "Who is Mrs Green to either of us? Fie on her—let us attend to our own pleasures instead."

Though he teased, Elizabeth thought there might be some truth to his pretend pique. Indeed, she wished to spend her morning with him too, but she feared that too much time and distance would result in an irremediable breach. So she explained to Darcy the strangeness of Mrs Green, how they had first been fast friends until odd silences and avoidance separated them.

"I feel that she has perhaps lied to me on occasion as well," said Elizabeth. "She told me her employer was the aunt of Lady Catherine, but Fitzwilliam said no such lady was living in these parts."

"Who is her employer?"

"A Mrs Lawrence."

"Ah yes. Well, I can answer for that much at least." Darcy motioned to Mrs Reynolds, beckoning her close and issuing some instruction to bring his hat and coat to him. "I know Mrs Lawrence, and she is indeed Lady Catherine's aunt but on her late husband's side."

"Oh!" Elizabeth considered that. "So perhaps Mrs Green was not lying but merely confused about the family tree."

"It seems likely," said Darcy. "However, I should very much like to attend you on this visit to Mrs Green if you would not dislike the notion."

"What are we doing?" Saye asked, entering the room. "Something entertaining please, for if there is a duller time than the festive season, I know not what it is. We should have had a ball, Darcy, something to keep us amused."

"The last time I had a ball, you said my friends were so stupid they made you want to put your own eyes out," Darcy reminded him.

"I was hoping you would get rid of the friends, not stop having balls." Saye heaved himself into a nearby chair, which groaned with the agony of receiving him. "I suppose you must have made a heap of American friends?"

"Scores of them," Darcy replied. "In any case, it is not my friends to concern yourself with; Miss Bennet and I are going to see her friend, Mrs Green."

"Mrs Green? Excellent, let us go."

"I hardly know whether she is expecting so many with me," Elizabeth interjected. "After all, she is imagining that I shall call alone, for amusements particular to ladies."

"Is she married?" Saye asked.

"No, she is a wid—"

"In my experience, a spinster is never of a mind to turn away handsome men, invited or not. Let us go with you, Lizzy, and if we are interfering, we shall walk the grounds or something like that."

Demurral was not to be heard apparently, and so it was that in short time, the three of them were in the carriage, intent on a visit Mrs Lawrence's house.

"Green, Green, Green," Saye sighed out the window. "Why do I know that name?"

"You used to have that friend called Peter Green," Darcy offered.

"No, he was my brother's friend. I found him rather common if you must know. Gambled his fortune away in a most unseemly manner."

Darcy shrugged. "Half of our school chums have done the same."

"Precisely." Saye sniffed haughtily. "Common."

"Whatever became of him?"

"Dead. Married dreadfully young I think—right after he left university, or thereabouts, and then ... What is that strange countenance on you?"

Elizabeth had noticed it too—the odd, strangled look that came upon Darcy's face. He tried to evade Saye's question. "I may have met her once at a house party—"

"Not that party in Lancashire! That was Green's widow?" Saye looked like he might burst with the delight of it, though Darcy seemed like he had swallowed something that was threatening to come back up.

The infamous house party in Lancashire. So it was Mrs Green? Did he once like her?

Elizabeth watched as Darcy's discomfiture turned to hauteur. He gave his cousin only a short, tight nod. "Yes, that party." He turned to Elizabeth then, providing unnecessary clarification. "The party I went to when I should have... I believe I told you this already."

"You did," she confirmed softly while Saye cackled from his side of the carriage. Darcy turned his face to look out the window, seeming unwilling to say anything more of the matter.

"Darcy, you simply must tell the story," Saye urged, but Darcy was implacable, giving no indication that he had even heard his cousin's entreaty.

When it was clear Darcy was not going to speak, Saye announced,

"Then I shall tell the story myself. About five years ago there was a party, quite a large one, in Lancashire."

"At Gawthorpe," said Darcy, speaking to the window.

"Gawthorpe." Saye made a little frown. "Such an inelegant name, like the sound a corpulent old man would make whilst choking to death. In any case, thither went our two young heroes, then-Colonel Fitzwilliam and his trusty companion, Mr Fitz Darcy."

Darcy shot him a glare but said nothing.

"Our dear colonel believed he was coming to the aid of young Mrs Green, who had recently learnt she was a penniless widow. The reason she gave was that she was in dire need of the dear colonel's assistance, but what a surprise she received when our prime article Darcy showed himself!"

"Pray, stop."

"Oh, he only wanted to help, but how can one help a woman who lures you into a hedgerow and bares her—"

"Saye!"

"Soul. She bared her soul." Saye smirked all around the carriage, and his meaning was not lost on Elizabeth.

I might be a maiden, but I am not an idiot.

"Of course, the real difficulty when one begins to bare things"— Saye paused and rearranged himself on the bench in a methodical and ostentatious manner—"is that a crowd does at times assemble. Our dear girl, who wished to be caught in flagrante delicto, was instead the subject of an excessively public humiliation atop a not-private-enough rejection."

"Poor dear" said Elizabeth. "How humiliating."

"Our host asked her to leave," said Darcy. "And her friends refused to depart with her. They left her to her ignominy with the excuse of keeping their own reputations unsullied."

A woman who had been so exceedingly embarrassed would likely go to any lengths to avoid seeing the people who witnessed it. Suddenly a great deal made sense to Elizabeth: Mrs Green knew some things about Darcy, but not others, she wished to humiliate him, she wanted Elizabeth to exact a revenge on him. At once, it seemed utterly nonsensical to arrive with Saye and Darcy in tow and subject Mrs Green to her past miseries.

"Perhaps we should not go," said Elizabeth. "I might have done better to send a note asking her whether—"

"Too late," Saye announced, leaning forward to peer out the window. "We are arrived."

When Mrs Green met them in the drawing room, it was the work of a moment to see the mortification spread over her face. She was introduced to Saye, and she was polite, in a mumbling, lowered-head sort of way, to Darcy. Elizabeth lost no time in sending the two gentlemen out of the room so she could apologise.

"I had no idea," she said, once the ladies were alone, "that there had been some trouble in the past."

"Trouble?" Mrs Green laughed weakly even as tears filled her eyes. "Oh, trouble does not begin to describe it. I had never imagined I could be so mortified; I felt it in my bones, I assure you. Wish to die? Absolutely. Would have descended into hell right then and there if the choice had been given to me."

She sighed. "No, you could not have known. It was stupid in any case. For some time I blamed Mr Darcy, but really, all he did was fail to succumb to my temptations. Even his cousin only came because of his association with my late husband. I pretended some sort of crisis, and sure enough, it brought them to me.

"In any case, it is long gone now, and the fate I was so desperate to avoid has proved to be tolerable. Indeed, I find I quite like my independence."

"It does have much to recommend it," said Elizabeth.

"Oh," said Mrs Green with a light in her eye. "I do not think you will be enjoying independence for long, Miss Bennet. Perhaps you have something to tell me even now?"

"I do not, I assure you," Elizabeth cried with a laugh just as the gentlemen entered.

Shortly before they departed, Darcy asked Mrs Green to speak with him a moment. Elizabeth went with Saye to await the carriage in the entrance hall while Darcy remained behind. He joined them a few moments later. Elizabeth only looked at him, but Saye had no scruple in demanding some sort of explanation.

"I am finding myself compelled to right the wrongs I have left behind me," said Darcy. "I am glad to see Mrs Green content in her situation, but I wished to be assured that I had not injured her. She convinced me I had not, and we have decided to remain as friends forthwith."

He smiled at Elizabeth. "I daresay she will not hide from you the next time we see her in Bakewell."

UPON THEIR RETURN, Darcy excused himself to attend to some things in his study. Elizabeth went to Charles, finding him engaged in hijinks in the nursery with Saye's daughters. It was delightful how they all got on, and Elizabeth thought how sad he would be when they left.

He needs brothers and sisters.

The thought came to her before she could stop it, and when she realised it, she blushed deeply.

"Why are you red, Lizzy?" Charles stopped and stared up at her. "Are you sick?"

"No, no sweetling, just…just warm. I thank you for asking. What are you playing?"

"We play ghost," cried out little Claire. "I a ghost!"

"You are not a ghost," Charles insisted. "You are George, who is like a ghost but not really a ghost." Claire was not impressed by this clarification.

It was an opening Elizabeth was quick to seize. "Has George come by lately?" Elizabeth asked. "I confess I would very much like to see George." It had occurred to Elizabeth—although the notion was exceedingly unlikely—that perhaps George was Miss Darcy. It seemed extraordinary to imagine she was alive and well enough to be paying nocturnal visits to Pemberley with her family none the wiser, but the coincidence was too much to disregard.

Charles had espied Annabelle edging too near his tin soldiers and so moved in that direction. "George only sees me."

"Oh, well, perhaps the next time you see George, you might call for me, and I could come to see you both."

Charles nodded while quickly scooping his soldiers under the bed. Annabelle cried out in protest, but he was firm. "Soldiers are not for girls. Soldiers like to play war, and girls cannot play war."

"Girls can play war," Elizabeth said, walking towards them and gently removing some of the soldiers from his grasp. "Is it not nice to have a friend to play with, be it a girl friend or a boy friend?"

Charles watched with dismay as his aunt handed some of the soldiers to Annabelle, who promptly wrapped them in a handkerchief and declared them her babies. "I singing them to sleep," she proclaimed, setting forth on some high-pitched warble of a lullaby while Charles gave his aunt a look of utter disgust.

Repressing her grin, Elizabeth said, "Once they awaken from their nap, I have no doubt they will be able to go to war very fiercely."

FROM THE NURSERY, Elizabeth went to the drawing room and found Saye there with his wife and brother, along with Lord and Lady Matlock. All were at their leisure, chatting amiably about various goings-on in town.

When the conversation paused, Elizabeth ventured, "And how is it, my lord, that you came to know so illustrious a personage as Gertie?"

Saye leant back in his chair chuckling as he changed glances with the others in the room.

Lord Matlock interjected saying, "We all know Gertie, or at least know of him."

"Miss Bennet," announced Fitzwilliam, "has a keen nose for sniffing out family scandal."

"Scandal." Lord Matlock was dismissive. "Hardly a scandal."

"If no one knows about it, then it is not really a scandal," Lady Matlock opined.

"People know," Lord Matlock assured them. "But Sir Lewis is dead, so why should it matter?"

"How can it be a scandal when Old George knighted him for it?" Fitzwilliam said. "Last I knew, one did not receive a knighthood for causing scandal."

"An excellent point." Saye crossed his legs comfortably. "Though relations in high places do not hurt."

"Sir Lewis always said that he had low friends and high friends," Lord Matlock began, "and of the two of them—"

"The low had always proven the most useful," Saye and Fitzwilliam finished with him. All three men broke into a chuckle.

"It is really not so amusing," Lady Matlock said. "He courted danger with every step, and look where it got him! In an early grave, that is where."

"'Tis like this, Miss Bennet," said Fitzwilliam. "Lady Catherine's late husband was a smuggler."

"Smuggler is such a dreadful word," Lady Matlock interjected. "He was not *really* a smuggler."

"He supported the efforts of the smugglers then," said Fitzwilliam. "Do not skewer me with those looks. Sir Lewis played an integral role in the development of a new harbour for Ramsgate both in financial backing and in design. It proved to be of good use to the navy once the wars began. In military circles, Sir Lewis is still very well regarded."

"And whilst he was so virtuously building the harbour for the navy," Saye added, "he was so good as to simultaneously develop channels through that harbour for the smugglers. Tunnels and caves for the importing and hiding of French wines and perfumes and fashions and all manner of good things."

"And of a means to move money to the army who were fighting on the continent," Fitzwilliam added. Elizabeth noticed he did not seem to find it as amusing as his brother did. "Smuggling can go both ways you know, and rather than believe Sir Lewis intended for illegal goods to be brought in, we might consider that without those channels, our very own army might have been cut off from supplies and money."

"And the aristocracy might have been cut off from brandy," Saye said with a smirk. "Of the two, I daresay it was the latter that got old Lewis knighted. In any case, the head of the biggest gang was a man called Birdie, and he was Gertie's father."

Elizabeth, struck by the names, was unable to conceal her giggle. "Birdie and Gertie? Those do not sound like the names of smugglers."

Saye nodded at her to acknowledge her mirth. "Rather amusing names for two decidedly serious figures. Urdwell is the last name;

Gertie's father was Barnard and Gertie is Gabriel, hence Birdie and
Gertie."

"So they owe a debt to Sir Lewis," Fitzwilliam added. "And for as
much as a gentleman's word means, you may believe me when I say
that honour among thieves is undeniable and irrefutable. I do not
even know what Sir Lewis did for Birdie, but I do know that he and
his son would likely kill someone if Sir Lewis asked them to do."

This roused something in Elizabeth's mind, some little tweak of
interest, but Lady Matlock hurried to say, "Sir Lewis never ordered
anyone killed, nor would he. In any case, Sir Lewis and Birdie are
both dead, and Gertie is happily living in Derbyshire."

Saye grinned, offering "Heaven knows, if Sir Lewis would have
ordered anyone killed, it probably would have been his wife."

This aroused contention among the others in the drawing room. A
vigorous debate between Saye and his parents ensued in which Lady
Matlock insisted Lady Catherine was all that was benevolent and
good, while Saye and his father said Lady Catherine was a shrew.

In the midst of it, Elizabeth speculated, "I wonder what might
have made a smuggler from Kent come to Derbyshire. Was
Napoleon's surrender so bad for business?"

Lord Matlock gave a snorting laugh. "I doubt it. Where there is
law, there will always be people willing to make their livings
breaking it. It is curious; though who knows what seems like good
sense to such people as these."

"He has been here for five years now, so he must like it," Saye
opined. "You know, I have never understood these people who just
froth at the mouth at the mere mention of the seaside. Give me good
forestland any day."

"Oh yes," said Fitzwilliam drily. "People are just flocking to the
forests for their good health."

"People are cows," Saye replied. "I have made it the study of my
life to avoid doing as the heaving masses do."

"I am just saying that the sea offers better air, and the benefits of
taking the waters are well known."

It seemed another squabble would come forth save for the fact
that Lady Saye rose, complaining of exhaustion and begging her
husband to go with her to their apartment.

Elizabeth found herself puzzling over the unusual notion of a smuggler moving so far away from the sea routes. Perhaps it was of no consequence, but it seemed important to Elizabeth. Gertie arrived at about the same time as Lady Catherine came to Pemberley. Important? Of course, she had no reason to think Lady Catherine had any association with Gertie just because her husband had.

She thought again about the dissected pictures that her father so enjoyed. He told her once that when it seemed the pieces would not fall in place, maybe it was the ones you thought you knew that were incorrect. "No matter how certain you are," he had cautioned her, "never be afraid to doubt the place of each piece. Assumptions are your enemy."

Of course, the vagaries of Gertie's life likely had no bearing whatsoever to Georgiana Darcy. She wondered whether Gertie had known Wickham and Mrs Younge. Darcy told her Wickham had arranged for falsified marriage papers to wed his young sister, and it stood to reason that a man who did such things would likely know people like Gertie. In any case, there was one way to find out. She wondered whether she had the courage to return to the smuggler's den.

The door to the drawing room opened and Darcy entered. His eyes found hers immediately, and she smiled at him. *I shall get to the bottom of this. For you, I shall find the answers.*

No kissing today. In this Darcy was determined. He would not dishonour her, and until they were engaged, stolen liberties were the act of a rake.

He had taken her off on another of their walks. Miss Bennet, he found, enjoyed walking no matter what the weather. While they strolled amiably through the woods, he found himself rattling away to avoid thoughts of kissing her, likely boring her to tears with his family history, the various species of fern they saw, and his thoughts on Twelfth Night. When at last he paused, he found they had already gone quite a distance from the house.

"I fear I have quite commanded our conversation."

"Think nothing of that," she said with a beguiling smile. "I enjoyed everything you had to say."

He laughed. "Oh dear. Pray, tell me you will not become one of these society misses."

"A society miss?"

"Sweet smiles and agreeing with everything I say." He shuddered dramatically. "Positively awful."

"Have no fear," she said in a tone rich with amusement. "I could never do that. If I did just now, it was a temporary union of our interests, that is all."

"Good." He grinned down at her. "Because I find I am quite fond of your arguing with me—and your accusations of murder."

She laughed. "To think I once believed you taciturn and grave, Mr Darcy! How little I knew, and I understood you even less."

"I am taciturn and grave," he said, feeling at once sobered. "Even before…"

She grew more serious. Although he loved when she laughed, he loved even more that she was never silly. When subjects of consequence arose, she did not shy away from them; she was always as ready to consider and ponder as she was to laugh and tease.

"Before Ramsgate?" she asked gently.

"I have always had a quiet, sober temperament even in my happiest times. And what about you?"

Elizabeth considered it for a moment. "You did not know my family, and I suppose my character makes more sense if you do."

"How so?"

"When you are one of five sisters close in age, everyone becomes a certain something. Jane was the beauty, the prettiest sister with the sweetest temper."

"I should have guessed as much by Bingley marrying her." He smiled so she would not think he meant it as an insult.

She smiled back. "Mary, my next younger sister, was the serious one, always with a heavy book in her hand, forever sober, always moralising. Then came Kitty, who was always seen as very delicate. She was exceedingly slender, always had some cold or fever, always being fussed over by Hill, our housekeeper.

"Then came Lydia." She sighed a little after she said it. "Lydia was exceedingly pretty, almost as lovely as Jane. We treated her as our little doll when she was young, dressing her up in the most elaborate way, much too elaborate for a child, doing her hair, making her sing little songs and do little dances. We spoilt her in all the worst ways. Mama simply could not say no to her no matter what she asked."

There was a wistful half-smile on her lips and she was quiet a few moments before she continued. "But you wanted to know about me, not my sisters. I was the sister that was a little bit of all things. A little bit pretty but nothing to Jane or Lydia. A little bit bookish but not so much as Mary. I was not sickly"—she laughed—"never that. So I had my good humour, my enjoyment of lively conversation, and my ease and friendliness no matter my company. So there it is."

"I think you are the most beautiful woman of my acquaintance." It emerged from his mouth before he had any notion of stopping it, but once he saw her pretty blush, he was glad he had not. "But it is a rare treasure to find that besides that,, you are a person I genuinely enjoy spending time with."

This pleased her. She looked up at him, tilting her head sideways. "I like spending time with you, too."

She continued looking at him like that—it was particularly hand-some, showing her eyes to advantage—and the desire to lean over and kiss her was nearly undeniable. He felt himself falling under the power of her gaze and at last wrenched himself away by looking to the side. "Stop that," he told her.

"Stop what?"

"Stop being so irresistible." More in command of himself, he looked back at her. "You make me want to forget I am a gentleman."

He hoped that would make her laugh, but instead she grew pensive, lowering her eyes to the path at her feet. He watched her for a few moments before asking, "What is it?"

"I hope you do not think ill of me for kissing you."

"No!" He said it so loudly, they heard a little echo. "No, not at all. But having come to know my feelings for you, I am loath to dishonour you. I cannot take liberties that are not mine to take."

"Of course," she said with an uncertain smile. "But it does bring a concern to my mind."

"What is that?"

"Until Lady Catherine returns," she said, "I must consider how it is that I should remain at Pemberley. Your family will leave after

Twelfth Night, and I must go with them or else find myself some other situation."

A proposal was nearly on the tip of his tongue, but he stopped himself. He did not wish to propose because time or space dictated it. He wanted her to be courted appropriately, seen with him about town. It would not do them well to have some mysterious attachment created among the muddy autumn in Derbyshire that suddenly became a marriage.

"As much as I hate the prospect," he said, "it is best. Do not doubt my intentions for a minute; I only wish for things to begin well to save us trouble later on."

She nodded.

Inspiration struck him as he considered it. He had received an invitation, given to them all, for a party nearby, an enormous Twelfth Night Ball. He despised the man hosting the party, but it was likely that a hundred or so people would attend, all people who would see and admire her and then be unsurprised when they found he was engaged to her later in the year.

"Let us begin with a ball."

"A ball?" She looked doubtful. "Where?"

"Quite close. A place called Halliday Abbey."

TWENTY-FOUR

It was clear to Elizabeth that she would require the assistance of Lord Saye in Bakewell, but it took two days before she could find him alone and ask for it. He was rarely alone, nearly always in the company of his wife or his father, but as she saw him stand at the end of one evening, she realised she would need to create her own opportunity.

Rising hastily, she mumbled some words of excuse and followed him from the drawing room, praying no one else would come after her. Fortune smiled upon her; they were alone in the hall.

"My lord," she murmured. "May I speak with you a moment?"

"Of course," he said, much too loudly.

She winced and then gestured towards the stairs. "I shall walk with you." On his inquiring glance, she explained, "I need privacy."

"You do not intend to tell me you are in love with me, do you?" he asked as they strolled. "Because I am very happily married."

"No, of course not."

"I do not even have a mistress," he told her, as if conveying some astonishing fact. "You might have presumed that I did."

"No, it is very clear to me that you are besotted with Lady Saye."

"Yes, I rather am." He smiled and chuckled. "Has me right tied to her apron, she does. In any case, what is it?"

"I need to go to Bakewell," she said, "with only you to accompany me. Is tomorrow agreeable?"

He studied her a moment, then leant back against the wall. "Why?"

Elizabeth, hiding a little sigh, gave him a quick recounting of the various tidbits of information she had gleaned. He smiled indulgently at her throughout, diminishing her hope somewhat, but undaunted, she continued.

"I admire your spirit, Miss Bennet, but as you know, my brother has spent a great deal of time trying to find her. He has come up empty-handed for years despite all his resources."

"I know it has all been done before and done better that I could hope to do it," she owned. "Likely, I shall find the same bits of nothing. But would it not be dreadful if there were something to all of this and I did not heed my suspicions?"

Saye chuckled. "You are an unusual female. No wonder Darcy likes you so."

"He will not like me if he knows I persist in this," Elizabeth replied. "He prefers to accept her death and move on."

"He has earned that much, to be sure." Saye nodded decisively. "I shall take you to Bakewell, and we shall keep it to ourselves."

SAYE ENTERED the carriage the next morning with clear evidence of a sleepless night on his countenance. He immediately sank into a corner and tugged his hat over his face. "Wake me when we arrive," he mumbled, adding something about two hours' sleep.

"Did you not retire when I saw you?" Elizabeth asked him with no little astonishment.

"No."

After a pause, she asked, "But you were on your way to your bedchamber when I saw you, were you not?"

With a sigh, he pushed his hat back enough to peer at her with his right eye. "I was going to don my lucky billiards waistcoat to play with Darcy and my brother. Served me well, I might add, found myself two hundred pounds the richer thanks to Darcy."

"Two hundred pounds!" Elizabeth exclaimed. "You played high, then."

"Hardly." Saye sniffed.

"In any case, I hope you are not too fatigued from your exertions," Elizabeth said trying to conceal her concern. "We need to pay a visit to your friend Gertie."

"I could deal with Gertie whilst fighting off consumption with one leg amputated," he assured her.

Elizabeth thought surely that the pin would prove significant, and thus she wished to first see Mrs Giles and learn why she had thought Elizabeth would know something about it. Saye was not averse to the idea, being immediately interested in the thought of coffee and bread.

They took a seat at one of the long tables in the shop and waited, hoping to catch sight of the proprietress, but alas, she was not to be found. When a quarter of an hour had elapsed, Saye made hints that he would seek her husband, and Elizabeth immediately rose. "Allow me to summon Mr Giles."

Mr Giles was a fresh-faced boy who scarcely looked old enough to have said his vows of marriage. He came to them at once on their request, no doubt perceiving by Saye's manner and dress that they were persons of consequence. His deferential ease faded immediately and a hard, suspicious look came over him when Elizabeth asked about Mrs Giles.

"Who wants her?"

"I am a friend," Elizabeth explained. "Miss Elizabeth Bennet? Perhaps she has mentioned me."

"No," he murmured, turning his head away. "She han't. Excuse—"

Saye pulled some coins from his pocket, thrusting them into Mr Giles's hand. "See that she gets here, immediately," Saye ordered with a quirk of his brow, "if not sooner."

Mr Giles stared at the coins a moment, seeming offended by them. With calm civility, he handed them back to Saye, "She is unwell, sir."

"Unwell?" Saye raised one brow. "What ails her?"

The boy pressed his lips together tightly. "I am loath to disoblige you, but my concern must be for my wife at this time."

Saye rose to his feet, saying, "Boy, do you know who I am?"

Elizabeth knew she must intervene, and she rose beside Saye, laying a hand on his arm and whispering, "Allow me."

She gave their host her most amiable smile. "Mr Giles?"

He simply looked at her.

"Mrs Giles gave me something, a pin, and I only needed to ask her a few questions about it. But, as you said, she is not well, so perhaps I could ask you instead? And if you know the answers to those questions, maybe you would be so good as to tell me?"

He gave a grudging little nod and gestured to her to follow him. Saye moved to accompany them, but Elizabeth forestalled him with a raised hand. "I shall return directly. Have a biscuit or two, you seem a little peckish."

Mr Giles led Elizabeth down the very same hall that his wife had a few days prior. Instead of passing near the kitchens, however, he led her out a side door into an alleyway. It was cramped and small, but the heat from the kitchens rendered it quite pleasant.

"Please leave us alone," said Mr Giles as soon as the door closed behind them. "I ain't wanting any trouble."

"And I do not wish to give you any," said Elizabeth. "I only wish to understand more about the pin your wife gave me." She extended her hand, showing it to him.

He scarcely afforded it a glance. "I dunno nothing about it." "You do not know where she might have gotten it?"

"No, ma'am."

"Did she buy it? Or did someone give it to her?"

He shrugged.

"Did your wife know a lady called Mrs Younge?"

He shook his head.

"What about Mr George Wickham?"

"No."

"Georgiana Darcy?"

"We all know who the Darcys is. Don't mean we know 'em."

Elizabeth thought that she was very close to grasping hold of his collar and shaking him until some information came loose. Very patiently, she said, "You must know then that Miss Darcy has been missing for some years."

"Aye. Don't have nothing to do with me or the missus or that pin though."

"Of course not," said Elizabeth with a sigh. Defeated, she allowed her head to fall back, closing her eyes a moment. Then she straightened. "Very well. I shall not bother you needlessly. I can see you are exceedingly busy there." She gave him a kindly smile. "For the soup donation, is it still?"

Mr Giles hesitated a moment before cautiously replying, "Aye. That what Lady Catherine's gave to us, and we's grateful for it."

His words gave her pause. Strange, was it not, that Lady Catherine should lay claim to the good will brought about by Mr Darcy's good works? Elizabeth gave him a reassuring smile. "Forgive me. I do not mean to speak out of turn, but I do have it on excellent authority that in truth, it was not Lady Catherine who funded the venture but Mr Darcy."

Mr Giles only grunted sceptically but Elizabeth saw some of interest in his eyes.

"And Mr Darcy will likely be exceedingly grateful to anyone or anything that provides information about his sister."

Mr Giles dropped his gaze to his feet. "I don't know nothing about his sister."

"But perhaps you do know something else," Elizabeth entreated. "Something that seems inconsequential to you but might be very important to me or to Mr Darcy."

He was silent.

"This pin, for example." She thrust it towards him again, pushing it nearly beneath his nose. "I did not know what it was, and none of the family knew what it was, but then a lady recognised it and said it was a pin that was given out for the girl with the best comportment at Miss Darcy's school. So you see, information that did not seem important to her made me think that perhaps this was Miss Darcy's pin."

He still did not speak but used the toe of his boot to press at the muck on the ground.

"And then your wife said to me—and in this point I am certain—

that I would know what to do with it. An odd turn of phrase if it is nothing more than a mere gift, is it not?" Having said that much, Elizabeth waited, watchful and silent, hoping he was wrestling with his conscience.

"We just want to find her," she urged gently. "Or at least know what happened to her. It is a dreadful thing, the not knowing."

Mr Giles looked around him again as if he expected the stone walls to have sprouted ears, then heaved a sigh worthy of any Shakespearean tragedy. "I don't know nothing," he said, emphasising each word. "All's what I know is that we waren't to marry for a time. Jenny was in the scullery at Halliday, trying to save what she could, but it ain't never enough. Her pa was sick, and she was paying for the medicine, and it just don't leave much besides. But Lady Catherine, she did give Mrs Giles the money so's she could leave service and took care of her pa too. So now we's married, and we have the money for the bread, and we're doing right good. Right good indeed."

Elizabeth considered all of this for a moment. "Who is Lady Catherine to you?" she asked. "Is there some reason she should act so generously to you?"

He shook his head. "None whatever. When it happened, me and Jenny was too afraid to believe it, but the condition was we kept our mouths shut. Now Jenny's gone and give this to you, and all the questions come about."

"Do not blame your wife," Elizabeth said hastily. "You may be assured that I shall not reveal you. I am a curious person but discreet too. Your secret is safe with me."

He was not persuaded in the least, shaking his head mournfully. Elizabeth did her best to convince him but soon realised only time would reassure him that no ill would come of his confidence. She departed soon after, Saye at her side and questions whirling about madly in her mind.

As they strolled down the street towards the place where Gertie could be found, Elizabeth asked Saye if he knew anything of the matter. "None whatever," he replied idly. "Lady Catherine is not generous nor is she concerned for the plight of servants. I daresay we shall need to ask her about it."

They found Gertie where they had before, in the dark, dank, odiferous room, surrounded by idle men who somehow managed to appear uniformly menacing.

"Gertie, answer some questions from my friend here, will you?" Saye entreated after the obligatory greetings. "She thinks it strange that a smuggler lives in Derbyshire."

"What is it to you?" Gertie's tone was more curious than hostile.

"Well, ah, when did you come here?" Elizabeth asked.

"Dunno Maybe '12? P'raps '13."

"It does seem unusual," said Elizabeth hesitantly, "that you should move your business so far from the ships and ports."

Gertie shrugged. "Time to be respectable, I guess you might say. Got me a wife, some little 'uns."

Frustrated, Elizabeth hid a little sigh. Instinct told her there was more to the story, but Gertie was thoroughly disinclined to be of assistance. She glanced at Saye who did and said nothing.

"Do you know George Wickham?" she asked.

"'Course."

"What about Mrs Younge?"

"Aye."

She gave him a tentative smile. "No doubt General Fitzwilliam has already wondered whether you knew about what happened with…with Mr Wickham's, uh, wife and the elopement and—"

"I dunno nuthin' about it 'cept what I've been told. Wickham's a lunatic now, and Mrs Younge is disappeared, so that's long done in my opinion."

"Yes," she agreed faintly, giving Saye another glance.

Saye appeared terminally disinterested throughout. He examined his fingernails, he drifted over towards the soot-crusted window, and he even went so far as to yawn—loudly and with his mouth wide open—several times. Elizabeth despaired of him and cast several beseeching glances his way before at last conceding that it was Saye's intention to be useless, as he settled himself against the wall, appearing to be nearly asleep.

She asked Gertie more odd questions that even she knew were irrelevant and stupid. Gertie answered in the least syllables possible, showing no sign of involvement or at least none that she could discern. At long last, it was time to admit defeat. "Mr Gertie, sir, I wish to thank you for your time," she said with a heavy sigh. "Pray, if you do think of anything that might be of use, will you send word to us at Pemberley?"

Gertie made some sound that was close enough to assent to Elizabeth. She nodded and turned, beckoning Saye, who peeled himself away from the wall and shuffled slowly after her. As they neared the door, he stopped, turned around, and said, in a tone of supreme civility and ennui, "Gertie, I daresay this might be our last meeting. Allow me to wish you well in your journey."

The room seemed to go unnaturally still around them. Gertie stared at Saye, and Elizabeth felt a frisson of excitement as she realised Gertie had the look of a trapped mouse.

"'Fraid I don't know what you's talking about, my lord."

Saye lifted one shoulder up, then down, insouciance personified. "Italy, is it?"

There was again a prolonged staring between the pair of them until Gertie sighed. "The very sight of you brings me trouble."

"I love you, too," Saye replied. "Let us go away from your men."

It took Gertie a moment to consent, but at last he nodded, flicked his hand lightly at his colleagues around the room, and gestured towards the back. Elizabeth followed behind them and through a door that opened to a staircase.

Saye looped an arm around Gertie's bony shoulders as they climbed the dark stairs. "When I came of age," he said, in a confiding tone, "my father gave me some invaluable advice. He is an art collector, my father—did you know that?"

Gertie did not reply.

"Just loves art, sculpture, painting, sketches, what have you. Says his collection is valuable to him in ways that exceed its worth in pounds because the pieces are uplifting to his soul. So that was his advice to me. 'Son,' he said, 'find something in your life that brings you joy, that makes you delight in it each time you hear, taste, touch, or behold it.' So I thought about what delights me. Was it women? Brandy? Horses? Because it certainly was not art or music or anything of that sort."

Gertie grunted.

"I find art tedious if you must know. Landscapes? Yawn. Portraiture? I should rather be shot in the head. The worst of all—animals! Good lord above, is not one horse about the same as the next?" Saye shuddered theatrically. "Music is all well and good so long as I can dance to it, but my interest ends there, I assure you. I only go to concerts so people can see how handsome I look in whatever new coat I have commissioned for the evening."

No one replied to him, so after a moment he continued his introspective tale. "So then I was faced with the question of what it was exactly that set my soul aloft. I took some months to deliberate it, but then one day it simply came to me. Popped right into my head, what it was I truly love."

Reaching the top of the stairs, they entered a surprisingly comfortable room with windows, a fire, and several well-stuffed chairs. Even the smell was tolerable. Elizabeth took a seat while Saye perched on the windowsill and Gertie stood glowering at them both. As Saye would do nothing, it seemed, but stare at them expectantly, she cleared her throat and said, "What is it, Saye?"

After a moment to breathe, look at them, and in other ways build their anticipation, Saye announced, "I like stories." He gave a modest little shrug. "So I collect them."

"What kind of stories?" Elizabeth asked while Gertie stared sullenly out the window.

"Any kind, but my favourite by far are the stories that people wish to remain unknown. Scandals, secrets, salacious tidbits of people I know, people I do not know, people who are dead, people who live in Van Dieman's Land. I love them all."

Gertie had begun to look interested in a concerned sort of way. Saye gave him an arrogant little wink. "And it was because of this love of stories and the people behind them that I have gathered up a little tidbit you might like, Gertie. Something about a sunken ship in the winter of '12, some overextended credit, and the Hastings brothers."

Elizabeth watched with amazement as Gertie turned the colour of filthy snow.

"It was Miss Bennet who thought of it," Saye remarked carelessly. "Asked us just the other day why on earth a smuggler should wish to live in Derbyshire? An excellent question indeed, Miss Bennet."

Gertie's only concession to distress was the clenching of his fists by his side and the muttering of one quiet oath.

"So I did a little exploring, one might say. A brief but glorious search of my aunt's apartments just to see what I might find."

"What do you want?" Gertie hissed through clenched teeth. "Aye, that miserable old crone you call a lady has held it over me these many years, and aye, I intend to run before the Hastings boys catch up to me. What pound of my flesh will you take that she has not already taken?"

"Been blackmailing you, has she?" Saye nodded understandingly. "Dreadful old bat."

Gertie scoffed. "Hiding me, that's all, and I have done her good many times over for it."

"Hiding you from what?"

"From my former friends, my associates such as it was."

"Why hide from them?"

"They have a bounty on me, those Hastings, and they do not merely kill a man, they like to torture him first." Gertie sounded oddly proud of this savage truth.

"Well this is awkward." Saye paused a moment, looking skyward and then returning his attention to Gertie. "No one is trying to find you, Gertie. She paid them."

Elizabeth's mind whirled, trying to make sense of it all, but she could not. Lady Catherine, paying this smuggler here and hiding that smuggler there, but why? To what purpose?

Gertie immediately refuted the notion that he was not being sought by dangerous smugglers. Saye immediately told him it was so. The two gentlemen engaged in a stare-down of sorts until Saye at last held up his hand, and in a tone of indelicate amusement said, "Back in '12, she did pay them. Had I known that you did not know, I would have brought her receipts with me."

"They have a bounty on me," Gertie insisted.

Saye shook his head sorrowfully. "Alas, they do not. Actually, the leader of that gang...Reginald? Ronald?"

"Roland."

"Executed in '14. Hung him up in chains, which I find an abhorrent practice that serves very little purpose in my humble estimation."

Gertie began to curse and mutter, his grey face gradually becoming increasingly flushed.

"Why would she do it?" Elizabeth asked, though it seemed her presence had been mostly forgotten.

"I cannot answer that," Saye replied, his eyes still on Gertie. "But I daresay Lady Catherine wanted Gertie to be here and alive, and she did not wish the Hastings boys to get in the way. But why did Lady Catherine want you here, Gertie? What were her reasons?"

Gertie paused in the midst of his cursing and muttering to cut a quick glance towards Elizabeth. "Send her out. This is men's business."

"I cannot send her out there alone," Saye replied. "But she has a strong constitution. I daresay she will survive the telling of it."

THE TALE that Gertie had to tell, the colours he inserted into what had heretofore been Elizabeth's sketch, amazed them both. Even Saye could not have foretold the likes of it.

They entered the carriage in silence, settled themselves, and then, once they were moving, they began to speak to one another using hushed voices so that the coachmen would not overhear.

In tones that conveyed her astonishment, Elizabeth said, "Mrs Younge snatched Miss Darcy with the intention of ransoming her to Darcy. Lady Catherine somehow intervened, and Mrs Younge died as the result of it."

"No matter how he denied it," said Saye, "I am sure Gertie killed her."

Elizabeth shuddered for a moment, thinking she had just been in the presence of a murderer. "So Mrs Younge was—"

"Disposed of." Saye made a little grimace. "In the Thames, perhaps."

"Mrs Younge was thus gone, and Miss Darcy was…hidden?"

"Taken elsewhere," Saye replied grimly. "Hidden in a place known only to my aunt."

"Gertie must know. He was the one who hid her the first time."

"No, I think he told us the truth. He has no personal stake in this matter with Georgiana. Indeed, he might like to betray my aunt, given how she has swindled him these many years."

"But why should Lady Catherine have done this?" Elizabeth asked. "With Darcy gone to America thinking he had killed Wickham and every other wrong thing, why did she never admit this to him? She might have saved him years of misery!"

"If the truth about Georgiana came out, the entire family should have partaken in her disgrace. I can assure you, Lady Catherine would not have wanted any such share in the humiliation."

"You think she hid her to disguise the truth?" Elizabeth asked. "Her own niece?"

Saye shook his head. "No other explanation will do. No matter how we toss this about, Lady Catherine knew what became of her and said nothing to us about it. She wanted Georgiana gone."

"Mr and Mrs Giles must be involved somehow," Elizabeth mused. "Their part, I cannot imagine, but everything points to them. The havercakes, the fact that Mrs Giles had the pin. Perhaps she can lead us to Miss Darcy?"

"Lady Catherine might confess once confronted. She is, I suppose, the only person who knows for certain."

They had arrived back at the house by then, both of them absent-minded and lost in their own deliberations of the matter. Their plans were destined to be forestalled, however, by an uproar they found within Pemberley. Mrs Reynolds was awaiting them in the vestibule, calm and proper but with worry marking the lines of her countenance. They looked past her to see maids racing about the halls.

"What is going on here?" Saye asked.

"We have had word from Matlock. Lady Catherine has suffered apoplexy and is not conscious. They think she is unlikely to recover."

TWENTY-FIVE

"Ding-dong the witch is dead," Saye remarked with a little smirk. "Say, is there any hot soup anywhere? I could use a bite to eat. Miss Bennet did insist that we gad all about without so much as a bun to sustain us. Perhaps some venison?"

"Saye!" Elizabeth cried out in surprise. Turning to Mrs Reynolds, she asked, "Where are the rest of the family? Have they gone to her bedside?"

"They have, save for the children who remain in their nursery."

Elizabeth turned to Saye. "You will want to go at once, I presume? I shall—"

"You presume too much," Saye replied in a disinterested tone. "I do not intend to go anywhere."

Elizabeth took a moment to gather her wits through the shock of his words. "She is your relation."

Saye levelled a serious look at her. "Have you already forgotten all we learnt this morning?"

"Perhaps there were other considerations that—"

"Oh pooh," Saye replied. "In any case, I have despised her for years. You know what she gave me for Christmas one year? A rotten orange. I was scarcely in long pants, and she gave me a rotten orange. What sort of aunt is that? Better to give nothing at all in my opinion. In any case, if even half of it is true, I still say she should rot in hell."

Alarmed, Elizabeth cut her eyes immediately towards Mrs Reynolds. Saye, who was hungry and angry, suffered no such discretion. "Please feel free to send word to them, Mrs Reynolds. I do not care two straws if she dies, and in fact, I hope she does."

Elizabeth gasped with surprise but hardly knew what to do with him. It was surely not her place to order him about, and in any case, it seemed Lady Catherine had made her own bed. In one last attempt, she said, "Will not your conscience be assuaged—"

"I have no patience nor a conscience for those who do not deserve it. I have never understood why we think people should be granted our benevolence simply because they are relations. After all, does not Napoleon have nieces and nephews? Did not Vlad the Impaler have many children?"

"They did, true, but for the sake of Christian mercy—"

"Christian mercy." Saye sniffed and scoffed dramatically. "How about this: hypocrisy. I have faults enough, Miss Bennet, but being a hypocrite is not one of them."

Elizabeth hardly knew what to say or think. She supposed, in some sense, he was correct. Why pay homage to a person who it seemed had an essential hardness of heart? She herself would have, she supposed. The bonds of family were too tightly wound about her. She wondered whether it presumed too much to go herself—would Darcy wish her there? Or would he wish her to stay at Pemberley? Her head soon ached with wondering about it.

In any case, she need not have thought of it overmuch, for shortly after dinner, Lady Saye returned to Pemberley with bad news. "She is gone," she said softly, though her eyes remained dry and un-reddened.

Saye, who had removed himself from his newspaper to kiss his wife, immediately picked it up again, muttering, "My regrets, Uncle Lewis, but you knew it was too good to last. She's a'coming for you, old boy."

"How is Mrs Fitzwilliam?" Elizabeth asked.

"Quiet and grave but calm," Lady Saye told her. "Her mother was not always kind to her, if you must know the truth. Lady Catherine wished for different things for her daughter and never allowed her to forget it."

"Like what?" Elizabeth asked curiously while Saye began to read aloud from his news sheet. A party for the festive season had captured his interest, and he spoke with increasing volume over the ladies, who nevertheless disregarded him.

"She wished to make a true society lady of Anne, and the truth was, Anne was never interested in that. Even her hair! Anne's hair, so dark and poker straight, and Lady Catherine was always having the maids curl it, even when she was very small, and once she put some potion on it that was supposed to turn it flaxen but instead only made it mouse brown and very, very dry. Oh, she was forever criticising her figure and form, she deplored that Anne could not play or sing, and French bored her to tears. She blamed Anne's health, but I think it was merely an excuse. She preferred to think her daughter sickly before accepting that her talents lay elsewhere. Anne is fond of math, which Lady Catherine found abhorrent in a lady, and she is quite a fast runner too."

"A fast runner," Elizabeth echoed her faintly. Well did she know how it was to wish in vain for a mother's approbation. It pained a daughter to know that she was not the daughter her mother wished for! Sympathy bloomed in Elizabeth's chest as she recalled the particular agony of watching her mother die, knowing she would not ever receive the feelings of maternal affection that she longed for.

Such thoughts remained with her throughout the day and into the night, even in her dreams. Mrs Bennet became Mrs Younge—whom Elizabeth had never seen but somehow knew exactly who she was in the dream—and was trying to steal little Charles, grabbing him and running away into the woods, threatening to chop off his fingers if Elizabeth came too close. She chased after them, cold and anxious and always missing him by fractions of an inch, right up until they all leapt headlong into a roaring river. She awoke with a jolt.

Just a dream, she told herself, sitting upright and looking around her at all the reassuring, now-familiar sights of her bedchamber. Only a dream.

But she could not quite dispel the uneasiness in her heart. As she had often done when awakened by fearful dreams and night terrors, she got out of her bed, donned her dressing gown, and went to her nephew's room. She had often found in cases such as these that simply laying her eyes upon him would do her well.

She entered the room, almost immediately stumbling over the toy soldiers that were scattered about the floor. Beside them was Charles, also on the floor, sound asleep. Clearly someone had decided to have some night-time diversion.

Elizabeth bent, heaving Charles into her arms with a quiet grunt. Charles mumbled some sleepy nonsense in response. "Up in the middle of the night," she whispered. "My silly little prince."

"Where is George?" he mumbled as she laid him on his bed. "Not done soldiers." He turned into his pillow as he said it, instantly falling back into deep slumber.

George? Her nerves fairly jangled with trepidation—or was it delight?— as she tucked the coverlet around Charles. George. Was she here? How long ago had she left? Which way had she gone?

Elizabeth left the room on the tips of her toes, hasty but silent and scarcely breathing in the effort to hear something, anything that would lead her to the elusive George. Outside? Inside? Down this hall or that one? But perhaps George was long gone, maybe did not even exist. Elizabeth resisted the impulse to growl with frustration.

On an instinct, she chose to move, silent and swift, towards the blue room, flying up the stairs on her toes, straining to listen for any noise no matter how soft or small to guide her. The blue room was no longer boarded up—she had no idea when Darcy had removed the board, but at some point he had—but neither was it occupied. When she pressed the door open, it was silent and dark with a musty, unoccupied air.

Darcy's bedchamber was across the small sitting room, and she moved towards it, telling herself she should not but somehow unable to stop herself. She was thankful for the small sliver of grey moonlight that enabled her to navigate the space. Darcy's door was slightly ajar, and she pushed it open quietly.

At first, she saw nothing to alarm her, then her eyes adjusted, and she saw a grey, ghost-like shape standing by his bedside. It was a woman with her head bowed, appearing to look at something on his bed table.

Some part of her wondered whether the woman was a dream. Elizabeth thought perhaps she was still in her bed and had never quit her dream of running after Charles. Another part of her supposed she might be seeing things that were not there.

But no, for the apparition moved. She raised her head, turning and facing Elizabeth. She startled in a distinctly real and un-ghostly manner and dropped something from her hand.

"Who are you?" Elizabeth whispered. "Is it you? Are you George?"

A fraction of a second too late, the girl spoke, her voice having a forced, almost-Irish accent. "Begging your pardon, miss, I'm to light the fire in here." She moved towards Darcy's fireplace, her eyes trained on Elizabeth like a frightened animal.

Elizabeth took a step towards her, her hand stretched outwards. "Miss Darcy?"

"No miss, me name's Nan. I am new in the scullery, and Mrs Reynolds sent me to light the fire."

Elizabeth took several slow steps, at last drawing near to her. "Mr Darcy is not here, so there is no need for a fire."

The girl's head dropped for a moment, but she soon raised it again. "I...I must have the wrong room then. 'Scuse me."

She moved as if to push past Elizabeth, but Elizabeth stopped her by placing her hand on her upper arm. "Miss Darcy, I know it is you."

There was not enough moonlight to see the expression in the girl's eyes, but Elizabeth could sense her warring within herself. Was the game up? Could she fake her way out of this?

"I know what happened to you," Elizabeth said softly but firmly. "I know you were lied to and betrayed by your companion, I know you consented to an elopement, and I know all about your hand."

Reaching down, Elizabeth grabbed at the girl's hand, hoping she would find the injured one. Fortune was with her and she felt a hand that was missing a digit, though in a fraction of an instant, the girl yanked her hand away.

"Georgiana Darcy is dead," she hissed. "She died many years ago. Let her be dead."

"She is not dead. She lives on in the hearts and souls of those who still love her dearly."

"What do you want from me?"

"I wish only to have a conversation with you." Elizabeth took a step backwards. "Will you not come and speak to me?"

The girl hesitated but Elizabeth pressed the opportunity. "Not for long. Just a few minutes."

Elizabeth backed slowly into the sitting area, keeping her eyes on Miss Darcy. She could not make out her face in the dark room and hastened to light a lamp the moment she found one. The light was long unused but gave off a decent glow. Elizabeth sat down in a comfortable chair, relieved when Miss Darcy eventually came to join her, perching on the edge of a sofa as if she might bolt at any moment.

Her head had been lowered throughout, but once she was seated she raised it, her lips set and her jaw tight. She did not utter one sound.

"Lady Catherine died this morning," Elizabeth said.

Miss Darcy nodded stonily.

"I understand that…that she has been hiding you these years. From the very beginning, after Mrs Younge injured you."

"Yes," said Miss Darcy, fury curling her lip, "she did. I made a deal with the devil herself, and the joke is on me. Mrs Younge would have killed me too, but she would have done it a lot quicker than Lady Catherine has."

"Will you tell me about it?"

In a flat, dispassionate tone, Miss Darcy related her side of the dreadful tale. Gertie had taken her off, handing her into the care of her aunt, who then proceeded to place her into service, threatening her with death should she ever reveal herself. Mrs Jenkinson became her shadow, quick to correct her if she showed any signs of her prior 'airs,' as the woman termed it, At last, she had enough and decided to take her fate into her own hands.

"So you come to Pemberley at night?" Elizabeth asked.

Miss Darcy bristled. "I take what was once mine and no one

else's. Nothing that has any value except the little bit it gives me to get away. I daresay my brother would wish that much for me. You are his mistress, are you not?"

The change in subject was so abrupt it threw Elizabeth off. She stumbled a moment before saying, "No, of course not."

Miss Darcy sniffed, then leant forward, a strange, feral look on her countenance. Elizabeth noticed that she did not have the look of a gentlewoman any more. Her skin was rough and spotted, and her hair looked dull and lank. "Sure looked like it to me, the way I saw you kiss him."

"You…you saw me kiss him?"

She did not answer Elizabeth directly, instead challenging her further. "Can you deny it?"

Elizabeth could not deny it so said only, "I am not his mistress."

Miss Darcy raised one eyebrow, the shadow of her former, perhaps haughtier self emerging. "If you say so."

"I love him." It was a strange and awkward admission particularly to someone who received it with such scepticism. "I truly do. I love your brother and he…he loves me."

Miss Darcy said nothing for a moment. "Love is not always what you think it is. Maybe you are in love, but maybe you are just stupid. A woman never really knows until it is too late."

"Let me help you," Elizabeth said impetuously. "Miss Darcy, surely—"

"Stop calling me that," she said sharply. "See here; we all have secrets, and the guardian of mine just took them with her to hell. Just keep your mouth closed about me, and I shall not care two straws for what you and my brother do here. You start telling people about me, and I might just have to pass along some little rumours about Mr Darcy's mistress. Do we understand each other?"

For whatever Elizabeth had expected, it was not hostility. She scarcely had time to think of it before Miss Darcy stood, evidently meaning to disappear again.

Elizabeth leapt to her feet, at the girl's side in a trice. "You cannot leave!"

"Who says I cannot?" Somehow Miss Darcy turned them about, playing the aggressor and moving such that she had backed Elizabeth against a wall. "You think you have any power over me? I have survived beatings and humiliations, betrayals, mutilations—there is nothing you can do to me. Do you understand that? I am not Georgiana Darcy. I do not know what or who I am, but that girl is dead; she died in London years ago, and I am what was left behind."

"I have no wish to hold power over you," Elizabeth cried, her heart thudding. "Do you not know how he misses you? How losing you haunts him?"

"Then there is no good to come from stirring any of this up again, is there?" Miss Darcy sneered. "Do not be an idiot. Can you not comprehend what will come if 'Miss Darcy' is found again after so many years?"

Her words gave Elizabeth pause. "But you must have wanted him to find you? Your journals—"

"She took those from me. Brought them here to make Fitzwilliam read them so he would feel what his failures had done to me." She shrugged. "She likes guilt, heaps it on in full measures."

"But she is gone now," Elizabeth said earnestly. "You are safe."

"I am not hiding because that old shrew made me," Miss Darcy said with an excess of derision.

"Then why?" Elizabeth asked. "Why not go to him, show him you are well, or as well as can be, after all? Let him help you, he can—"

"No, no, no." Miss Darcy shook her head. "You do not understand any of this do you? I hid because she was right. Nothing good can come of finding me. My shame will ruin them all. No decent person will ever receive any Darcy again. You would not wish to marry into such scandal as this, would you?"

As was her custom, Elizabeth had thought only of sating her curiosity; it had not occurred to her—not in any serious way, anyway —to imagine the consequences of Miss Darcy's re-emergence. Stupid really. Had she imagined Miss Darcy could come from hiding, brush off her skirts, and resume her old life?

Miss Darcy had watched her face closely, rage fading into cold acceptance as she saw Elizabeth reach the same understanding that obviously she herself had reached so long ago.

"I hide because I love him." In a gentler tone, she said, "I have no idea why you persisted in this, asking so many questions when it would have been so much easier to stay silent. In any case, it is not my wish either. I have long since reconciled myself to being a solitary female making her own way in the world. I intend to be gone within a week."

"Within a week?"

Miss Darcy nodded. "There is a ball at my house for Twelfth Night, and the scullery is close to where they have the carriages kept. I only need to get to Derby, and the rest shall go from there."

She glanced over at the window, and Elizabeth followed her eyes, seeing the first pale fingerlings of dawn touching Pemberley's Wood.

"I shall go now," she said. "Keep quiet about me, for both of our sakes."

DARCY THOUGHT that he must surely go straight to hell for standing in the very same room where his dead aunt was laid out and thinking of Elizabeth. At one point, he found himself wondering how this latest in a long string of ill-timed interferences of his aunt would affect his courtship of her; he immediately chastised himself for thinking such things, but all too soon, his mind had again wandered to the sweet curve of her lips and the feel of her body pressed against his.

Have I not had sufficient guilt and misery? A man in love most naturally wishes to enjoy that splendour and spend time with his beloved. I wish for lightness of heart and glad feelings and—

Stolen kisses in the woods. Darcy winced. His conscience would insist on full honesty.

It was the sound of Fitzwilliam sitting down with a thud in the chair next to his that interrupted what surely would have become pleasantly lascivious thoughts. "Anne wants her brought to Hunsford Parsonage, but I say let us be done with it here at Matlock. She is a daughter of the house, after all. It seems perfectly proper to me."

"Faster, easier, and less expensive too," Darcy agreed. "Can we have his lordship insist on it?"

"He has no objection, but Saye does." Fitzwilliam rolled his eyes. "He thinks it will induce the witches to hold their black rituals here. Says it should bring on dark magic and curses with the likes of her entombed therein, plagues of black flies and grasshoppers, all manner of dreadful things."

Darcy shook his head. "He does always take a dramatic stance,"

"He just told Anne that if Lady Catherine is left here, then the very moment he inherits, he will have her dug up and burnt or sanctified or whatever is required in such cases. Then he told my father he would sell Matlock to a tradesman and have them put a factory over her ladyship's grave just to spite her." Fitzwilliam laughed, somewhat ruefully. "Nothing is done easily in this family, but you knew that."

Darcy smiled. "That is true."

They sat in companionable silence for several minutes until Fitzwilliam, with a little poke, said, "I do hope mourning will not affect your plans too grievously."

"I have no plans," said Darcy. He had to admit to himself, however, his disavowal might have been more persuasive had he not broken into a broad grin as he said it.

"Three months puts us into Lent, does it not?"

Darcy shrugged. "So it does."

"Would be unseemly to have a wedding during Lent."

"Frowned upon in church, though with a licence…"

"You would not be the first to do it. Lord Bratten-Jones married the week prior to Easter. But Miss Bennet seems like the church-wedding sort."

"I have no intention of marrying during Lent. "After the Season, perhaps."

Fitzwilliam turned to look at him squarely, his countenance expressing every bit of astonishment he felt and then some. "After the Season? That is months away, Darcy!"

The explanation came easy to Darcy for he had thought of little else through the long night's vigil by her ladyship's bedside. "When Lady Catherine is laid to rest, I intend to put up a marker for Georgiana. Lay her to rest as well, so to speak. Lay the whole of these last five years to rest. So I shall mourn, and when it is done; I shall put away the weeds and be me again."

"Be you?"

"She knows me not."

"Of course she knows you! She has been living in your house for months now."

"She knows the sad, forlorn man, the man cast out of his own home, the man who was exiled, the man who…who had no certainty. The man who held no command of his own life." He sighed. "I shall not have her pity me."

"Pity you?" Fitzwilliam laughed. "Darcy, you suffered a great tragedy."

"I did," Darcy replied firmly. "But it did not define me. I must have her meet Fitzwilliam Darcy as he is and was. If she loves that man, then our future will be settled."

"IT OCCURS TO ME," said Lord Saye, "that we never did learn precisely where Georgiana might be found."

Elizabeth and Saye had, at length, confided in Lady Saye what they had learnt in Bakewell. They had sat in the drawing room until all hours, relating the dreadful tale to her.

"So what do we do now?" asked Lady Saye.

"I shall tell you what we cannot do," Saye replied, pacing and gesturing grandly. "And that is to honour the old witch in death. I shall not do it."

Elizabeth was grateful to leave the subject of Miss Darcy. "But we must," Elizabeth argued. "For the sake of Mrs Fitzwilliam, if none other."

Saye immediately entered into the debate with spirit, insisting that he and his wife would pay no deference to Lady Catherine. He pronounced that he despised a hypocrite over and over until Elizabeth thought she might hit him.

Lady Saye was silent, until eventually, she pronounced her judgment. She turned to her husband. "Funerals are for the living not the dead," she scolded her petulant husband. "We must think of Anne and Richard."

"Richard!" Saye protested. "He is delighted!"

"Oh Saye," Lady Saye admonished.

"I shall not have her at Rosings," he announced. "I would not have the shades of Matlock polluted by her presence in my churchyard. Indeed, I should think Gertie might just sink her offshore somewhere, but Gertie has gone missing; he is probably halfway to Greece by now."

Of course, what Elizabeth had told no one was the tale of her meeting with Georgiana. She hugged the secret close to her, reliving and replaying it until she was at last compelled to write it down, not wishing to neglect any detail.

She was at a crossroads; she knew it, and she felt it. If they told Darcy what they had learnt from Gertie and the Gileses, he might try again to find her, but by then, it would be surely too late. Miss Darcy intended to run in the next few days, and Elizabeth had no doubt that she would nevermore be seen in England.

But if Elizabeth took Darcy to find her, if she flung wide the door and induced him to see his sister again, then would ruin follow. Pandora's Box would be agape, and the secrets of Pemberley would spill out and stain everyone they touched.

Would you wish to marry him still? Elizabeth asked herself. She had seen much lesser scandal than this and knew the pain it brought to families.

Am I prepared to stand beside him in the tides of shame that will persist forevermore?

TWENTY-SIX

ALTHOUGH MISS DARCY HAD NEVER SAID SO HERSELF, ELIZABETH FELT quite sure that she was in service at Halliday Abbey. It was in Loxley, hence the lynx drawing, and it was the site of the Twelfth Night ball. Elizabeth had learnt that the approximate distance from Pemberley was 15 miles; not exactly an easy distance to cover in a dark night, but for an accomplished horsewoman—as Miss Darcy once was—not impossible.

Elizabeth sat at the pianoforte, her fingers running idly through well-worn songs while Charles and the young Miss Fitzwilliams sang beside her. She wondered what the true consequence would be should Miss Darcy re-emerge. Elizabeth supposed it depended upon how much of the story became known. She winced knowing how little Darcy would wish for any sort of attention, talk of any kind to be bandied about. But it would be inevitable. The ton, believing her dead these many years, would be alit with discussion of her, and once it was known she had eloped and then disappeared... well, the salacious tidbits would be passed around at dinner parties for years to come.

Her fingers drifted, unattended, into a favourite song. Actually, it had been Jane's favourite tune, a light, sweet melody that had much of the character of Jane herself. Elizabeth smiled, her eyes landing on little Charles as he played with his new friends on the rug even as her mind moved towards her last, most painful memory of this song. She had been at Netherfield, in the music room, with Jane sitting in a chair with baby Charles nestled to her bosom.

"Play my song for me, Lizzy."

Elizabeth smiled from her perch on the piano bench. "Is it not a bit energetic for now? Charles looks like he is ready to fall asleep."

"Oh, it will not disturb him."

And indeed, it did not. Elizabeth took some care not to sing over-loud, but it did not signify; Charles took a few moments to see how much of his chubby fist could be shoved into his mouth, but when that was done, he fell quickly into slumber.

And then Jane rose to take him to the nursery, stumbling and nearly dropping him in the process. "Lizzy?"

Elizabeth halted in the middle of the song and rose to go to assist her. "Jane, what is it?"

Jane was suddenly glassy-eyed and pale, with two bright red spots staining her cheeks. "I do not feel well."

"Go rest," Elizabeth urged. "Give me the baby."

And Jane agreed, which was the most frightening thing of all. Elizabeth removed Charles from her arms, taking him up to his nursemaid, and then returning to find Jane still in the same chair. She gave Jane her arm and help her into the care of her maid up in her bedchamber while trying not to notice how heavily Jane had leant on her.

Returning to the present, Elizabeth said with a little sigh, "And that was the last time she heard her song." And the last time she had held her son, though Elizabeth tried not to think of that. Oh, to have just one more day with Jane! It would never signify if Jane were scorned or degraded, or if she brought shame along with her, Elizabeth would delight in the moment she laid eyes upon her.

And it was in that moment that she knew her feelings for Mr Darcy, for no matter what, she wished the same for him, that he might be able to lay eyes on his precious sister once more. She delighted in being that person that would give him so precious a gift no matter what it cost her.

"And no matter what shame is upon him," she murmured aloud, "it should be far better to be with him in shame than without him in honour."

DARCY FOUND himself nearly aloft with relief on the road returning him to Pemberley from Matlock. The death of Lady Catherine had proven a strange and oppressive affair; indeed, he felt guilty for not feeling more sorrow at her passing. But the rest of the family seemed to share his sentiments. In such cases as these, people would often reminisce fondly about the deceased, but in this particular case, that had been impossible. Any episodes of fond remembrance that had been related had been in amusement at her more severe or outlandish actions.

Anne had been, in turns, a hysteric and a dry-eyed realist. Fitzwilliam had put his full energies into soothing her, and it had begun to wear on him. Darcy saw him turn peevish and impatient as the days of mourning wore on. When at last the plans had been made to send her to Rosings, Fitzwilliam seemed relieved to be able to take some action, even if that action involved a long journey accompanied by his aunt's corpse.

A chill wind blew hard upon him as he exited his carriage and hurried towards the door, shocked to find Elizabeth awaiting him on the other side—shocked but delighted. "Miss Bennet!"

"Mr Darcy." She smiled, but he immediately saw it seemed a trifle forced.

"Are you well?"

"I am. May I…that is…I wonder if I might speak to you?" She was excessively formal, perhaps even a touch cool, and a pang of fear struck him. What did she intend to say to him?

Anxiety rendered him likewise cool. "Of course. The library perhaps? I need only a few moments to change my attire."

She nodded. "I shall go there directly and await you."

He went immediately to his bedchamber, glad to find his man already waiting to help him into attire more amenable to a day at home. He was quiet as he changed, worries assailing him like a flock of black crows. Did she intend to leave? She was grave, her manner impenetrable. Perhaps her arrangements had been already made? Yet, damnation, he could not help but recall how very beguiling she looked in the way she held her shoulders so straight and elegant, her beautiful eyes filled with some emotion even though he did not comprehend what it was.

In minutes, he was ready. He entered the library to find Elizabeth standing by the window, lit by a beam of sunlight as she perused a book. She closed it and straightened as soon as she heard him enter. Again, she gave him a forced smile.

He had not closed the door behind him, and she surprised him by crossing the room to push it entirely shut.

"It is important that we not be disturbed," she said.

"Very well. I am at your mercy."

He gestured to the comfortable sofas upon which he had whiled away many pleasant hours. She went and sat very primly, her eyes fixed on her shoes. He joined her, sitting across from her and observing her for a few moments. He had come to know her very well, and he delighted in the small details of her: her habit of tucking her hair behind one ear and the way he could, at times, detect her pulse in her neck.

As I can now. He realised she must be very nervous as her heart was beating so hard that he could plainly see it. Surely if she was nervous, her subject could not be heartbreak.

"How are you?" She raised her eyes to him. "The last days must have been exhausting."

"They were. Very much so, but such is life…uh, death rather."

After a short pause in which she seemed disinclined to speak, he said, "You are no doubt concerned for your arrangements here with Lady Catherine gone."

She raised her head, seeming surprised. "Oh. Yes, that."

"Saye and Lady Saye would have you go with Charles to London and spend some time with them there."

She looked faintly interested by that thought. After a moment's contemplation, she asked, "And what are your plans?"

"Does that signify?" He was teasing her, but he did wish to know.

Her eyes searched his face. "For as much as I would like to go to London, it is a poor prospect if you are in Derbyshire."

Her daring seemed to astonish her. He watched her blush and then turn her head to the side, such that her curls blocked his view of her countenance. It did not matter however, for the memory of her confession would be enough for happy dreams for nights to come. He smiled, broad and easy, then said, "Then I shall come to London."

"Perhaps you will," she said quietly. "But perhaps not."

"Elizabeth," he said, suddenly understanding the reason for her sombre attitude, "if you are in doubt of my affections—"

"No, no," she stopped him.

"Then what?"

"I do not know how to begin."

"I have always found it best to start at the beginning."

She turned her face back to his, searching his eyes for a moment before she began to speak.

"The beginning, I suppose, would be when I read Miss Darcy's journals...," she said and then continued on an extraordinary tale of lynxes, the tea shop in Bakewell, havercakes, and ghostly hoof beats in the night.

She went on to tell him that a lady called Mrs Giles gave her a pin that was recognised by Lady Saye, and how queries in Bakewell and a visit to Saye's smuggler friend Gertie furthered the notion that Georgiana was alive—and implicated Lady Catherine in her disappearance.

He was silent as she spoke, at first with more interest than alarm, wholly unable to connect the fantastic tale with himself. It was a strange sense that he was hearing about something that happened to someone else, someone in a faraway place in a time long past—one of the frightful tales from the Brothers Grimm perhaps, terrible but nothing to do with him.

Then it pierced his consciousness: Lady Catherine, his own aunt, had harmed his sister, had hidden her from him.

"No!" He leapt to his feet, shouting and protesting. "You are quite mistaken."

"Sir—"

"This Gertie person has... You know those people are criminals, do you not? Respectable people do not linger about dark alleys telling such tales!"

"I know this seems incredible but—"

"They likely killed her themselves! They could have been in league with Wickham or Mrs Younge or any manner of... Lady Catherine was my aunt!"

Elizabeth rose, coming close to him, laying her hand on his arm, and squeezing him lightly. "I know," she said gently. "I do know, and it pains me to hurt you with this information. I could not do it save for one thing."

He looked down at her hand gently caressing his arm and then at her lovely dark eyes fraught with concern on his behalf. His breath came in fast gasps from the exertion of his protests and from the fear that had risen within him, fear of what else Elizabeth intended to tell him.

"I have seen her," she said softly. "Your sister is alive."

He removed his arm from hers with a shake, turning and going to the window where he stared at the lifeless gardens.

She came and stood beside him, a calm presence in the midst of his tumult. He was very cold, he realised suddenly, and his hands had clenched into fists by his side. "Where?"

"She comes to Pemberley sometimes in the night. I came upon her when I had awoken from a bad dream and went to see Charles."

"And you let her leave? You should have kept her here! In her home! How could you let her go?

"No." He began to pace, arguing with Elizabeth, God, and himself. "A dream. It must have been a dream. There is simply no way—Fitzwilliam has searched everywhere for five years! All the resources of his military, and he never saw any sign of her."

Elizabeth cleared her throat gently. "Your cousin had the decided disadvantage of having the malefactor—or malefactress, such as it is —in his confidence. No doubt Lady Catherine insisted on full knowl- edge of his activities and used them to move Miss Darcy hither and yon, such as was needed to keep her hidden from you."

He cursed and immediately repented of it, apologising to Eliza- beth, who only nodded.

"She has been coming to Pemberley and taking some small items that belonged to her—she did not say so explicitly, but I think she has sold them, intending to flee England and begin a new life."

"Where is she now?" He was already moving towards the door. "A new life? Nonsense. She belongs here."

"If she knows you are coming for her, she will run." Elizabeth offered him a small smile. "She has no wish to be found."

"No wish to be found? That is absurd. Of course, she must wish to resume her old life and with Lady Catherine gone..." He was ranting like a madman, and he knew it.

"I daresay her old life, such as she knew it, is gone," Elizabeth said gently. "Perhaps it is best to consider her new life, the life she had set her eyes upon, and not attempt to force her to become Miss Darcy again."

Her words, so gentle but correct, halted him in his steps. What was he thinking? That Georgiana could emerge from the shadows of ruin and go about the ballrooms of London as if nothing had ever happened to her? The ton thought she had died in Ramsgate. Her friends from school had written him many, many letters of condolence. He sank into the nearest chair.

Elizabeth remained on her feet and, in sweet, soft tones, told him of her meeting with Georgiana. That Georgiana should have been so fierce amazed him.

"But she has been through so much," said Elizabeth. "No doubt she felt cornered by my appearance. She has learnt to fight, sir."

When she concluded the details of that visit, she told him why she thought it likely that Georgiana was at Halliday Abbey. "She will leave on Twelfth Night after the ball. No doubt she wishes to leave amid the hubbub of carriages and partygoers to escape the notice of Mrs Jenkinson."

"But Lady Catherine is dead and can do her no harm Surely if she knew that—"

"She knows," said Elizabeth. "I told her, but her concern now is you and the Darcy name. She does not wish to be the cause of shame and scandal."

The rage that had been with him so long, the regret and exquisitely painful sorrow, welled up within his chest. He covered his face with one hand, unwilling to allow her to see his weakness. When he was at last in command of himself, he raised his head and found her kneeling at his feet, earnestly looking into his eyes.

"A lady, once she has seized hold of her destiny, is not easy to persuade in another direction. You can fix this for her, but on one matter she was definite—she refuses to accept the name of Miss Darcy."

"Perhaps it was not even her," said Darcy, suddenly recalling that Elizabeth did not know what his sister looked like. "It might have been some thief, coming in the night to steal! A former servant or the like."

Elizabeth rose to her feet and smiled encouragingly at him. "I know only one way that we can find out."

"You know that I would never object," Saye informed them. "But my father, should he learn of it, will be scandalised. So we must keep the excursion between us."

The reason for the excursion was to attend the ball at Halliday Abbey. Being ostensibly in mourning, none of them should have even considered it, no matter how much they despised Lady Catherine for what she did. Lord and Lady Saye had been shocked to hear of Elizabeth's encounter with Miss Darcy in the night, but unlike Darcy, they had been less doubtful of it. Evidently, nothing Lady Catherine had done would ever surprise them again.

"No one knows that she died yet," Lady Saye mentioned. "She did not attend services in Derbyshire, and no doubt they will make more of it once she is back at Rosings."

"My father still would not like it known that we disrespected any member of the family, no matter how little that person deserved respect."

"So we shall not tell him," Darcy said impatiently. Elizabeth touched his arm gently. Since the afternoon of her startling revelations about Miss Darcy when he realised his sister might be found, he had wished to storm off and snatch her bodily back to Pemberley. Elizabeth persuaded him to take better care, such that her removal would not raise any hue and cry. "Quietly," she reminded him. "For later considerations."

"I shudder to think that Georgiana was in that house," Lady Saye mentioned. "Halliday is quite the libertine when it comes to his servants."

Darcy's face darkened, and he looked like he was about to hit something. Elizabeth said quickly, "She said nothing of that to me. Now let us make our plans to get her away from there."

In Lady Saye's increasingly round state, attending a ball was out of the question, so it would be Elizabeth, Darcy, and Saye who did the necessary. Once they arrived, Darcy and Saye would mingle about, seeking Miss Darcy above stairs, while Elizabeth played the confused miss below stairs, appearing to be lost so she could look around.

Elizabeth's hands shook while she prepared for the ball, so much so that Lady Saye's maid, Boucher, had to scold her several times to sit still. Lady Saye had given Elizabeth a gown. "I assure you, when I am not laden down with child, I am about the same size as you," she said with a little laugh. "It will do very well."

And indeed, Elizabeth thought it the most beautiful gown she had ever worn. It was a deep blue with a gauzy, silvery overdress upon it, and Boucher did her hair high on her head with small ringlets framing her face. She descended the staircase feeling like quite the lady of society, if only for an hour or so.

Darcy awaited her at the bottom, standing with one hand tucked into his pocket and staring at her quite unabashedly.

"Shall I do?" she asked.

He reached out, taking her hand for the last step or two. "Yes," he said huskily. "You will do very, very well."

He leant forward as if he intended to kiss her, and she tilted her head up, quite willing to be kissed, but he only rested his cheek against hers. "You are irresistible," he murmured.

"Yet you resist me," she whispered in reply.

"Will you dance with me?"

She laughed, sounding a little throaty even to herself. "Should the opportunity arise, I would be honoured."

He pulled back with a deep sigh. He drew his hand from his pocket, and in his grasp was a beautiful necklace of exquisite sapphires. She gasped.

"Will you honour me and wear my mother's necklace this evening?"

She did not gasp again, though she considered it. Wear his mother's jewels? Could there be any more obvious statement of affection?

"Turn," he said. "Allow me to put it on you."

She turned, and he stepped close behind her, but before he began, she looked back over her shoulder, her eyes meeting his. For a moment, she wished desperately that he would kiss her.

"In case I have not said so…" She swallowed. "Come what may, I shall be here. I shall be beside you."

His eyes closed a moment, and he laid his lips within her curls. His breath whispered along her neck; it was not a kiss but near enough, and she closed her eyes, simply relishing in it.

"You are the love of my life," he said, in a voice so low as to be scarcely heard.

Alas, male footsteps were heard too soon, and Darcy busied himself with the necklace. Saye entered just as Darcy discovered the complexities of ringlets, necks, and jewellery that was determined to become entangled.

"Why Boucher, how tall you have gotten!" Saye snickered. "Good lord, no wonder you are not married, Darcy. You cannot even attach a necklace properly." He shoved his cousin to the side, taking command of the necklace. Saye spun Elizabeth around once the necklace was successfully fastened, examining her critically.

"Nice," was his final judgment.

For his own attire, he had chosen a jacket of scarlet velvet. A multitude of lace erupted from his sleeves, and his trousers seemed to have been painted on him. "No one could accuse you of being in mourning," was Darcy's only remark as they boarded the carriage to take them to Halliday Abbey.

"Beau Brummell be hanged," Saye replied blithely. "I am tired of going about like a black crow all the time."

The three fell into silence as they travelled. Elizabeth was worried, worried she was wrong, that Miss Darcy would not be at Halliday Abbey. After all, Twelfth Night was a popular night for a ball, why had she not considered that before telling Darcy so assuredly that he would find his sister there. Her heart began to pound as she realised that if they missed her, she would likely be gone off to wherever her purloined jewels would take her.

I shall not fail him. Elizabeth clenched her hands into fists underneath her reticule. Miss Darcy would be found at Halliday, and Elizabeth would search the servants' halls and scullery until she saw her. Mrs Giles had been in the scullery before her marriage, and perhaps Miss Darcy had taken her place.

It seemed to take an eternity to enter the house, to greet their host, and utter all the required utterances: how delightful the evening, how easy their travels, how wondrous her arrangements. The lecherous Lord Halliday gave Elizabeth a look over that made Darcy's jaw go tight, but he said nothing about it, simply steering her down the line. Saye was gone as soon as it was done, off to find what he could while Darcy offered his arm to Elizabeth, and they made a slow perambulation of the room.

They had been careful to time their arrival such that there was a crush, and the bustle of partygoers would hide their doings. Elizabeth immediately observed the door at one side of the ballroom where the servants went in and out, and as soon as she deemed it safe, she gave Darcy a look, slipped her arm from his, and followed a man with an enormous tray of used glasses.

She went silently down the stairs after him and found herself in a vestibule with a long hall to the right and the kitchens to the left. The man went left, so she went right, into a hall containing several bedchambers, presumably for the servants.

There was a large bed in each, likely for two girls, and Elizabeth thought they looked clean and well kept; Miss Darcy had not been mistreated, at least not so far as her lodgings were concerned. Alas, the rooms were also wholly unoccupied, but she might have guessed as much. What servant, on such a night as this, would be permitted to languish about in her bedchamber?

The kitchens showed all the disarray expected of a house in the middle of a party. Pots and pans, wine glasses, and plates were all stacked in precarious ways on every surface. Elizabeth walked over to the sink, which was likewise piled high.

Surprisingly, despite the apparent work that needed doing, the kitchens were empty of human habitation. A spaniel with chocolate-

coloured ears and soulful eyes stood on her hind legs, working diligently to obtain the remains of a ham; she cast a look in Elizabeth's
direction but did not stop her feast. Elizabeth smiled, stroking one of
her ears. "I do not suppose, ma'am, that you have seen Miss Darcy
hereabouts?"

Just as the words left her mouth, the door to outside swung open,
and a young girl, round-faced and merry-looking, walked in. She did
not look at Elizabeth but at the spaniel. "Miss Bessie! You get on out
of here now! Oh!"

She bobbed an absent curtsey towards Elizabeth as she set down
the large pails she carried; they were full of water. She then took a
hold of the dog by the scruff of her neck and began to tug her
outside. "Nan! Miss Bessie is getting in the dishes again!"

In the door, Miss Darcy appeared, her eyes having a more cheerful
look than when Elizabeth had seen her last. "Miss Bessie," she
scolded laughingly. "Not again! You threw up for—"

Her words died as she caught sight of Elizabeth standing there.
Her face hardened, and her eyes changed from a sparkling cerulean
to a stormy blue. "Martha, take Miss Bessie to the barn for me, will
you?"

She did not take her gaze from Elizabeth while Martha did as
asked. As soon as the door closed, Miss Darcy said, evenly, "Why are
you here? I thought we understood one another."

"Miss Darcy, I think if you—"

She crossed the room with quick paces. "I said," she poked Elizabeth on the arm, "do not call me that."

"I beg your pardon." Earnestly, Elizabeth entreated her. "Come
back with me. Come back to Pemberley and see your brother, please,
I beg you."

Miss Darcy shook her head. "Obstinate, headstrong girl! I—"

But her words died as the door to the kitchen was pushed open.
Colour drained from her face as she looked over Elizabeth's shoulder
at whomever had entered. Elizabeth turned to see that Darcy had
arrived.

His colour matched that of his sister, and he remained as stock-
still as she did. Elizabeth realised she was, in some manner, between

them. She took a step back, and her small movement seemed to break their enthralment.

In a choked voice, a child's voice, Miss Darcy whimpered, "Fitzwilliam?"

Darcy crossed the room in a trice, his arms reaching for his sister, pulling her into his chest. Tears sprung to Elizabeth's eyes just watching their reunion, hearing as Miss Darcy choked out repentant syllables and Darcy replied, soothing her, murmuring that he loved her, and above all, assuring her that he would fix everything.

TWENTY-SEVEN

AFTER SOME MINUTES WATCHING THE DARCYS' REUNION, ELIZABETH went to retrieve Miss Darcy's small case and find Saye. Elizabeth and Saye called for the carriage; Darcy and his sister slipped from the kitchens by a back door, narrowly missing the happily noisy Martha on her return from the barn. Saye was uncommonly grave when he beheld Miss Darcy, seeming unable to utter a syllable, only giving her a kiss on her cheek and then, following a deep inhale, said, "Let us get you home then."

They began the ride in silence. In the darkened carriage, the expression on Miss Darcy's countenance could not be seen, but at length, she said, "I am glad to see you all, but you must know nothing can change. I shall sail later this week."

The silence in the carriage was heavy and foreboding, but Elizabeth silently lauded both men for refraining from an immediate protest. "We wish only to help you, Miss Darcy, but perhaps there might be other possibilities for your future?" Miss Darcy stiffened beside her.

"Your father's illegitimate child," Saye pronounced from his corner of the carriage. "That was my idea."

"And a dreadful idea it was," Darcy responded. "Why should I bring dishonour to my father? People would surely recognise—"

"Who among us does not have a by-blow?"

"Do you? No. Do I? No. Does Miss Bennet? She does not and neither does Georgiana. So there you go—not everyone has a by-blow, and my father certainly will not have one given to him posthumously. On to the next idea."

"What do people think happened to me?" Miss Darcy asked.

There was a slight pause until Saye said, "Died at Ramsgate. Boating accident."

Elizabeth cleared her throat. "I had thought that perhaps we might say she had been recovered after all this time. Maybe she had been found by some kindly fisherman or the like but had suffered some injury that made her forget who she was."

"Lizzy." Saye chuckled indulgently. "You are a sweet girl, but you read too many novels. Let's let the menfolk do the thinking, shall we?"

Elizabeth—by now too accustomed to Saye's outrageous speeches to be offended—said, "The menfolk doing the thinking is why it's taken five years to find her."

Miss Darcy gave a surprised yelp of laughter, following which she hurriedly clapped her hand to her mouth.

Darcy said leant forward, "Georgie, Wickham is in a cottage on the outer reaches of Pemberley."

"I know," said Miss Darcy. "I was the one who wrote to you, asking you to retrieve him."

Darcy had told Elizabeth once some time ago that Wickham had been placed in a lunatic asylum, and he had received a letter from an unknown person, likely female, informing him of it. Guilt had induced him to go see him, and what he had seen was appalling. "People placed in circumstances worse than I should keep my cattle," he had told her. "Chains, sitting in their own excrement, infection, disease... Death should be far preferable to the poor creatures." So he had removed him and placed him in a cottage, knowing it was far better than the man deserved.

"Why did you write the letter?" Saye asked curiously. "I should have thought you of all people would be glad to leave him to suffer."

Miss Darcy sighed. "I was dreadfully angry and bitter when I saw where he was. I knew he would not live very long in such conditions. I wished him removed—not to save him from the asylum but to prohibit him from the relief of quick death. I am ashamed to admit that, but it is true. I wished to prolong his agony."

She shrugged. "In any case, the joke is on me. He is living a fine life, out of his wits but happy enough."

"It is a great deal more than he deserves," Darcy said gravely. "I shall remove him directly."

In a soft, strong voice she said, "Keep him where he is."

"I shall not have him—"

"Fitzwilliam. I cannot stay at Pemberley, so whether George Wickham is there or not there does not signify."

"Georgiana, we shall find a way—"

"No." Her words stopped his at once. "It will not do. Pray, Fitzwilliam, I should never have boarded this carriage if I thought you would understand it to mean I intended to remain at Pemberley."

The silence that followed was nearly deafening. Although the carriage was dark, Elizabeth could readily comprehend the distress marking Darcy's countenance. It was a great relief to find they were turning into the drive to Pemberley.

Lady Catherine had done one good service to them. Nearly all of Darcy's servants had been, in some manner, replaced during her tenure. Only Mrs Reynolds and three or four others had known Miss Georgiana Darcy. Of these, only Mrs Reynolds was entrusted with the knowledge of their secret visitor.

They entered quietly, going immediately to the sitting room that adjoined the blue room and Darcy's bedchamber. Therein stood Mrs Reynolds, tears in her eyes and a smile on her lips. Elizabeth perceived immediately that the blue room stood open, a fire in the fireplace and a clean, sweet smell emanating from within. The bed looked plump and inviting.

Miss Darcy recoiled from it.

Her mouth and chin trembled alarmingly, and she took a step

backwards. "No, no… may I sleep in the attic room? What about…in fact, I am not tired; perhaps I should just while away a few hours, um…on the grounds, perhaps?"

Darcy looked at her as if she were mad while Mrs Reynolds began to fret about her possible error. Elizabeth stepped into the sitting room and quickly closed the door to the blue room. It seemed to bring some relief to the scene.

"Georgiana, see here," Darcy began, "I do understand—"

"There is too much in that room," Miss Darcy replied, still trembling. "I do not want to be in there with all the ghosts of my past."

"Ghosts? There are certainly not ghosts—"

She wrapped her arms tightly around herself. "I cannot—"

"George!" A small voice was heard at the door. They all turned to find Charles standing there in his nightshirt. "What is everyone doing?"

Before anyone could answer he crossed the room. Elizabeth watched as Miss Darcy exhaled a deep sigh and then knelt to be at his level.

"I thought you said you could not play with me any more? Did you already go on the big ship?"

Elizabeth watched Miss Darcy take another deep breath. "Not yet. Soon, my sweet. Very soon."

Charles looked up at Elizabeth, his round cheeks still flushed with sleep. "I asked George if I could go, but she said you would miss me too much."

Elizabeth laughed. "Yes, that is true. I would miss you to the point of madness."

"We should all go on the ship," Charles suggested enthusiastically.

"That would be fun, would it not?" Elizabeth reached down and scooped him into her arms. "But first, my beloved, you must stop wandering about in the middle of the night. You are meant to be asleep! Let us get you back to your bed."

"May I come too?" Miss Darcy asked. Darcy, who had been conferring quietly with Mrs Reynolds, looked up with some surprise.

"Of course," Elizabeth said.

Charles, in the artless manner of a child, leant from Elizabeth's arms to reach for Miss Darcy, and Miss Darcy, after a moment of hesitation, took him.

They went towards the nursery, Charles's eyes already beginning to droop. His blankets were in disarray, as if a tornado had gone through them, and Elizabeth took a moment to straighten and fix the bed. When she straightened, she found Miss Darcy clasping a sleeping Charles to her, gently rocking back and forth. Elizabeth stepped aside, allowing Miss Darcy to place him on the bed, to tuck the blankets around his small form, and to take a moment to behold him, so vulnerable and innocent in his slumber.

"I was once with child," she whispered, her eyes far away.

Elizabeth placed her hand on Miss Darcy's arm lightly, and the girl continued to speak, her gaze still aimed at Charles but her sight elsewhere. "Wickham did not like it. It was...well, it is a very bad memory. I cannot speak of it, but I do like to think of the child I might have had. He would have been just a wee bit younger than Charles, I think, but not by much."

Elizabeth could not reply to such as this. That it had caused the girl great pain was undeniable, but it was a pain that she had, it seemed, walled over with great determination. Elizabeth wondered how many other sealed vaults of misery lay within the poor dear.

"Perhaps you would wish to stay with me," she said, scarcely without thinking of it.

Miss Darcy turned to her, her eyes bright, though her voice remained soft for Charles's benefit. "Yes! In your dressing room perhaps? Or is your maid in there already?"

"Oh, um, no, not in my dressing room. With me—I used to share a bed with my sister Jane, and I confess I have been lonely ever since she left me. Much better to be warm with another in these winter months." Elizabeth wondered whether she was mad for having suggested it, but Miss Darcy appeared so relieved and delighted, there was no turning back.

They found Darcy and Mrs Reynolds awaiting them outside the nursery, Darcy pacing anxiously while Mrs Reynolds had the quiet air of a servant who feared she had displeased her master. Miss Darcy halted in her steps on seeing them. Elizabeth put her hand on Miss

Darcy's back, announcing, "We have hit on the perfect solution. Miss Darcy will share with me tonight."

Though seeming dubious, Miss Darcy's pleasure in the idea forced its acceptance on the others. From thence, Mrs Reynolds bustled her off for a bath and a change of clothing—causing another minor bit of difficulty when it seemed Miss Darcy intended to wear some threadbare nightshift not even a servant at Pemberley would have found acceptable. Elizabeth was again called upon to step into the breach, offering up one of her own nightgowns.

Elizabeth could hardly imagine what time it was when at last she and Miss Darcy lay in the bed together. Miss Darcy was silent while Elizabeth extinguished the lamp and settled on her pillows. Despite the hour, Elizabeth did not expect to sleep for some time.

"You must love him very much," said Miss Darcy, "to endure such as this."

Elizabeth turned over on her back, staring at the canopy above before replying. "I did think about what you said to me," she admitted. "I could not discount it—we both know it to be true. But then I realised that I would do anything for him, suffer any amount of shame alongside him, because to be without him was unimaginable."

She reached out in the darkness, hoping to find Miss Darcy's hand. "Having searched my heart, I want you to know that I am prepared to weather any storm."

"Even the shame of a sister so disgraced?"

"Even so," said Elizabeth. "You see, I was raised in the country. I was rarely in London, certainly not in any exalted society, so should society shun us, it would not matter to me. I am happy in obscurity."

"I am glad you think that," said Miss Darcy. "But for myself, I do not agree. I have suffered for my mistake, truly I have, in ways none of you will ever know. But I am determined I shall begin anew. I am twenty… Oh!"

"What is it?"

The girl gave a little chuckle. "My birthday. I had quite forgotten it although it was the reason I chose to leave when I did. I am one and twenty now."

"You are full grown." Such an absurd statement, Elizabeth mused.

Georgiana Darcy had lived a lifetime, surely more than she herself could ever comprehend.

"Full grown and in full understanding of my heart and mind. It grieves me to bring more pain to my brother, and I am gratified to know that he is willing to bear a lifetime of shame on my behalf. I, however, am not. I must leave, go somewhere no one has ever heard of any Darcys and would not care if they did."

"Where do you want to go?"

Miss Darcy hesitated a moment before answering. "America." She paused again, then added, "I thought I could be a school teacher."

"That sounds nice." Elizabeth waited a moment, then pressed gently, saying, "Let him help you."

"He wants only for me to stay," she said immediately.

"I think once he knew your mind, he would understand—"

"Miss Bennet, you heard him. He wants only to restrain me."

"What he wants right now is to clutch you to his chest and never let you go. But I think he can be prevailed on to do what he can for you—even if it means letting you go."

DARCY PACED HIS BEDCHAMBER, his emotions too high to be wrestled into slumber. Georgiana was here, she was alive! It elated him until he recollected that she wanted to leave him again, a crashing, disappointed sensation.

But she is here, she is safe, she is whole.

Was she whole? Or had Wickham damaged her beyond what could be seen? He could not bear to see her hand, once so lovely and delicate, now scarred and mutilated. Could she still play the pianoforte? She had been so gifted. The loss of what she had been made him long to weep, to scream and hit someone or something...

But then he reminded himself, she is here at Pemberley. She will be well.

So went the night, his thoughts run amok in his mind, circuitous and sometimes contrary thoughts, thoughts laced with delight and fear and anger and sorrow and joy. His steps ran along with his thoughts: sometimes quick, sometimes lively, sometimes dragging to a stop.

One thing was certain. She could not just leave. She belonged in her rightful place at Pemberley, and he was quite certain that with careful planning and careful execution of those plans, the past five years would soon be no more than a bad memory.

Into his fears and cares, pleasanter thoughts would intrude, most of which concerned Elizabeth. What she had done for him, for his sister, made his eyes sting with happy, grateful tears. He blessed the day that Bingley had, no doubt absentmindedly and unadvisedly, made him the guardian of Charles, for had he not, likely Darcy should never have known the name Elizabeth Bennet. Never to know her… The idea made him shudder. What a bleak life he should have without her!

He turned his chair to the window, watching the leisurely retreat of night and the languid approach of sunrise, first grey and then rosy-pink. It was this time, he felt, when Pemberley was best seen, its majesty made golden and splendid. Surely Georgiana could never wish to leave such a place as this?

He heard a light knock and moments later a click. He smiled to think that Elizabeth would let herself in. "Mr Darcy? I hope you do not mind. I knocked several times."

"I was lost in my thoughts," he said. "Come sit." He offered her his chair and then dragged another over to sit with her.

"Is my sister—"

"Still sleeping. I confess, it took a good bit of time for sleep to find us. We had too much to say to surrender immediately to Morpheus."

He availed himself of her hand, bending within his chair to kiss it once, twice, three times. "I can never, ever repay what you have done for me."

"I would not wish you to. "I am glad she is back. I am glad to do any part in relieving her sorrow. But most of all, I was moved to act because…"

He raised his head from her hand, meeting her eyes that were steady and sure. "Because I love you," she said in a voice scarcely above a whisper. "Above all, I wished to please you."

"You do please me." He bent over her hand once again. "You please me very much."

So caught was he in his lovemaking that he nearly missed her next words.

"I am afraid when I tell you the content of our discussion, it will not be very pleasing to you."

He sat up with a sigh. "She wants to leave."

"She wants a new life."

"She will have a new life!" He rose to his feet, agitation bringing a prickly flush to his skin that made him want to move. "She was a child when last she lived here, and now she is twenty—"

"Twenty-one."

"Twenty-one!" He muttered a soft oath, falling back into his chair.

"And possessed of an experience the rest of us can never imagine."

He watched the fingerlings of sunlight coming through the window caress Elizabeth's cheek and make marvellous hues appear in her hair. "She is all the family I have."

"I understand." She studied him, those deeply compassionate eyes seemed to bore into him. "Have not I felt it too? Jane and I should have married gentleman who were brothers or, if not, then dearest friends, and we were all to live near enough to visit often. We would spend happy days on the lawns with our children, watching them tumble about while our husbands did gentlemanly things in the background."

"Gentlemanly things?" Darcy permitted her a half-smile. "Talk of horses and cricket perhaps?"

"But as it is, it will never be. Jane died, her husband died, and that life I thought we should all have died too. Life took a turn, and it does me no good to repine what was lost."

"I care nothing for the scandal," he said. "You yourself said once, 'my family and how dearly I love them will always prevail over the dictates of society.' I think it was then that I began to love you, for saying so clearly what I had always felt."

Elizabeth enfolded his hand in hers. "But you see, she does care. She does not wish to live out her days under the shadow of her mistakes."

Darcy yearned to protest. For years, he had wanted nothing more than to see Georgiana's beloved face, to hold her near, and help her, heal her. Now, it seemed he must set her free. "What have I not learnt from you, my dearest, loveliest girl? First, you taught me to accept Georgiana's death. Now, you are teaching me to accept her life."

Elizabeth gently chafed his hand with hers. "Whether or not you accept it, she will go. She intends to go to America. The only thing that remains is to decide whether you will help her or hinder her."

"I shall help her," he said, mortified to feel something very much like a sob rising up in his chest. He coughed, forcing back his emotions. "Of course, I shall help her."

Very boldly, Elizabeth then leant over, kissing his cheek. "Shall I go see if she is awake? Perhaps you two should talk soon, to reassure her."

"Very well."

On the wall of his study immediately next to his door was a simple charcoal sketch of Hickory Hill, the place he had called home while he was exiled in America. Elizabeth paused to examine it, tilting her head in that way he found so beguiling.

"What house is this?"

He came to stand beside her. "Hickory Hill. In the county of Fairfax, in Virginia." On her questioning look, he added, "America."

"Is it yours?"

"For a time, it was. I settled there and bought some little piece of land. It was not worth much, but it was prettily situated near Alexandria, which is a port, and they are establishing their capital city there. I daresay it might be worth something someday."

"It sounds very pleasant."

"America is not England," he said quickly. "It can never be England."

"I think that was rather their point in going to war for independence," she said with a little smile. "Because they did not wish to be England."

"In one way, America is exactly like England: a bachelor must be always agreeable to flirting and dancing with any eligible young lady in sight else he is thought uncivil. Mr George Walter, a taciturn bloke who wished mostly to be alone, angered everyone in sight by neglecting his attentions to their daughters."

"Heaven forbid!" Elizabeth said with a little laugh. "So it is still yours then."

"For now."

"Very nice." And with one last touch of her fingers to the picture, she departed.

TWENTY-EIGHT

FOLLOWING BREAKFAST, DARCY RETIRED TO HIS UPSTAIRS SITTING ROOM with his sister. Knowing all they needed to say and decide, Elizabeth did not expect to see them for the remainder of the day.

Lady Saye's maid, Boucher, along with Jones, Saye's valet, were bustling about; the Sayes would be departing soon, wishing to be in London with ample time for Lady Saye to prepare for her confinement. She called Elizabeth into her dressing room in the morning to speak to her about their intentions.

"What is your plan, Lizzy?"

"My plan?"

"We would be absolutely incandescent with delight if you would consent to join us in London."

"Right, of course." Catching sight of herself in Lady Saye's looking glass, Elizabeth saw herself flush. What was her plan after all? The lot of a spinster, she reminded herself. Shuffled to and fro with whosoever would take her. Of course, being a spinster was much less agreeable to her now that she had someone she wished to be married to.

Lady Saye was busy rubbing some sort of potion from a beautiful cut-glass bottle onto her skin. "Darcy thought it might be agreeable to you to have fun this Season. You never had a Season in London, did you?"

Darcy wishes me to have a Season in London? "Um, no, I did not."

"So there you go!" Her ladyship beamed. "Clearly I could not be with you"—she gestured towards her abdomen—"but Saye would have ever so much fun taking you about. The concerts, the plays, the balls!"

"I do enjoy those things, though I should find it much more agreeable when…" She stopped herself. It was too uncomfortable to mention Mr Darcy when he had not actually declared himself, not formally in any case.

"Why did you never go to London? There must have been an enormous number of eligible bachelors in Hertfordshire for your father to think he would marry you all off without taking you out."

"I do not think he thought of it much at all," Elizabeth replied. "But it is true, we were never in want of suitors."

"Even so," Lady Saye urged, "it would be unfair to you to marry before you have had your fill of beaux."

"You are very kind," Elizabeth replied woodenly.

The shame of it was she knew Lady Saye meant it kindly. But why would she be urging Elizabeth towards other gentlemen? Were these her ideas or Darcy's? What did she know that Elizabeth was failing to see?

DARCY WAS CLOSETED with his sister for several hours, not again appearing until it was nearly time to dress for dinner. When he did at last emerge, his face pale and drawn, he invited Elizabeth to join him in his study.

"You look very tired," she observed when the door had closed behind them.

He gave her a wan smile even while he escorted her to a comfortable chair by the fire. He chose the chair next to hers. "I confess I am.

Everything of these past days, from exultation to desperation, has drained me. She is determined to leave me."

Elizabeth watched him as he stared into the fire, his face unreadable. "She is alive, and she will be well. I daresay no more can be hoped."

He did not reply directly. "She wants to go to America, and I must accompany her. I simply could not live with myself if I did not at the very least sail with her, see her situated..." He shook his head. "A young lady, alone in such a savage country. I wonder whether I have gone mad to even ponder it."

Elizabeth said gently, "I daresay it is the best you can do by her, else she will simply hie off on her own."

"You are correct." From his pocket, he withdrew a folded piece of paper. "Here. This is for you."

Elizabeth opened it and gasped. It was a bank draft made out for three thousand pounds. Heat rose in her cheeks at the sight of it. "What is this about?"

Darcy waved his hand tiredly at it, stretching his legs towards the fire. "Georgie wished for you to have that—she was quite surprised to learn her fortune is largely intact. A token of gratitude perhaps, but I am sure she is hoping she can depend upon your silence."

"Count on my silence?" she asked carefully, examining the paper in her hands as if she expected it to turn into a live serpent.

"About the events, the things you have witnessed here at Pemberley." He smiled tiredly.

"I see."

"In any case, will you not find it useful as a means of establishing yourself in London while I am gone? I have not found your father's interest in yours or Charles's well-being in any way satisfactory."

Elizabeth swallowed against the indignation such a statement produced. "In such cases as these," she said, "I believe gratitude is the common mode, and if I could feel gratitude, I would now thank you. But I cannot—I have never desired your money, or your sister's, for any deeds I performed for your interests."

"What do you mean?"

She rose with purpose and stepped close to the fire. Without looking at him, she crumpled the bank draft and tossed it into the fire. She turned back to look at him. "Is that more clear?"

"Elizabeth!" He leapt from his chair. "Have you gone mad?"

"Have you?" she retorted. "Your sister I can excuse—she scarcely knows me. But you! Surely you must have seen this is an offence and an insult against my character?"

"How is money an offence and an insult against your character?" Darcy bent, retrieving the barely-burnt paper from the fire, then rose again and turned to Elizabeth. "Yes, I do know you, and I also know your situation. You have no fortune to speak of, nothing to—"

"So you make love to me in the morning and then in the afternoon you come and hand me a cheque. Am I some sort of prostitute then?"

The door pushed open just then, and Saye stood framed in the doorway, a bowl of soup in his hand. "Well, this sounds like a promising show!"

Darcy did not remove his eyes from Elizabeth. "Saye, this is a private matter."

Saye paid no attention, settling himself onto the couch nearest them. "Hardly private when someone two rooms over can hear the shouting."

He took a large, noisy slurp of soup, then said to Elizabeth, "Do go on. You were at something about a prostitute?"

Darcy carefully unfolded the paper, smoothed it out, and handed it back to Elizabeth.

"You know why I did as I did," Elizabeth said, accepting it from him. She knelt, shoving it as far as she could into the fire without setting her arm alight, then stood again. "And it was not because I wished for money or even gratitude! I did it because I love you, and I wished to see you reunited with her. And now you wish to take that feeling on your behalf and reward it with a 'Farewell. I am off to America, and here is your payment for services rendered'."

The cheque had taken fire and was burning vigorously. Saye, behind her, whistled long and low. "Badly done, Darcy."

"Saye, get out of here."

"And leave Miss Bennet unchaperoned?" Saye asked, "I could not think of it." Reaching into his coat, he removed an enormous chunk of brown bread, biting into it with undisguised glee.

"It is clear I have misjudged our attachment if you think you need to pay me for goodness and mercy."

"It was not my intention, nor was it Georgiana's, to insult you," said Darcy. "But I might ask why you must reject this benevolence with such incivility. How do you intend to live?"

He was correct, of course, insofar as she had no means to support her and Charles save to return to her father—who did not wish for that in any regard. Of course, what she could not say was that she had hoped he would want her to stay with him as his wife. Evidently, that was a fool's wish.

"As much as I would prefer to situate you in town myself, should it become known I had made and paid for your arrangements..."

"People would think I was your mistress," she finished for him, in a flat angry tone.

"With that money, you can keep yourself in town, reliant on no one."

Elizabeth turned away from him, indignation giving way to humiliated sorrow. What a fool she was! Marriage—he had never spoken of it. Instead, he intended to leave for parts unknown for an indeterminate length of time, while she was expected to gad about the ton? So much for kisses and love and promises of a future.

"Darcy, this is not going well," Saye opined. "You should know, Lilly spoke to her about the plan to go to London for the Season and reported to me that Miss Bennet was decidedly unenthusiastic. Is that not right, Miss Bennet? You made some comment about knowing plenty of gentlemen already."

"Yes," Elizabeth said warmly. "Indeed, I feel like I may know one too many of them already."

With a wink towards Darcy, Saye said, "That's an insult for either you or me old boy. Let us hope it's me, because if it is you, then I fear you will have an uphill climb."

Darcy came to her, reaching for her hands and holding them close. "Elizabeth, I have only your best interests in heart. You have not been in London—"

"And I never felt I was wanting for it either," Elizabeth replied, tugging her hands away. "I am five and twenty, and I have been in plenty of ballrooms, have had my share of suitors. I am not unaware of what I want and need."

Darcy rubbed his forehead with one hand, and Saye groaned quietly. "This is difficult to watch. Darcy, stop faffing about and ask the girl to marry you."

Darcy gave Saye a look while Elizabeth felt her face blaze with embarrassment.

"What?" Saye took another spoonful of soup. "You are in love with her. We have all seen it from the moment we saw you with her. Let us put an end to this pointless drivel."

"People who love people," said Elizabeth in acid tones, "do not always wish to marry those people."

"You cannot doubt I wish to marry you," Darcy said quickly.

"Of course, I can. You just told me you intend to hie off and leave me to dangle about London all Season."

Darcy sighed heavily. "You do not know me, not as I really am."

It was such an incredible statement, she knew not what to say in reply.

"The man you know has been enmeshed in this tragedy for years now, hiding and uncertain and sad and angry. You know not the person I really am. Indeed, I scarcely know that person anymore."

"If I love you at your worst, does it not follow that I should still love you at your best?"

She turned then, making plain her desire to flee, but he begged her to stop. "Elizabeth, wait," Darcy said behind her. "I do wish to marry—"

"Pray, say nothing more. I do not want any measure of obligation from you, not money, not some proposal that I have persuaded and induced you to give me."

She turned and exited the room, leaving the two stunned gentleman behind her. She ran to her bedchamber, where from actual weakness, she sat down and cried for half an hour.

"Pray, do not speak another word," Darcy snarled at his cousin. He hardly knew what to do next, whether to chase her or allow her some time to herself. Though the former was his preference, he suspected the latter might be more wise. He had no idea what he would say to her once he had her, and he feared above all that he would likely make the situation worse.

Saye departed and Darcy found himself wearing a hole in his carpet, fretting and pacing about what had just happened. Georgiana had been so firm, so definite in her wish to offer Elizabeth some financial reward for what she had done, that Darcy had scarcely taken any time to think of how it might seem—how Elizabeth might take it to mean he believed she had mercenary motives. He thought nothing of the sort and wished he had told her so. It was nothing more than a solution of sorts to the problem of how to keep her while he was gone.

Of course, he wanted her to go with him, but he had presumed she would loathe the idea of taking herself and Charles so far away. He groaned. It seemed he could not have botched it more thoroughly if he had set out to do so.

"I must fix this," he said to no one. "I must speak to her and tell her…" What? He knew not what he should say. I love you, and you are coming with me? But Elizabeth did not like to be ordered about, that much he had learnt of her.

He quit his study merely because he could no longer stay on the scene of his blunder. Not knowing where his footsteps might take him, he found himself seeking out his sister, finding her in the sitting room between his bedchamber and the apartment she once called her own. She had what appeared to be one of Elizabeth's gowns in her hands and was stitching away at it.

"What are you doing?"

"Lizzy gave me this, but she is smaller than I am, so I need to change it a little."

He bit his tongue to keep from saying what she no doubt already knew: there were many much finer gowns in the wardrobe in the blue room, and those gowns would already be fitted to her.

"In any case," she said with a sly glance in his direction, "Mrs Darcy would not wear a gown like this, would she? It is a pretty gown but not fitting to such a station as Mrs Darcy should occupy."

He rolled his eyes and muttered a soft word of lament. Georgiana stilled immediately. "Have I said something wrong?"

He did not answer immediately, and she pressed him, saying, "It is clear to me she loves you, and you appear to be in love with her too. I thought surely a proposal must be soon in the offing."

"Yes," he said tiredly. "But I just I hardly know what I did but we argued, and it is…complicated. I was so pleased with your wish to give her recompense for all she did, but she found it offensive."

"I offended her?" Georgiana's eyes went wide with horror.

"Not you. Me. She said that you scarcely know her, so it is natural you would wish to ensure her silence—"

"But no! You did not tell her I wished to buy her silence? Because I only wished to…to help her. You said she had no fortune, that her father had all but cast her off, and I wanted to help in some way as she has helped me!"

"I hardly know what I said," he admitted. "Whatever I said, I said it wrongly, and she is angry with me. I think she might have been upset at the idea I would leave for America with you, and she would remain here."

"No doubt she believed it meant you did not love her," she said, her eyes on her sewing. "As you were willing to leave her for months and allow her to roam about London meeting other gentlemen."

The idea of Elizabeth with other men made his stomach clench immediately. "I thought it would be agreeable to her. It is surely not agreeable to me."

"Perhaps you should tell her so."

"And deny her the chance to find—"

"To find what? Someone better than you? She could search the world over and never find a man like you, Brother."

"I fear you are too partial to me."

Georgiana did not deny that, simply lowering her head and stitching away at her gown. At length, she continued, "She was willing to remain by you, enduring whatever ignominy I brought to you both. I do not think you could find a greater love than that."

Darcy nodded, aware she could not see him but unable to say anything more.

"If you love her…"

"I do."

Georgiana smiled gently. "If you love her, and she loves you, then pray, do not risk losing it on my account. There is too much that is ugly and bad in this world; we must nurture what is precious and good. All you need to tell her is that you love her and wish never to be parted from her."

Darcy leant over and kissed her cheek, seeing with no little satisfaction that her bloom was returning. "You are very wise, dear sister."

Georgiana had been delighted by the idea of Hickory Hill being her home even though it required extensive and persistent conversation to persuade her not to enter it as a servant. "The people there do not know me," he told her. "They had no idea I had a sister, so your appearance will be no shock to them."

Hickory Hill, he explained, had been arranged much as Pemberley was, though on a smaller scale. Most of the original acreage had been designated for smaller farms leased by the farmers who were under the protection of the estate—freed men whose papers had been purchased by Darcy, granting them the right to live and work as any man did.

What delighted Georgiana most of all was that Darcy had seen fit to erect a small schoolhouse. "Some of the parents do not wish the children sent there," he said. "There are many old superstitions among them, and one is: to learn to write as the English do would bring damnation to their souls. But for those who wish it, it is there, and they can learn to read and write and do sums."

"It is difficult to imagine being housekeeper for such a place."

"Then perhaps you would do better to imagine yourself as mistress, because that is what you should be.

"It seems it's all settled, then" she said. "And far more advantageously than I should deserve."

With Georgiana settled as well as she could be, Darcy found his mind racing, thinking of his missteps with Elizabeth. What was she doing even now? She had taken her dinner from a tray in her bedchamber and had not been seen since. He waited in the drawing room, hoping she might emerge, but she did not. Was she angry?

Sad? Crying? Making plans to run off? The possibilities were endless and infinitely anxiety provoking.

Lady Saye was drooping from her exertions and preparations over the day and soon left Saye and Darcy to their own amusements. "Shall we play some cards, Darcy?"

"I cannot. I have no mind for them this evening and no inclination to let you win money from me, not after that disaster you enjoyed in my study earlier."

"You are not still angry, surely?"

Darcy rolled his eyes. "Implacable resentment has always been my fault, as you well know."

"Then allow me to do you a good turn. Perhaps it will appease that resentment of yours." Saye was busy shuffling a deck of cards but paused long enough to say, "I saw her walking towards the library only moments ago. Go on then; see what you can make of it."

Unprepared, Darcy nearly said he would not; then he decried his own stupidity, rose, and went to find her.

As Saye reported, she was in the library with her back to the door as she sought something among the shelves. Her fingers trailed back and forth along the titles to no avail. Darcy watched her a moment wishing he knew what to say but finally thinking that if he stood there all night, he would likely be no better prepared than he was at that moment.

Darcy moved soundlessly through the room, managing to come close to her without her realising he was there. When he put his arm around her, she startled, whirling to see him nearly toe to toe with her.

"You frightened me!" she scolded him. "I did not hear you."

"We must add that to the list of things for which I shall beg your forgiveness." He smiled tentatively, relieved to see she awarded him a small smile in return before turning her head away.

Silence stretched awkwardly between them while he frantically tried to find something to say. His eyes followed her hands, touching this book and tapping that one, until she found a former favourite of his. It was an old book that had belonged to his father, a token of George Darcy's grand tour and time in Italy. Darcy had not read it since he studied Italian, but if memory served, it would be perfect.

She watched him while he pulled the book down, then opened and paged through it gently. He found exactly what he wished for and raised his eyes to her. "Would you permit me to read something to you? I have found myself thinking of it very often these days."

"Of course." He had inspired her curiosity just as he had hoped he would.

With a slight clearing of his throat, he began:

> In paradiso el cor n'hanno portato
> que' begli occhi ridenti,
> ov'io ti vidi, Amore, star celato
> con le tue fiamme ardenti.
> O vaghi occhi lucenti
> che 'l cor tolto m'avete,
> onde traete - sì dolce valore?

IT WAS NOT easy to raise his eyes from the page and thus comprehend her response, but he did. She stood transfixed, her eyes on him and her colour high. In the event there was any confusion, he translated for her in soft tones.

> Those lovely laughing eyes have carried my heart to Paradise,
> Where, Love, I saw how you hide there, among your ardent
> fires,
> O lovely shining eyes that snatched my heart away,
> How, say - does such sweet power move?

"AS YOU SAW EARLIER, I have not the talent of recommending myself to a woman I love. I said nothing of what I meant and meant little of what I said. I hope Signor Poliziano will better express how I feel to you, since I made such a dreadful jumble of it myself this morning."

He took a step towards her, drawing near enough to hear the soft exhalations of her breath and catch the sweet, light scent of her. He continued to read.

I' ero già della mia vita in forse:
madonna in bianca vesta
con un riso amoroso mi soccorse,
lieta bella et onesta:
dipinta avea la testa
di rose e di viole,
gli occhi che 'l sole - avanzan di splendore

I had grave doubts for my life: my lady dressed in white,
With her loving smile, she saved me, pure, beautiful and happy,
Her hair was decked with roses and violets, and her eyes yet -
brighter than sunlight prove

WHEN HE LOOKED UP, she had moved towards him, and he lowered the book and placed his other hand on her waist. He bent, touching his lips to hers, first softly but then with rising passion. He felt her melt into his embrace.

"I want you to marry me," he murmured against her mouth, punctuating his words with soft kisses. "Immediately. And come to America with me."

"I thought you wanted me to remain in London and—"

"No," he stopped her words with a kiss. "No, I said that only because I thought it would make you happy. The very notion of it fills me with misery, but I would do it if it would bring you pleasure."

"What brings me pleasure is being with you. Nothing else. Only you."

"Will you marry me?"

She smiled, looking up into his eyes with all the love he could have ever wished for. "Yes," she said. "I shall."

TWENTY-NINE

THE MAN STRAIGHTENED AS HALLIDAY ABBEY CAME INTO VIEW. NO ONE could see him ensconced as he was within the luxuriously appointed carriage, but appearances began within. He brushed at an imaginary spot on his trousers, then reached up to ensure his hat was on, tilted at just the precise angle that those among The Quality wore their hats.

The sting of having failed Mr Darcy had not yet left him. He had been so sure Miss Darcy was dead—and now, it seemed she had been found. All quite secret of course and he was honoured to have been one of the very few entrusted with the information, but nevertheless, it should have been he who found her. Instead, it was some slip of a girl from the country who earned the master's gratitude.

Not just his gratitude either. Mr Pritchard sniffed. Miss Bennet was not what he thought suitable for the likes of Mr Darcy of Pemberley, but it was not for him to question the gentleman's wishes. No, the only thing on his mind was this recent bit of business. It would be done and done for the absolute best. Nothing would be neglected. All instructions should be heeded to the very letter.

The carriage stopped, and moments later, the coachman opened the door. With his lips pursed, Mr Pritchard withdrew a card and said, "Please tell the housekeeper my first order is with Lady Halliday herself. Following that, I shall see Mrs Jenkinson, Sarah Jones, and Joseph Cooper." He laid it into the coachman's hand and added, "Quickly, please, I do not have all day."

The coachman returned in a trice. "The housekeeper went to get them, sir, and asked whether you would like to wait in the sitting room."

Mr Pritchard descended from the carriage with all the pomp of a monarch. He moved into the house and down the hall with a slow, measured gait, his nose aloft. His hat and gloves he surrendered to the maid, but the rest remained with him.

The dowager Lady Halliday was quick to meet him. He found he liked her; there was no swooning or silliness over the facts he related to her. She merely heard him, read the letter from Lord Matlock, then set about doing what needed to be done.

Shortly, Miss Sarah Jones entered the room, Mrs Jenkinson immediately behind her. Miss Jones appeared terrified, glancing back at Mrs Jenkinson as if she expected the worst but knew not from which direction it should come. "I don't know this man," she protested in a loud whisper. "I couldna did nothin' to him, I don't even know him!"

"Quiet, girl," Mrs Jenkinson hissed. With a sickly sweet smile, she said, "Why Mr Pritchard, how do you do?"

"Where," Mr Pritchard asked, with a little frown of displeasure, "is Mr Cooper?"

"Well naturally, I told him he must go and clean himself, put on some proper attire to meet such a distinguished—"

"Yes, well, I do not have all day, so pray, do go and tell him to hurry along."

"Oh, um, well, of course. Of course." Mrs Jenkinson excused herself, going into the hall and no doubt ordering some maid or footman to do his bidding. Mr, Pritchard smiled at the consternation he caused her, knowing she deserved far worse.

Miss Jones had retreated to the farthest corner of the room and stood twisting her apron in her hand and regarding him with terror.

Mr Pritchard, trying to be kindly, turned his head and looked out the window. It was a fair prospect, a rolling lawn leading towards the meadow, but it bored him in an instant.

Fortunately, Mr Cooper presented himself moments later. Mr Pritchard did not miss the smile he shot towards Miss Jones or the light blush that arose on Miss Jones's face at the sight of him. Young love. He almost smiled at the thought of it.

"Miss Jones, pray come here to me," he said, reaching into his pocket.

The terror was back, but with a few reassuring nods from Mr Cooper, Miss Jones was able to have courage sufficient to approach him. From his pocket, he withdrew something: a small, cheap pin fashioned to look like a lily. He handed it to her.

That she recognised it was undeniable. He knew enough about people to know when they were hiding something, and Miss Jones decidedly tried to conceal her recognition of the pin. "I don't know..." she began, but he would have none of it.

"The person who sent the pin," he said, "also wished me to give you this."

He reached into his pocket again and withdrew a folded packet. He handed her the bundle.

Miss Jones took the packet, curiosity poking through her alarm. She looked into the packet, and her eyes flew wide. Mr Pritchard saw her pallor and immediately called out, "Stand her, Mr Cooper!" just in time to see her collapse onto the floor. She released the packet when she fainted and some of the pound notes fell out. Mr Pritchard bent and calmly scooped them back into their packet whilst Mrs Jenkinson, no doubt smelling opportunity in the air, began to fuss over Miss Jones.

"A vinaigrette would be in order, Mrs Jenkinson," he said smoothly as he returned to a standing position. "I daresay you must have one on your person. All the most distinguished ladies' maids do."

Mrs Jenkinson, suddenly complaisant, was quick to produce the vinaigrette, and Miss Jones was forced to inhale. She sat up sputtering and coughing, her posture inelegant and her countenance bewildered. Her eyes immediately went to her little parcel. "What... what is that?"

"That," said Mr Pritchard, "is for you. It is but a fraction...your benefactor has set up an account for you with the rest. You will find the details therein."

"That cannot be."

"I am afraid," said Mr Pritchard, "it is."

"But...but who? But..."

Mr Pritchard said, "I am not at liberty to reveal my employer's identity. I can only tell you she is a lady who is grateful to have had your friendship in a time when she had no one else. Mr Cooper?"

Mr Cooper looked up from where he knelt next to Miss Jones. Mr Pritchard handed him a similar packet to the one Miss Jones had received. "This, sir, is yours, and this"—Mr Pritchard pulled an apple from his pocket—"is for Lady Angel."

Mr Cooper's mouth fell open as he received the packet and the apple. He appeared reluctant to open the packet, so Mr Pritchard informed him, "You will find the same sum and arrangement as Miss Jones received. If you think you might swoon, pray sit first."

"But...I don't understand." Mr Cooper looked like a fish, his mouth opening and closing as his mind struggled to comprehend this bit of good fortune.

"Allow me to explain it to you," said Mr Pritchard tartly. "You are not wealthy nor are you a gentleman. But you have a tidy sum to fix yourself in some nice trade, perhaps even marry." He looked at Miss Jones, pleased to see the expected blush. "Your lot has been improved, young man, and I suggest you make good of it."

Mr Pritchard turned on his heel. All had gone splendidly well, but the ending was the most essential part of all. He heard excited murmurings behind him and said, "Follow me out, Mrs Jenkinson. I have something for you as well."

"Of course, sir."

Mr Pritchard stopped to allow Mrs Jenkinson to walk ahead of him, noting an almost girlish skip to her steps. He despised her for that. He overheard a conversation—beneath him to listen, but he had —in which Miss Darcy told Miss Bennet of Mrs Jenkinson's participation in some of the more terrible acts perpetrated upon her person.

When they were outside beside the carriage, Mrs Jenkinson stopped. She turned, attempting to school her glee into humility but failing dreadfully.

"Lady Catherine is dead," he said bluntly. "Perhaps you already knew."

"I...I, yes, I had heard the...the sad, sad—"

"No." Mr Pritchard held up his hand. "Let us not lament the removal of the scourge. Oftentimes a mistress of such a grand estate will leave something to her faithful servants on death."

"Yes," breathed Mrs Jenkinson, her eyes lit with anticipation.

"Well, Lady Catherine is *not* one of them."

"What?" Mrs Jenkinson went from a humble pink colour to an enraged, disappointed purple. "You mean to tell me, after all I did—"

"Yes, it seems your foul deeds must be their own reward. She has done nothing for you, and it may leave you in difficulty."

"Difficulty? How?"

"This dreadful business with Miss Darcy and Mr George Wickham—who could ever believe one of noble birth would have done such terrible things? No, much easier to think it was some lunatic nurse who killed Miss Darcy, is it not?"

"I killed no one!" Mrs Jenkinson drew up. "I shall not have my reputation—"

"Soiled? Oh, I fear it already is. Indeed, Mrs Fitzwilliam, the former Miss de Bourgh, already has some questions about the nature of her supposed ill health and the role you played in that for so many years. She declares she has never been in such good health since her nurse left her. Oh, the tales of your madness, your treachery, will spread far and wide, Mrs Jenkinson."

From the corner of his eye, Mr Pritchard saw a young nervous footman appear with a bag. Splendid. The timing of all of it was quite a triumph.

"Ah, there is your bag. So there you are, Mrs Jenkinson. The kindness of my employer has granted you the opportunity to exile yourself, for in England, I fear there is nothing left to you but the opportunity to swing from a scaffold. I do not think you should like that, do you?"

Mrs Jenkinson had gone white. Rage? Fear? Whatever it was, Mr Pritchard enjoyed it—rather more than he should, he suspected.

"However, I do have one last message to deliver from the lady who sent me."

Mr Pritchard breathed deeply. It was the coup de grace, and he girded himself, wishing to imbue the delivery of it with as much theatrical dignity as he could.

"What is it then?"

"It is only this: go straight to hell, Mrs Jenkinson. I have not the least doubt Lady Catherine is arranging your place there too."

He climbed into the carriage, not bothering to look back at her. The door slammed closed, and he was soon tootling merrily down the lane.

Bakewell was next. He had heard word of a delightful bake shop and looked forward to meeting the baker and his wife.

WITH A SIGH, Elizabeth raised her head, resting her cheek on her hand as she looked out the window. She was at the desk of Lady Anne Darcy, the spot where she had worked on all of her correspondence, and the place Darcy had told her was now hers. She had resisted a little, protesting they were not yet married, but he was persistent.

Persistent in other things too. She smiled, recalling how he had stolen off with her earlier that morning, walking in the chill of the early hours with her, talking and laughing together. They had walked by the scene of their first kiss, the old well—now safely filled in and covered—and it was there, he had taken her in his arms. He had whispered the sweet endearments of a lover in her ear while kissing her to the brink of madness.

A sketch lay to the side of her letters, and she picked it up, looking over it with satisfaction. It was the sketch of what would be their new bedchamber. Darcy wished to move from his bedchamber, and so they would go one floor below. She liked how it would look, one bedchamber with separate dressing rooms—which Lady Saye had told her was absolutely necessary for marital harmony—an enormous bed (that made her blush), and a roaring fireplace. It would be their sanctuary.

Of course, it would be some time before they enjoyed it. They would sail for America shortly after their wedding, leaving Pemberley in the care of Saye and Lord Matlock. It had all been settled easily.

One dreaded task lay before her: a letter to her father.

She had always considered herself her father's beloved—his favourite daughter—and perhaps she still was, for in truth, he did not like his other daughters very much. He had never missed the opportunity to scorn them, to call them silly, or to mock any other's praise of them. Had she been a true favourite or merely the least vexing?

There had been scarcely any time to think about his rejection of her and the manner in which he had neatly cast her off and gone off to another entirely unsuitable marriage. There was a blessing in that, for she had spared herself a great deal of pain simply by not allowing herself to consider it.

So what might one say in such a letter as this? Should she tell him she had learnt the true meaning of love and sacrifice and care for family? Should she say she realised now that her father, learned though he was, was silly and thoughtless in his choice of wives? Could a daughter tell her father that she felt he was a slave to his pleasures, whether found in the flesh or in a book?

In the end, she could not give way to the darker sentiments within her. Instead, she wrote a coolly polite little missive, wondering as she did if her father would even read it in due time.

Dearest Father and Mrs Bennet,

I hope this letter finds you both well. We are all very well at Pemberley and already anticipating an improvement in the landscape and fields with the coming of spring.

Mr Darcy has asked me to marry him, and I have accepted him. He is an excellent guardian to Charles, indeed more a father than merely a guardian, and we are exceedingly happy here. We intend to engage in a journey following our wedding. We will travel to America to visit a property Mr Darcy owns. We are not likely to return to England until the autumn comes.

Perhaps, when we are returned, we shall all gather at Pemberley.

Fondly,
Elizabeth

Such a strained, stifled little note! She hardly knew how to address her father's new wife—had she been Charlotte Lucas, or even Collins, it would read "Dearest Charlotte," but those times were behind them now. Elizabeth read over her words several times, feeling the concealed disgust contained within the polite words. At the last, she decided to make one alteration to it—the invitation to come to Pemberley. She carefully copied the letter, omitting the last sentence, then sealed it and took it for mailing.

HER BROTHER HAD DEEMED it safe for her to go on limited walks outside of Pemberley, and Georgiana was heartily glad for it. The days of remaining out of sight proved trying to her spirits, no matter how well she understood the necessity. They had decided it should not raise undue talk if they spoke of a Fitzwilliam cousin who had come to visit.

She struck out in the direction where she believed she would find him, near the ruins of old Pemberton. She had seen him there before, but this time, she would speak to him.

The day was warm for January, and she had grown unused to the many layers ladies were required to wear: the stockings, the petticoats, the skirts, the overdresses. It made her smirk a little to imagine there was anything from her time in service she missed, but in truth, the gowns were less adorned and lighter, and she wished for one of them now.

Despite the fact she was looking for him, it was still a jolt when she saw him. He was so altered now; gone was his former, assured stride, replaced by a shuffling, shambling sort of gait. He kept his eyes lowered, and his arms swung like an ape. It might have been sad had she not known of the blackness within his soul.

Some strapping young lad accompanied him, but Georgiana paid him no mind, calling out, "George."

He did not hear her, so she repeated herself, still to no avail until his companion touched his arm.

"Forgive him, miss," said the lad. "He don't hear so good on that side."

She smiled at him absently and bid him give them some privacy. He nodded and walked some short distance away, still in sight but not within earshot. Georgiana returned her gaze to the bereft figure she had once believed was her husband. She had no idea what to say. It is good to see you? Except it was not. How do you do? But alas, she did not care.

"Have we met?" Wickham swept into a deep, courtly bow. "I am sure I should have remembered such loveliness had I known you before."

He does not know me. Georgiana hardly knew whether to laugh or cry.

"Perhaps," she said tightly, "you will recall me better if you think of the fortune you wished to steal from me. Or possibly you remember beating me, pushing me down the stairs, pulling my hair, and locking me in my bedchamber like a naughty child."

He stared at her blankly.

She sighed, crossing her arms over her chest. "Are you even in there? Or am I wasting my words on a shell?"

"A shell!" He brightened. "Have you walked the shore this morning? I was much delighted by the shells I found, though I must say, none I found were anything to your beauty."

"Oh, please stop." Georgiana chewed her lip a moment. She had been angry, so angry, for so long. She had eagerly anticipated this moment to vent her spleen, to say all the things she had wanted to say starting from the very moment when she realised what a terrible mistake she had made in eloping. That had been the first time she found herself with a bruised cheek because he had slapped her, and she had sat at her dressing table, filled with remorse and wondering what trials lay ahead of her.

Yes, it was that young girl she needed to remember. Young Georgiana, only sixteen, who stared into her looking glass at the mark on her face and wondered what would become of her, wondered whether the beatings would get worse and how she would stand it.

Well, she had stood it—that and much worse—but here she was, standing on two good legs with her brother's love still behind her. She knew what it was to walk through the fire and come out on the other side, changed but not destroyed.

"You did not break me," she hissed at him. "Your love for money, your wish to revenge yourself on the Darcy family—you failed. Do you understand me? You failed. I am going to be perfectly well. I shall live and love and laugh, and the truth is…"

A sting of tears in her eyes interrupted her, and she paused a moment. She would not cry. No, she had cried and begged and screamed—she had already given him plenty of that sort of satisfaction.

He seemed confused by her words, but when she paused, he smiled. "Would you fancy a turn about the room?"

She sighed and motioned to the lad, who came over at once. "I am finished with him," she said, and she truly was. The hatred in her heart was seeping away, and she was glad to see it go. A hateful heart was never happy, and she wanted to be happy more than anything. "What is wrong with him?"

The lad shrugged. "Bit o'everything, the truth been told. He had some injuries, I don't know why—maybe from the war? And he gets beat in the village fairly regular. That's why I am here, to keep him from trouble."

"Why does he get beaten?"

"Acts up with the ladies sometimes, and their brothers and fathers don't like it much. But now he's got the French disease, pretty far along, so I daresay that's the worst of it."

"The French disease?"

"He was in the madhouse, ma'am, p'raps Bedlam, though I don't rightly know. But those inmates, they all get the French disease, if you forgive me for speaking so to a lady. A lot goes on in those places that ain't fit for genteel ears, but they figure it finishes 'em off sooner so might as well let them go."

"My goodness," said Georgiana. She would not speak it aloud, but in truth, it did not surprise her. What was held within George Wickham's trousers was always destined to finish him off in one way or another. "In any case, I shall bid you a good day."

She turned and headed off in the other direction, feeling a lightness in her step she scarcely recognised. She would be well, she realised. She had faced down her devil and found he was merely a pathetic man.

It was just after noon when Saye arrived in Bakewell, and he knew he was early. He stopped at a little shop he liked and got some cheese and bread, then it was off to the stable to wait. Happily, he was not required to wait long.

Gertie was attired in the respectable clothing of a gentleman when he trotted into the yard on what Saye considered one of the most excellent pieces of horseflesh he had ever seen. An Arabian. Gertie told him he won the beast in a game, and Saye dearly hoped one day Gertie would wager it to him. Buying it was out of the question; Saye had already tried many times.

"How do, Gertie," he said, surprising the man as he dismounted. "Why, if it is not Arion! Gertie, I simply long to own this horse. Please tell me you will sell it to me?"

"What do you want?" Gertie said, stripping off his hat and gloves and taking a brush from the groom.

"Your horse! Please? Come now, I simply must have it. Name your price."

"Never."

"I was just telling someone the other day about the marvels of this horse. The fastest horse I have ever seen! Why, I daresay I could be from here to Matlock inside half an hour. Do you think so?"

"P'raps."

Saye fondly rubbed the animal's neck. "There's a good animal. No one fast as your Arion."

"What do you want, my lord?" Gertie spat on the ground near his horse, continuing with his gentle grooming.

Saye took an uninvited seat on a nearby hay bale. "I do not suppose you knew Lady Catherine passed away."

Gertie grunted. "Whats'at to me?"

"Oh, nothing. Nothing at all. Scarcely anything to me, if you must know. I just thought it strange that she passed the very same day I came to see you. Quite unanticipated!"

Gertie tossed a narrow-eyed, steely gaze at Saye but said nothing.

"My brother," said Saye, "told me that the old girl was having a bit of Veuve Clicquot before she suffered her attack. Quite strange—she was not known to drink it. No, Lady Catherine liked her gin, plain and simple. She never did have any use for wine. Ever."

"Sometimes even the most devoted gin drinker wishes for a change. In any case, it is not so rare these days, not with Napoleon in his place and the French beaten back."

"That is true. Before long, I daresay it will be in every corner of the kingdom—though it is not now. My father, of course, would not have it at Matlock. He is firm in his resolution to never line the pockets of the French."

"Yet, there it was," said Gertie. "At Matlock. In the hand of his sister."

"Just so," Saye replied with a sage nod. "It made me think—"

"You, think?" Gertie chuckled meanly. "Well, I daresay there is a first time for everything."

"Gertie, if you keep on in such a way, people will begin to think we are not best friends." Saye smiled genially.

Gertie turned on him, anger flashing in his eyes. "If you will recall, I was with you."

"Aye, you were. And I heard of her stroke as soon as I returned to Pemberley."

"So there you have it. Quite impossible for me to have gone to Matlock in the time it took you to travel to Pemberley."

"Quite impossible indeed—for *you*. For your men ..." He shrugged elaborately, then reached out and gave Arion a loving pat. "Perhaps someone might have ridden this magnificent creature to Matlock on your behalf, and perhaps that same person gave my aunt the gift of some champagne. And if perhaps that champagne had something in it that disagreed with her..."

Gertie lit on him in a trice, grasping his lapels and pulling him near, where he growled in an angry, feral way, "You want to accuse my men? 'Tis the same as accusing me, and you will answer for it."

Saye shook him off with ease, removing a step back. "I accuse you of nothing, but I daresay I applaud you for everything."

Reaching down to the place where he had stashed it, Saye tossed a small purse Gertie's way. "This is for the champagne."

With that, he turned and exited the stable.

THIRTY

For however much Darcy and Elizabeth wished to marry with expedience, there were things that would thwart them. The first was an express from Fitzwilliam begging them to delay so he might attend and see Georgiana before she left the country.

"I suppose we must concede that much to him," Darcy acknowledged. "In any case, the closer we are to spring, the better it is to sail." It was determined the nuptials should happen at the end of February, and the Darcys would sail in March.

Their greatest concern was that Georgiana should be discovered. but while the neighbours might have wondered why this visiting Fitzwilliam cousin had no wish to attend the few gatherings happening in Derbyshire in the winter, no one from Pemberley was around to hear them.

The second concern proved to be Elizabeth's gown. "I have just the thing," Georgiana told her shyly. "It was meant for my coming-out ball."

"Oh I could not—"

"Do not be silly," Georgiana admonished. "It would give me great pleasure. I was exceedingly fond of it, and I could not bear to imagine it, in so much splendour, rotting away in my wardrobe for all eternity."

The gown was the palest peach with a silk gauze overlay picked out in silver thread. It was perhaps extravagant for a morning affair but not uncommon for a wedding gown. "It is very beautiful," Elizabeth said. "I wonder if Boucher could fit it to me."

"Oh, I can do it."

Elizabeth looked at Georgiana with surprise.

"Truly I can. In fact, I am a good seamstress now. I was well enough…um, before, but my duties to the houses I served made me quite an expert. I enjoy it; one loses the desire to think as much when your fingers are busy." She laughed and added, "And mine are busier than most as I have only nine of them to do the same work as ten."

Elizabeth was not quite sure she should join her in laughing and merely nodded. Minutes later, she found herself wearing the gown, standing on a little step so Georgiana could pin and tuck and assess. Watching Georgiana perform her little tasks made Elizabeth realise it was a kindness to consent to wearing the gown—not that she would have needed further inducement anyway—for the girl set about her work with sedate cheer, humming lightly under her breath while she worked. When Georgiana stepped back and looked at how it was, she had true satisfaction in her eyes.

"That will do very well, I think."

"It is lovely." Elizabeth stepped down and gingerly embraced Georgiana. "Thank you. I am sure I have never had such a beautiful gown before."

Georgiana blushed. "I am just happy to see it worn, and what better occasion than the marriage of my brother…and my sister."

Elizabeth smiled as she leant towards her and, for the first time, kissed her on the cheek. Although they had shared a bed these past weeks and Elizabeth knew her deepest secrets, Georgiana still had the demeanour of a frightened animal around Elizabeth. She acted eager to please but fearful of any advance that was too sudden or too close. But the kiss, she accepted, even tilting her cheek a bit to receive it.

The wedding day itself had an inauspicious beginning. Rain,

heavy and relentless, poured down, making a trip to the chapel in Kympton difficult if not impossible. "You will not make half the journey before being bogged down in the mud," Fitzwilliam insisted. "The road has scarcely been passable as it is."

"So we shall walk," Elizabeth announced cheerfully.

"Walk?" Lady Saye stared at her. "In all this rain? You will not be fit to be seen when you get there."

"If my bridegroom does not mind," she said with a little smile at him, "then I daresay no one else should object. I shall wear my proper clothes when I return for our little breakfast. But I should much prefer to walk to my vows than to give up saying them altogether."

"Yes indeed," Darcy said warmly. "We cannot let rain and mud prevent what is the most important order of the day."

Elizabeth thus retired to her bedchamber where the maid helped her into an older gown, her sensible outdoor boots, and an arrangement for her hair that would bear up well under damp weather. "You can try as you wish," Elizabeth warned her with a little laugh, "but my curls are likely to thwart you no matter what you do."

Darcy was quiet as they set out walking huddled under an umbrella, which necessitated Elizabeth being tucked close into his side. Fitzwilliam and Georgiana accompanied them under their own umbrella to serve as witnesses to the event.

"An umbrella is a handy thing for providing privacy, is it not?" Elizabeth at last remarked.

"It is; although generally, one walking in such a rain as this is unable to enjoy whatever privacy might be afforded."

"But just think," she teased, "if you were to kiss me just feet away from Fitzwilliam and your sister, neither of them would be any the wiser."

He looked at her, clearly deliberating the idea.

"It is our wedding day after all. Surely a few stolen kisses would not be remarked upon?"

That made him smile at last. He lightly squeezed the hand that rested on his arm and . "In under an hour, I shall not have to steal them any more; they will all belong to me."

"They already do," she said, tilting her chin upwards to make it easier for him to kiss her. It worked. He could not resist such an invitation, and kissed her once, twice, then a third time before his efforts caused him to move the umbrella and get the back of his greatcoat soaked.

"Forgive my bad humour," he said when they began again to walk. "I cannot help but think this could not be the wedding you dreamt of—rain and mud and walking through the forest to a country church. We should have married at St Georges and had the breakfast at my house in town. Or perhaps at Longbourn? Yes, you likely would have wished to marry at Longbourn."

"In truth, I never did dream of any such thing. Even as a girl. Jane liked to think of her wedding and imagine how it would be, but I could never get past wondering who this faceless man would be who would become my husband. And in that regard, we have surpassed even my wildest imaginings."

He obviously liked that. She saw the smile flicker across his face even as the rain seemed to come down even harder upon them.

"My mother was forever scolding me for scampering about the countryside like some untamed creature," Elizabeth continued. "Always distressed that my gowns and shoes were muddy, and always concerned that no man would ever want me because of my wild ways."

"This man wants you particularly for your wild ways," Darcy replied with a grin. "I daresay she would not have approved of me."

"My mother would have delighted in you. You are two things she likes the most of anything: wealthy and tall. And a house in town? Goodness me, she would have wished to marry you herself."

Darcy chuckled and chanced to kiss her again.

"We see you," Fitzwilliam called from behind them. "Darcy, with your height, every time you do that, the umbrella dips down. Quite plain to the disinterested observers behind you what you are doing. In any case, here we are at the church. Let us get this business done."

IT WAS a simple affair but Elizabeth—his Elizabeth now—did not seem aggrieved by it. It almost made him laugh to contrast it with what he had always imagined his wedding would be. Back then, as a young bachelor about town, he had believed he would avoid marriage as long as was possible, then decide upon some society beauty from a good family—preferably someone who was as fond of reading and good conversation as he was—then settle in at Pemberley to produce an heir.

He had known none of that could ever come to pass from the moment Georgiana eloped. He had thought of it often while he was in America, wondering what sort of life awaited him. He had not expected anything good; certainly he had no expectation of happiness such as he felt now, lying in bed with her sleeping peacefully in his arms.

He looked down at her, remembering how she looked when she pledged her troth to him. It had not mattered one bit that the gown was old or that her hair was damp and curling wildly in all directions. All that mattered was that her eyes shone with joy as she said, "to love, cherish, and to obey, till death us do part, according to God's holy ordinance; and thereto I give thee my troth."

For some reason it struck him then: she really did love him. How it had come about, why it had happened, he could not imagine. But she did. She loved him.

"How on earth," he murmured, kissing her hair gently, "did I ever earn your love?"

"What?" she asked, almost instantly awake.

She is a light sleeper, he added to the growing list of things he was learning about his new wife. The slightest noise wakes her.

"My apologies, Mrs Darcy; I did not intend to wake you."

She smiled, shifting slightly so she could see him. "I would much rather be awake and enjoying my husband than asleep. Can you not sleep?"

"My mind was too full," he admitted. "Thinking of the day—our wedding and our breakfast."

The breakfast had been a delight. Mrs Reynolds had been determined to do things properly, and there was food in abundance. The children, delighted with the novelty of making merry with the adults, had eaten too much cake and gambolled about uproariously. The adults had been likewise merry, drinking and eating and talking. It ended when Georgiana, shockingly, asked whether she might play a song for them.

Everyone got quiet to see her approach the instrument; she seemed hesitant, even a bit fearful, as she sat, picking up the music and rifling through it. "All my old songs," she said to the room at large with a little nervous smile. "It is like having old friends waiting for me."

A moment later, she found what she wished for. "One of my brother's favourites," she announced. "Elizabeth, perhaps you will sing with me? Your voice is so much nicer than mine, and I think it will require all my courage just to play."

Back in the present moment, Darcy said, "It was good of you to sing for Georgiana while she played. She was once quite accomplished."

"She still is," said Elizabeth with a little yawn. "All she wants for is some time to practice. Does Hickory Hill have a pianoforte?"

"I never bought one. I am sure whatever I might find in America will be vastly inferior to what she has here."

"The joy in being able to play will make it up to her," Elizabeth assured him.

She turned over onto her stomach, and in so doing, he felt the silk of her bare leg brush against his. That was all that was required; instantly all thoughts of pianofortes and sisters were driven from his mind. "Elizabeth," he murmured, taking care not to groan lustfully.

In reply, she slid her leg beside his again. "Yes, Mr Darcy?"

"Have I told you today I love you?"

She glanced towards the clock on his mantel. In the low glow of the fire, it was barely visible, but she could likely still see it was well past the midnight hour. "As it turns out," she said, "you have not."

"Then you must allow me to tell you how ardently I admire and love you."

With a light touch, she ran her hand up his chest, ending with her hand on the side of his face. "Telling me is nice, but showing me would be even better."

ABOUT THE AUTHOR

Amy D'Orazio is a long time devotee of Jane Austen and fiction related to her characters. She began writing her own little stories to amuse herself during hours spent at sports practices and the like and soon discovered a passion for it. By far, however, the thing she loves most is the connections she has made with readers and other writers of Austenesque fiction.

Amy currently lives in Pittsburgh with her husband and daughters, as well as three Jack Russell terriers who often make appearances (in a human form) in her book.

For more information about new releases, sales and promotions on books by Amy and other great authors, please visit www. QuillsAndQuartos.com.

Quills & Quartos
PUBLISHING

Quills & Quartos Publishing thanks you for reading this book.

To receive special offers, bonus content, and information on sales and new releases, we invite you to sign up for our newsletter at www.QuillsandQuartos.com.

resolves to meet her with indifference. He is determined that he will not demand answers to the questions that plague him. Elizabeth is also resolved to remain silent and hold fast to the secret behind her refusal. Once they are together, however, it proves difficult to deny the intense passion that still exists. Fury, grief, and profound love prove to be a combustible mixture. But will the secrets between them be their undoing?

The Best Part of Love

Avoiding the truth does not change the truth.

When Fitzwilliam Darcy meets Miss Elizabeth Bennet, his heart is almost immediately engaged. Seeing the pretty lady before him, a lady of no consequence or fortune, he believes he should not form an attachment to her, unsuitable as such a woman is to be his wife.

What he cannot see, however, is the truth, that the simple country girl harbours a secret. Before she meets Darcy, Elizabeth has spent two years hiding from the men who killed her beloved first husband. Feeling herself destroyed by love, Elizabeth is certain she will never love again, certainly not the arrogant man who has offended her from the first moment of their acquaintance.

In time, Elizabeth surprises herself by finding in Darcy a friend; even greater is her surprise to find herself gradually coming to love him and even accepting an offer of marriage from him. As the newly married couple is beginning to settle into their happily-ever-after, a condemned man on his way to the gallows divulges a shattering truth, a secret that contradicts everything Elizabeth thought she knew about the tragic circumstances of her first marriage. Against the advice of everyone who loves her—including Darcy—Elizabeth begins to seek the truth, knowing she must have it even if it may destroy her newfound happiness with Darcy.

Printed in Great Britain
by Amazon

11968664R00226